Eagles of the Grand Kingdom

Rage of Lions Book Four

Matt Barron

BLADE OF TRUTH PUBLISHING COMPANY

PROLOGUE

Dawn wasn't much more than an hour away, but the Rampart—the ribbon of light that shone across the night sky from east to west—was already beginning to fade. The moon had long set. Soon it would be the darkest part of the night.

"Be ready, Vesta," whispered Larriman to his companion. "It's almost time."

"I will be," she answered, unseen in the shadows beside him.

Even with the darkness to hide them, the two runaways pressed themselves down into the long grasses where they'd spent the whole of the night hiding. Darkness was a cover against mortal eyes, but the two young peasant-folk knew there was more than mere men to fear in the night. Just over a hundred paces from where they lay, the flowing waters of the Murr River promised safety, if they could only make it. Larriman reached out, and finding Vesta's slender hand, squeezed it. He meant it to comfort her, and he hoped and prayed she couldn't feel him shaking through their grasp. He and Vesta were lifelong friends, having shared their childhoods, and were now on the verge of adulthood together. Talk in the village had been that they would likely be betrothed in a year or two.

That was before the invaders and the war.

"You're sure we need to cross the river?" he asked for the umpteenth time, unable to stop himself.

"You know we must," Vesta answered, her tone unmistakably exasperated in the darkness.

What Larriman knew was that he annoyed her with his fretting, but the river was more than a geographical feature for him; it was the edge of his world. His vision had never stretched very far beyond the village boundaries. Vesta was the one who followed the gossip and the tales of far-off lands. On market days, she was the one in the village square listening to the merchants or the occasional visiting minstrels as they traded tales of distant places for a tapster's brew. Larriman loved the flocks and always stuck with the shepherds, learning everything he could. He dreamed of a Carders Guild pin, the mark of a very respectable man in the village.

It was Vesta who knew the tales from the north of a foreign invader attacking the Western Reach and its renegade duchess who had raised banners against the Prince of Rhales. When he'd heard it from her mouth over a year ago, Larriman had scoffed. What woman led an army against a prince, even if she was a duchess? Vesta had known though, and when the invaders sailed down the Murr from the unknown west in their shallow draught boats, she listened to the tales of the refugees who were fleeing the conquered frontier land of Radengon beyond Dwelt.

When the elders gathered the whole village to discuss what to do and decided to send to Lord Wolden for aid, it was Vesta who reminded them that Viscount Wolden had died in the north. She said that day they should all flee, but word came of King Chrostmer, High King of the Grand Kingdom, marching with his army to defend the frontier. The village elders spread the word that there was nothing to fear then. The king would defend them, and there was no need to flee.

That was a mistake.

The first raiders who came to the village hadn't been invaders from the west; they were knights from the Kingdom. Steel-clad noblemen, they levied a harsh tax in grain and service from the farms of the village. Vesta pulled Larriman under a haystack that morning, and while they hid, nearly a third of the hale villagers were bound with ropes and dragged off to labor in service to the king's army. And with them went almost the whole of the village stores. The folk who remained were forced to eat straw bread, saving what little grain they had so that there would be seed to plant in the next sowing season.

And the Kingdom army's presence had done little to hold the invaders back. Strange, monstrous soldiers from the west were already raiding the farmsteads at the edge of the village—especially the ones near the river. Every day, it seemed, word came that someone else had been taken, and while servitude to the king might have been harsh, the rumors Vesta heard of the invaders were terrifying. They were witches and sorcerers that melded the flesh of men and beasts to create monsters. They were cannibals, bloodthirsty and savage. And they hated the peoples of the Grand Kingdom, from the highest born noble to the lowliest serf. Folk might have dismissed Vesta's stories before—Larriman certainly had—but when she'd come to him yesterday and said they could wait no longer, he took her word for it. The invaders were in the west, the king's army was to the east, and the north was in rebellion.

That only left the south, the Vec princedoms, who the village sacrist taught were all debauched, ungodly souls damned to hell. Officially, the Vec were enemies of the Grand Kingdom, having rebelled against the Denay throne centuries before, and they were supposed to be always at war with each other, but at least their people weren't starving. So Larriman accepted Vesta's plan, and the two of them were about to become "wayward"—peasants who had travelled more than four leagues from their village without their lord's express permission.

But first they had to cross the Murr.

"We can't wait anymore," said Vesta.

Larriman nodded, but when he realized she couldn't see him in the darkness, he tapped her on the shoulder. "Let's go."

Crouching, hands groping ahead of them in the blackness, they crept toward the sounds of the river, the buzzing of insects, and the calls of the night birds. Soon, their slow going was even further restrained as they began to slip and slither through the muddy fen grasses at the river's edge.

"Once we're in the water, we'll be safe," Vesta whispered, but Larriman didn't share her confidence.

They both knew how to swim—almost everyone in the village did—and the Murr had a pretty sedate flow at this point. But the invaders had used the river to come out of the west, hadn't they? And they still raided the riverside farms, so what made the river safe?

"Just a quick dip and we'll be newly baptized citizens of the Princedom of Aubrey," Vesta went on.

"I thought you said the Prince of Aubrey had fled."

"He has but not his son. The man's a coward, but the young prince has mettle."

"How can you know so much?" Larriman asked, astonished by the extent of her knowledge, despite himself.

"Hush! I think I heard something."

They both froze and turned their heads about, ears pricked and eyes straining to pierce the darkness. For a long moment there were no strange sounds, and they saw nothing out of the ordinary. But in the west, the horizon was beginning to lighten.

"Dawn!" said Vesta. "We have to hurry." She began to clamber more recklessly through the rushes, her feet squelching in the sucking mud.

"Wait, Vesta," Larriman hissed after her but doubted she heard him.

The light was growing too quickly, and they had missed their chance to cross safely. Worse than that, Larriman thought he could hear the sound that had caught Vesta's ear a moment before. He cocked his head once more and a moment later felt himself knocked sideways into the mud. The force of the blow drove the breath from his lungs, and he thought he saw a blur of motion in the corner of his eye as he rolled over, groaning. He felt the wetness of the mud soaking through his clothes, and he tried to lever himself upright.

A panicked cry from Vesta told him that whatever had attacked him was now after her. He shook his head as he pushed himself painfully to his feet, trying to regain his bearings, but before he could, he was knocked down once more. This time, whatever had struck him held on as he fell, its weight pressing down on him, sticking him fast to the mud. In the timid, predawn light he could only just make out the silhouette of a man above him, but even in the dimness, something was not right about the proportions. And there was a strange smell.

"We have, we have found meat," the attacker said, his voice making a strange slurping, clicking sound. Worse than that, the man drooled as he leaned over Larriman's prone form. The liquid dripped on his face, and it stung where it fell.

"Get off me," Larriman said in a loud voice. There was no more point trying to be stealthy. He had to help Vesta. He pushed at the man on top of him, but his assailant was skilled at wrestling, and no matter what he did, the man shifted his limbs and kept him down.

"This way," called a voice from some distance, and Larriman despaired to realize how many attackers were hunting them—too many for two wayward villagers to escape. He groaned pitifully but was surprised to feel a hand press down on his mouth.

"Silence, meat," slurred the attacker, pressing fully down on Larriman's body in the grass, hiding from the new voice.

Larriman wondered what that meant. Was it a Grand Kingdom man-at-arms? Or had some of the Prince of Aubrey's son's men crossed the river, perhaps scouting the invaded north bank?

As Larriman worried at all these possibilities, he realized there was much more light suddenly playing across the tops of the grasses. Someone had a lantern, a bullseye that could send a longer beam farther into the dark. A flash of the lamplight danced through the shadows and lit the man on top of him for just a moment. Larriman screamed into the man's hand, terrified by what he saw. The creature on top of him was no mere mortal. It had arms and legs, two of each like any man, but its face was nothing nature could produce. It was distended by two enormous eyes that bulged from the sockets, the size of fists, like the eyes of a mantis. Each inhuman orb twisted independently of the other. Only the sparsest tufts of dark hair sprouted on his scalp, which was bizarrely crested, catching the light with its ridges. Despite his nearly bald pate, the insect-man had a beard of sorts, though it seemed more of a mat of tendrils than true facial hair. And in the midst of that growth was a lipless mouth, stretched and contorted by pincer-like teeth that moved of their own accord, slobbering a viscous ichor that Larriman was sure must be poisonous. That was what he'd felt dripping on his cheek. In a panic, he shoved again, harder, and the distracted monster was raised up above the grass for a moment.

"There!" shouted the voice again.

Suddenly, there was the clash of armor and the splash of running feet as someone unseen charged toward Larriman and his hideous mantis-man assailant.

The creature cursed and seemed caught between wanting to escape and wanting to punish its prisoner for giving away its hiding place. That indecision was its doom, and Larriman was suddenly sprayed with gore as a spear tip drove fully into the monster's chest, lifting it bodily and throwing it from on top of him. He scrambled away on hands and knees through the long grass as an armored man crashed into the speared creature, swinging savage strokes with his sword. For a long time, Larriman pressed his face into the grass while the combat beat around him. Then it moved on, continuing a short distance away.

"There's others over here," came a cry and more rushing bodies, along with shouts and the clash of arms.

Then there was quiet.

Fearfully, Larriman opened his eyes and saw that he was alone. The sky was lightening, but the long grasses were still in shadow. He listened without moving and was sure he could hear muddy footfalls. The men-at-arms, whoever they were, were hunting through the reeds for any other threats. After seeing his first beastman, Larriman was thankful to the bottom of his toes that these soldiers had shown up to save them, but that didn't mean he wanted to be dragged away to serve as some knight's indenture. He decided to hide and wait for them to go. Then, he would find Vesta and they could head back to the village. If she wanted, they could try to cross again another night, or else she might come up with a different plan.

"Methinks that's all of 'em," said a voice some distance away.

"Thanks to God for that," said another. "Ugly bastards they are. Seein' one of them comin' out of the shadows at you, don't that make you want to soil your britches?"

"True enough. We best tidy this up and report back."

They were leaving, and Larriman smiled hopefully. He'd be able to move soon.

"Damn, this'un's a girl," said the voice that feared messing his pants.

"Farmgirl by the looks of her."

Vesta. Larriman was certain they'd found her. He listened, poised and tense, like a hunting hound that's caught wind of prey. Were they going to escape the monsters only for Vesta to fall victim to men?

"Was she with 'em, d'ya think?" asked the other voice.

"I wouldn't say so. Looks like that thing was trying to eat her. Look, her arm's almost come away from the shoulder where he was chewin' on her."

"Poor little hen."

"Wasn't there another...?"

Even before the man could finish, panic in Larriman's chest made him spring upright, the terror that his best friend and dearest love was dead controlling his motions as if he were a mere puppet.

"No," he cried out as he splashed through the muddy reeds.

Although only two men had been talking, there were eight soldiers in total standing about in the early morning light. They turned with surprise at Larriman's appearance, weapons held ready. All were clad in white, with dark blue accents sewn into the cloth and polished steel armor. Some had helmets, others didn't, but all wore gauntlets and arm plates, as well as riveted brigandines on their chests. Between them they had spears and long-handled war axes, and two had swords, with small shields in their off hands. One man had some kind of club made of metal and wood, but he held it back to front, and there was a slow match burning on top of it. The sight of the strange object would have puzzled Larriman if he had thought to spare for any question but one. He scanned the armed men, and seeing two close together, one crouched in the grass, he was sure that was where he had to go. He charged amongst them, knowing in the back of his mind that if they thought he was a threat he would be dead in a trice, but still he could not stop himself.

He had to see Vesta.

He was still several paces away when one of them caught him. It was like running into ancient oak or karri. He was stopped hard but tried to break away.

"Let me go," he all but screamed. "I have to see her! You have to let me see her!"

"What's this?" asked one of the men, but Larriman couldn't tell which. He could barely hear the question, so fixed was he on reaching Vesta. "She your sweet, lad?"

"No," he answered reflexively, embarrassed as ever he had been when village children had mocked his young love. "Yes. I don't...yes. I love her."

There was no mockery in the tone or stances of the men around him.

"Hush, boy, it's alright," said the one crouched by her body. "She's not dead, 'though she'll lose that arm, I'd wager. But she's still breathing. She'll live, if she's strong in heart."

"The strongest," Larriman breathed, and tears of relief started to flow down his cheeks.

The arms that gripped him released, and he fell beside the unconscious form of the young woman he hoped one day to marry. She was bloody and torn, her left arm a ruin of flesh. Larriman had no idea how to help her, but even as he watched, the men around him tended her wounds and arranged to carry her off to a healer.

"Step back, lad," one ordered him, and Larriman recognized the man's voice as the one who'd spoken of soiling his pants.

Larriman wiped his eyes as he got to his feet and gave the soldiers room to make a stretcher to carry Vesta. They used two of their spears as poles and tied blankets to them. Soon she was being carried out of the marsh, with a clean bandage tied around her shoulder.

"Where will you take her?" the young man asked.

"We'll be camping to the north and west," answered the soldier. "We can get her there and send for a healer to tend her. You should come with us. She'll want to see a friendly face when she wakes."

"The north and west?" Larriman repeated as he followed the stretcher-bearers. "I didn't think we were that close to the king's camp."

"T'ain't the king's camp, lad," said another soldier. "We're duchess' men, Lions of the Reach."

"What's that then?"

The men around Larriman chuckled as if they were sharing a private joke. "Soiled pants" clapped him on the shoulder with a gauntleted hand.

"We're Reachermen, lad. Freed men of the west." He paused and seemed to revise his thoughts for a moment. "Well, sworn men of the west. We've been fighting these monsters two years now. We're getting quite good at it. And now the Duchess Amelia, Lioness of the Reach, has sent her pride south to help defend the Grand Kingdom. The west marches to victory."

"The Reach!" exclaimed every man as one loudly, each clapping his fist to his chest.

Larriman looked to each one in turn, marveling at these competent, well-armed men who had saved them and, it seemed, had no plan to drag them away to serve a foreign lord. Unless it was this lioness they spoke of, this Duchess Amelia. Larriman had never heard of her, but he was sure Vesta would know. When she awoke, he would ask her. He looked down at her pale, unconscious face covered in mud, blood, and sweat, and his heart broke. The loss of her arm would be brutal to have to wake to, both the pain and the horrible stigma of being crippled for life. Larriman knew that many folks were crushed in their spirit by such wounds, dying slowly inside or else taking their own lives. But not Vesta, he was sure of it. He couldn't imagine anything that could break her.

These rescuers talked about lionesses. Well, Vesta was such a creature, and Larriman loved her. He'd declared it to these strange, hard men, and he would never take it back.

"We're close enough to signal," said one of the soldiers.

The man with the smoldering club lifted it to his shoulder, and suddenly a gout of smoke and flame erupted from its end, sending a loud crack echoing into the morning air that set marsh birds aloft for half a league. Larriman flinched in shock, but none of the other men even seemed to notice. A short moment later, the sound was answered by a similar noise, coming from some distance to the north. Larriman watched in astonishment as the man wielding the burning club placed one end upon the ground and proceeded to work upon it with tools.

"It's not magic, lad," said the man walking beside him, seeing his wonderment.

"What is it?"

"The roar of the lions," the man answered cryptically. "The sound that heralds death for the enemies of the Reach and the Grand Kingdom."

Larriman shook his head and looked down again at Vesta. This was something even she had never heard of, he would bet. What a thing to tell her about when she came round.

"Wake up, Vesta," he whispered to her. "Promise me you'll wake up."

CHAPTER 1

"Bug men?" Captain Prentice Ash asked, repeating the report but not really understanding it.

"That's the tale the patrols are telling," Sergeant Felix answered. "Big eyes bulging out the sides of their heads like a praying mantis, they say. Mouths dripping venom from giant pincers."

"Mandibles," said Prentice, reflexively providing the correct term from some deep part of his memory where his education slept, occasionally coughing up obscure details like the word for an insect's strange teeth. It had been more than ten years since he'd been convicted of heresy and transported, banished from his education, and still those tiny facts floated up like motes of dust in a beam of sunlight.

"How quickly does the venom kill?" he followed up. If these new beastmen could slay with a single bite, they were a threat he needed to understand. Could a handful of them slay a cohort of a hundred in mere moments? The thought made him shudder.

Sergeant Felix stroked his long, dark beard. The man's thick facial hair hid his mouth so that Prentice couldn't ever see if he was smiling or frowning, but the seriousness in his eyes made it clear he understood his captain's concerns.

"It don't look like it's a poison that kills," he said, which Prentice was glad to hear. "The men that were bitten got vile sickly, but that's about the whole of it. They retched out their guts for an hour or so, but a night's sleep seems to see them right. Course, a man chucking up on a battlefield is as good as slain to us as a man full of venom, so I suppose it's not that much of a mercy. And God only knows what's to happen to the wounds yet. They may still turn septic from the venom in the next days."

Felix shrugged and Prentice nodded, agreeing with the dour sentiment. The initial sickness from these insect-men's bite could be just the start. The wounds might refuse to heal and then the victim was just as dead, only more slowly and painfully.

"Still, at least it's not serpent-women," said the sergeant, and Prentice turned away.

In the weeks since the army had started its southward march, following the course of the River Dwelt, they'd encountered one serpent-woman, and the fight was already legendary amongst his soldiers. Posing as a Reacherman's widow, the enemy woman had hidden her face's distinctive markings and tattoos under a veil and managed to infiltrate the march, looking for officers, and ultimately looking for Captain Prentice Ash, as it turned out.

The core of Prentice's army was a cadre of reformed convicts, over two thousand, exiled and transported west across the mountains to pay their debt of justice in the Western Reach, the Grand Kingdom's far frontier. They'd been hard-forged by their lives and were barely restrained by the army's strict discipline. Turning convicts into soldiers was Prentice's alchemy, forging perfect steel out of waste iron, as it were, making soldiers out of convicts hoping to serve long enough to be free and frontiersmen. Many of the Reach's yeomen were descended from convicts who had won their freedom in years past. But since the invaders had come from the west, the entire province had risen in arms, and now Prentice's army swelled with volunteers, two yeomen at least for every convict soldier. Both kinds of men were tough folk, accustomed to the hardest lives, and they were all naturally cunning and suspicious. In the heartland of the Grand Kingdom, a company of peasants would be almost exclusively made up of serfs and convicted men who had no hope of winning their freedom. Such beaten-down folk showed no initiative or loyalty. They tugged the forelock, bowed their heads, and did only what they were told.

That was the difference with Prentice's soldiers, and it was what saved his life.

When the serpent-woman had demanded to see the army's leader, the captain of the White Lions, the soldiers escorting her brought her into camp. When she refused to unveil herself as they walked, they grew suspicious, and as they neared the captain's tent, they became insistent, trying to force the issue, pulling back the woman's hood. There was a moment as they recognized the tattoos on her skin, but then she changed and suddenly she had the head of a serpent, eyes yellow and slitted, tongue flickering like a viper's. Even as her escort yelled for assistance, she drew forth a pair of daggers from under her skirts and swung at them, spitting actual venom from fang-split lips. Men struck in the face with the deadly poison screamed as their skin and eyes burned, clawing futilely at their injuries as the agony took them to their deaths. By the time the assassin was finally slain, sixteen men were dead, twice as many from her venom as from her blades.

"Remember the days when the worst we had to face were the Horned Man and his skin-changer wolves?" Prentice asked with a sour smile and looked away again to the south toward the Murr River. The Horned Man had been the commander of the first Redlander army to invade the Grand Kingdom out of the west three years ago. It seemed an age had passed since then.

"Whoever would have thought those were our halcyon days?" Felix agreed, following Prentice's sentiment. "Still, we beat 'em then, and we've beat 'em since. We'll beat these ones now."

Prentice appreciated his sergeant's confidence, even if he wasn't sure he shared it. He kicked at the grass under his feet and looked to the west where the River Dwelt rolled southward to meet up with the silver ribbon of the Murr, wending its way east through the green grass of the riverside pasturelands. Behind him and to his left were the last foothills of the Azure Mountains, the boundary that separated the Grand Kingdom proper from the lands of the Western Reach, the fiefdom of his mistress, the Duchess Amelia, widow of Duke Marne. Looking to the southeast, Prentice could see a stone keep on the spur of a ridge. A watchtower built centuries before to guard against incursion across the river to the south, it would be the strongpoint where the duchess would sleep when she joined her army. The soldiers themselves, around five thousand, would camp in the pastures at the bottom of the ridge.

"Once the camp is set, make sure no one moves east of that tower," Prentice ordered. "Not one man. Pass the word to the corporals and set provosts to keep that watch."

By King's Law, no convict transported west over the Azures could return to the Grand Kingdom while under their sentence. Any such man or woman, soldier or not, who moved east of the keep would be liable for summary execution.

"Like as not we'll have to march east at some time to meet up with King Chrostmer's army," Felix objected.

Prentice turned to look at him, steel-blue eyes narrowing coldly. "The whether and the when of that decision is for the duchess to say," he declared bluntly. "In the meantime, make sure they keep west of that pile of stones. I would rather have to flog a few as an example than lose any to some petty nobleman overeager to test the edge of his blade on a wayward convict. You know they will do it."

Sergeant Felix was not a native of the Grand Kingdom, having been born in the Vec, but he was familiar with the privileges and abuses of Kingdom nobility. That was why both he and Prentice were so loyal in their service to Duchess Amelia. She was one of the rare high-ranked folk who did not see judgement and punishment as a mere privilege of rank—maybe because she had risen to her status and not actually born to it.

"Righto, I'll pass the word."

"How far back is the duchess and her escort?" Prentice asked.

Duchess Amelia had ordered the bulk of her army, the five thousand under Prentice's command, to march south as soon as the winter began to turn to spring. She herself remained behind to oversee the gathering of supplies, sending them down the River Dwelt on skiffs and barges. Now, she was coming south with the rest of her forces, another thousand soldiers and knights.

"They're three or four days behind us," said Felix. "Now that spring's full, they'll make good time. It's going to be a fine year if it keeps up like this." He looked up at the bright, cloudless sky.

"Then that's how long we've got to get that keep livable for her. I want it cleaned, furnished, and defensible when she arrives."

"That's a lot of work in a short time."

"And we've got a lot of strong hands at our disposal, so we will get it done."

As if to emphasize Prentice's words, the first ranks of the vanguard cohort marched past, one hundred foot soldiers in twenty ranks of five, carrying pike and halberds, swords and bucklers, or the Lions' secret weapon—matchlock serpentines, handguns of a new design that could punch an iron ball the size of a child's marble through the breastplate of a knight's armor if fired from close enough range. Even if it did not penetrate, the force could knock a man off his mount. The cohort's lead corporal shouted an order and a drummer beat "present arms." One hundred soldiers brought their weapons to order and clapped their right fists across their hearts, the salute of the White Lions. Prentice and Felix returned the salute as the ranks marched past. Then the drum beat again and the arms relaxed in unison.

"With your permission, Captain, I'll get cohorts to setting camp. You want everyone in close to that ridge?"

"Yes."

With the two rivers to the south and west, and the mountains to the east, this was the perfect defensive location for the army to camp, with the only open ground to the north, and that merely led to the Griffith Pale and the rest of the duchess's lands. Nevertheless, somewhere in the surrounding regions was a vast army of invaders from the west that had been terrorizing these lands since the previous summer—an army that counted wolf-men, horned-men, and serpent-women amongst its number. And now, according to the previous night's patrols, mantis-men as well. Who knew if they didn't have soldiers that wouldn't even notice a river as a barrier or who climbed along mountain ridges like fleet-footed goats? No matter the advantages the ground gave him, Prentice was not going to relax for a moment.

And even if his advantages neutralized the invaders entirely, on the other side of that ridge was the army of King Chrostmer IV and the nobility of the Grand Kingdom. Duchess Amelia had as many enemies there as she had friends, not the least of whom was Crown Prince Daven Marcus, Prince of the West, Prince of Rhales and, supposedly, the duchess's wedded husband. Daven Marcus, the man who had had the duchess chained and tried on false charges, then attempted to marry her in order to steal her lands and their riches out from under her. His final plan had been to execute her and "inherit her lands," but loyal men and women had rescued her and brought her safely into the protection of the army Prentice had been training for her. Rumors from the other side of the Azure Mountains said Prince Daven Marcus had brought charges before Church courts, claiming that Duchess Amelia was a wayward wife and that she should be returned to his "care." It was only a matter of time until his father, the king, would be forced to act on the matter.

No, as long as they camped this far south, Prentice was not going to relax for a moment.

CHAPTER 2

"I suppose it qualifies as a solar," said Lady Dalflitch. "But just barely."

Looking around the keep's upper floor, Duchess Amelia had to agree with her. Prentice's men had been laboring for days to make the long-deserted watchpoint habitable for the ruler of the Western Reach. Having arrived by horse not an hour before, Amelia and Dalflitch had been escorted into a ground floor that had once stabled horses. The broken wooden stalls had been torn out and the flagstone floor swept and washed, but the space still smelled vaguely of manure and rotting wood. Now ushered upstairs, they found themselves in a dark room, the only windows being arrow slits looking south or north to watch for enemies. Rush lights had been lit, but their oily flames only seemed to make the air more close and cloying. "We'll need those oil lamps out of the baggage as soon as we can," Amelia told her lady's companion, and Dalflitch accepted the instruction with a dutiful bob and nod of the head. "And the blankets and mattresses."

The room contained three newly made beds, rudely constructed but serviceable. There was a far nicer bed for the duchess in the barges that brought her baggage south, but Amelia would not insist men haul finer furniture up the ridge and into the tower just to satisfy her vanity. Bedding, though, was a different matter. At present, the three new beds were simply stacked with rushes covered with thin canvas sheets. Surely it wasn't too much self-indulgence to want a proper mattress.

The duchess turned at the sound of footsteps climbing the stairs to see her other two ladies-in-waiting arrive. Both were lean and slender, and in spite of the lace of their bodices and the fineness of their hairstyles, they moved with a predatory grace that reminded Amelia more of hunting animals than pampered household pets. One was a quiet, watchful creature who wore a half mask of fine, black lace that fully covered one side of her face and head. The flesh beneath the lace was horribly scarred, Amelia knew, though she'd only seen it once late at night. Save for this one blemish, the woman was pretty, and she knew her needlework. The mask's embroidered surface accented the same patterns on her skirt and bodice and lent the dark eyes behind the mask a mystique as feminine as any unmarred beauty. The woman's name was Tress, but she insisted on being called Spindle. Her companion was as richly dressed as she was but in a far less feminine manner.

"Righteous, are you wearing trousers again?" Amelia asked archly, looking the second lady up and down. "Where are the skirts I paid for?"

"Torn again," replied the young woman named Righteous, bobbing up and down in a vague approximation of a curtsey. "I just ain't got the knack of wearing 'em back, Your Grace. I'm so sorry."

For all her formal regret, Righteous's mischievous expression was not in the least bit apologetic. Amelia was certain the woman was tearing the skirts on purpose. Years ago, back when Righteous was a convicted criminal named Cutter Sal, she'd had to conceal her sex, posing as a boy among men. She had grown accustomed to trousers then and never seemed to want to go back. Other than this refusal though, Righteous was as impeccably turned out as her companion—strawberry hair arranged properly under a silver net and bodice suitably laced.

Given the choice, Amelia knew the woman would rather be wearing a gambeson or arming doublet with a belt at her waist and a fighting knife hanging in a scabbard.

Spindle and Righteous. Officially, they were simply her lady's companions, but in fact, the pair were skilled knife fighters and practiced killers. Righteous even had a judicial brand on her cheek, having been convicted of killing a man in a public brawl. Unlike Spindle, hers was a scar she chose not to conceal. Ever since Amelia had escaped from captivity at the hands of Prince Daven Marcus, this pair had been given the twin roles of lady's companions and bodyguards hidden in plain sight.

"We're not in Dweltford anymore, Righteous," Amelia chided. "The closer we get to the king's court, the more scrutiny we come under. The more scrutiny *I* come under. You understand?"

Righteous nodded, but her smirk made it clear she didn't care.

"The prince has sent to the Church to name me a defiant and wayward wife, living free of my rightful husband's authority," Amelia continued, grinding out the words, her hatred for the prince twisting her lips into a sneer. "Sometime soon I'll have to answer his charges, and when I do, it will not help my case to have a member of my household flouting decorum so publicly in the face of the fathers of Mother Church. So, please, Righteous, do me a favor...and wear the damned skirts!"

Dalflitch sighed genteelly at the sound of her mistress cursing so vehemently, but Righteous met the duchess's eyes and there was a moment of true recognition between them.

"As you say, Your Grace." Then Righteous smirked again. "Course I don't know what you're worried about. Ain't no one looking at me when Dalflitch is next to you."

Amelia cast a glance over her shoulder at Lady Dalflitch. It was true. Spindle wore her fine and mysterious mask, and Righteous had her peasant-girl prettiness that she covered with boyish habits of dress. And with her own straw-colored hair and unremarkable features, Amelia knew she herself to be pleasant enough to look upon, but Dalflitch was a true beauty and justifiably renowned for it. The woman's hair was black as a starless night and her skin pale as the moon, with fine-boned features and flashing dark brown eyes. She had been a countess once and a lover of the prince. When she was found out, her husband, the count, had divorced her. Soon after, Daven Marcus had thrown her from his bed, leaving the woman destitute, without allies or influence. Despite previous bad blood between them, Amelia had had sympathy on Dalflitch, and in return, the former countess became an unswervingly loyal ally. Infamous as an inveterate gossip, Dalflitch was in fact an expert in sifting secret information from false tales, making her a spymaster in all but name. Just as Spindle and Righteous guarded Amelia physically, Dalflitch guarded her politically, and the young duchess wasn't sure which service she valued more.

"At least this will be better than sleeping in muddy tents," the former countess said.

"But what will you complain about if the dirt isn't staining your slippers and hems?" Righteous mocked.

She and Dalflitch sniped at each other often, but Amelia was reasonably confident that it was good natured. Of course, there were days when she wondered if she would wake up to find Dalflitch dead from a clean, quiet dagger thrust or watch as Righteous choked to death on a cup of poisoned tea.

More footsteps heralded the arrival of Turley, Duchess Amelia's burly chief steward. He clasped the forelock of his tangled mop of dark hair with his right hand, his left hand tucked into his belt. That was his crippled hand. During the desperate escape that had rescued her from the prince's control, Turley had taken a savage sword cut to his left forearm, a wound that had turned septic and threatened to take the whole limb. A healer had saved the arm, but the hand would never work properly again. Nonetheless, he managed to maintain his infamously roguish good humor.

"Beggin' your pardon, Your Grace," he said, announcing himself. "These men are set to watch from the battlements and need to go up through these stairs." He gestured to four armed men in ducal livery coming up the stairs behind him.

"Of course," Amelia said reflexively. She assumed the men had been set to that post by either Captain Prentice or her knight captain, Sir Gant. In military matters like this, she trusted their judgement absolutely.

"Is there no other way up to the battlements?" Dalflitch asked.

"No, m'lady," said Turley. "This is the only stair."

"Well, that is just unacceptable," the ex-countess continued. "Her grace cannot be expected to sleep and change her garb in a room with armed men marching back and forth through it."

"There's cloth in the baggage," Spindle offered. "I could sew some quick curtains, if that would help."

"And rods could be put up quick enough," the chief steward agreed.

"That will do for now," Dalflitch said imperiously. "But you should also send for carpenters and have a paneled wall built as soon as possible. Something behind which ladies might feel secure."

Turley cocked an eyebrow at this instruction but bowed his head to Amelia. "If that's your wish, Your Grace?"

"I think it a good solution," Amelia agreed, heartened by the notion that she would not have to share her sleeping and dressing quarters with her own men-at-arms. Additionally, having a private space to which she could withdraw was an asset she had grown to value over the years since her husband died.

"I'll see to it at once," Turley said.

"Is there anything else you need to ask Her Grace, steward?" Dalflitch asked, and there was a new edge to her tone.

Amelia thought she saw Turley flash the lady a hard-edged glance, and looking over her shoulder, she thought she saw something equally cutting reflected in Dalflitch's expression.

She hoped the pair weren't developing a secret enmity. She valued both their services and did not want unspoken rivalries undermining her household.

"Nothin' at this time," Turley responded flatly, eyes askance at Amelia's companion. He looked back to the duchess. "With your permission, Your Grace."

She dismissed him with a wave, and when he was gone, she sat on the edge of one of the beds. Dalflitch lounged on a chest that had already been brought from the luggage and placed under one of the slit windows. Righteous and Spindle remained standing, moving back and forth uncomfortably in the space. Amelia watched them both for a moment, but was soon exasperated.

"Don't fret so, you two," she insisted.

"They're like a pair of war horses who've been left in the stalls too long," Dalflitch agreed. "They want for a good long run."

"And what's wrong with wanting to run?" Righteous demanded.

"Ladies of birth do not run," Dalflitch declared. She could not have sounded more regal if she had been an empress issuing an edict. "They are creatures of dignity."

"Is that right...?" Righteous thrust out her lip, but Spindle cut across her.

"And a run's not the activity you're wanting anyway."

Righteous looked at her and then to the other women all around. Each one met her eyes in turn.

"Well," she said with a shrug and a dismissive sniff, "I'm a married woman. It's exactly right that I miss my husband, being away from him this long."

Righteous was married to Amelia's captain, Prentice Ash, a fellow freed convict and the only man Amelia knew whom she could imagine as both strong and gentle enough to hold this wild young woman's affections. They never argued, but Righteous mocked at him frequently, like a playful scold. And many times since they married, the duchess had seen man and wife dressed in quilted doublets and armed with wooden weapons, sparring furiously on the training ground. As near as Amelia could tell, Righteous never gave an inch, coming at her husband with the full force of her skill, but he only ever seemed to smile at her assaults and laughed when she managed to land a full touch, no matter how painful the blow. She was the woman who was never afraid of the icy fury within him, and he was the man who would never mistreat her, no matter how wildly or hotly she ill-used him.

There were days when the duchess envied them. She missed her own husband dearly, dead from assassination three years now. Inevitably, thoughts of her husband led her mind around once more to the prince's wretched suit against her and the damage his foul stories did to her reputation with the royal courts.

"They'll come soon," she said, lost in her thoughts.

"Your Grace?" asked Spindle attentively.

Dalflitch was quicker on the uptake. "I'm surprised they haven't sent to you already, Your Grace," she said.

"Who?" asked Righteous.

"The men of the king's court, or of the Church, or both," Dalflitch explained.

"Are they like to come?"

"Soon," Amelia said with a firm nod.

"What for?" Righteous liked an opponent in front of her. Her mind didn't take to politics as quickly as the others.

"They'll want to resolve the fracture between the Western Reach and the court in Rhales. The prince's failed crusade makes him look weak."

"His own stupid fault," Righteous sneered, but bowed her head when the duchess gave her a stern look.

"It doesn't matter," Amelia went on. "The kingdom's at war and the king cannot afford to have such a split in his army, not on the eve of a conclusive battle. The hash Daven Marcus made of his crusade west was bad enough, but what he did to me with the sham marriage and treason confession is embarrassing for King Chrostmer. His son looks like a fool and has poisoned the whole Western Reach against the throne. Every one of my nobles knows the tale and has taken my side. Between them and my own men-at-arms, that's a third of the total soldiery of the Grand Kingdom. The king cannot afford to risk losing my support."

"Would he?" asked Spindle. "He's the king. He just commands and you have to obey, don't you?"

"How could he make her?" Dalflitch answered. "With so many loyal men at her back, he'd break his own kingdom before he brought her to heel."

"But he's the king. She can't just defy him, can she?"

"Nobles do it to each other all the time. To you or me, the king is just short of God himself, but to the highest-ranking nobles, a king is just another one of them, the one lucky enough to have the fanciest chair."

Spindle whistled in disbelief, but Dalflitch's assessment matched Amelia's own. Righteous also seemed to be coming to grips with the broader situation, nodding along as she listened and then offering her own summation.

"So, the king needs the Reach's nobles and boys wit' swords. But those boys're all loyal to you because of the way Prince Daven Marcus insulted them, and you stood up to him during his useless crusade. The king needs *you*, because they're on *your* side. So, he'll send some of his own boys, all sweetness and pretty words, to make sure you're on *his* side. The 'right' side of things. What's the Church got to do with it?"

"Mother Church is involved because that's where the prince has taken his complaints," Amelia explained. She could feel her lips twist in a sneer. "The same way a parish court would be called to judge ordinary matters between a husband and wife."

"Oh ay? And some parish sacrist is going to sit judgement over a duchess and a prince, is he?"

"Not a sacrist, no," Amelia conceded. She smiled at that thought, and she heard Dalflitch sniff in amused derision.

"A synod would have to be called," Dalflitch explained. "It would take a council of the ecclesiarchs to decide between a duchess and a prince. But it won't come to that."

"Why not?"

"The king will not let it."

"Cause of the shame?" Spindle put in.

Dalflitch nodded. She still leaned back languidly on the chest by the window, but her eyes were focused and calculating. She may have been a true natural beauty and superbly trained in courtly manners, but Amelia knew the former countess nonetheless possessed the same cold knife-fighter's heart that beat in the breasts of her two lower-born ladies-in-waiting. Dalflitch didn't know one end of a blade from the other, but she had an inner edge as tempered as any steel.

"The conflict between Her Grace and Daven Marcus is already an embarrassment to the royal house of Denay," Dalflitch observed. "The prince has tried to claim the part of a spurned husband, merely seeking to have his wayward bride returned to him. But do not doubt, every man of rank can see the naked ambition the prince is trying to hide. King's court and Rhales both, they all know this is about the Reach's wealth—the duchess's lands, the iron, and the silver."

"Don't wait for the prince to worry how others see him," said Amelia. She'd spent enough time with Daven Marcus to know that the crown prince thought of life as a game and everyone else as merely the pieces for him to play with. "To him the Church courts are just another rod to beat me."

"As you say, Your Grace," Dalflitch nodded.

Righteous sneered this time and finally sat down on the bed opposite Amelia. "So, if he doesn't care what others think, then like as not he doesn't know how weak it makes him look, going crying to the Church that his wife has run off, him being a prince with an army and a court and all? All that backing him up, and he can't keep a wife at home for one night? Not even his wedding night? He looks a fool. And Your Grace's still gone more than a year now and he's not got you back? No true man would put up with that. He's weak and a fool."

"No matter how others see him, we shouldn't rush to call him weak," Amelia said quietly.

She still vividly remembered the weight of humiliation when he had struck her, punching her in the stomach and driving her to the ground. She'd defeated him eventually, undermining his plans through a combination of cunning and the loyalty of her people, but it had cost too many lives. Good lives. Amelia had cried many nights since her escape, weeping for those who'd sacrificed so much on her behalf. She felt the urge to weep now as well, but as her gaze met Righteous's, she saw the stern resolve there and the tears in her eyes dried away.

A sudden image of Daven Marcus trying to punch Righteous in the same way leaped into Amelia's mind and she knew instantly what that would lead to. The prince would find himself with a concealed poniard buried in his throat. As the two women shared their look, Amelia was sure Righteous knew what she was thinking, and the street-fighting lady-in-waiting nodded her head ever so slightly. They all knew the stories of how the prince had treated Amelia.

"No, you wouldn't," Spindle said to Righteous quietly. "You're too canny to try and stick a prince."

Amelia broke from Righteous's gaze to look around the room. She could see that each woman there was sharing the same thought, imagining the same action against the crown prince.

"Course," the masked woman went on, "if you waited for the night, you could do it quiet, when no one would know it was you."

"Oh sure," Righteous scoffed. "If you could find a moment when he had no men guarding him. No grooms or slatterns sharing his rooms." She cast a glance at Dalflitch. "No offence."

Dalflitch did not seem offended at being reminded of her old relationship with the prince and, by extension, being called a slut. Rather, the lady clutched at her breast and sighed loudly.

"Oh, it was terrible," she cried out as if terrified. "Lady Spindle and I were only seeing to the prince's *regal needs* when a shadow, a dark, beastly thing, stole between us and slew him, as if sticking him with a dagger. See how the blood has stained our hands. We have done all we might to save him, to stop the bleeding, but alas. It was witchcraft, assassination by witchcraft, I swear. Summoned from the depths of hell, it must have been, for it flew from the window into the air, his royal blood dripping from its talons." She sighed once more and then slumped, feigning being overwhelmed with fear and emotion. Lying artificially unconscious, Lady Dalflitch's lips curled into a cunning smile. Looking at her other companions, Amelia saw them likewise smiling openly.

"It seems I'm not the only one to have this particular daydream," she said to them, her own lips twitching despite her efforts to keep them under control. It was not seemly for a duchess of the realm to enjoy the thought of the crown prince being assassinated, no matter how much she felt he utterly deserved it.

"There's not so much acting in my version," Righteous muttered, but her expression showed more of a grudging respect than any disdain.

"I slept with the fool for over a year," said Dalflitch, levering herself back upright. "You'd better bet I know how to act."

The four women shared a quiet chuckle. Although only one of them was married at present, none of them was a maiden, and they all understood what private relations between men and women could be like. Amelia let herself smile at last. For her, this knowing, womanly laughter was a sign of the bonds she shared with these three who served her but were so much more to her than servants. After her husband died, she had shared her household with only servile retainers or handmaids too young, foolish, or selfish to be true friends. These three were the true companions she had longed for—loyal but worldly and cunning as well. Women with whom she could talk openly, share plans and unravel plots. Counselors and friends. For too long, she'd only had Prentice to rely upon. He was more than up to the task, wise and shrewd in equal measure, but there was only one of him, and she needed him at the head of her military.

"So, the king will send to me soon," said Amelia casting her eyes about like a captain looking to his sergeants in a council of war. "Who do we think he will send?"

"Someone high up?" offered Spindle.

"Lady Dalflitch?" Amelia cocked an eyebrow.

"Indeed, no one less than a count," Dalflitch agreed. When she noticed Amelia's surprised expression, she shook her head with a chuckle. "No, not my ex-husband. He's too old to be camping with the army these days. Even if he was available, that would be too impolite for King Chrostmer. His son's a brute, but the king is a man of gentle manners."

"Do you have any more specific ideas who the king might look to for the duty?"

Dalflitch shook her head with a regretful expression.

"So, we have only the full list of peers of the realm from which to guess." Amelia wracked her brains, trying to remember the names of the highest-ranking nobles of the Grand Kingdom. There had once been a time when she could recite the order of succession from the king down through the royal family and every ducal house in the Denay and Rhales courts, but it was such a long time since that information had seemed relevant. She had her own lands to rule and defend, and her own nobles to care about. Courtly intrigues seemed so far away.

"It won't be anyone from Rhales," Righteous said with a certainty that surprised Amelia.

"How can you be so sure?"

"Cause they're all the prince's boys. The king wants to make peace between his gang and your gang. He can't send one of the prince's as go between. 'S'gotta be someone neutral.'"

Amelia could not help wondering how the king and the prince would react to hearing themselves described as part of rival criminal gangs, but there was no denying the sense of Righteous's analysis. Thoughtful silence settled over the room. The truth was that they were making plans with too little information. Having spent years now defending her province against invaders from the west who were still mostly an enigma, Amelia knew how fruitless such musings could be.

The quiet was disturbed as a stocky man in undyed jerkin and trews under a thick leather apron mounted the stairs, stopping on the landing and respectfully tugging his forelock. Behind him came a lanky, shaven-headed youth carrying a wooden box full of tools. Not looking, the younger man nearly ran into the back of the older. When he looked up and saw the four ladies seated about the room, he too ducked his head and knuckled his hairline where his forelock should have been but was missing.

"Begging your pardons, m'ladies," said the older man awkwardly. "They sent me to make curtain rods and take measures for a panel wall. I didn't know there'd be anyone here."

Amelia smiled gently. "What is your name?"

"Bryars, m'lady," the man answered. "Master carpenter." He pointed to the silver guild pin on his breast, then nodded his head over his shoulder at the younger man. "This'un's my apprentice, Pollur. He's a year from his journeyman's and a sound lad, if a bit distractible."

Amelia nodded, but before she could say anything more, her ladies sprang to their own duties, forming a social boundary between her and the lower orders.

"The duchess thanks you for your service, Master Bryars, apprentice Pollur," Dalflitch said with a formal tone, standing quickly and straightening her skirts. "We will not interfere with your work, and you likewise will respect the privacy of her grace's chambers, seeing and hearing nothing and never speaking of anything you do see or hear. Do you understand?"

Bryars touched a finger to the pin on his chest. "I carry the honor of the guild with me, m'lady. I understand."

"Very good."

Bryars was turning to put his apprentice to his work when Righteous added one more set of instructions.

"Also, master carpenter, in future, when you come into the duchess' presence, you will not address her direct. Nor the Lady Dalflitch here." Righteous nodded to the dark-haired woman so that Bryars knew whom she meant. "You come to me or to the lady in the mask there. You don't tug a forelock to us, but you show us the deference. Understand?"

Bryars nodded.

Righteous's hard tone made it clear she would brook no mistake in manners, and the carpenter's nervous expression showed he accepted her authority in this matter without question. He looked her up and down once, clearly noting that she was a woman in trousers, a strangeness that seemed only to make her more threatening to him, if his expression was anything to go by.

Righteous gave her final instructions. "If by some quirk of fate you are forced to address the duchess directly, then you call her 'Your Grace,' not m'lady. M'lady is for lessers, like we three. The Duchess Amelia is 'Your Grace.' Tell me you understand."

"I understand." The master craftsman swallowed heavily.

"And your apprentice?"

Bryars gave Pollur a cold glance. "He knows to keep his mouth well shut, don't you?"

Pollur nodded with wide eyes and knuckled his missing hairline again.

"Then go to, Master Carpenter."

Righteous turned her back on the two workmen with such regal disdain that it took all of Amelia's self-control not to burst out laughing. Whatever the hostility between them,

Righteous had obviously been studying Dalflitch's mores and manners, and had learned a great deal. The duchess cocked an eyebrow in the ex-countess's direction. Dalflitch acknowledged Righteous's performance with a gracious nod.

"I could have done no better myself."

Maybe there was hope for peace between the two women after all, Amelia thought. In the meantime, there were other things to do.

"I have a codex of the noble houses in my luggage," she told them. "Make that a priority in the unloading, along with the other legal papers. Dalflitch you'll have to see to that." She was the only one of Amelia's ladies who could read. "Spindle, you'll go with her to fetch the cloth for making the curtains. And when you do, seek as many maidservants and camp women as you can to help you."

"I can sew, Your Grace," Spindle started to object, but Amelia raised her hand for quiet.

"I've never known a surer or finer hand, Lady Spindle, but you are only one, and I want the curtains up before we bed tonight. See to it."

Spindle curtseyed. The duchess turned to her last lady's maid. "Righteous, you'll come with me, and we'll go seek out your husband. You can have a moment with him, and I can find out how the soldiers are disposed."

"I was hoping for a bit more than a moment, Your Grace," Righteous said, but Amelia shook her head.

"Later. For now, we all have duties."

Righteous's expression showed her disappointment, but she nodded nonetheless. Amelia felt a strange mixture of sympathy and jealousy. She had compassion for the young woman's desire to be reunited with her spouse, but it only reminded her of her own dead husband. Duchesses had time for neither compassion nor jealousy, however. Amelia had duties to her people to fulfill, and she had to be ready for whomever the king would send, hoping to reconcile her conflict with the crown prince—a conflict that threatened to split the Western Reach from the rest of the kingdom, dividing it before the invaders, ripe for conquest.

CHAPTER 3

As it happened, the king sent two envoys to the duchess, and they arrived late that afternoon.

In the middle of the day, Amelia and Righteous had located Prentice Ash in the soldiers' camp, giving orders and setting duties. He reported on the status of the camp and the tales from the scouts and patrols. The stories of yet more forms of beastmen among the invaders chilled Amelia, and she was glad when Prentice ordered a sergeant and two corporals to show her the dispositions of her soldiers.

Three years ago, she had been at the mercy of arrogant knights to protect her lands and people, men who thought as much or more of their own ambitions than of their supposed loyalty to her. Now, Captain Ash had trained her a company of thousands, all skilled and disciplined. The core force was comprised of convicts, serving their years of exile in this new military of wasted men and some women, discarded by the Grand Kingdom, but Prentice had forged them into something powerful. At least that was the hope. Knighthood and military service were the essence of Grand Kingdom nobility, and those high-born nobles had a simple philosophy: you could not make a fine blade out of scrap iron, and you could not make a true man-at-arms out of a worthless rogue. When the Grand Kingdom was forced to arm peasants, they were always called rogues, and rogues were all but disposable. Prentice proposed to prove this all wrong, and so far, he had succeeded. However, with the invaders' army now so near, the toughest test was yet to come.

Amelia knew Prentice trusted his officers, so she chose to as well, and with several as escort she was happy to release Righteous to spend a private moment with her husband. The duchess saw them both as a strange yet utterly suitable pair. Prentice was hard and cold in all his dealings and Righteous was much the same. Yet when the pair came together, they revealed unexpected sides of their scarred hearts. Righteous became almost wickedly cruel, her normally sharp tongue becoming barbed in its teasing, but Prentice looked at her as a man looked at a beautiful wild animal, smiling in a way Amelia never saw him do in any other circumstance. And though his wife showed herself thorny, he reached out and grasped the nettle with all his strength and seemed all the happier for the stings.

Amelia watched the pair embrace as she was escorted away, unable to fully quash the envy she felt for Righteous. She also felt a prayerful hope that if two so damaged and unlikely lovers might find each other in the world, then perhaps she could find something like that for herself again. She did not want a future of only growing from a young widow to an old widow. Nonetheless, she would die childless and alone before she allowed Prince Daven Marcus to try to take her hand in marriage.

After her tour of inspection, Amelia returned to the watchtower, escorted by Prentice and Righteous, just in time to hear news of the approaching royal envoys.

"Who and how many?" she asked.

"Some in colors," the messenger reported, meaning men of noble birth with their own household regalia. A mere herald would wear the king's livery, rich red and gold. Just as her maids had predicted, King Chrostmer had sent high-ranking nobles to bring his greetings. "Also, there's churchmen among them, with lots of gold on their robes."

That meant ecclesiarchs, high-ranking sacrists who were rulers in the Church, coming at the same time as King Chrostmer's own political envoys. It seemed the king meant business.

"With your permission, Your Grace," said Prentice, "we can set a chair for you to receive them in the bottom floor of the tower. It'll be rough, but we'll make it suitable to your dignity."

"Will I need a chair?" she asked. "We do not know the rank of the king's envoys."

"We are still within the boundaries of the Western Reach, Your Grace," Prentice explained. "These are your lands, and in your domain you stand only in the presence of the king and the Prince of Rhales. All others are beneath you."

Amelia accepted the advice with a nod and a smile and retired upstairs to change her clothes. In her new chambers she found that the master carpenter and his apprentice had already set the curtain rod and were now gone to make the panels for the wall that would replace it. Spindle sat with four seamstresses on the beds and floor, all working swiftly to sew the curtains from two rolls of undyed linen. The lace-masked lady cut the lengths herself with a long-bladed dagger.

"I've set them to the hems and loops first, Your Grace," Spindle reported. "You said the hanging was more important than prettying them with lace or embroidery."

"Quite so," said Amelia. She then called Dalflitch to help her wash her face and hands, change her dress and set her hair. She told her ladies to keep watch so she wasn't disturbed, and Spindle immediately sent two of the women sewing on the floor to go and sit at the head of the stairs and to warn them all if anyone tried to come up.

"What about them ones on the roof?" asked one.

"If you see one of them coming down, then give us a shout for them, too," Spindle instructed. The two seamstresses smiled to hear the elegantly dressed lady-in-waiting speaking to them like an ordinary charwoman, but they soon sobered when they saw Spindle's cold-eyed expression. Her mask gave her an air of mystery, but it was also strange and intimidating and, when she wanted, Spindle Tress projected a cold, regal visage that easily cowed yeoman-folk.

An hour later, half the curtains were already in place and hanging, and Amelia was ready to receive the king's envoys. She left Spindle to supervise the rest of the sewing and descended the tower stairs to find the ground level space almost transformed. The earth floor had been swept and fresh rushes laid, giving a sweet aroma to the air. Iron braziers had been set, as well as four tall, carved wooden candelabras with high banks of thick wax candles that could burn for hours. Near the rear wall of the chamber, a dais of sorts had been improvised from wooden crates covered in a carpet, and upon this was set a heavy wooden chair with graven panels on the back and sides, as near to a throne as any watchtower ever held. The wooden arms were carved as lion's heads, and that pleased Amelia when she saw it.

Behind the chair, a banner of blue and cream cloth hung from an upright pike driven into the earthen floor. Embroidered with a rampant lion, it was the banner of Amelia's army, her household colors and heraldry. Prentice must have had it fetched up from the camp the moment she had withdrawn to change her clothes.

As she descended the stairs and took her place on the chair, Prentice stood at a respectful distance from the dais, awaiting her, dressed in his armored brigandine—a leather tunic with steel plates riveted underneath. On a battlefield, he would augment this protection with steel plates on his legs and arms, as well as gauntlets and a helmet, but for now he wore only the brigandine with his sword belted about his waist. The other man nearby was her chief steward Turley, standing formally at the corner of the dais, wearing a black doublet with a silver pin featuring the ducal lion on his breast. There was a second silver pin on the sleeve of his left arm, but the folds of the cloth made it harder to see. He waited on his mistress like the captain, but facing away, fulfilling the role of herald, ready to greet her guests.

"You were right, Captain Prentice," the duchess said as she watched two lesser chairs brought for her two ladies-in-waiting.

Dalflitch sat with perfect dignity, arranging her skirts precisely, as if the task were the most important in all the world. When she was done, she looked up with an impassive face that would rival a marble statue for its reserve. On the duchess's other side Righteous sat with much less grace. Though she had changed into a skirt, the slender young woman fidgeted and cast her eyes about continually, giving no sign of comfort whatsoever. Amelia was certain that Righteous would much rather be standing next to her husband than seated in this place of honor, as well as dressed in trousers. Nonetheless, the woman said nothing and gradually settled herself.

"Right, Your Grace?" Prentice asked, not understanding Amelia's statement.

"You have made a respectable space for the Duchess of the Reach to receive king's envoys."

"Much of the credit goes to your stewards and their chief."

"Then thanks to you, Master Turley," Amelia said to Turley, who half turned and bowed to receive the thanks. He and Prentice were the closest of friends, going back to years spent together as convicts, and they were ferociously loyal to each other and to their liege.

"Captain Prentice did have the pretty banner sent for," Turley said with a straight face and a glint in his eye. "Some of the thanks could go to him if Your Grace wished it. 'Course it was other men that did the actual fetching, so he'd have to share the praise with them, if we're being fair." He looked back at Prentice, who glared at him. Although she could not see his face, Amelia knew that Turley would have a roguish grin. It was the nature of their friendship: Prentice was dangerous; Turley was trouble. It occurred to the duchess that Turley was like

Righteous in that regard, and she wondered that Prentice drew such people to himself so often.

Did he do it deliberately?

"I'm sure you can sort the division of reward between yourselves at a later time," Amelia said, gathering herself and putting a sober expression on her own face. "In the meantime, let us bring the envoys in. Evening is pressing upon us, and it is not seemly that they should be left on my doorstep."

Prentice and Turley accepted the instruction, and the captain turned to give a nod to two men standing guard at the door. They went out and returned ahead of a clutch of four more men. Three were tall and proud, dressed in long gambesons of knightly colors. The fourth was short and stout, and if anything, more richly dressed in embroidered vestments of a high churchman. A gold cross at least a handspan wide sat on his barreled chest, hanging from a glittering chain over a black robe of deep velvet that was surely too warm for spring. Of the three knights in the group, two were young and wore longswords with the confidence of men who knew how to wield them. The third was older, with a fully grey beard and moustache, neatly groomed and his hair trimmed. Despite his age, he still stood straight-backed and strong.

The four paused a moment just inside the door, and from behind them a fifth emerged, another knight, but one wearing Amelia's colors rather than any of his own. This was Knight Captain Sir Gant, instantly recognizable by his red hair and long moustache. Prentice would have set him to accompany the envoys, Amelia was sure, as a man of sufficiently high rank to escort them through the camp without insulting their dignity. Sir Gant gestured with an open hand and led the envoys to the space in front of Amelia's chair.

"Your Grace," Sir Gant said, formally bowing in front of her, "may I present the chosen envoy of King Chrostmer the Fourth, Count Lark-Stross of Ashfield." He stood aside and made space for the older man who stepped forward and bowed with perfect formality. In that short moment, Amelia wracked her brain for any information she could remember about Lark-Stross or his place in the king's court, but nothing came to mind. She cast a side glance at Dalflitch to see if her attendant had anything she could communicate, but except for a tiny shake of her head, the former countess had nothing to offer.

"You are welcome, My Lord," Amelia said formally. "I apologize for the crudeness of my hospitality, but I am sure you understand the limitations of armies marching to war."

"I do, of course, Your Grace," Lark-Stross replied, his voice rich and deep. "But I would not dream of calling your hospitality crude. We have been well disposed as we waited. Food and wine were set for us and chairs beside a cheering fire. We have been quite comfortable."

You're a smooth one, Amelia thought. No wonder the king sent Lark-Stross. This was a man who understood diplomacy.

"With your permission, Your Grace," the count went on. "I would introduce my companions."

Amelia nodded. The count ushered the first of the other two knights forward.

"This is my son, Marken." The young man bowed, and when he straightened again, Amelia could see immediately the family resemblance. Both men had the same rich brown eyes and firm, set jaws. The two could only be father and son. The count continued. "He is my pride. Already he handles much of my estate business in Ashfield and one day soon will take the whole of the county upon his shoulders."

"A competent man, then," Amelia complimented the young knight. "Such a son must be a source of great pride to his father."

"Indeed, he is, Your Grace."

Sir Marken stood back again, and Amelia expected Lark-Stross to introduce the other knight next, but instead he turned to the churchman.

"This is Reverend Master Faldmoor."

The ecclesiarch stood forward but bowed with a deal less formality than the men who preceded him. As he straightened up, he touched his hands to the gold cross on his chest in a way that seemed deliberately significant to Amelia's eye.

"The reverend master is primarch elder of the Church Academy in Ashfield." As the count finished the introduction, it seemed to the duchess that he hung some special emphasis on the name of Ashfield.

That's twice he's mentioned the town, she thought. *Why?*

For a long moment there was silence, and caught in her thoughts, Amelia took some time before she noticed. Fearing she had somehow been impolite, she looked at the fourth and final man, by far the youngest of them all.

"And who is this last knight?" she asked before she even really looked at him.

Turning her eyes upon the man, Amelia realized he was quite young, with a long, narrow face and skin and hair so fair that he looked almost feminine in the candlelight. As she regarded him, she also noticed that his long gambeson was white, with two overlapping crosses on the chest, one black and one green. Two crosses was an emblem, a sign that this was a knight of the Church, sworn sword to defend the faith. Realizing this, it was less of a surprise that Ecclesiarch Faldmoor made the man's introduction.

"This man is sworn to Mother Church," said the patriarch. "And his name is Sir..."

"Pallas?" exclaimed Prentice suddenly, his shocked tone drawing every eye in the room.

CHAPTER 4

S ir Pallas?

Even before the duchess had sat down in her improvised throne, Prentice felt like a rope pulled taut and kept under tension, his nerves singing like a cable in a high wind. This was the first time the duchess would meet with any Grand Kingdom nobles since Prince Daven Marcus had fled back east with his tail between his legs. No one from west of the mountains had any clear idea what the nobility of the inner kingdom thought of the Duchess of the Western Reach and the accusations of her waywardness. It was suicidally unlikely that these men sent by King Chrostmer were assassins, but that didn't mean Prentice trusted them. He had a cohort line of Fangs, the White Lions' specialist swordsmen, waiting just outside, unseen but ready to be summoned should there be violence.

His first duty was always to defend his liege's life.

Prentice watched her seat herself with the dignity he had grown to respect more and more as the years of his service passed. She was still a young woman really, but there was nothing immature or ill-considered in what she did. Beside her, the older, dark-haired Lady Dalflitch was equally poised, seated forward on her lesser chair, hands folded delicately on her lap. It took all Prentice's will not to grin at his wife Righteous as she fidgeted herself into her own seat. It was surprising enough for him just to see her in a dress, and though she was obviously doing everything to project a similar air of dignity as the other two ladies beside her, she just could not do it. There was something about her that was too unpolished. Dalflitch and the duchess were tended roses, perfectly suited to a courtly arrangement. Righteous was a wildflower, pretty in her way but uncultivated, far more suited to a rougher setting.

As much as he delighted in her, Prentice pushed his feelings for his wife to the back of his mind and forced his thoughts to focus on the coming envoys. He'd wanted to punch Turley when they'd had their little moment of banter, but this was not the time. Then his watchful nervousness climbed to an even higher pitch as the king's representatives were finally admitted. Prentice surreptitiously met Sir Gant's eye as the knight escorted the envoys in front of the dais, and there was a flicker of recognition, the slightest of signals. The messenger nobles had made no trouble and there were no other signs of treachery. That was something.

Then came the introductions, and as the duchess and Count Lark-Stross exchanged pleasantries, something about one of the representatives caught Prentice's attention. He studied the man in Church knight garb, trying to pin down what was wrong. With so many candles, the light was not terrible, but somehow the young knight conspired to keep his face hidden from Prentice's gaze. It wasn't obvious, but the man was certainly turning away from Prentice, keeping his head down, even though that meant he was not paying attention to the duchess either. His posture wasn't insulting to her grace, but it was far from polite in such noble company.

Prentice was beginning to wonder if this was the treachery he feared, somehow brewing in this Church knight's head, when he heard the count mention that the ecclesiarch present was primarch elder of the Ashfield Academy. Prentice had been a student at Ashfield when he had been convicted of heresy almost fourteen years ago. When Faldmoor made to introduce the mysterious knight, the young Church man-at-arms turned to Prentice and lifted his eyes, and Prentice knew in a shocking instant why the man had captured his attention.

It was his brother.

"Pallas?" he barked out before he could stop himself. Prentice's youngest brother, Pallas, had not even been eight years old the last time Prentice had seen him back before his exile. During his trial, Prentice's ambitious father had disowned him to protect the family from the shame of his son's heresy conviction, and Prentice had not laid eyes on any member of his family since. Nevertheless, the face that looked at him now was unmistakably that of his youngest sibling. Pallas wore his fair hair long in the knightly fashion, but his high cheekbones and narrow features were as they had been in his childhood.

And the blue eyes in that face were full of furious hatred.

"Is something wrong, Captain Prentice?" the duchess asked, and Prentice could hear the concern in her voice, mixed with annoyance.

Speaking out of turn was a breach of protocol that could offend a noble of the count's rank. Still, Prentice could not break his eyes from his brother's.

"Perhaps he is experiencing an agony of guilt," Ecclesiarch Faldmoor mused loudly, the archness in his tone unmistakable. "It is common among convicts not fully purged of their sin, especially heretics and apostates."

That comment penetrated Prentice's confused surprise, and he glared at the patriarch through slitted eyes.

"Bastard," he whispered quietly.

Then he realized how close he was to saying something rash and he physically bit his own tongue to shut himself up. The duchess could not afford to have him embarrassing her.

"Revered Master, I think you are mistaken," the duchess said, and it was clear from her tone she was not pleased. "Captain Prentice is a reformed convict and a trusted man. He is fully purged under law; his conviction is spent."

"Only the Church can forgive apostasy."

"The duchess is addressed as 'Your Grace,' even by fat churchmen," said Righteous.

Dalflitch and the duchess both gave her a stern glance, and Prentice wanted her to shut up as well before she compounded his rudeness. But he was still watching Faldmoor's expression as the primarch elder turned to face the dais. The man was not in the least bit insulted; he was smiling. Prentice was sure this was all part of some plan of his. But what?

"I see respect for the Church is somewhat lax throughout your house, *Your Grace*," Faldmoor addressed the duchess. His demeanor showed not the slightest deference to her rank. "It is as I said earlier, Count Lark-Stross. Heresy is a devil's rot that spreads so easily from the apostate to whomever he beds, from servant to mistress. The west is a house that needs a master's strength, not the dainty restraint of a mere woman."

Prentice saw the burning fury in his liege's eyes and he cursed himself inwardly. Faldmoor was insulting the duchess to her face, using Prentice's heresy as an excuse, and he and Righteous's outbursts had given the churchman the perfect opening.

"Forgive my lady-in-waiting, Master," Amelia apologized to the ecclesiarch through gritted teeth. "She is sometimes overzealous for my dignity. She is not however, a heretic. Neither, indeed, is any member of my household. As for the firmness of my grasp upon the Western Reach, I would point out that under my guidance we have repelled multiple assaults of the invaders which now beset the rest of the south of the Grand Kingdom. The Redlanders have not found my grip so light or dainty that they could wrest my province from me. Neither has any other man."

That was a reference to Prince Daven Marcus, Prentice knew. Everyone in the room had to know it.

"As you say, Your Grace," Faldmoor answered her in a tone that conceded nothing. "Nonetheless, Mother Church will keep her own counsel on all such subjects."

Prentice knew his mistress was being goaded by Faldmoor, but he could not help looking back to Pallas, who continued to glare like a hunting dog held back by an invisible leash. The young man wanted him dead, there could be no doubt. Prentice had never been especially close to his younger brother, but he had never imagined that their normal fraternal affection could be twisted into such contempt. For his own part, Prentice had absorbed the rejection of his father disowning him and buried all those feelings under the ice cold will he cultivated to survive, like the darkness of deep-frozen water buried under thick frost in the dead of winter. Watching his brother's expression, it took all Prentice's will not to put his hand to his own sword. Such a gesture could easily be interpreted as a threat, and looking into that loathing gaze, Prentice was sure Pallas would love nothing more than an excuse to draw his own blade.

How would he react if Pallas did attack him? Prentice realized he had no answer for that question.

"Did you have a point to reach, sacrist, or do you visit me simply to sermonize while being rude?" Prentice heard the duchess ask and realized that he hadn't been listening as the conversation moved on without him.

He turned his attention back to it, one eye still drawn to keep watch on his brother. He could tell by the duchess's tone that she was reaching the limit of her patience with Faldmoor. Moreover, it was obvious that this was likely the ecclesiarch's intent. He wanted her to lose her temper.

"Even kings and princes have spent many willing hours listening to my sermons, Duchess, and been thankful for the opportunity. Perhaps if you had more love for the Church and her truth, you would not bristle so at instruction."

"Is that so, sacrist?"

Duchess Amelia's eyes were narrowed as she stripped the churchman down in address to the rank of a mere parish cleric again, and her mouth twisted in so deep a frown she could have blistered paint. Any minute the reverend master would provoke her into insulting him directly, or the Church, and that would confirm all the rumors that Prince Daven Marcus was circulating about her. In a flash of insight, Prentice became certain that was Faldmoor's entire purpose in this meeting.

He cast a swift glance at Lark-Stross and his son. The two noblemen stood watching impassively. They were in on this, Prentice was certain. Officially, they were here as envoys of the king. Reverend Master Faldmoor's rudeness should be as embarrassing to them as it was to the duchess, but it clearly was not. That was not why they were here; they were here as witnesses. Faldmoor would provoke Amelia to insult the Church, and Lark-Stross, an ostensibly neutral third party, would be shocked to see the extent of the duchess's lack of morals and propriety, which would be taken as a sign of weakness, waywardness, and possibly even heresy. This entire envoy was sent by the king, but it had come to support the prince's Church lawsuit against the duchess. Prentice knew the duchess was wise enough to see the trap, but as the sniping continued between noblewoman and Church leader, it was becoming obvious she could not find a dignified way to get clear of the hectoring cleric. Her temper would soon undo her.

Dignity, Prentice thought. *That's the key*.

Faldmoor was pushing her to be undignified, rude even, with his own rudeness being so well couched in the guise of theological teaching. The duchess could not afford to be rude to the Church, even in the guise of this self-righteous boor.

But a heretic could.

CHAPTER 5

"What word of the invaders from the west, My Lord Lark-Stross?" Prentice asked so loudly that everyone in the room started, even his glaring brother. Every eye fell on him again, and the duchess's expression turned all her fury in his direction.

Trust me one moment, he pleaded with his liege lady in his heart.

"Captain Prentice, you speak out of turn," Lady Dalflitch rebuked him, speaking on the duchess's behalf before Amelia herself could. Prentice gave a shallow, polite bow to the dais and as he did so, he saw something in Dalflitch's eyes. In that one look he was sure he recognized in her expression the same concern that he felt. They both wanted to get their mistress out of this fool theological trap.

"Your Grace, forgive my rudeness, but the invaders rampage on Grand Kingdom soil, and Count Lark-Stross has been sent as envoy from the crown and throne. While I do not doubt that King Chrostmer, may God favor his reign, wants every issue of Church law pursued to its fullest extent, it is an unconscionable waste of the count's time with Redlanders assailing the king's peace at this very moment. Perhaps, with your permission and as your captain, I might receive the king's instructions from the count for the dispensation of your army while the revered master continues his sermon to you in private, if you wished."

"You imagine yourself of a rank to receive a count, Captain? And you rudely interrupt Church discourse! And then you think to direct your liege lady? You forget yourself," Dalflitch said sternly, feeding Prentice his next line. He was certain now she knew what he was doing. Together, they were rewriting this little morality play, improvising their lines.

Just don't say anything stupid, Prentice thought to himself, and he nodded to Dalflitch.

"Of course, My Lady, you are completely correct. But I feared to insult the count, not to mention the royal house itself, by treating his envoy as something that could wait. Church teaching is fundamental to all that is good in life. My purging service here in the west has taught me that well, under the duchess' firm hand. But the king's envoy is the king's dignity, and that cannot be delayed. And the Grand Kingdom is at war."

Prentice looked to Lark-Stross and then to Faldmoor. The churchman's smile was gone now, replaced with a scowl every bit as hateful as Pallas's expression. Now he was trapped in the same net he had spread for the duchess. So was the count. If either man pressed to continue the theological lecturing, then they effectively insulted the king, and Lark-Stross would be dishonored for failing the dignity of his office. They had to release the trap now or else be caught in it, and the duchess had not had to be rude to get out from it.

Of course, that meant that Prentice *had* been rude, and the full weight of the trap fell on him.

"You dare rebuke your betters?" Dalflitch demanded.

"Only from zeal for the king and the kingdom," Prentice pleaded insincerely.

He looked to the duchess, and every eye in the room followed. Seated on her throne, Amelia straightened her back and looked down on the whole room. For a fleeting instant her lightly freckled nose crinkled, and it looked as if she were suppressing a smile. Then her face was a dignified mask once more. Prentice knew then that he had succeeded; he had bought her that moment's breath to recover her self-control.

"Zeal is admirable, as Revered Master Faldmoor is demonstrating," Amelia conceded with a reserved nod in Prentice's direction. "Nonetheless, to interrupt an audience in this manner is most improper, and you will be chastised. This is not a battlefield, Captain."

Prentice bowed to accept the duchess's rebuke, but Faldmoor thought he saw an opening to continue his hectoring.

"Even on a battlefield, this disrespect would show a corrupted spirit."

Prentice saw his wife open her mouth to speak in his defense, but this time Duchess Amelia was ready, and she spoke first.

"You speak as one who thinks to know. My captain has stood ground beside princes and knight commanders," she said mildly but with firmness, mimicking Faldmoor's boast about his sermons. "He fought beside the late Prince Mercad, and the champion Carron Ironworth, at the Battle of the Brook. Sir Carron took this man's hand fondly after the battle as a brotherly comrade. As men who had fought and won together."

"They didn't fight well enough to save the prince's life though, did they?" Faldmoor retorted sourly, but it was a misstep. Both Lark-Stross and Marken drew in angry breaths to hear that level of disrespect for men like the old prince and Sir Carron.

"Prince Mercad was King Chrostmer's brother, and he gave his life saving the Reach and the Grand Kingdom from invaders," Amelia declared imperiously. "He died a hero of the west, as did many knights of Rhales and the Reach. We who are left thank God daily for the safety their sacrifice won for us. Perhaps it is you who forget yourself if you would speak so disdainfully of one so revered."

"He was a prince, not a saint, slattern!" Pallas declared suddenly, his voice dripping with contempt. He sneered up at Amelia, all pretense of manners stripped away. Faldmoor wheeled on him and hissed for silence, but it was too late. The damage was done. Veiled hostility had given way to naked insult, and it had not been the duchess who had broken protocol. Her honor was secure, at least for now.

"Fool boy!" Faldmoor spat, and he dismissed the knight with a wave of his hand. Pallas seemed confused, no sign of regret in his expression for how he had spoken. Nonetheless, he accepted the dismissal and turned to go without acknowledging the duchess's rank or the count's, for that matter. He certainly made no effort to apologize for insulting her grace.

Like a sudden change in the weather, the mood in the room shifted. With little more than a bare nod, Reverend Master Faldmoor withdrew as well, also offering no apology, and not even waiting for permission to go. As the tower door closed behind him, Amelia turned to the count.

"What would His Majesty have of my forces, My Lord envoy?" she asked as if the ecclesiarch's exit had been a model of decorum. Lark-Stross blinked several times, seemingly taking a moment to adjust to the changed circumstances.

"His majesty instructs that you attend his court tomorrow for a council of war," the count explained finally.

"A forfeits council?" Amelia asked.

The count shook his head. "Forfeiture is an old practice, Your Grace," he said. "It is more honored in the breach than the observance in the Denay court."

During the first campaign against the invaders, Prince Mercad, the previous crown prince, had held a forfeits council, following the old tradition of Grand Kingdom armies. Duchess Amelia had turned the whole event to her advantage politically, and Prentice wondered if King Chrostmer had heard tell of that achievement. Perhaps his majesty might fear that she could do it again, and the count's explanation for why there would not be one in this war was a polite, if plausible, lie. Or the king could simply hold no value in the practice; it was an old tradition.

"This is only a council of strategems, Your Grace," Lark-Stross went on. "You are welcome to attend. Your bent for martial leadership, in spite of your alleged daintiness, is well reported. Your knight captain and the…" The count paused to look at Prentice. "The man in charge of your rogues can also attend."

"There are no rogues in the Western Reach," said Amelia. "Only knights and my sworn company, the White Lions."

"As you say, Your Grace."

"My Lord, please tell his majesty that I and my men will attend his council readily, and we thank him for his invitation."

"I will, Your Grace." The count bowed, as did his son. "With your permission?"

The duchess nodded and Lark-Stross turned to go, but Prentice's voice stopped him.

"Might I speak, Your Grace?" he asked, looking not to her, but to the two envoy knights. When he heard her give him permission, there was a strained tone in her voice. He was sure she wanted the whole encounter finished, but this was something he had to do. "My Lord Count, I apologize to you and to your son unreservedly. I have been rude and have no excuse. If it seems good to you, let me offer you any recompense you see fit to demand."

"Recompense?" repeated Lark-Stross. "What recompense can a convict offer?"

"I was a convict, My Lord, but am no longer. My conviction and service in the west has reformed me, as the duchess attests. I have my own purse and some small means. I invite you to name a price within those to satisfy your honor."

"You think to buy my father's forgiveness?" asked Marken, but Prentice shook his head.

"Forgiveness, like honor, cannot be bought," Prentice conceded. "I would not insult the count with bribery. But an appropriate gift, perhaps a donation to the academy under his care in Ashfield, would be a suitable recompense to honor."

For a long moment the count held Prentice's eyes, and the ex-convict wondered what was going through the noble envoy's mind. Then, the count looked to the duchess and gave her a truly respectful nod, as of an opponent who appreciates that he has been outplayed. Lark-Stross looked back at Prentice.

"You are unfailingly polite," he said, "for a rude man."

Then the count turned on his heel and led his son from the room into the torchlit night outside. Prentice stood silently, watching as the door closed after them. From behind him he heard a whistle, and when he turned back was surprised to see it had come from Lady Dalflitch.

"Captain Prentice," she said, shaking her head in appreciative disbelief and whistling again. "I've gambled the whole table on the turn of a card in my time, and I've heard of the fool who falls in a puddle and comes up having found a crown of gold, but I never thought I'd see it played out so readily."

Prentice looked at the duchess and saw in her expression the same mix of relief and wonderment that colored Lady Dalflitch's tone, and he was glad. The whole short conversation with the envoys had been a petty, vicious battle of manners, maneuvering for honor or humiliation, like so many of the interactions between Grand Kingdom nobility. And this had just been the first foray. Even as the king summoned the duchess's army to war, so he called her into more and more of these social combats—less bloody than true battle, but no less dangerous.

CHAPTER 6

"Whoo-wee but that boy hated your guts," Righteous declared from the dais. "Who was he?"

Prentice wasn't sure if she was talking to him or to the duchess. Either would qualify. For her part, Duchess Amelia had closed her eyes and was pinching the bridge of her nose. Prentice knew it as a sign that she was thinking deeply, considering all the implications of what had just passed.

"You knew him, Captain Ash?" Dalflitch asked.

"He is my brother, Pallas, Lady Dalflitch" Prentice admitted, feeling strangely shame-faced. "I have not seen him since my conviction. Since well before that, in fact."

"No wonder you spoke out of turn. We should be thankful that you managed to wrestle your tongue as well as you did. Your heart must have been driving you to say much more."

"It is kind of you to think so, My Lady," Prentice acknowledged.

"I'd have told him to stop making eyes and either pull his head in or skin his blade, see if his steel has the edge he thinks it does," Righteous chimed in. "Even if he was my brother.

"Oh, and surely that would have served Her Grace," said Dalflitch archly. "Your little comment to the primarch elder did enough damage as it was."

"The twit was being rude."

"He's an ecclesiarch of the Church, not a carpenter building a curtain rod. He gets to be rude. He was being provocative deliberately, and you took the bait like a fish in a hurry to know what air tastes like."

Righteous frowned, eyebrows knitted.

"I'd just point out that Sir Gant and I were the solers of discretion," Turley said quietly and loyally as he sidled next to Prentice. "We never said a word."

"Souls of discretion," Prentice said, correcting his friend's grammar.

"What?"

"Never mind." This wasn't the time for old comrades to console each other. Prentice looked to the duchess, and she met his eyes.

"My thanks to you all for your service this evening," she said as they shared that look, but addressing the room as a whole. "Especially you and Sir Gant, Chief Steward. You both were, indeed, the souls of discretion." She smiled affectionately for a moment, then sighed and her face became stern. "I would speak with the captain now. The rest may go to their duties and thence their rests."

Everyone else in the room bowed, curtseyed, or tugged the forelock as rank required, and then withdrew. As he went past, Turley clapped Prentice on the shoulder gently.

"Your brother became a Church knight instead of you, eh?" he said.

"So it would seem," Prentice replied, feeling weary and wanting to be dismissed as well.

"Your brother became a Brother," Turley joked lamely, but Prentice didn't laugh or smile. "Better him than you."

Prentice cocked an eyebrow.

"You'd have looked a right twat with your hair cut like that. And one of them white robes? Like a maid on her wedding day."

That made Prentice smile, and he was thankful at last for his friend's efforts. The duchess, however, had no more patience for breaches of decorum, it seemed.

"Do not tarry, master steward," she said firmly. "You have your duties to go to."

Turley tugged his forelock again and departed quickly. Soon enough the whole ground floor of the watchtower was empty again, even the two guards at the door stepping outside, leaving just Prentice and Amelia. Upstairs, a gentle sound of women conversing could be heard, the seamstresses finishing the curtains and doubtless asking Lady Dalflitch and Righteous what a meeting with a king's envoy had been like. The sound of someone loudly shushing them floated down, stilling all voices. For a long moment, Prentice waited as the duchess sat looking at him in silence. Then she offered him the seat beside her, the one his wife had just vacated.

Time for my bollocking, he thought as he sat down. When the duchess finally spoke, he was surprised by the softness of her tone.

"He really did look like he wanted to kill you," she said.

"He's not the first."

The duchess's eyes went wide, but her expression remained gentle. Prentice shrugged. He was a heretic that had shamed his family. What else was there to say?

"That could have gone much worse than it did," the duchess went on, changing the subject.

"I'm truly sorry, Your Grace..." Prentice began to apologize, but she held up a hand to stop him.

"You were provoked. They'll have done it on purpose, bringing your brother to this meeting to throw us off."

"But why?" Prentice understood her reasoning but was surprised to imagine that high-ranking nobles and the Church hierarchy would bother to include him in their plans. He expected to be beneath their notice. "Have I risen so far?"

His liege lady nodded. "It seems you have. Also, they have only gossip and the prince's vicious accusations by which to judge my house. Remember who had the prince's ear when he was last in the west?"

"Liam."

Prentice nodded, remembering the ambitious nobleman who had undermined him and the duchess so often. Baron Liam was dead almost two years now, and not for the first time, Prentice was glad it was so.

"The now-departed baron was obsessed with the idea that you and I were laying together," the duchess said. "He accused me of it more than once, even to the prince."

Prentice snorted in derision at the idea. Even if he had thought to want such a thing, Duchess Amelia was too aware of the political needs of her position to condescend to marry an ex-convict and too moral a woman to lay with him just for the thrill of it. In all his life, this young noble woman who married up from the hoi poloi was the only person he'd ever known with a similar level of self-control as his own—not that his had served him all that well this night. As he thought about it, Prentice shook his head and berated himself inwardly for being too critical. He had spoken out of turn from surprise, but he'd done little enough real damage. And as a new silence extended between them, he realized the duchess thought much the same.

There wasn't going to be a bollocking after all.

"At least we gave them nothing new to report," he ventured. "I am still in your household, but they knew that. You received them as a decorous widow, with ladies-in-waiting at your side and no heretical lover whispering in your ear. Your house had some unruly underlings, but so are all Reachermen to them. No one in the king's court would expect any different. We were far from perfect, but we did not give them the salacious new gossip for which they were hoping."

The duchess watched him as he spoke and then smiled slightly. "They wanted to come back with new tales to tell, at least the churchmen did," she agreed. "Faldmoor was here to provoke me, there is no doubt. But Count Lark-Stross was more watchful, I thought."

"To be a neutral witness, probably."

This time she did not fully agree with him. "Perhaps, but I believe that is not all."

Prentice considered what else it might be. "You wonder exactly what he will be reporting back to the king?"

"Yes." The duchess pondered quietly for a moment longer. "I'll have to ask Dalflitch what she knows of the man. Her experience with the royal courts far exceeds mine."

"My own experience in Ashfield never led me across the count's path, sorry to say, Your Grace," Prentice said. Duchess Amelia looked up from her thoughts with surprise.

"Of course, you were at the academy there, weren't you?" Her wonder turned to a look of shrewd thought mixed with concern. "Are you hurt that I did not think to ask you? That I wanted her opinion but not yours?"

"Your Grace?" Even knowing the duchess as he did, this question caught Prentice out.

"For a long time now, you have been my highest counselor, the voice I listen to first and most closely. I wonder if you fear losing your influence now that others have grown in my service, especially Lady Dalflitch."

Prentice frowned and pressed his hand upon his thigh absentmindedly as he considered his response.

"I serve at your pleasure, Your Grace," he explained at last. "And I have always encouraged you to know your own mind; you know that. Listen to me. Listen to Lady Dalflitch. Listen to every voice, weigh them by your own wisdom and then decide as you see fit. As you say, the lady knows the royal courts, Rhales and Denay, better than I ever will. And she is shrewd the way a fox wishes it could be."

"Do you think I should trust her?"

"Yes, Your Grace." Prentice fixed his liege with a level gaze. In private she still accepted him as a near equal, so long as he never forgot that when they stood up from these quiet conversations, she became the duchess once more and he her sworn man. He gave the duchess his honest assessment of her high-born lady. "She is loyal. You have only to hear her tell the tale of your desperate retreat together across the grasslands to know that. Whatever she was before you met her, Your Grace, Lady Dalflitch knows she owes you everything, even her life. As do I."

The duchess reached out a hand and placed it on his. "Thank you. I think there is some point of conflict between Dalflitch and Turley, and I was nervous that she was rubbing you all the wrong way."

It did not surprise Prentice to hear that exactly, especially knowing Turley and his predilection for cheek, but he had no specific information. He shook his head.

"The lady and I have rarely spoken, and this evening she did her best to support me against the primarch elder."

"By rebuking you publicly?"

"I was an underling being rude. By rebuking me, she showed that you keep your house in order. When your captain was unruly, you did not even need to speak a single word to bring things back to appropriate equanimity. You have servants for that."

"And meanwhile, your censure is the cost to buy me a moment to gather my thoughts." The duchess looked truly regretful as she spoke. Prentice waved away any coming apology.

"I'm only thankful it worked, Your Grace. Normally you are quite the equal of sharp-tongued exchanges like that."

"Not with Faldmoor though. Are the courtiers of the inner kingdom that much more cunning? Or just sacrists?"

Prentice smiled but shook his head. "A man does not rise to primarch elder of the Academy without having lived a life of constant debate and theological battle. Reverend Master Faldmoor is exceptional, I promise you, Your Grace. And..." He gave her a conspiratorial nod. "I'd bet silvers to saddle soap that he spent hours plotting and planning everything he said. He came with a sermon in mind and a dozen honed barbs with which to pin you, whichever way you twisted."

That seemed to comfort her, and she smiled, lowering her head with a sigh. Her arms and shoulders visibly relaxed.

"As to a conflict between Turley and Lady Dalflitch," Prentice went on, "he's not said anything to me about it. And do not discount the possibility that he is the one rubbing her the wrong way. This is Turley we're talking about."

That made her chuckle. "I'll have to talk to Dalflitch directly about it."

"Better that than to let it trouble your mind."

The duchess breathed deeply for a moment and Prentice waited quietly. She would dismiss him soon, he expected. Then he would go back to his tent in the camp and see that the night watches were set. He would also have to plan for when they went to the king's strategy council tomorrow. Would the duchess need an armed escort? A show of strength might help. No matter how many victories her forces won, there would always be some who only saw her as a silly young woman, unsuited to war councils. But too forceful a show of strength might be taken as an insult. Yet another political needle for the duchess to thread.

I'm not going to sleep well tonight, he thought. *I could do with my wife's company.*

"Do you ever wish you could just run away from all this?" she asked him suddenly, as if reading or sharing his thoughts.

"Not for an instant, Your Grace," he answered readily. "Like no one before you, even your departed husband, you have protected the Western Reach. I could not live with myself if I abandoned you in that task."

"What happened to your ambition, Prentice?"

"You fulfilled it, Your Grace, when you let me off the chain. Now I have the debt to pay."

"We've come a long way from that night when we hid together in a church and wondered if we were to be slaughtered along with those villagers, haven't we?"

"Yes, we have, Your Grace."

From the look in her eyes, Prentice was sure she was remembering the cries and screams of the dying from that horrific night years ago. Sometimes in his dreams he was still haunted by those anguished voices, but often enough they were only a few among many crying souls from a dozen such brutal days and nights. And there were always his own tormented screams among the voices. The scars in his flesh told the tales, but it was his dreams that recalled the sufferings most vividly. The Inquisition had not been kind when it interrogated him. It never was.

"Tomorrow the king will make known his plan to drive the Redlanders back up the Murr River for good," said the duchess. "Then I will have only the prince and his matrimonial ambitions to cope with. I think it will be good to have one less enemy to fight."

"Until the next one arises," said Prentice without thinking.

"Thank you for that pessimism, Prentice. I wouldn't want too much hope in my thoughts." She cocked an eyebrow at him and the pair of them laughed.

"Ten years on a chain makes hope an unfamiliar habit, Your Grace. Forgive me."

She nodded. "Your wife misses you," she said, changing the subject.

"I miss her."

"I could send her to you tonight, if you wish."

"I would enjoy nothing more, but you are safer with her in your chamber. Until we return north, it will be better she stays with you."

"I appreciate your sacrifice. Will you go now to your bed?"

"Eventually, Your Grace," Prentice admitted. "But there are many duties first."

"Then you are dismissed, Captain."

Prentice stood and gave her the White Lions' salute, slapping his right fist to his brigandine, over his heart. The duchess nodded, accepting the honor, and Prentice withdrew. As he left, she called after him.

"And give Sir Gant my thanks."

"For what specifically, Your Grace?" Prentice asked.

"For his escort duty on the road. And his dignity in the midst of that fracas tonight. Turley was right, the pair of them were the 'solers' of discretion."

Prentice nodded with a smile, then ducked through the tower door out into the night.

CHAPTER 7

The warm spring night made for a pleasant walk down from the tower back into the camp proper. Prentice was even more pleased when a patrol challenged him at the edge of the encampment. They were doing their work diligently.

"Who goes?" came the call, and a lantern hood was pulled to shine light suddenly in his face.

"Captain Ash," he answered readily and waited while his uniform was recognized. The sudden light meant he couldn't make out the men challenging him very well, but he heard their fists slap their chests.

"Sorry, Cap'n," said one. "Didn't know you in the dark."

"Do not apologize. You know your orders. Everyone is challenged until they are known."

"That's right, sir."

"Very good. Back to your patrol."

The light was shuttered once more, and the patrol moved off. Prentice could understand the soldiers' uncertainty. A Grand Kingdom noble challenged like that by a low-born man would likely have been offended. Even a mere knight, accustomed to the rougher manners of a military camp, could easily have been insulted, or at least indignant, and then the cruelty of the social order would fall on the heads of a simple group of men doing their duty in the late hours of the night. But Prentice was no knight.

And I never will be, he thought to himself.

The heart of the military order he was trying to create in the White Lions made knights irrelevant. Any man could rise to any rank, even the captaincy itself. Birth was not to matter, only success or failure. Of course, all of this was in service of the duchess, a noblewoman. How irrelevant had he really made birth, if the ultimate service was to protect a noble? Prentice did not have an answer, and he didn't let himself dwell on the question, turning his mind to practical matters as he approached his tent. Two men were waiting for him, silhouetted by the nearby campfires.

"Ho, Captain," one called softly, and Prentice recognized the voice as belonging to Fostermae, the sacrist who served as the White Lions' de facto chaplain.

The slender man with thinning hair around his tonsured head was a skilled healer and devout servant of the gospel. For his services to her militia, the duchess provided Fostermae with a generous stipend, but apart from buying a warmer robe without patches or holes, the sacrist refused to spend the guilders on himself, instead sending it to his old parish in the town of Dweltford where it was used to feed widows and orphans.

Prentice didn't recognize the other figure with the sacrist and in the dark could only make out that whoever he was, he was also dressed in a clerical robe. That did not bode well. They had already sent his brother after him this night. Was this another clergyman sent by the Church to undermine his place with the duchess or the White Lions? Prentice trusted Fostermae as an honest man of faith but counted him a rare exception amongst the churchmen of the Grand Kingdom.

"You've brought me a visitor, have you sacrist?" he asked Fostermae. Before Fostermae could answer, Prentice held up a hand and stepped past the two men into his tent. Returning a moment later with the stub of a candle, he waved them over with him as he took a twig from the fire and used it as a taper to light the wick. As it glowed into flame, he lifted it and took a closer look at Fostermae's companion. The man's hair was cut bowl-style, hanging simply about his face. He was pale, soft, and solid, nothing like the scarecrow-thin Fostermae. He had an intense expression and looked to be covering his discomfort at being so closely examined by smoothing his dark, silk-edged jacket and arranging his slashed sleeves. Whoever this man was, he was significantly wealthier than the sacrist he was with. Wealthier than Prentice too, for that matter.

"Captain Prentice Ash," Fostermae said formally, tugging his wispy forelock as if Prentice was a nobleman. "May I introduce Solft of Lower Otney, my friend and frater sacrist."

That explains his wealth, Prentice thought.

Lower Otney was a small but rich town close to the capital Denay. All Prentice knew of the place, other than its wealth and proximity to the center of Grand Kingdom power, was that by quirk of history, there had never been an Upper Otney. It was *Lower* Otney for reasons no scholar could name.

"Sacrist Solft," Prentice greeted the man, but Solft immediately waved that away, shaking his head so that his hanging hair danced about his shadowed face.

"I have not taken vows," Solft explained. "I am a mere scholar, I fear."

Prentice looked to Fostermae. "You said..."

"I'm sorry, Captain," Fostermae apologized. "I forget so often. Master Solft and I studied together under the same rector. They were goodly years, but I took orders elsewhere and..." He trailed off.

"And forget you have different trades?" Prentice finished for him.

"Trades?" repeated Solft, plainly surprised to hear religious devotion referred to as a trade.

"Captain Prentice has an arch turn of phrase," Fostermae explained.

The two companions looked at each other, as if they were each trying to silently urge the other to speak. Prentice found his patience for their hesitancy running thin. There were times in the past he had enjoyed theological conversations with Fostermae and more than once had prayed with the man, but he had neither time nor inclination this night.

"A pleasure to meet you, Master Solft," he said crisply. "If you will excuse me, I have had a busy day and expect to rise to an even busier one. Moreover, I will be very busy before I can sleep." He made to leave the two men, but Fostermae stopped him with a gentle hand on his arm.

"Please, Captain. My friend has some matters he must discuss with you. Important matters. Church matters."

Prentice almost sighed out loud. Solft *had been* sent by the Mother Church, it seemed. Two men in one night. His brother in knightly garb had been a shock. In comparison, this scholar should be easily dismissed.

"The duchess has already suffered her night's sermon," he said coldly, blowing out the candle. "And I suffered it with her. If you have come to follow Reverend Master Faldmoor's words, I have no interest."

"Faldmoor is here?" Solft asked, and even in the darkness the man's fear was palpable.

"He met with the duchess this evening," Prentice answered, not really thinking about the scholar's response. "But he has gone now."

"Perhaps now is not a good time, after all."

"Do not lose your nerve," Fostermae urged his friend. "You're here now. The Lord has given you this opportunity. You must not shrink from it."

"What is this about?" Prentice felt a renewed wariness, coupled with intellectual curiosity, pressing the fatigue out of his mind momentarily. Neither man answered him for a long moment. Prentice waited, looking back and forth between the two, and still the quiet stretched so that his impatience began to assert itself again. "Well, one of you say something."

The man Solft made a sound, nearly like a yelp, and Prentice was astonished. *This one jumps at his own shadow*, he thought. Surely this man could not be sent by the Church proper? He seemed too timid by far.

"I am...that is..." Solft stammered, his voice shrinking down to almost a whisper as he spoke.

"You know that it is an open secret why you were convicted, Captain?" Fostermae said suddenly, as if to help his friend broach the subject. "It was for heresy, and many in the west know it, even the duchess and her nobles."

"Nobles of the Denay and Rhales courts too, it seems," Prentice said through gritted teeth, thinking of the envoys.

"We mean no disrespect, raising the issue," Fostermae went on. "But it is for this that we've come to you."

"Why?"

"I am a heretic as well," Solft squeaked suddenly, as if barely summoning the courage to speak.

Prentice wished the man had never found his tongue. All thought of sleep fled, and he could feel his jaw clench with a new tension. For a moment he looked from one shadowed face to the other, as if by staring he could divine fresh truths from these two silhouetted figures. Lacking any new information, he decided to trust Fostermae, at least this far, but also do what he could to protect himself. He stepped to his tent and lifted the flap.

"Inside," he commanded them.

As they entered, he stepped back to the fire and re-lit his candle. Then he followed them and closed the flap behind him. Inside, all three were hunched under the cloth roof. Prentice had a cot and small table that took up most of the space. He pointed the two men to the bed, and they sat while he took up a small oil lamp and lit it from the candle. In the increased light, he faced them both, eyes narrowed as he looked back and forth between them.

"First of all, what heresy is it that you committed?"

"Does that matter?" asked Solft.

"It does if you don't want me to hand you directly to the Inquisition."

CHAPTER 8

Prentice could feel fury rising in him. How could Fostermae be so foolish? If this man Solft really was a heretic, then bringing him here like this was incredibly dangerous. The Western Reach was a freer place than the inner Kingdom, true enough, but it was still under the spiritual authority of the Church. A convicted heretic like Prentice might rise in status in this less civilized frontier province. Still, that did not mean the ecclesiarchs would suffer him fostering further heresy. The Inquisition was not afraid to cross the Azure Mountains.

And that assumed Prentice would *want* to be involved. Heresy was a catch-all term for all manner of beliefs that ran contrary to Church teaching—some benign, some vile.

"I was convicted by the Inquisition and transported for Argensianism," Prentice explained tersely to the two men who both looked at him with eyes wide in terror. That was the power that even the mention of Inquisitorial involvement had on men, especially men well versed in theology. "Mother Church and I disagree on the finer points of the nature of salvation and the disposition of a man's soul before God. That does not mean that I am a pagan or an unbeliever. I do not pray to spirits in forest glades or study blood arts under the light of black candles."

"Neither I," Fostermae protested reflexively, his indignation overcoming his fear. He looked to his friend. "Neither does Solft."

Solft was still too terrified to speak easily, but he shook his head readily. The man looked more timid than a mouse, unless it was all an act. Prentice trusted Fostermae. The sacrist never played false, but he could be duped. He was a soft touch at times, easily swayed by his compassion and ready to listen to a sob story. Was that what Solft was? And was his sob story sincere? Could the man be a cunning actor, feigning heresy and playing upon an old friendship with Fostermae, just as Faldmoor had used Prentice's brother, Pallas? The Church supported the crown prince's case against the duchess, it seemed, and because of Prentice's position in her household, the ecclesiarchs clearly suspected her of heresy. But they would have no evidence. Someone like Solft, pitiable and weak-seeming, might be the kind of bait they would offer to get Prentice to reveal himself and condemn the duchess thereby.

"So, what is your heresy?" he pressed Solft. "Speak for yourself, man."

The scholar swallowed heavily. By all impressions, he looked genuinely intimidated by Prentice and the circumstances of this late-night interview. Prentice needed more than impressions though. His duty to the duchess demanded no less.

"Have you heard of the seventh house, Captain?" Solft asked at last, and that caught Prentice by surprise. He had expected to hear talk of Second Flood or Argensius, or even something more esoteric like Whittanism. But seventh house? Even though it teased at his memory, Prentice could not be sure he had even heard of it. Seventh house? What heresy was that?

"I have not," he conceded after wracking his memories.

"Not surprising," said Solft. "It is an obscure belief, pertaining to the histories."

One of the histories? Prentice thought.

He could feel his brow wrinkling. The histories were a separate part of Church teaching, generally regarded as lesser than scripture and usually not tied to issues of heresy. Contending over the accuracy of historical doctrine was not usually something the Inquisition concerned itself with.

"I am not by nature a venal man," Solft went on. "I find passing temptation in drink or food, and none in pleasures of the flesh. Knowledge is the light that draws me, like a moth to a flame."

"Love of learning is no sin," said Fostermae.

"What then when what is learned is evil?"

"That is why we pray daily. Lead us not into temptation."

Prentice had a sense this conversation was an old one the two men had shared for many years, perhaps all the way back to their early life as students together.

"Seventh house is about the love of learning?" he asked, trying to weave what was being discussed into a coherent thread.

"No, no, Captain," Solft responded. "Love of learning explains how I find myself knowing what I wish I did not."

He drew in a deep breath, and to Prentice it seemed he must be finally deciding to share what he knew. A war between doubt, conviction, and resolution fought its way across the man's soft features. Prentice recognized the flow of emotions from his own experience of times he had recounted the story of his conviction to others, such as his friend Turley or Duchess Amelia. The sight of it all but convinced Prentice. If this man Solft truly was a fraud, then his act was flawless. More likely by far that he was what he said.

"I love history," Solft explained. "The farther back, the better. It's like treasure hunting, sifting through ancient sources to piece together the truth of the past. Books and scrolls so old that a stiff breeze might crack them and scatter them to dust. The story of the Grand Kingdom's foundation most especially fascinates me. Do you know it?"

Prentice nodded. "The royal house of Denay, led by the man who would become the first king, Creshess Holl-Benneth, united all the noble houses and they campaigned from Denay; the First Crusade. They drove out dark tribes and irredeemable fey, and by their victories, they forged the Grand Kingdom, ordained by God, blessed through the hand of the first ecclesiarch, a new holy land far from lost Jerusalem."

"You recite it almost word for word," said Solft, and for the first time he smiled.

Prentice accepted the compliment. "They drilled it into us at Ashfield. So, what about it is not true, according to your heresy?"

Fostermae flinched at so bald a use of that one terrible word, but Solft accepted the question without protest.

"It's all wrong," he said. "At least, I think it is. Seeking first manuscripts of the laws of kings, I found a page copied by an unknown scholar and glued between two other pages of an unrelated volume. It told of a cypher that when applied to some ancient texts would reveal a true history of the founding of the Grand Kingdom."

"Which texts?"

"I would rather not say."

Prentice cocked an eyebrow, but Solft merely shrugged.

"Very well," Prentice conceded with a wave of his hand. "Say what you would rather."

The scholar swallowed, and with a heavy sigh, went on. "I found one of the books, an illuminated manuscript, in a small archive held by a mercantile scriptorium. Theirs was in fine condition, being a copy that had been recopied many times, but an over-diligent archivist in the document's long history had decided to restructure the original, reordering the chapters and lines to fit a more modern folio shape. The text was recorded, but the cypher was useless. I could not apply it."

"Perhaps the cypher is false," said Prentice.

Solft shook his head vehemently, and Prentice noticed that now that the conversation had turned to his subject of specialty, Solft seemed far less timid. Like most folk, in an area where he was confident, the scholar was willing to stand his ground.

"The cypher is true," Solft insisted. "It would be no simple matter to explain how I know, but I am sure."

"But it does not work, you say."

"It didn't that time, but I've found other sources."

"And they say what?" Prentice was losing his patience again. He had work to do and wanted to sleep, and Solft seemed intent on making him draw out every piece of the story like a chirurgeon pulling teeth.

"The forging of the Grand Kingdom was not the act of the royal house of Denay, at least not they alone. It was a confederation of seven royal houses."

"Seven kings?" Prentice made no effort to keep his skepticism a secret. "With seven kingdoms, I presume?"

"Not exactly. It was a less civilized age. A king of that time ruled his own town and immediate lands and little else."

"You make a king sound like little more than a petty baron."

"It may well have been the case," Fostermae offered. "Why else would a kingdom become known as the Grand Kingdom if not compared to smaller, lesser kingdoms."

That certainly made some sense to Prentice. He'd never really thought about it before. The Grand Kingdom had always been the Grand Kingdom, so far as he knew, but what made its founders call it grand? This explanation made as much sense as any other. It did raise one clear question, however.

"If the kingdom was founded by seven kings in confederacy, then where are the other six kings? Why do we not remember them?"

"We do," said Solft sitting forward, warming even further to his subject. "You said it yourself; Denay united other nobles under them."

"Other nobles, not kings. There's a difference. Even the Vec is only princedoms. When the southern lords rebelled, even they dared not take the title king for themselves."

"Except when they unite to make war."

That was true. The Vec princes did sometimes unite behind a king, such as when King Kolber had invaded the Western Reach just over a decade earlier.

"But that is not the only change history has made," Solft continued. "The first king of the Grand Kingdom was not of the house of Denay."

"What?" That seemed impossible to Prentice's mind.

Solft reached into a pocket of his coat and drew forth a folded packet of papers. He opened it out, explaining as he did so. "These seven kings were known by their icons. Each one had a heraldic animal, just like the nobles of today. I found these in another manuscript, an unadulterated one. I copied them down as faithfully as I could."

Spreading one sheet flat, he held it up in the sparse lamplight for Prentice to see. In three rows on the page were excerpts from illuminated page borders redrawn in charcoal. Prentice examined them closely and was immediately impressed with the level of detail. Whatever quality of scholar or heretic Solft was, he was a talented artist, of that there was no doubt.

"Do you see it?" the scholar asked earnestly.

The first line showed seven animals in a row, with the lion first and the eagle, the Denay eagle, second. Each beast wore a small crown, but in the midst of the line was a larger crown, glowing with glory. The artwork could symbolize a confederacy of kings forging a single, grander kingdom. The second line showed the lion as the only one wearing a crown, but it was running away from the others. They were hunting the lion as king, with the eagle leading the pursuit. The third line showed the lion slain, the eagle wearing the crown and standing over the broken body. The other five beasts were bowing to the eagle.

In heraldic language, the three pictures told the story that Solft claimed was forgotten history.

"You see the significance?" Solft pressed.

"I was persuaded," Fostermae offered. "But to challenge history set as true by Mother Church is heresy. Lesser heresy, but still. There were no other educated men I could trust to ask. That is why I pressed Master Solft to come to you."

Prentice nodded, not fully listening to the two men. He was examining the pictures and their import. A kingly lion, slain by a kingly eagle and its five supporting beasts—a serpent, a mantis, a bull, an elk and... a wolf. Taking them all in as a whole, Prentice was overwhelmed by a sudden memory so powerful that it was as if he were transported back in time.

Years before, he had had a moonlit vision, a terrifying revelation of a monstrous serpent with six necks and five heads. Each of those heads had been one of these five beasts—snake, mantis, bull, elk, and wolf. That mighty serpent had represented the Redlander army, coming from the west to invade the Reach. The creature's sixth neck had been a severed stump, the final head cut away. Prentice looked at the three pictures in his hand and wondered. Was the severed stump the lion? Had the eagle of Denay betrayed the lion and cut it from the rest of the royal houses? No, that made the least sense. The Redlanders weren't from the Grand Kingdom. They came from the far west, over the sea.

How could they be the royal houses that united under the eagle?

Even more perplexing, it was the lion who'd fought the many-headed serpent in his vision. How could the lion be a part of the serpent, the missing sixth head, if it was the one that fought back? And the lion was an angel, Prentice knew that. He had seen it in other visions since—an angel of God and the inspiration to create the militia he now commanded. He tried to reconcile the ideas and images in his mind. A six-headed Redlander monster, missing one head and fighting a mighty lion in his vision, the Denay eagle leading a bestial hunt against a lion in history.

What did it all mean?

"Captain Ash? Prentice?"

Prentice blinked as Fostermae's voice penetrated his thoughts.

"I am sorry, masters," he said, blinking as his focus returned to the tent around him and the visions receded back into his memories.

"You were as a man sleeping but awake," said Solft.

"Forgive me."

"Was it the visions?" asked Fostermae, and Prentice wanted to curse the man. He had confided in the sacrist about his visions and dreams some years ago. It was not information he wanted to share with a heretic he had just met.

"Visions?" asked Solft, seeing the significance immediately.

"The captain has seen visions of angels and even the Lord," Fostermae went on before Prentice could stop him. Solft's expression showed keen interest mixed with professional reserve. He was a Church-trained scholar; testing visions and dreams against known revelation was one of his essential skills.

"Tell me," he urged, but Prentice had had enough for one night. He shook his head.

"You need to leave now." The vehemence in his tone surprised them.

"We do not mean to offend," said Fostermae.

"Please, Captain," Solft pleaded, the timidity flooding back into his tone and manner. "Please."

"No," Prentice insisted, his decision firm. "I need to think about what you have said. I need...to think." He waved them toward the tent flap.

"Do you think to inform the Inquisition about me?" asked Solft.

Fostermae shook his head sympathetically, taking his friend gently by the arm. Prentice could see the fear in the scholar's eyes and he felt a momentary compassion in the midst of his confusion.

"I would not trust a feral beast to the mercy of the inquisitors," he said, trying to assuage the man's fear. "Much less you, sir."

"You will not tell what I told you?"

"To whom would I tell it, this matter of truth? To the men who lied to convict me? No, Master Solft. I will contemplate what you said, but I will not speak of it, I think."

"Thank you." Solft tugged his forelock, and just before he allowed Fostermae to pull him from the tent, he handed Prentice the folded sheet of paper with the three heraldic illuminations.

"To aid your contemplation," he said simply. "I have other copies."

I should put this to the fire and forget I ever met you, Prentice thought as he watched the tent flap fall closed behind the departing pair.

He held the paper in his hand a moment and then thrust it away in his belt pouch. In his mind, the five kingly, heraldic animals merged with the types of beasts that were part of the Redlander magics. He'd slain the Horned Man, the mighty elk champion with his gold-chased antlers and massive strength. Since that day, he and the Reach had faced wolf-men and serpent-women, and now came reports of mantis-men. All these were among Master Solft's ancient, forgotten kings. What did that mean?

And where were the bull-men? What would it mean to face one or more of them on a battlefield?

CHAPTER 9

"I am sorry, I did not hear you," said Prentice. Sir Gant had been talking, but Prentice's mind still dwelt on his conversation with Fostermae and Solft the night before. The scholar's revelations raised many questions that would not quite settle in his mind. He had to force himself to pay attention to the matters at hand.

"I was saying that it was a pity there would be no forfeits this time. I was rather looking forward to that." Sir Gant flicked his moustache from his lip as he smiled at Prentice.

"Really?" Prentice asked, cocking one eyebrow. "What have you got to offer in forfeiture? Were you not a mere hedge knight not so long ago? I seem to remember someone so poor he had to carry his own saddle, having lost his horse and with no silver to buy a new one."

"I wasn't going to offer my own forfeit," Gant responded dismissively, ignoring Prentice's jibe. "I just thought to enjoy the offers of greater men. There's something appealing about the notion of the kingdom's highest men groveling before the throne, begging and competing for the chance to risk the greatest portion of their wealth. We former hedge knights think it good that they should feel the breath of poverty on their necks as we have, even if only for the space of one forfeits council and the battle to follow."

"It does have an appeal, doesn't it?" Prentice smiled, but in his thoughts he remembered the vivid image of the five wild beasts bowing to the Denay eagle, bloodied talons over the slain regal lion.

The manuscript the illumination came from was centuries old, if not millennia, but the imagery could almost be prophetic. The ancient lion was not the same as Duchess Amelia's white lion, but otherwise the imagery suited the current conflicts of the Reach completely, with the one strange exception. The other five beasts, the beasts of the Redlanders, were not bowing down to the eagle or the lion. These five beasts had come to slay.

Prentice and Sir Gant were waiting in front of the captain's tent in the center of the White Lions' camp. In every direction, neat rows of canvas squares filled the spring-green swarded vale. Dawn was cresting the horizon, and the company was awakening. Watchfires were being stirred to cook breakfasts, and stiff bodies stretched and yawned. Somewhere in the direction of the river, a tentative thump of a drum sounded, as of a drummer confirming he was warmed sufficiently for his duty. There was a pause, and then the beat of the daybreak call hammered out. It was picked up by another drum nearby and then another. Every hundred-man cohort in the White Lions had their own drummer—usually a youth, little more than a boy, often—and soon every lad from every cohort had taken up the duty so that all across the camp dozens of drums beat the unrelenting rhythm of daybreak. No one overslept in Duchess Amelia's army.

"The question is, who does the duchess take with her to this meeting with the king?" Gant mused as the din ended with a dramatic single beat struck at exactly the same time from every point in the camp. "Any Reachermen of rank will have the right to go, whether she takes them or not."

"Even so, that's little more than a dozen earls, counts and barons," said Prentice. "And their sons. The prince may have offended the Reach and her nobility, but even the most

indignant Reacherman won't miss a chance to present his heir
to the king."

"No indeed. But what of the duchess' own house? Does she
bring bannermen like me? Or guards? Or some lions? Knights
are one thing, but if she wants to make an impression, then some
of the company's frontlines are the finest and newest-minted
footmen in the whole Grand Kingdom."

Prentice nodded in agreement as he looked about the camp,
watching corporals and line-firsts in their midnight-blue quilted
gambesons and blued-steel gorgets, driving the lax or slow out
of beds and tents to their morning duties. Ordinary men had
off-white uniforms made from undyed cloth; only officers wore
the blue. For two years now, building the White Lions militia
had threatened to drain the duchy's coffers of their last silver
guilder and driven a small town's worth of weapon smiths and
armorers almost to exhaustion. But every man in the militia
was well armed and equipped with better protection than any
non-knight of the Grand Kingdom had ever enjoyed. And
the frontline of every cohort—a halberdier, typically, with a
bright steel polearm for a weapon—was the best armored and
equipped of all. Frontlines were formed with the cohort's best
fighters—men who had to prove and re-prove themselves in
training, all for the right to stand closest to the enemy on the
day of battle. It was a dangerous privilege, and it came with extra
pay and the best armor.

These soldiers were the sharp main weapon of the Lions, and
so they were called Claws. Each of their ranking officers wore
an embossed steel pauldron on his left shoulder, polished until
it shone like silver—a plate with the symbol of a lion's paw
upon it, claws out. Claws in the ranks farther back wielded pikes
over their frontline comrades' shoulders. Then, in amongst the
Claws on the battlefield were the Fangs, swordsmen equipped
with long, thrusting swords and small buckler shields. They
wore less armor because they had a different role. When an
enemy bullied his way past the Claws, usually because his armor

was too good, like say a knight in full steel, then the Fangs came out, meeting the enemy in the tight gaps between the pikes and halberds. Quickly out and quickly withdrawn, these soldiers moved fast and fought tight. Their officers had a lion's mouth embossed on their shoulders, teeth bared and snarling.

There was one other kind of soldier in the company—the Roar—and on their shoulders was the lion in profile, head back and mouth open, as in a mighty roaring. These men wielded the serpentines, the company's matchlock firearms. On the battlefield, the Roars came out first, firing their iron balls at the charging enemy. Then they withdrew into the lines of their cohort to be protected by the Claws and, if the enemy pressed hard, the Fangs. It was an order of battle designed to fight knights, as well as the ranks of the Redlander invaders, and in their one battle against Prince Daven Marcus's treacherous nobles, the newly formed White Lions had proved almost ludicrously effective. Duchess Amelia had not liked the notion that Prentice would build her a militia that could fight effectively against the Grand Kingdom's rightful rulers, but Prentice was a pragmatist. In the dark days when she escaped from Daven Marcus's clutches and fled from the force of knights he sent to recapture her, the duchess realized Prentice's wisdom. His first five hundred White Lions had thrashed the prince's force. They were so superior that many Reacher nobles had begun sending their own houseguards to train with the company, swelling the numbers under Prentice's command even further.

"Soon, we test ourselves against the real enemy," Prentice said aloud, trying to force aside thoughts of heraldic animals for a moment.

Prophetic or not, and even with his resentment against the self-indulgent nobility of the Grand Kingdom, Prentice held no illusions as to the Redlanders being the greater threat. The nobles were rapacious, by and large, but the invaders were unspeakably ruthless. Redlanders thought nothing of torturing whole towns to death—man, woman, and child—just to make a point. The eagle might be hunting the lion again, but the other five beasts planned to slaughter one and all.

"Just to be clear," said Gant, as the company's first sergeant, Felix, approached to make his morning report. "You're talking about the invaders, not the king and his courtiers?"

"Bad odds and even money," Prentice joked.

"And for the war council? Guards or knights or what?"

"Another difficult needle to thread. Let's give it a moment's more thought." Prentice turned to receive Felix's salute. "What's the report, Sergeant?"

"Camp is in order, and the night held no new encounters with the invaders."

That was good news.

"Any deserters?" With the core of his army made up of convicts in forced service, desertion was another of Prentice's fears, not only because it weakened his forces but because it would mean he had failed the duchess in his first duty. King's Law entrusted convicts into the duchy's charge, and letting even one escape was a shame upon the province's honor, upon Duchess Amelia's honor. After so many years as a convict on a chain, not daring to dream of escape, now Prentice was the Reach's chief jailer. The thought made him scowl.

"Just one. Some twit," said Felix. "Local boy who figured he'd sneak off and have a good time with his old flame. Swore he'd have been back in the morning."

"Unless a bailiff found him, damned fool," Prentice cursed.

"Yea, well he never made it past the night patrol, so there's that. He'll get the rod on his back this morning in front of his whole cohort and be put back to the least line. His first'll have him digging the slit trenches for the rest of the campaign, I'd wager."

"He's lucky he's not dead," said Sir Gant.

An ordinary convict who attempted an escape, no matter the reason, was subject to summary execution. A bounty was frequently offered on escapees' heads, so anyone they met was usually eager to put them to the blade.

"Is he the only one?" asked Prentice.

"Only one since before winter, if you can believe it."

Prentice barely could, but when he thought about it, he remembered that ordinary convict life was bitterly harsh. By contrast, a White Lion recruit was issued a uniform, had a tent in which to sleep, or barracks when they were back in the north of the Reach, not to mention regular food. Soldiery was a better life than convictry by far, at least until they had to face the enemy in battle.

"I'm keeping 'em busy," Felix said, referring to the company as a whole with a wave of his hand. "But now things are well set, I'm running out of jobs to have 'em do. There's weapon training and marching, 'course, but it'd be good to have another duty. Variation's the best weapon 'gainst boredom, and boredom's our main enemy right now, at least until them painted oddities from the west take the field against us. Bored soldiers are a threat to themselves and the local folks—allies and enemies alike."

"They can't be set to make camp defenses?" asked Sir Gant.

Felix shrugged and looked to the west and south. "Rivers in those directions make the ground too boggy to dig a trench or put up a palisade, and isn't that the point? The rivers and their marshes make a better defense than we could build for ourselves, short of bringing in stones from somewhere else."

Gant and Prentice nodded as they followed the sergeant's reasoning.

Felix went on. "'Course we could do trench and fence on the east side of the camp 'tween the hills and the Murr, but that way's where the king and the rest of his army is. I figure the high and mighty knights of the Grand Kingdom might take it amiss if we started building defenses facing against them."

"It would be an insult to the throne, no mistake," Sir Gant agreed.

"More's the pity," Prentice said quietly, but he knew Felix was right.

"There's always the north, but that's our homefront. Who're we protecting against there?" After pointing in that direction, Felix dropped his arms like a tutor who had stopped teaching a moment to let his pupils fully absorb the truths he was imparting.

"Notwithstanding those reasons, I do not like leaving sides of the camp undefended," Prentice thought aloud. "And even if those were not all good excuses, any wood we take to build a palisade is wood the local villages won't have to rebuild with once the enemy's driven off, at least not until the army breaks up. And that could be a year or more still."

"You think so long?" asked Felix.

"Even if we break the Redlanders in one great battle, many of them will flee and we will have to hunt them down. We cannot let them just run off. Can you imagine what they would be like in small companies if they turned to banditry?"

All three men shook their heads. The Redlanders were no mere soldiers who could be defeated and expected to head back to their farms and towns, tails between their legs. The sorcery-backed forces would have to be broken and driven off thoroughly. Anything less would only leave the Grand Kingdom and the Western Reach weakened and vulnerable. The same was true for the Vec princedoms south of the river, but they were not Prentice's concern. They had their own rulers and armies.

"No defenses then?" asked Felix.

"What about the gate at Fallenhill?" Prentice mused.

Gant and Felix both frowned.

"D'you want the actual gate, or are you talking 'bout the bloody wagon out the front?" asked Felix. All three men had been part of a force that spent a winter besieged in the fortress town of Fallenhill. One of the things that had slowed the besieger's assault was a heavy, up-tipped wagon blocking the main gate. Any time the besiegers wanted to assault the gate, they had to clear the wagon away first, and that made them vulnerable to attacks from the wall.

"You want us to make a defensive wall out of wagons?" asked Gant, following Prentice's thoughts quicker than the sergeant. "How do we do that? And how is that any better for wasting wood? Any wagon we overturn is likely to lose one or more wheels. Better to just take the raw wood."

"What if we don't have to tip them up?" Prentice said, an idea forming. "We have the supply wagons bringing everything from Griffith. Even with the barges, there's a train going back and forth on the road too."

"'Bout fifty wagons, last I counted," Felix agreed, but his furrowed brow said he still didn't understand Prentice's notion.

"When they are unloaded on the next turnaround, set carpenters to build thick, wooden sides, like a palisade's wall."

"They'll get in the way of the wheels, won't they?"

"Not if they put the bottom half on hinges. They can fold up for travel, then fold down to be walls."

"So, we make them tiny wooden forts?" asked Gant, clearly working to stretch his mind to the new notion.

"Exactly so," Prentice confirmed. The idea of turning heavy-sided wagons into mobile fortifications had leapt into his mind so quickly that he felt like he was running to catch up with it just like his lieutenants. Nonetheless, the more he thought about it, the more he was convinced such wagons could work, at least in certain circumstances. "We can have shuttered slits for Roar gunners to fire through, like archer's loops in a castle wall, and Claws with pike over the top to prevent men from just clambering up the sides."

"But they'll just be by themselves. Won't they be easily overwhelmed?"

"Not if we line them up," said Felix, starting to see the potential as well. "And if they aren't neat in the line, we can plug the gaps with more claws and fangs. It could work."

Sir Gant still looked skeptical. "Do we convert all the wagons? And if we do, what happens to supplies coming down from Griffith by road? That all stops. We'll have to pay the merchants for their wagons as well, or they'll get wind of this plan, and your fifty or more heavy wagons will be *mysteriously* all caught in a bog somewhere north, unable to be converted and unable to bring supplies. Is this really what we want?"

"What I want is for the duchess to be back north in Dweltford Castle, safe from the Redlanders and from the prince," Prentice said flatly. "But since she is here and not there, I want her to have the best protection we can muster."

"And the White Lions aren't enough on their own?"

Prentice's scowl returned and hardened at the implicit criticism in Gant's question. "If knights were enough, no one would build castles," he snapped back. "I will not allow the duchess' house to fall because I was too overconfident to shore up the roof!"

Sir Gant accepted the rebuke with a polite nod.

"So, we set our woodworkers to make a mobile wall," said Felix. "Do we still dig that trench?"

"From the hill line there all the way to the river." Prentice pointed to the line he was describing.

"You want it north of where the path to the watchtower goes?"

"Closer than that."

"That'll mean the duchess is outside the camp," said Sir Gant. The other two looked at him. "Any trench you make will become the north boundary of the camp. If the path up to the watchtower comes down out of the hills beyond that trench, then she'll effectively be outside the camp. It could be taken as an insult."

Prentice doubted the duchess would see it that way, but Gant's reasoning would be sound for most highborn, even the Reachermen nobility. And if one of them thought it looked like an insult, Duchess Amelia would be shamed just for accepting it. Even so, Prentice did not want works being done too far from the center of the camp; it would make desertion that much easier. Despite Felix's positive assessment of the discipline situation, desertion would always be a fear never far from the captain's mind.

"We could build a second path, one inside the camp," Felix offered, even as Prentice was considering the political and security implications. The sergeant nodded to a part of the hill that sloped under the tower, the long feather on his hat waving like a flag in the breeze. "A switchback there, between them rock outcrops, would work fine. And it would be a good second duty to set the company to. Some can dig a trench and others can hack out that slope. What do you say, Captain?"

"That's good for now. How long will all that take?"

"More than five thousand men, most still marching and training as well? All them jobs'll keep them busy maybe a week, more if we let 'em slack."

"Do we ever let them slack?" asked Prentice with a wry smile.

"No, Captain, we do not."

CHAPTER 10

Word came to the duchess a little after mid-morning that an escort was ready at her convenience to accompany her to the king's war council. By that stage, several of her land's nobles, including an earl from the Pale and the brother of the former Griffith viscount, along with some of their closest companions, had petitioned to accompany her, and she accepted them. When the time came to head to the council, Duchess Amelia's entourage had grown to nearly twenty, and that did not include the two lines of ten Fangs in full armor that Prentice had assigned as escort, along with a standard-bearer, a man named Markas, and two drummer boys.

Amelia descended the tower to find everyone waiting for her. She was dressed in a simple cream gown beneath an overdress of midnight blue with slashed and gathered sleeves—her ducal colors. Both were made of fine linen, as light as could be managed, but still felt heavy for a warm morning. Every nobleman at a king's council of war would be dressed in his own house colors, just as he would on the battlefield. Amelia could do no less. The darkly dyed cloth was further embroidered by Spindle's expert hand, with a complex edge pattern in silver thread, and on the skirt, two rampant silver lions facing each other. One had the mane of the ducal male lion, but the other was a she-lion. The heraldic implication would be clear to any noble who saw it; the Western Reach was equally secure in the hands of a duke or a duchess. Lion or she-lion, the Reach was well ruled. Her straw-colored hair was crisply plaited and tucked under a silver-threaded coif set with tiny pearls and fine sapphires.

Behind Amelia, Lady Dalflitch was dressed in an under-gown of deep scarlet and an elegant overdress of brown silk sewn with a pattern of orange flowers. Her dark hair was also plaited and covered with a simpler coif, with only the barest of embroidery. Her appearance was more than the equal of a king's court but carefully calculated to be a fraction less impressive than Amelia's. It would not do for a duchess to be upstaged by a lady-in-waiting.

Righteous and Spindle were dressed in their finest gowns as well, though measurably less impressively than the two ladies of rank. The duchess had overheard them both remarking on how much easier it was to conceal a blade, or even blades, under such full skirts. Both were waiting by the duchess's open-topped carriage seeming awkward, less than comfortable at the prospect of the coming journey. Until they had been raised to their new status as ladies a little over a year ago, neither had ever sat a horse or ridden in a carriage in their lives. Yeomen and serfs might own carthorses or plough animals, but riding was a noble's pastime and a privilege closely guarded in the Grand Kingdom. Sumptuary laws forbade any low-born folk to even mount a horse in the presence of a ranking noble.

Turley stood by next to a steward holding one of the two carriage horses' bridles. As Amelia approached, he waved her politely toward the other side of the carriage.

"Begging your pardon, Your Grace, but she's a might spirited, this one," he explained. "Something spooked her this morning, and now the swish of the ladies' skirts is making her skittish. Best not to clear her blinders."

"With thanks, steward." Amelia accepted the guidance, giving a genteel nod.

In truth, she would much rather have ridden her own mare, Silvermane, but she had decided the carriage presented a more dignified impression for her arrival at the king's audience. Silvermane was like the carriage horse that Turley held so tightly—spirited, skittish even. Riding the mare was a wild experience and one that Amelia enjoyed, but it was not conducive to the dignity of a duchess. She could not arrive at the king's court with her hair disarrayed and her cheeks flushed from the effort of bending a high-spirited mount to the reins. Her previous pony had been a much more placid creature called Meadow Dancer, but Amelia had been forced to ride that poor animal to death in her escape from the prince's clutches. There was a part of her that would never forgive Daven Marcus for that. Silvermane reminded her to never let her spirit be fully broken, no matter who held the reins.

Turley followed the two ladies a pace behind as they made their way to the carriage step. Standing in attendance at the carriage's little door was a stern young man with a neatly trimmed beard and long hair, wearing white and grey livery with green bull's heads embroidered on his doublet. When news of the king's summons had circulated amongst the duchess's nobles, requests had poured in, asking for the honor of being her escort to the court. Amelia had only needed to see this man's name on his letter to know that she would choose him.

"Viscount Gullden," she greeted him, and he bowed. "You look well this morning."

"Fully well and fully honored, Your Grace," the viscount replied. "Thank you for this privilege."

"Your brother was dear to me. You have this honor by his service. It is his privilege you enjoy."

"I know it is true, Your Grace," Gullden said and bowed again, his tone and posture indicating that he fully accepted the debt he owed to his late brother, the former viscount.

"If you offer the Reach even half the service he did, you will be a valued, honored man indeed," Amelia said, and then she accepted his hand as he helped her aboard the carriage.

Once she was in her seat, he offered his hand to Dalflitch, after which he stepped away with a bow and Turley took the role, helping first Righteous and then Spindle into the carriage. Helping the duchess into her carriage was an honor for a viscount, but performing the same service for the duchess's low-born ladies would have been an indignity. As Spindle pulled herself into her seat, Amelia caught another flash of a meaningful look in Turley's eyes, and she glanced quickly to see the look shared by Dalflitch. There was so much in that unspoken communication, and she was about to demand an explanation to have done with the secrets when Spindle asked a question of her own.

"Which nobleman was that?" she said, watching the viscount move to his own horse and mount up.

"Viscount Gullden," Dalflitch answered.

"Is he special?"

Dalflitch cocked her eyebrow, but Amelia answered this question.

"His brother, Viscount Wolden, died in a duel over my honor," she explained, "during the prince's crusade."

Spindle nodded solemnly and Righteous frowned as well. All the duchess's ladies knew the stories from the crusade, and mention of Lord Wolden's death sobered the festive air in the carriage. Amelia decided she didn't want to deal with Dalflitch and Turley right at that moment after all. The carriage rocked as Turley climbed up next to the driver on the bench.

"I trust everything is ready, steward?" Amelia asked sternly.

"Indeed so, Your Grace."

"Captain Prentice is not here?"

Turley looked over his shoulder and tugged his forelock in polite apology. "He begs your pardon, Your Grace, and says he'll meet up with you before you reach the edge of the camp."

"Very well. We will leave."

Turley gave the driver a signal and the carriage moved off, the escort of nobles forming up behind them. Word was passed and the drummers beat a march. The banner was lifted high, and the small parade commenced the short journey from the Western Reach camp to the encampment of the king.

CHAPTER 11

The sound of cheering told Prentice of the duchess's approach before he saw her carriage or even the White Lion banner being carried ahead of her. He had passed the word that militiamen should not hold back when she entered the main of the camp. They were her men-at-arms, and she was their liege. For years now she had led the Western Reach in defense against the Redlanders. A duke who had done as much would be acclaimed a war hero. The duchess was due no less honor. Even with his order though, Prentice was pleased at the enthusiasm of the cheering he heard. Men stopped in their duties and raised their hands to shout huzzahs. Duchess Amelia waved to them as she passed, and many of her escorting nobles likewise acknowledged the praise.

The two lines of White Lion swordsmen who led the escort were utterly po-faced however, showing not the least emotion. Sergeant Felix had made it clear to them that discipline and dignity were to be their watchwords. If they did their duty well, the captain had passed the word that casks of brandy would be their reward, as well as a night to enjoy them. Prentice was pleased to see their faces set like stone, their marching order flawless.

He tromped out to meet the entourage, coming alongside the carriage at an easy jog, even wearing his brigandine and its shoulder and throat plates, pauldrons and gorget. He wore this much armor so often these days that it felt like little more than winter clothing. It was natural to him.

"Like a knight," Sir Gant had reflected when they discussed it.

"Are you trying to insult me?" was all Prentice had said in reply, scowling darkly.

Seeing him approach, the duchess gave the order for the carriage to stop. The drummers beat the halt.

"Are all the house of Ash stiff-necked rebels, Captain?" she asked him, casting a glance at Righteous before looking back.

Prentice didn't understand her meaning. "Your Grace?"

"I give your wife skirts and find her almost always in trousers. I gave you a horse and yet you do not ride it." The duchess flashed him a sly smile that did not disrupt her dignity and he returned it.

"I fear, Your Grace, that while you are able to bestow a mount upon me, even you cannot provide me the skill to ride it better than a sack of grain."

Prentice thought he heard a number of quiet chuckles from the nobles seated on their own horses behind the carriage.

Let them laugh, he thought.

It was true that he was a wretched horseman. It was a skill of knighthood that he had never drawn close to mastering. But more importantly, it helped the duchess. He was her captain, but to have a reformed convict riding beside her, even one as respected as he had become, might be a step too far for a nobleman's dignity. Even if not for the duchess's own nobles, then definitely for those of the two royal courts, Denay and Rhales. It was risk enough for her to have him go with her to the court as it was. Why chance salting the wound by having him ride up like a man of rank? Prentice knew, of course, that the duchess did not see it that way.

"Perhaps you could take the time to learn to ride, Captain," she said.

"I will devote my every spare moment to the task, Your Grace."

What spare moments?

The journey to the king's council took somewhat more than an hour, and Prentice felt his tension growing with every moment. It took all his will not to stare at the tower looming from its spur as they marched east. Not letting himself look, he felt it pass on his left, and its presence seemed to sit behind his shoulder the farther they went. He was now over the border, back in the Grand Kingdom proper for the first time in over a decade. As a reformed convict, pardoned by the duchess of the Western Reach and serving in her household, he might be within the law to be here. But as Reverend Master Faldmoor had delighted in pointing out, as a heretic his pardon had to be ratified by the Church before it was fully legal. And if Faldmoor represented the overall position of the ecclesiarchy, then that ratification would likely never come. Just by marching next to his liege, Prentice was risking a death sentence.

Heading east, they approached a pair of heralds in royal livery acting as outriders for the king's camp. The men didn't allow the duchess's entourage to draw too close before riding away, doubtless to announce the Reach contingent's approach to the court.

"What? They don't even introduce themselves?" Prentice heard his wife demand.

"They're just squires," Dalflitch explained. "They'll have ridden off to announce our coming. Nobles who wish the introduction won't meet us out here. They'll wait until Her Grace is presented to the king, then they'll know how to present themselves to her."

"Their manners'll change based on that?"

"Certainly. If the king is not welcoming, then they cannot be too polite or the throne might take it amiss."

"Doesn't anyone in a royal court know their own mind?"

There was a moment of silence following Righteous's question. The duchess herself answered it ultimately. "They know that their own thoughts don't matter as much as the king's."

"So only the king speaks his own mind?"

"Not even he, many times."

"Who holds a king to account?"

"Mother Church," said Dalflitch flatly, and that made Prentice shiver involuntarily for a moment despite the warmth of the late morning sun and his heavy armor.

The Church held its power over even the throne of the Grand Kingdom itself. The Church was supposedly the Kingdom of God but was ruled by men like Ecclesiarch Faldmoor and served by men-at-arms like Prentice's brother Pallas, who hated him with a fury that gave even an ex-convict pause. Then an unexpected thought occurred to him. If Mother Church could limit even kings and princes, what had happened to let the ancient lion king be thrown down by the Denay eagle? If the scholar Solft's history was true, then at some point the Church had approved one king overthrowing another. Was that the secret history? Had the Church approved a right king to take the throne from a wrong king? And if that had happened, how had the wrong king gotten the throne in the first place? Why hadn't Mother Church protected the nation from that crime?

"What's that thing?" Righteous asked, and her tone made Prentice look for a moment.

"It's from the duchess' luggage," Spindle answered, holding up a leather- and board-bound book about the size of a dinner plate. "She said I could bring it."

"What for? You can't even read it."

Spindle sniffed at Righteous's disdain. "I can learn. Besides, this one's full of pictures and they're beautiful."

Illuminated, thought Prentice, and he wondered what the tome might be. Its presence felt vaguely ominous in light of his other thoughts.

"Some of these patterns are really fine, but I bet I could sow them," said Spindle. "Or something like them."

"It's full of knights' badges and emblems, eh?" Righteous asked, looking closely as the seamstress flicked the pages.

"Heraldry," Dalflitch said. "And best not to copy them. Ranking houses are jealous about such things."

"Then why do they put them in a book like this?"

"It's the Bell Knight's Codex," the duchess said, finally joining the conversation.

"That sounds fancy," said Righteous. "What's a bell knight?"

"Not a what, a who. The Bell Knight was the man who composed the original copy of the codex. No one remembers his name, but his book has been remade for centuries. It lists every family of rank, with their titles, lands, and heraldry. Every noble house maintains their own list, and every ten years they send a copy to the royal court in Denay to be composed in a new codex. Then, new copies of the entire codex are made and circulated."

Prentice listened to the duchess and found himself wondering if there were a bull or an elk or a serpent in amongst the Bell Knight's records. Probably dozens of each. But were any of them Solft's ancient beasts? And what would it mean if they were?

"Why?" asked Spindle, but she was not contemplating the same questions that troubled Prentice's mind. "I mean, why, *Your Grace*? If they are all so jealous of their pictures, why share them?"

There was a moment of silence and Prentice wondered if the duchess had taken offence. He stole another glance and saw that Amelia and Dalflitch were smiling together.

"Why don't *you* tell *me*," said the duchess.

"But I don't know."

"You want us to figure it out?" asked Righteous, cocking an eyebrow.

"Surely you can do it," prompted Dalflitch, a sardonic half-smile on her lips. "If you give it a moment's thought."

He didn't look, but Prentice could imagine how his wife would respond to such a challenge.

You can do it, he silently willed her. *Do not let the fancy woman intimidate you.*

Quiet stretched for a long moment, the soft groan of the carriage's wheels and the shuffling of men's feet over the grass settling in the air, more merging with the peace of the day than disturbing it. Armor harness creaked and metal pieces scraped against each other occasionally. Even the thuds of the horses' hoofs were dulled. For all their martial aspect, the entire entourage felt quiet and gentle as it passed over the sward.

The moment stretched on and on, and Prentice began to fear for his wife's answer. He knew that Righteous and Dalflitch conflicted often. It was almost inevitable since the two women had had such vastly different lives. Prentice and Righteous were sworn to serve the duchess, and fostering conflict in her household was anything but good service. And Dalflitch was an important source of advice. Good relations between the duchess's ladies were paramount. But Prentice wanted his wife to win. He couldn't help it.

"It's so they know each other, isn't it, Your Grace?" Righteous declared suddenly, and Prentice had to hide a smile.

"But nobles know each other, don't they Your Grace?" Spindle objected. "Perhaps not everyone, but anyone that you don't know, Lady Dalflitch does, doesn't she?"

"It's not for them," Righteous explained, and it was clear she had figured it out. "Nobles know each other, that's right. This is for their boys and girls, their soldiers and servants and whatnot. It's for folk like us, ain't that right?"

"That's correct," the duchess agreed, and Prentice was sure he heard satisfaction in her tone. That made him proud. His wife was a streetfighter, but she was as worthy to be Duchess Amelia's lady-in-waiting as any other woman.

"But what good is it if we can't read?" asked Spindle.

"That's why we get to look at pictures."

"And most heralds can read. That's who the Bell Knight is aimed at mostly," Dalflitch explained.

The conversation lapsed once more. Prentice cast an eye over his shoulder at the train of nobles on horseback. There were no women there, and each man was dressed in his house colors in the finest clothing he could afford. An audience with the king required no less.

"This golden eagle is beautiful," Spindle said. "The wings stretched out on the rich red is so fine."

"That's the Denay eagle," said Dalflitch. "Symbol of the royal house."

"Then what's this one? This second eagle?"

"What second eagle?"

The book was handed across the carriage and pages were flicked back and forth.

"I don't know what this is," said Dalflitch ultimately. "Two pages, two gold eagles, both listed as the royal house but no explanation of the difference. Do you know, Your Grace?"

"No," answered the duchess, and Prentice could hear the book passed once more. "Captain Prentice, do you know the explanation?"

"Two eagles, Your Grace?" Prentice answered, without looking. "Both with their wings spread but facing different ways?"

"Yes."

"Yes, Your Grace, I know. One is the Denay eagle, and the other is the Rhales eagle."

"The royal house has two heraldic animals? Or the same animal twice?" the duchess pressed.

"What's the difference?" asked Righteous.

A swift smile played on Prentice's lips as he enjoyed the prospect of showing off his knowledge for his wife. "The eagle facing to the left is the Rhales eagle, the heraldry of the crown prince. The Denay eagle faces right. That is the king's eagle. There should be a crown on that eagle's head, though sometimes it is shown in the eagle's claw instead."

Or on the head of a slaughtered lion?

"Yes, the one facing right has a small crown on its head. It's difficult to see."

"Then you have a copy of the Height Codex there, Your Grace, produced thirty or so years ago. A rare book indeed."

"The Height Codex?"

"Ecclesiarch Height, a senior churchman of the time, sponsored a copy of the codex from his own purse, ostensibly as a mark of respect to the throne, but he instructed the illuminator to draw the crown of the Denay eagle smaller than usual."

"Why would he do that?"

"As a quiet insult to the newly crowned King Chrostmer."

"He insulted the king? Publicly?" The duchess' tone made it clear she was utterly shocked by the notion. Prentice turned to see all four women in the open carriage rapt with his story. "Why would he do such a thing?"

"The official story told by the Church is that it was a rebuke for the king's support of a heretic, an old friend of his. There is a rumor, though, that the two men were rivals for the same mistress."

"He insulted the king over a woman?"

"She must have been quite the mistress," said Dalflitch with an awestruck tone. Duchess Amelia turned to look at her and she held up her hands diffidently. "What? It wasn't me. I wasn't even born then."

The women shared a laugh at Dalflitch's defensiveness, and then the duchess turned back to Prentice.

"Do you believe the rumor?" she asked.

"I do not know, Your Grace," he answered her honestly. "But I do know that Ecclesiarch Height was killed two years later, ambushed by 'bandits' while on a hunt with the royal court. Within a year, the king had collected and burned every copy of that edition of the codex he could find. Hence, the rarity of your copy, Your Grace."

"That is quite the tale, Captain," said the duchess.

"He is a wise man, your husband," said Dalflitch to Righteous.

"That he is," she replied in an appreciative tone, and Prentice felt an involuntary moment of pride.

"Where did you obtain such knowledge, Captain Ash?" Dalflitch asked lightly, making conversation.

"The captain attended the academy in Ashfield," Duchess Amelia said quickly. Prentice knew she was trying to maintain the mood, but it was already too late for him. His pride was almost instantly boiling away like spittle on a hot skillet.

"You studied with Mother Church?" Dalflitch followed up, uncharacteristically missing the shift in mood.

"Until they convicted me of heresy and threw me out!" he answered her, his bitterness coming out before he could get it fully under control.

"Oh, I am sorry." Lady Dalflitch frowned, but Prentice looked away again, clenching his jaw to keep from saying anything else.

"Well, the captain has done good service by us today, helping to understand some finer points of heraldry and entertaining us with a salacious story," said the duchess, obviously trying to restore some sense of equanimity. "Good service, as he always does for the Reach and its people."

"Hear, hear," Dalflitch agreed, but Prentice hardly heard.

A somber mood settled over him and all the conversation died. Inwardly he cursed himself. Not a moment ago he had been flushed with pride and the joy of his wife's satisfaction in him, and all that had been blown away by the memories of his conviction and exile. No one had meant him any shame, but they were marching toward a whole court of nobles and churchmen who would intend to show him, and his liege lady, nothing but shame and humiliation. A decade on the chain, followed by years now fighting to preserve the duchess and to rise in her service, and still the stain of heresy would not be washed away. What had Faldmoor said? "Only the Church can forgive apostasy?"

Prentice had seen visions and received messages from angels. He had lived out prophetic experiences in recent years and even spoken with the Lord himself. Yet still the Church thought to keep forgiveness from him.

Only the Church could forgive apostasy? What if the men of the Church were the apostates? And that thought flashed to another. *What if the Church had backed the wrong king? What if the secret of Solft's history was the tale of a Church compromised with a usurper king, like the prophets who lied to King Ahab in far lost Israel?*

Prentice shook his head and thrust all those thoughts to the back of his mind. He had immediate duties to the duchess and her people. Lifting his gaze, he looked eastward for the heralds that should be coming to escort Duchess Amelia to the king's council. Heretic or no, he was not the only one walking into danger.

Chapter 12

As Amelia's entourage reached the edge of the Grand Kingdom encampment, two heralds, squires in royal livery, rode out to meet them once more.

"They've got crowns over their eagles," Spindle observed, whipping her head around to study them as they approached. "They've come from the king."

"Dignity, Spindle," Amelia chided gently, but she found her lady's enthusiasm infectious after the somber mood of the last part of the journey.

The lace-masked woman settled herself back into her seat while the two men on horses rode to within a few paces of the standard-bearer leading the procession. One of them stood in the stirrups and lifted his head to make a loud pronouncement.

"You enter the encampment of King Chrostmer the Fourth, long may he reign, unchallenged sovereign of the Grand Kingdom and all her subjects. Name yourself and be recognized in his sight."

Unchallenged sovereign? That was a new title to Amelia's ears. She wondered if it had been prompted by the invaders' coming. Raids on a kingdom's border would be a good reason to remind folk of the king's unquestionable rule. She watched as Prentice went forward to stand beside her standard-bearer.

"This is Amelia," he answered them just as volubly, announcing her, "Duchess of the Western Reach, defender of the frontier and thrice victor over the Redlanders, cursed interlopers from beyond the shallow sea."

Thrice victor sounded like a bold claim to Amelia's ears. The three victories certainly were not hers alone. The first was the Battle of the Brook where Amelia's forces had fought but had been led by the old Prince of Rhales, Mercad, Daven Marcus's precedent. He died that day and that was why the youthful Daven Marcus was now prince. The second victory had been in a battle on the coast of the shallow sea, far in the west. That battle had no name, and it, too, had been fought under the command of a prince—Daven Marcus that time. The third victory had been driving the Redlander raiders south ahead of them as the White Lions marched to the Murr River this spring. Amelia felt she had little right to claim glory from any of these, but Prentice had reassured her.

"These were successes for the Western Reach," he had told her. "*Your* lands, *your* victories; it is a ruler's right to claim. That is how it is with princes and kings."

"I am neither prince nor king," she had said, objecting.

"But you go to face them, and with a powerful army at your back."

Whatever the boldness of the claim, the heralds accepted Prentice's words without question and politely offered to escort the duchess into the king's presence. They then turned and began to call for way through the encampment.

The Grand Kingdom camp was significantly different from the White Lions' camp. It sprawled over a wide sloping vale, with a tile-roofed manor house at its center. The king had taken residence in that building, which was encircled by vineyards and walled gardens. In the surrounding fields, ranking nobles had their own pavilions, all made from brightly colored cloths. The camp had been in place for over a year, opposing the Redlander army across the Murr, and in that time many of the richer nobles had begun adding wooden walls and a sense of permanency to their camp dwellings, just as Amelia was installing curtains and dividing walls in her tower residence. The vineyards and gardens showed spring green, but everywhere else was earthen brown, any possible plant growth churned under the feet of the frustrated army, their servants, and animals.

There were other significant differences between the royal encampment and the White Lions' bivouac. The Lions had tents all made of the same cloth and the same color, established in strict ranks and rows. The Western Reach nobles who rode with the company had their own private tents in a small clutch near the foot of the ridge, but the majority of the camp was a uniform field of undyed cotton—white, squared tents in squared formation, well ordered, like every other part of the Lions' discipline.

In contrast, King Chrostmer's camp was more organic. Each significant noble had their own tent or pavilion, shaped and colored according to their own whims. Around them clustered the smaller tents of their closest allies and retainers, lesser nobles and sworn men-at-arms. And around them clustered the still smaller tents of even lesser nobles and their retainers, like smaller and smaller spores budding from the central great plant. It was a cloth reflection of the intricacies of Grand Kingdom politics, of the fealties each noble owed and was owed.

And because of its wild nature, there was no straight road through the camp for Duchess Amelia's entourage to follow. The entire procession needed the two heralds on horseback leading the way, the path twisted and turned so much. It felt so convoluted that even after some time they seemed no more than halfway to the manor house in the center, and Amelia began to wonder if they were deliberately taking a more circuitous route.

Perhaps they think to show me off, she thought. *The curious, wayward woman from the west.*

There would be no way for her to know for sure if they were, but ultimately she dismissed the idea. The heralds were too low in status to risk spurning her in such a fashion. The fact that she'd even thought of the possibility troubled her, though.

Was she becoming paranoid? And even if she was, was that necessarily a bad thing? If only one in every ten nobles in this camp thought of her the way Reverend Master Faldmoor did, then there was a large number here who meant her ill.

The carriage swayed as it bumped and bounced over the churned, rutted ground, and the duchess swayed with it, searching the faces of those who watched her pass. There were no cheers and or waves here, just impassive expressions—some curious, most disinterested. There was a dejected air over the whole populace, though at one point they passed a small knot of knights who sat together chatting amiably and drinking from pewter goblets. These watched the entourage approach with smiles on their faces until one of them seemed to remember his manners. Amelia saw him stand, then turn to his fellows, slapping and waving at them to join him. Soon enough, the others levered themselves upright and they all stood in a vague semblance of respect as she passed, although none put down his cup and most let their free hands rest on the hilts of their longswords.

"You would almost think we weren't welcome," Dalflitch mused.

"Well, they ain't cheering for us, that's for sure," Righteous agreed.

"Is there much farther to go, Turley? Can you see?" Amelia asked. Her chief steward half stood in his higher seat, looking ahead of them.

"Almost there, I think, Your Grace," he answered. "And none too soon, if you'll pardon me saying so."

"The duchess will ask your opinion, should she want it," Dalflitch corrected him reflexively.

Amelia put her hand on her lady's arm. Everyone was tense, it seemed. "Something troubles you, steward?" she asked Turley.

"I don't think these folks like the sight of convicts in armor with swords, Your Grace," Turley explained. "True enough, Prentice has made sure the Fangs' blades're different enough to not be a straight insult to any knights we pass, but we're in the Grand Kingdom proper now. To these folk, a convict is supposed to have irons on his legs and a rag or two to cover his nakedness. And he's supposed to be thankful to have that much. I think your lions make 'em all nervous, Your Grace."

Trust Turley to see the practical realities in the midst of my political terrors, Amelia thought.

The impassive expressions on the denizens of the king's camp weren't for her moral character or her ongoing legal conflict with the crown prince. Armed convicts were marching past, and no more explanation than that was required. Traditionally, convicts that were sent to battle, the rogues 'foot, weren't given weapons until they were actually on the battlefield, and even then, they were never given much more than sharp sticks for the task. Armed convicts were a threat, and in that light, even the knights' behavior made sense. They'd stood to be respectful but kept their hands on their swords because they feared real trouble.

"Looks like we're just about here," said Turley, nodding to the two heralds who brought the little column to a halt at the corner of two walls of whitewashed brick. One of the riders consulted with Prentice while the other walked his mount back and spoke to Turley and the driver. Their conversation seemed overly long, and Amelia did not hear much of what was said.

"What word?" she asked as the herald withdrew and Turley dropped off the driver's board to get the door of the carriage.

"He says the gateway in the wall just ahead leads to the garden where the king is holding council. There's a path there and it runs straight to the seats and tables, so the herald says. Your Grace is expected to line her 'tourage up on the path and march in to present to the king. Other nobles will be about on a big square of pavement. After the bows and introductions, then there's a chair with an awning for you to sit on, Your Grace." Turley stopped and tugged his forelock. "Leastwise, that's what the heralds say to do. I wouldn't think to tell you how to behave, Your Grace."

He stood by with his hand on the door, waiting respectfully for Viscount Gullden to dismount and be ready to help the ladies down from the carriage. Once that was done, Amelia lifted her skirt out of the dust and allowed Turley and Gullden to escort her to the head of the line of soldiers. Prentice saluted and bowed at her approach, while from behind her nobles dismounted, handing reins off to squires and forming themselves into a column based on their own noble ranks. Presently, the entire party was arranged in procession, with the duchess at their head and then the White Lions as her immediate men-at-arms with their drummers leading. Behind them walked her ladies-in-waiting, and behind them the nobility of the Western Reach, with Sir Gant at their rear, serving as ceremonial rear-guard.

"At your convenience, Your Grace," Prentice whispered, pointing a guiding hand toward the gate in the wall.

Amelia blinked, realizing that she had been lost in her thoughts. "Will it always be like this?" she said quietly, not exactly talking to Prentice, but once the words were spoken, she looked to him for his thoughts.

"Like this, Your Grace?" he asked.

"Coming cap-in-hand to these vultures who want to peck me apart? Three years, nearly four, and I am still the young, upstart widow, clinging on to my husband's legacy by the tips of my fingernails." She turned to him for a moment and let him see the full strength of her fears and uncertainties in her expression. "My stomach is churning, and my hands are slick with sweat. It is all I can do to speak, my throat is so dry. Every time it is like this. Am I just a weak little girl who cannot find her strength?"

"You have found your strength in times like this before, Your Grace," he said to her. "More than one prince has learned not to underestimate you." He leaned in and Amelia felt her nervousness softened by the care in his eyes. At moments like this, he was like an older brother or dear uncle. Nevertheless.

"I've never faced a king before," she said.

"The day arrives, Your Grace, when the up-and-comer finally gets into the ring with the champion and learns for certain if they are worthy of the highest trophy."

"Am I the up-and-comer?" The duchess cocked an eyebrow at being compared to a professional wrestler or young knight in a tournament but smiled at the metaphor.

"Indeed, Your Grace. You have won all lesser bouts and earned your place in the list. You have proven your mettle and are the Reach's heroine. Time to challenge for the championship."

"Then why don't I feel confident? Why am I so nervous?"

"The trumpet, the horn, and the drum. These are the testers of men."

Amelia frowned at that. "And what does that mean?"

"On the day of battle, there comes a moment, Your Grace, when enemies are arrayed, watching one another, seeing the weapons that have been brought to cut, smash, and rend men's flesh. And both sides watch, waiting for the order to come, for the horn or trumpet to blow, for the drum to beat and the march to begin. It takes as much courage to stand and wait for that order, staring at the massed death readied for you, as it does to charge into the fray."

"How do you banish the fear?" she asked him, praying inwardly that he had an answer.

"You do not. You hold on to it. And when the trumpet sounds and the drum beats, you throw it all out at your foe, full force.

Amelia listened to Prentice's words, and a sudden feeling of shame came over her. How many battlefields had Prentice stood upon? Several in her service alone, as well as all the others in his years as a convict, not to mention all the lesser duels and petty fights he'd been a part of. And behind her were columns of men with similar pedigrees in conflict and warfare. How cowardly was she that she shied away from a little acid conversation in polite company?

I am no coward, she told herself. The feebleness of women, if there was such a thing, was not for her. She gritted her teeth and summoned her courage. *I can face a king.*

"Also, Your Grace, you have one other advantage," Prentice added, leaning closer and lowering his voice even further.

"What is that?"

"You do not have to wait any longer," he whispered. "You are the Duchess of the Western Reach, the *She* Lion. You give the order and the trumpet sounds the charge. And we all march with you."

He met her gaze directly, quietly, privately, in spite of all the people standing, waiting. That look told her that he fully trusted her and supported her in whatever action she took. She was his liege lady, and he would die for her. And if she had his loyalty, Amelia knew that every man behind him would follow her with him.

"Huzzah," she whispered, smiling at the irony of such a soft call for a charge.

"The trumpet sounds," Prentice replied, sharing her smile. Then he stood upright and his face became hard as iron, showing no emotion whatsoever.

Amelia turned to the gate and led her entourage to it without another word. She held her head high, and as she passed through, she did her best not to gawp at the beauty of the garden or the riot of color that danced in the midday sun. Under her feet, a pebble-laid path crunched softly, then began to grind beneath the heavy boots of her guards. On either side of the path were neatly trimmed lawns and well-tended flower beds. The grass was a rich green from the winter and spring rains, and the multi-colored flowers were in full bloom. Their perfume was heady in the air.

Despite the beauty of the garden, Amelia resisted every temptation to look to the left or right, fixing her eyes straight ahead. There, gathered on an open courtyard of paved stones, was the Denay Court of King Chrostmer IV. Nobles of the highest ranks flocked about a pair of stone fountains that bubbled unheard under the hum of conversation—men in rich doublets and hose, ladies in fine gowns. Slashed sleeves revealed second layers of silk and satin. The colors of the most ancient and respectable houses proclaimed the nobility of the highest court of the Grand Kingdom. The highest-born folk in all the world.

And directly opposite her, seated upon a gilded throne carved with eagle-headed armrests and feet like talons, was King Chrostmer IV himself. Amelia watched him as she approached, knowing that as she drew closer she would have to avert her eyes since it was beyond rude to look directly upon the king without invitation. But seizing the opportunity before she drew near, she did her best to assess this man, the final opponent in her long quest to keep her people and her lands safe.

No, not the final opponent, she thought. *Merely the next one.* After all, in the coming days the entire kingdom would have to face the Redlanders in battle. Until they were defeated, the Western Reach would never be safe.

Amelia's first impression was that Chrostmer was old, with long white hair and a thick, well-trimmed beard. She had known that, of course. Years before, she had met the king's brother, Prince Mercad, a man decrepit in his age. But where Mercad had been all skin and bones, with his fine robes hanging from his scarecrow frame like sheets draped over leafless branches, Chrostmer seemed strong and hale indeed. His barreled chest filled his doublet, and there was a solid fortitude to the way he sat, as if his limbs still retained the strength of youth. Prince Mercad had been a withered thing in the last days of his life, but Chrostmer looked as if he easily had another ten or twenty years remaining to him.

Looking away from the throne, Amelia noticed that many of the gathered nobles were of a similar age to the king, and it made sense as she thought about it. These were her husband's contemporaries, the nobles who had crusaded over the mountains to fully civilize the wild frontier that was now her duchy. When Daven Marcus had come to her lands two years past, he had come with his lesser court, which was full of the sons and daughters of this court. As the prince was heir of this king, so the Rhales court was made up of the heirs of the Denay court. Daven Marcus's nobles were the youth that had grown up in the shadow of this conquering generation that now ruled in the autumn of their glory.

Thoughts of Daven Marcus caused Amelia to look for the crown prince, and she was surprised not to see him anywhere about. When the king had summoned his son to join the defense of the south, Amelia had assumed that the two courts, Denay and Rhales, prince and king, were merged. From a quick survey of the gathered worthies, it seemed not so. Perhaps the prince maintained his court separately somewhere. Even so, surely he would have been summoned to his father's war council.

Amelia reached the edge of the pavement and paused. Every eye was upon her, though most tried to affect disinterest, pretending to be above so simple an emotion as curiosity. But they were looking, and the conversation had quieted to no more than a whisper. As she waited, the duchess began to wonder what would happen next. Had Turley said she would be announced, or would she have to provide her own herald? She couldn't remember. The quiet stretched and no announcement was made.

"Should I send for Viscount Gullden to announce me?" she whispered and was about to do just that when a sudden blast of trumpets ripped the quiet from the garden like a tent plucked away in a hurricane wind. The clarion echoed around the garden walls, but by the second blast it was clear from which direction the trumpet calls were coming. Every head turned to

Amelia's left to look away across the garden. The entire Denay court, from the least servant to the king himself, looked in one direction, away from the duchess and her entourage. Amelia looked as well, though as she did so, she was pleased to notice that Prentice had not, and she knew why. In truth, she hadn't really needed to look either. They were both fully aware what the trumpets signified.

Prince Daven Marcus had arrived at his father's council of war.

CHAPTER 13

Petty little snot, Prentice thought.

Daven Marcus's arrival was obviously calculated to upstage the duchess, and it was working. The trumpets' clarion call rang out one more time as the Prince of Rhales led his own entourage of nobles and worthies into the garden from a different entry point. The gathered courtiers watched them enter, moving aside to welcome them into the courtyard. The Rhales men wore festive clothes, with dyed feathers in their caps and ruffled silk on their sleeves and trews, embroidered capes across their shoulders, tied in place with golden threads. Every man had at least two fine jewels presented on themselves, pinned to their chests or set in rings on their fingers. The few women amongst them were even more finely garbed, their over-dresses embroidered and festooned with ribbons and ruffles. Heavy gold chains studded with gems hung at every throat, and their complex hairstyles were so wrapped in pearls and precious stones that the ladies of the prince's entourage all looked at a distance as if they had only just walked through a rain shower, and little drops of water were glistening in their hair.

Prentice held his eyes forward, facing the king's throne, but looking politely downward at a point halfway across the courtyard. He wanted to study the prince, but he had a duty to maintain the dignity of his liege. Eventually, the arriving cortege moved into his field of view, and he watched as the prince circulated amongst the crowd, greeting dukes and earls as old friends, shaking hands, and receiving bows. Close behind him, Prentice thought he recognized a young, fair-haired woman in a red velvet dress. Kirsten, former handmaid of Duchess Amelia, who had betrayed the duchess in hope of advancement. The young lady stood tall and dignified, but she seemed thinner than Prentice remembered her and much colder in demeanor. Recognizing her, Prentice could guess who her escort was—a dark-haired man with a perfectly groomed beard and almost foppish manner. That would be Baron Robant, Kirsten's new husband and the prince's champion. Robant had been Duchess Amelia's jailer, of sorts, during the failed crusade west, and Prentice recognized him from her grace's description. The two men had never met, but the Captain of the Lions felt an instant dislike for this chosen man of Daven Marcus's.

Even in the vibrant colors of the king's court, Daven Marcus's hangers-on seemed gaudily bright, as if bathed in rainbows. The prince himself, by contrast seemed almost reserved, his golden hair held with a simple coronet. He wore hose in royal red under a doublet that was patterned of squares of the same red and Reach blue. Prentice recognized this, too, from the duchess's stories of the crusade. On the doublet's front were two heraldic animals, the golden Royal eagle and the silver Reach lion. The eagle was above, wings spread and ascendant, the lion beneath, seemingly asleep and with its tail between its legs, a position called dormant and coward. The lion in that heraldry declared that the Reach was weak and defeated. This was the prince's wedding doublet, the jacket he'd worn to announce his intention to marry Duchess Amelia. Melding two heraldries into one was common with a high-born marriage, but to do it like this was as brutal an insult as the prince could deliver to the Western Reach, as well as to the duchess he proclaimed intent to marry.

Seeing the doublet, Prentice could not miss the parallel with Solft's illuminations. An eagle dominant over a lion. Unbidden, a piece of scripture came into his mind of God speaking through a prophet, "I am He who declares the end from the beginning." Prentice was sure it must have been something he'd read during his studies, but even as he remembered the words, another voice sounded in his head, so powerfully that he almost felt that he heard it in his ears.

As it began, so shall it end.

He had no idea what the words meant, but the sound of them in his thoughts made him shiver momentarily, despite the bright warmth of the day and his heavy armor. To keep control of his own mind, he watched how members of the court responded to the symbolism of the prince's doublet. Some seemed surprised, and curious glances were cast back at the duchess and her entourage, held up by the prince's arrival. One or two seemed to comment on the jacket directly, and these seemed to Prentice to be mostly amused. They would be the prince's allies in his father's court, the ones to watch most closely. Prentice risked a quick glance at the duchess. Her expression seemed to show she recognized the significance of Daven Marcus's doublet as well, though there was no sign she'd heard the inner voice Prentice had. She all but trembled with fury, her eyes slitted and hands clenched at her sides.

Daven Marcus reached the space in front of his father's throne. He bowed, and Prentice noticed for the first time that he had a cup in his hand. The prince toasted his father and drank the cup dry.

"Forgive my lateness, Father," he said grandly. He spun about gracefully, arms wide to take in the gathered courtiers. "My apologies to you all. We have been at my wedding celebration, hoping to finish the ritual that was interrupted in the boorish west. We just lacked one thing." He paused to look meaningfully at the duchess.

"What was that?" Prentice heard the duchess mutter under her breath. "A bed to publicly rape me on?" The prince had planned just such a "consummation" at his previous "marriage ceremony." Daven Marcus caught the duchess's gaze, and he sneered at her for an instant before turning back to the king.

"It's just a little matter, Father," he said unctuously. "I have a sacrist with me. We could have it settled in a trice. Then the ladies can withdraw, and we men can conduct the business of your war council."

"Perhaps that would be for the best, Your Majesty," offered an older nobleman from the other side of the courtyard. "Get the petty business put to bed and move to the defense of the Grand Kingdom."

Petty business? Put to bed? thought Prentice. *That was not subtle.*

Every courtier looked to the throne, and boldly as he dared, Prentice looked as well, watching the king's reaction. It seemed King Chrostmer was judging the matter seriously. His son was offering a swift resolution to the Grand Kingdom's problems in the west. If the king decreed the duchess should marry the prince, there was virtually nothing she could do about it. Her nobles might hate Daven Marcus, but they would have no authority to refuse him. And rushing the whole process was clever on Daven Marcus's part. This was the way he played the game, Prentice had heard—fast and treacherously, wielding his royal privilege like a weapon and daring any opponent to question his methods. The prince must defer to the king, but it seemed he had long ago learned to presume upon his father's affection so that Daven Marcus expected to manipulate even the king himself with these sorts of machinations.

"We cannot let him win," Prentice muttered to himself and he knew in an instant what he needed to do. "Your Grace, do you trust me?"

"What are you planning?" she whispered back. "This is not a Reach frontier tower where I can save you if you are rude."

"This is the championship, Your Grace," he returned. "No point coming this far just to concede."

An age stretched in silence as king and duchess thought. Prentice had to resist the temptation to hurry her, but if she waited until the king delivered his judgement, it could be too late. He watched the sovereign contemplating, and almost didn't realize he had met the king's gaze. Chrostmer was thinking, and as he did, he was regarding the duchess and her entourage. No doubt the canny ruler was weighing the outcomes in his thoughts, and Prentice was looking straight into the man's eyes. Any fear for this breach of protocol was immediately dispelled when he heard his mistress whisper her decision.

"Sound the trumpet, Captain. Huzzah."

Prentice smiled at her words and bowed to the king before breaking eye contact. He hoped that was polite enough for the highest sovereign in the whole world. Then, he turned to the two drummers standing behind him.

"Beat the march lads," he whispered his order. "March to ranks and present with all your strength. Make the walls tremble."

The two drummer boys looked pale and uncertain, and behind them the two ranks were equally unnerved. Farther back, the Reacher nobles likewise seemed to lack confidence, shifting uncomfortably under the amused gaze of the land's highest court. No one here knew what the right protocol was exactly, and Prentice realized in a flash that the uncertainty extended even to the king. That was why Chrostmer was not speaking. He wanted to see what this widow duchess, this unknown quantity from the west, would do.

The drummers struck the beat, pounding so forcefully that the entire courtyard jumped with surprise. Many flinched, and even the prince drew back an involuntary step. The familiar beat had an opposite effect on the two lines of Fangs. The rhythm of the march seized them, and all uncertainty fled. Months of drilling made their response automatic, visceral, rising up from their very feet. Their boots tromped on the earth, beating out the same cadence so that the very air was hammered by it. Then Prentice took his first step forward and the duchess moved with him. As if her bodyguard, he stayed a half pace ahead and picked the straightest path across the courtyard directly to the throne itself. The drumbeat went ahead of him like a storm front, clearing the way. Picking a point that seemed like the respectful distance for an audience with the king, Prentice stopped just two steps in front of Daven Marcus. Duchess Amelia came up beside him, eyes to the throne, refusing to even acknowledge the Prince of Rhales.

The drumbeat changed, and in immediate response, the two lines divided, spreading to the left and right in single file. They made no allowance for the rest of the courtiers, their discipline allowing them only obedience, as if this were the field of battle. A noble lady yelped in momentary panic as she was forced to jump aside. When the two lines were stretched before the throne, all twenty Fangs turned in place, facing forward. Another change in the beat sounded the "present," and twenty men put their right hands on the hilts of their swords. As one, they went down on one knee and bowed their heads. The beat continued for a few more hammers on the drums as behind the line of kneeling soldiers, the nobles of the Reach spread out in their own second, impromptu line. Then the drummers pounded one last stroke and silence fell. Prentice went down on one knee at the same moment, bowing his head as well.

"Her Grace, Amelia, Duchess of the Western Reach," he bellowed out, announcing her before anyone present could recover their wits to make a comment. "Widow of Marne, hero of the Reach. Scourge of the Redlanders and loyal servant of the throne of the Grand Kingdom. Unchallenged from the Azure Mountains to the Salt Sea. The Lioness." He was making up the titles as he went along but was confident the duchess would not object. "Presenting her fealty to King Chrostmer IV, unchallenged sovereign of the Grand Kingdom, first over all nobility. Defender of the Faith. The Lord's anointed king. Before the king, the Lioness and her pride."

"Huzzah!" cried one of the Reach nobles behind them. Then it was taken up by all of them for two more cheers. "Huzzah! Huzzah!"

CHAPTER 14

A melia felt her cheeks flushed in pride as silence washed in over the whole courtyard. Beside and behind her every Reacherman was on their knees, heads down in perfect deference to the king. She alone stood, as was her right as Duchess of the Reach. Nonetheless, she bowed her head and curtseyed.

"Your Majesty," she said in as clear a voice as she could muster. "The Reach presents its homage."

Then there really was silence in the courtyard. No one moved—not the courtiers from Rhales or Denay, not the prince. And not one of Amelia's people, noble or lion, so much as breathed too heavily. It was so quiet that not only could the duchess hear the two fountains bubbling away, but she could detect the buzz of a dragonfly's wings as it hovered over the surface of the water. The quiet would have been pleasant if it were not so tense. And still it stretched, as no one dared speak before the king. Amelia kept her head down, fighting the uncertainty that threatened her calm and made her stomach twist in knots.

Is he testing me? she wondered. *Does he want to see if he can tempt me to some rudeness? O king, I have waited more than three years to see you finally rouse yourself against these invaders. I can wait another five minutes, if that is what it takes.*

"Welcome, Duchess Amelia," King Chrostmer said at last, his voice rich and resonant in the quiet. "Quite the martial display you make."

"Thank you, Majesty, for your kind welcome. As to our display, we are the men and women of your Western Reach. We are a serious people. When our king summons us to war, we come with swords and armor, not ribbons and ruffles."

A quiet intake of breath, a fraction too polite to be a gasp, passed through the court as everyone present heard her implicit criticism of the prince and his supposed wedding plans.

Good. Let them see that she was ready to stand, even against the prince and his self-aggrandizing. Prentice was right. This was the championship, and she had come to fight. And win.

Assuming the king let her, of course.

Right now, he still seemed in two minds. It was all Amelia could do to keep herself from cursing out loud as Ecclesiarch Faldmoor stepped from the crowd and bowed before the throne.

"King Chrostmer, long may you reign," he declared, following the form of politeness but not actually waiting to be acknowledged before turning on the duchess. "Surely you do not mean to treat with a wayward wife who refuses the guidance of Mother Church and the rightful authority of her husband. She must be brought to heel."

Someone's got his confidence back, Amelia thought. *Feeling the home turf advantage, are we sacrist?* She managed to keep herself from sneering at the man.

"What say you, Duchess?" the king asked, and Amelia let herself smile for a moment.

Years before, she had stood in an audience similar to this in front of Chrostmer's brother, Prince Mercad, and she had watched the prince play this very game, setting courtiers off against each other. He was waiting for his own advantage. Like a table of card players, the king would bide his time, letting the others make the running until he was sure he held all the trumps; then he would play his winning hand.

So, let's give him some trumps to play.

"Majesty, I confess myself confused," Amelia said, affecting innocence in her voice. "Prince Daven Marcus comes to summon me to be a bride, yet the ecclesiarch names me as a wayward wife. How can both claims stand?"

Amelia risked a glance at the king directly and was sure she could see in his expression that he recognized the winning play she was offering him. With his pre-emptive wedding summons, the prince had admitted publicly that he and Amelia were not yet married. How could she be wayward from a marriage that had not yet happened? It seemed almost too easy. From the whispers rising around her, it seemed the whole court could suddenly see the mistake.

"You make an excellent point, Duchess Amelia," said the king. "Can you answer that, Reverend Faldmoor?"

Amelia noted that the king's question demoted the patriarch from reverend master to mere reverend. She wondered if anyone else realized. If Faldmoor did, he didn't mention it.

"I must concede, Your Majesty," said the churchman. "It seems that the charge of waywardness has been brought..." He paused, seemingly reaching for the right word.

Trying to agree with the king and keep the charge alive at the same time, Amelia thought.

After a moment it became clear Faldmoor could not find the right equivocation.

"Prematurely," he said through gritted teeth. "A woman cannot be a wayward wife and not yet married at the same time."

"So, we need not hear any more talk of ecclesiarchal synods and writs of judgement?" asked the king.

Faldmoor visibly ground his teeth. "Not on this matter, I would say, Majesty."

Amelia wanted to dare a glance at the prince to see if he recognized how fully he'd defeated himself, but she held her self-control. It seemed the prince was so used to using his personal charisma and privilege of birth to get his own way that he lacked even the basic skills at courtly negotiation of even the least Denay nobleman. No wonder Dalflitch had once thought to manipulate her way into a marriage with him.

"Good to put that business to bed, just as you say, Earl Gawestead." King Chrostmer nodded at the courtier who'd made the comment in support of the prince's claim.

This time, Amelia did look, as did most of the rest of the court, she noted. The nobleman in question, a middle-aged man with a fur-trimmed cape that must surely have been making him sweat in the spring warmth, scowled and bowed his head in submission.

"With your indulgence, Majesty," Faldmoor said before the king could say anything else. "There are yet matters of Church justice to resolve. Though the duchess might not be wayward, there are questions of heresy to answer."

There was another collective breath, but this time less shocked and more avid. The courtiers were enjoying their favorite sport, political wrangling. The fact that this clash involved both senior Church authority and the honor of the throne directly only made it more exciting for them.

Vultures, Amelia thought, and this time she did not hide her disdain, at least for a moment. Then she remembered her vision from years ago. *Rotting eagles.*

"How many times must this charge be answered, Majesty?" Amelia asked, her contempt for the gathered courts of Denay and Rhales making her more bold, more willing to try the offensive.

That, and her loyalty to her own people, especially Prentice Ash. Her captain had been tortured, reviled, and exiled. And in response, he had fought loyally to protect her life and the lives of her people. He had been more faithful to her than the child-man prince who professed to woo her. Yet the Church authorities wanted to back the prince, for whatever righteous authority the ecclesiarchy once possessed, in Amelia's eyes, they had forfeited it for the chance to play the dirty court politics of the kingdom. And they were just as grubby and low as a result.

"This charge has been answered?" asked the king. "Is that so?"

"Count Lark-Stross was witness," the duchess answered, "last night when the Reverend Master brought the charge against my man, claiming he remained a heretic in my household."

"Remained?"

"The man here at my side, my captain, was a convicted heretic, Majesty." Amelia nodded to Prentice still kneeling next to her. "He has served his time upon the chain, purged his soul in service to the Western Reach and the Grand Kingdom, and risen again as a free man."

"Only the Church can forgive heresy," Faldmoor insisted. "You know this, Majesty."

"Nothing is forgiven," Amelia countered. "The judgement has been rendered and the sentence served."

"You have no right to declare the sentence served. The Church reserves that judgement to itself."

"King's Law gives me the right as Duchess of the Reach."

"Not in this case, petty duchess. Heresy and apostasy are reserved to the Church. You should know King's Law better before you try to call upon it."

Amelia wanted to continue to argue, but the truth was she wasn't sure Faldmoor was wrong. The interaction between Church law and King's Law was arcane. It was possible that the ecclesiarch was completely correct. Prentice would know, but she couldn't very well ask him his advice in the midst of this company, especially since he was the subject of the legal question.

"Well, who can declare a sentence of heresy served?" asked King Chrostmer.

From his tone, he sounded genuinely curious. Given how brutal convict life was and how often the convicted died on the chain before their terms of service were completed, it occurred to Amelia that this could very well be the first time any heretic had survived long enough for this legal question to be raised.

"It is an authority reserved to ecclesiarchy alone," said Faldmoor, raising his chin.

"So you, as an ecclesiarch, could grant the declaration?"

"I...suppose." Faldmoor's eyes blinked, and his dignity slipped for a moment. Immediately, he cleared his throat and reset his demeanor, forcing a disdainful expression on his face once more. "Yes, I could, though a writ confirming the judgement would be needed from the full Council of Ecclesiarchs."

"Well, that seems simple enough." The king turned his eyes on Prentice. "You there, captain of the Reach militia. Stand up."

Prentice rose next to Amelia. Out of the corner of her eye she watched him release the hilt of his sword and put both hands behind his back. It would be almost an act of rebellion for a man of his birth to put his hand to his weapon while addressing the king. The duchess had no doubt her captain would know every law of courtesy. He might break them deliberately, as he had on her behalf last night, but he knew how to obey them as well.

"What is your name?" the king asked.

"Prentice Ash, Your Majesty," Prentice answered, head down at the correct angle.

"Ash? An odd family name. We do not recognize it."

"It is not a family name, Majesty. It is a battle name. I won it from the hands of the Redlanders."

"It is the name they fear, Majesty," Amelia said proudly.

"They do not fear the name of Chrostmer?" the king said mildly, but there was a barb in it, and immediately Amelia recoiled within herself. Her confidence dimmed and she realized that the game was still going on. The king hadn't played all his trumps yet.

"Not as well as they will soon, Majesty," said Prentice smoothly, and Amelia wanted to kiss him.

"Very good, Captain," said the king. "And you, Duchess, felt to grant this man release from the chain? He fights in your militia because you freed him?"

"I freed him because he already fought so well—by my judgement, as well as any man the Reach has seen." It was a risky boast to make, especially considering the nobility gathered behind her, but many changes had happened in the Reach since her husband had been murdered and the duchy passed into her hands. One of those was the honor this one convict soldier had earned amongst the people of the Western Reach. Amelia was confident no Reacherman would object to hearing him so described.

The courts of Rhales and Denay were another matter. Many of the nobles around her scoffed openly, and Daven Marcus, sensing an opportunity, it seemed, turned a circle, arms wide.

"See?" he demanded of the two courts. "This is what happens when fools trust military command to a woman. How many of the finest of Rhales gave their lives to save the Reach? How many houses of Denay lost their heirs? Lost because of him." Daven Marcus pointed straight at Prentice. "He commanded the rebels who ambushed and butchered so many good Rhales knights when I loaned them to that Reacher fool Liam. Tricked them and killed them without honor."

Next to her, Amelia thought she could sense the tension in Prentice's posture as he held himself back. The prince's account of the battle between the knights under Liam's command and Prentice's first five cohorts of lions was so false that she was almost certain Daven Marcus was deliberately insulting Prentice, trying to bait him to rash action. Just to the side, Amelia could see Baron Robant, the prince's loyal champion. Although he was dressed in his wedding clothes, Robant somehow had a sword to hand, holding it still sheathed but ready to draw. Either he and the prince had planned for the audience to take this turn or else the loyal attack dog knew his master's moods and was ready if the order to strike came. Amelia

wanted to warn Prentice but could not think of a way to do it
that wouldn't give Daven Marcus another, different advantage.
Everything balanced on the edge of that blade, it seemed.

"And this heretic, convict, coward," the prince was
continuing, pointing at Prentice but addressing the king
directly, "he was also present at the so-called Battle of the Brook.
Not only did he raise a banner against my man and slaughter
good men of my court, but he is responsible for that tragic loss
as well."

Tragic loss? Amelia felt her eyebrows rise in disbelief. *The
Brook was a victory.*

"She says he was there, then he is to blame," Daven Marcus
declared, his voice growing almost shrill. "It is because of him
that Prince Mercad is dead! Your brother, father. My uncle. The
Prince of Rhales."

Like actors in a morality play, the Rhales nobles all looked
suddenly mournful, shaking their heads. Amelia wanted to
scream at the flagrant falsehood. Not one of those nobles had
marched with Mercad or stood at the Battle of the Brook. She
doubted they'd even met the former prince. She was trying
to think how to respond when another voice, not yet heard,
sounded through the air from somewhere unseen at the side of
the king's throne.

"That is a lie," the resonant declaration rang out like a parade
ground command.

From amidst the courtiers in that corner, a tall, older man
with a full grey beard and wearing a breastplate of polished
white steel pressed forward. He was of an age and demeanor
with the king and showed a similar vigor. But where King
Chrostmer was thickset and barrel chested, this man had a
leanness that suggested ongoing training, like a soldier who had
grown older but was, if anything, a better warrior for the extra
years. It probably helped that, apart from her own guards, he
was the only man present in armor. Amelia recognized him

immediately, and it made her smile to see him amidst this pit of vipers.

"Sir Carron," she breathed. He had been Prince Mercad's champion, scion of a line of royal champions and knight commander at the Battle of the Brook. He was by far the most honorable and dutiful knight Amelia had ever met.

"You call our son and heir a liar, Lord Ironworth?" the king asked, seeming more curious than offended on behalf of the prince.

"I cannot say if he lies or has been lied to and repeats the words unknowingly, Your Majesty," Sir Carron admitted bluntly. "But the words he spoke are lies, and they do not deserve to stand."

"You jealous old fool," Daven Marcus began, clearly thinking to silence the older man.

When he had become Prince of Rhales, Daven Marcus had dismissed Sir Carron from court summarily. He tried to do the same now but misjudged his move once again. As a mere knight, Carron Ironworth was far beneath the prince in rank but not in reputation. In the Denay court, he was widely regarded as the kingdom's greatest living warrior, and with good cause.

Sir Carron ignored the prince's contempt, speaking only to the king. "Far be it for me to question the military competence of a man who wears ruffles and ribbons to a council of war, Your Majesty. But the prince is not correct in what he says. Prince Mercad did not lose the Battle of the Brook, though it cost him his life, and he had the victory by my hand and the hand of the man that the duchess has made her captain."

"You vouch for his skill?"

"And bravery, Majesty. He rallied our forces with me and slew the enemy general with his own hand."

"The idiot Liam killed the Horned Man; everyone knows that," the prince retorted with venom, almost spitting in his fury. "He had the damned antlers on his helmet."

"Were you there?" Sir Carron turned to the prince and asked flatly.

"No, and good thing I wasn't, given your talent for losing princes in battle!"

That was a genuine step too far for the Denay court. Any support among the older nobles that the prince had against Amelia dissolved in the acid of his contempt for Sir Carron Ironworth.

"Sir Carron has saved princes from many more battles than he lost them in," said the king and although his tone was still mild, Amelia felt that she could see a growing annoyance with his petty son. Perhaps even King Chrostmer was reaching the end of his patience. "And perhaps if you'd had more chances to march with him you would have lost fewer dragons?"

The Bronze Dragons were a company of enormous cannons maintained by the Royal house of Denay, phenomenally powerful and so ancient that the technique to manufacture them was now forgotten. The king had allowed his son to take five of them with him on his western campaign and all five had been irretrievably lost, captured, or destroyed. Apparently, King Chrostmer was unhappy about their loss, and perhaps rightly so. Five monstrous weapons that could level castles and could not be replaced were a loss to the whole kingdom. The royal house was permanently weakened.

"Am I not more important than some lumps of old metal? Do you love me or those damned bombards?" Daven Marcus demanded, spraying spittle in his fury. His handsome face was reddening, and he glared at his father. "I am the Prince of Rhales, heir to the throne. To *your* throne."

"Then start acting like it and not like a tantruming brat."

There were no more gasps or sighs or breaths amongst the courtiers. This was open conflict between the two highest ranking men in the Grand Kingdom. Clearly no one knew how to act so everyone held themselves as still as they could. For her part, Amelia felt embarrassed for the king. She'd seen Daven Marcus lose his temper before. To be on the receiving end of his rage was humiliating enough, but King Chrostmer was owed respect and fealty, as both the prince's father and as king. Yet he was receiving none.

"I am aggrieved, and you take their side?" Daven Marcus cried. "The woman thinks she's too good to lift her skirt. I've dirt under my fingernails worth more than all her bastard toy soldiers put together, and yet you let them stand here pretending to be real men-at-arms. Worst of all, you let this incontinent old lapdog yap at me instead of swatting his nose like he deserves."

"Enough, boy!" the king shouted, thrusting himself to his feet. "Be silent."

"I will not..."

"You will!" The king's voice rang with the same battlefield authority Sir Carron's had. "You will or you will be commanded from our presence."

Amelia blinked in surprise. The king had just threatened to exile his own son from the Denay court. It was unprecedented. She wondered if such a thing had ever happened before in the entire history of the Grand Kingdom.

"We have had enough of all of this. The crown will render judgement." From somewhere unseen behind the king's throne, a black-robed scholar stepped into view carrying a large, full gold crown on a red velvet cloth. The king took the crown and placed it on his own head, a sign that his next words would have the full force of law. In the face of this naked authority, even Daven Marcus stood quietly. Everyone present bowed, curtseyed, or knelt as rank required. Prentice started to go back down on his knee, but the king gestured for him to remain standing. "Sir Carron, you say that this man fought with honor?"

"I do, Your Majesty."

"And you, Faldmoor, say that an elder of Mother Church can forgive a charge of heresy?"

"I do, Majesty," Faldmoor answered, then added. "If I judge the heresy purged."

The king glared a moment at the religious man's insistent impertinence, but he seemed focused now on resolving the key question. He turned to Prentice.

"You, duchess' man, the one they call Ash. You were convicted of heresy?"

"I was, Majesty."

"And are you sorry?"

"Utterly," said Prentice.

Knowing the complexity of Prentice's thoughts, Amelia wondered for a moment if he was saying he was sorry for his heresy or sorry he was convicted. It was the kind of technical truth telling of which he was easily capable.

"Utterly?" the king repeated. "And do you accept the authority of Mother Church."

"I do."

This time Amelia had to believe he was lying, but she did not begrudge him that. The king turned back to the patriarch.

"There you go, Faldmoor. The man has served his time, purged his soul, and put his foolishness behind him. What cause have you to refuse to forgive the charge now?"

The reverend master drew in a long, labored breath, and for a moment Amelia wondered if he was about to refuse the king to his face. It threatened a schism between throne and Church, on top of estrangement between king and crown prince, all over her man Prentice. Faldmoor was not as proud as the prince it seemed, however. He bowed in acquiescence to the king's position.

"I cannot withhold, Your Majesty. I grant that the heresy is purged."

"Good. We will have the writ drawn this afternoon and you will affix your signature, good reverend." The king turned to his son once more. The prince still seemed on the verge of apoplexy, as if he could not quite believe the king's threat. "Now, my boy. Go change out of that silly doublet and then come back so we can get to the business of this war council. God in heaven preserve us, sorcerers and scoundrels have invaded our lands and we are forced to preside over the mewling of infants."

King Chrostmer sat back down in disgust, looking away at the sky over the garden wall. Taking the crown from his head with one hand, he all but threw it at the waiting lawyer, who wrapped it again in its cloth.

CHAPTER 15

Prince Daven Marcus's mouth opened and closed several times, as if he wanted to speak but couldn't think what to say. Finally, he turned away and left the court, accompanied by Baron Robant and a number of his closest companions. At least half of the Rhales court stayed, however, and several of them surreptitiously removed feathers, jewels, and ribbons from their clothes. When the prince was gone, the rest of the courtiers began to relax and conversation recommenced, although at first only at a whisper.

"You may dismiss the guard," the duchess commanded Prentice. "More gently than our arrival, I think."

He nodded and set about quietly giving the soldiers their orders. As he did so, she moved past him and them to her nobles and ladies-in-waiting. The honor guard withdrew from the courtyard, told to find the duchess's carriage and wait there until they were called for the return journey.

"This will take hours yet," Prentice told them. "You will get your brandy, just not for a while, I fear. You will have to be patient." The men accepted his words with po-faced equanimity, saluting and marching out in correct order without the need of the drummers' beat.

"Perhaps the king will allow me to introduce you individually later without too much loss of honor," the duchess said to her noble attendants apologetically.

Listening, Prentice understood her mood. A chance to be presented to the king was immensely precious to any noble. The duchess would hate the thought that all her loyal retainers had missed their opportunity because of the political wrangling. Her nobles had a different impression of the day's proceedings.

"The honor was to stand in the pride of the Lioness, Your Grace," said Viscount Gullden earnestly, and many of other the nobles nodded.

"Peacocks and popinjays," said the Earl of Querridin contemptuously, though quietly, looking at the courtiers around the fountains. "You'd think they didn't even know the land was invaded."

"Nevertheless, My Lord, we must conduct ourselves with the dignity of our rank." The duchess chided gently, and the earl accepted her words with a bow. "Now gentlemen and ladies, please feel free to make your own way about the court. However long it takes the prince to change his doublet, there will be some moments at least before the king calls us to his council, I'm sure."

Her nobles accepted the duchess's dismissal graciously, and all withdrew to mingle amongst the gathered worthies. Prentice watched them go and then followed the duchess as she sought out the chair she had been told would be kept for her. Once seated, her ladies gathered around her. Lady Dalflitch settled down elegantly to sit on a footstool at the duchess's feet, while Righteous and Spindle stood behind her, one at each shoulder. When all were neatly arranged, the duchess turned to Prentice and Sir Gant.

"With your permission, I will remain, Your Grace," said Sir Gant.

"You do not wish to circulate, sir?"

"I fear not. I have no relatives here. I suspect my nobility would not meet the measure of this august company."

He took up a position to the side of the duchess, facing outward like a bodyguard. Prentice gave him an approving smile and stood beside him. Together they would continue to project a suitably military image for the duchess.

"Dramatic things these royal courts," Righteous observed wryly and everyone smiled. "S'it always like this, or did they put on a special performance for us, d'you think?"

"Courtly life is typically theatrical," observed Dalflitch, her eyes constantly scanning the shifting of the crowd of nobles. "But today has been especially dramatic, even by usual standards. I've not heard of a prince threatened with exile before."

Prentice watched her a moment, trying to track what she was seeing as she regarded the courtiers, but he knew he was running to catch up to her skills at politicking. In this environment, she was the duchess's sentry, the watchful guard who would always see trouble coming first.

"Not a lot of kings forcing the Church to issue writs of pardon for heresy either," said Duchess Amelia.

"Yes, that was quite interesting as well."

"Maybe the king ain't forgotten 'bout his mistress and the bell knight insult," said Spindle.

"I wouldn't think so," Dalflitch disagreed. "That is a long grudge to still hold, especially against the Church as a whole."

"Maybe he's just sour on 'em," said Righteous. "Forgiveness is the teaching, but grudges are a habit that's hard to break."

Glad my torture, conviction, and exile could give his majesty a chance to vent his spleen, Prentice thought sourly, but he kept his face a mask. And he consoled himself with the knowledge that whatever the king's motive, his heresy was absolved. He wondered what that would mean and suddenly thought again of Pallas and the rest of his family.

"Let us not speak any more of the king's motives," the duchess told them all. "We are not in private now."

"Of course, Your Grace," said Dalflitch, and all concurred.

There was silence between them for a long moment.

"Lots of pretty dresses," Spindle said at last.

"Indeed, though none made with more skill than yours, Mistress Spindle," said Righteous.

"Quite so," the duchess agreed. "You have given us all a presentation equal to the occasion."

Dalflitch also agreed, nodding and smiling.

"You're all very kind," Spindle answered, obviously flattered.

Their conversation ceased again as a steward brought glass goblets with a sweet white wine, which the ladies each accepted. They sipped politely but watchfully. Standing in his place, Prentice felt like a part of a lion's pride, lazing in the afternoon sun, regally scanning the grasslands. Suddenly, his mind transformed the gently milling courtiers to a herd—prey for the lioness and her pride—and though the image amused him, he dismissed it. Even with the prince absent, there were too many other predators hidden in amongst that assembly to relax. As if to reinforce his thoughts, the individual figure of Sir Carron emerged from the general mass of folk and stood before the duchess.

"Your Grace, may I present my compliments to you and your household?" he said and bowed formally.

"With pleasure, Sir Carron," said the duchess. "It was a pleasant surprise to see you here today. And I must thank you for your support before the king. I'm sure Captain Prentice is thankful as well."

"I am, indeed, Your Grace."

Prentice met Sir Carron's eyes, and as the knight nodded, he reflexively gave the man the White Lion's salute. He surprised himself doing it, and he saw the emotion mirrored in Sir Carron's own expression. Nonetheless, the noble champion accepted the gesture in the courteous manner it was intended.

"I understood the politics of not broadcasting a convict's central involvement in the Battle of the Brook," Sir Carron said bluntly, "although it did not sit fully well with me. But when I started to hear that dog Liam telling false tales of 'his' great victory on that day, I nearly choked with fury. I spoke of it with Prince Daven Marcus, but I phrased myself poorly and the prince took offence. Liam's lies cost me my honor, but I realized I surrendered it when I allowed politics to hide the truth. I have been ashamed from that day to this. A chance to set right my mistake was welcome."

Prentice noted that Sir Carron didn't use any of Liam's noble titles, neither sir nor baron.

"Liam is dead," he said, and Sir Carron nodded solemnly.

"I had heard. At your hand?"

Prentice shook his head. "In battle against the duchess' militia. He refused to surrender, and the Lions put him down."

"Vain until the last?" said Sir Carron, not disapproving exactly, but not happy to hear it, apparently. "It is a grim thing when men of rank behave with such baseness. Too ambitious, too eager to rise, it seems." He turned to Sir Gant. "And you, sir? A fellow victor from the Brook, I hear."

"Sir Gant. Your servant, sir," said Gant, introducing himself with a bow. His stern expression brightened at being recognized by this hero of the Grand Kingdom. Sir Carron accepted the gesture of deference respectfully.

"I hear you won your spurs at Toading Creek," he said, shaking Sir Gant's offered hand and beginning the custom of two knights meeting formally for the first time.

They fell to telling the tales they had heard of each other's successes and valor in battle. An almost ritual practice, it kept the proud men from being forced to boast against one another to assert rank. If each knight took it as his duty to praise the other, then neither could be accused of pride above his station or seeking glory that didn't belong to him. At least that was the ideal. Proud younger knights with little renown often fell back into boasting, especially amongst themselves. But with mature and established men-at-arms like Sir Gant and Sir Carron, the practice worked well, and the two men were soon in warm conversation, each recounting the other's achievements.

Prentice found he liked Sir Carron, and he trusted Sir Gant utterly as a loyal comrade, but moments like this reminded him of the gap that still existed between himself and the noble warriors who dominated the Grand Kingdom—a gap that likely would always exist. Sir Carron respected him, considered him a fellow veteran in service to the kingdom, but he would never feel the comradely affection for Prentice that he offered so readily to Sir Gant. And there was no simple path from where Prentice stood to that fraternity that was being expressed only two paces from him. Commoners could only climb so high.

Of course, there was the exception of the knights of the Church. Devout and capable men were accepted from almost any echelon of society to try for their ranks. That had been Prentice's plan—well, his father's plan for him at least—to become a Church knight and rise from the commons to the nobility by that path. Except that Prentice had been convicted of heresy, and now the burden of lifting the family name above the base born fell to his younger brother Pallas.

As he thought about it, Prentice realized that Duchess Amelia would probably be willing to raise him to the rank of knight, if she could. She'd set him free from the convict chain and given him the right to his own family name as a patrician, but that was the highest honor she could offer. Only a prince or king could knight a man, usually only then because the man had been born to a knight himself or for a show of exceptional valor on the field. Even with the coming battle against the Redlanders, there was little chance of that. King Chrostmer had just arranged for Prentice's heresy to be expunged in law. It would be ungrateful to beg the further favor of being raised to the rank of knight, not to mention the additional insult it would give to Mother Church. All things considered, that was unlikely. And Prince Daven Marcus? Prentice would have a better chance crossing the Murr and trying to get one of the Vec princes to knight him.

He scoffed at the thought, a wry smile twisting his lips.

"Something amuses you, Captain?" asked the duchess, and Prentice realized that the entire of his liege lady's entourage were looking at him, as were Sir Gant and Sir Carron.

"Forgive me, Your Grace," he said with a bow. "I was remembering a joke I heard last night."

"Then by all means tell us that we may share in your amusement."

"I dare not, Your Grace," Prentice lied again. "It is not suitable for a lady's ears."

"Then best to keep it from your mind as well, do you not think?"

Prentice accepted the duchess's rebuke with another bow, but as he looked at her face, she didn't seem troubled or offended. He wondered if she was simply bored and happy for any distraction. Over her shoulder, Righteous was smirking openly. His wife liked nothing better than to see her husband get into trouble sometimes.

"I will do as you instruct, Your Grace," he said while raising an eyebrow at his wife. She responded by poking her tongue out at him.

"And you will remain dignified, Lady Righteous," the duchess commanded without turning to see what her lady-in-waiting was doing. Righteous stopped immediately and her eyes went wide in surprise.

"How did she know?" she mouthed to her husband.

Prentice only shook his head.

"Sir Carron, I see you are wearing royal red," the duchess said, taking note of the man's arming doublet under his shining breastplate. "Do I take it from this that you are restored to your position as Knight Commander of Rhales?"

"I fear not, Your Grace," Sir Carron apologized. "The prince's dismissal remains in force."

"But your livery?"

"When he heard that Daven Marcus had...dispensed with my service, the king sent messengers and offered me the post of Knight Marshall of the Grand Kingdom."

Duchess Amelia and Lady Dalflitch dutifully made approving noises, and Spindle and Righteous mimicked them a fraction later. The lesser born ladies obviously didn't recognize the significance of this news but dutifully followed their mistress's lead.

"So, you command the entire of the fighting force of the Grand Kingdom?" said the duchess, "Second only to the king himself."

"Quite so, Your Grace. It is a paramount honor and duty." From his smile, Sir Carron was justly proud of his promotion.

Especially after being dismissed by the prince, I'd wager, Prentice thought.

"I know of no more deserving man," the duchess pronounced, and Sir Carron bowed again.

"But *Sir* Carron?" Dalflitch objected with furrowed brow. "Does the rank of Knight Marshall not require a man of the rank of at least baronet? I ask from curiosity and mean no insult."

"I take none, m'lady," Carron replied without sign of indignation. "The king also saw fit to raise me to that rank to match my duty to his court."

Once again, the ladies oo'd and ah'd politely, and this time Righteous and Spindle kept up.

"Dear me," said the duchess, rising politely and offering her hand. "Here this whole time I have been calling you *Sir* Carron and you are actually Lord Ironworth. Please forgive me my rudeness."

"There is nothing to forgive, Your Grace," Lord Ironworth replied readily, although he accepted the duchess's hand and kissed it politely. "I am a man of many years and used to my old title. I still forget which name to use myself."

And much too polite to correct your betters, as well, thought Prentice, bowing once more to acknowledge the man's newly revealed higher rank.

"Your Grace, Duchess of the Western Reach?" asked a nearby male voice loudly, and all turned to see a herald in royal livery standing nearby. "The king calls all to his council of war. Lord Ironworth, you also are called, as are all the loyal noblemen of the Reach." The herald paused and the duchess, Lord Ironworth, and Sir Gant all acknowledged his word. There was a long moment as the man remained where he was rather than withdrawing.

"Is there aught else?" asked the duchess. The herald frowned, as if he were tasting something sour.

"Only those concerned with the defense of the realm are called," he said at last. "No other gentlefolk will be required."

He was telling the duchess to leave her ladies-in-waiting behind. Odds were that he had been instructed to do so by the king. That explained his unpleasant expression. It was a risky thing to deliver a direct order to one's superiors. But there was further reason for the man's distemper, which became clear with his next words.

"His majesty says that, if you feel you must, you may be accompanied by the...recently absolved...man in your household."

CHAPTER 16

The council of war was to be conducted inside the manor house, away from the rest of the court. One side of the building was given over to a banqueting hall, and that was now converted to an audience and council chamber for the king. At one end of the hall was a dais for a throne, bedecked with a curtained canopy and royal war banners. Along one long wall hung the banners of other ranking nobles, including right at the far end, farthest from the throne, the white lion of the Reach.

"Dukes and earls only," Duchess Amelia said as she entered, noting the ranks of the noble houses represented in the hanging regalia. "Do they wish to insult the Reach, putting us down the end, do you think? Or is it just that we come last to the feast?"

"I would not hazard a guess, Your Grace," Prentice answered quietly. He found himself looking at the banners for different reasons than his mistress. He studied the heraldic symbols to find the five animals that had hunted the lion with the Denay eagle. He saw bears and unicorns, along with seahorses and boars. There were, of course, a myriad of other symbols, swords and hammers, ships and wheels. There was one house with stags, but they were paired, facing each other. None of the others were readily apparent, certainly no serpents or mantises. Such creatures were not typically found among Grand Kingdom heraldry, at least not in this age.

Against the wall opposite the banners were three ranks of benches, rising almost to the ceiling like a grandstand, and these were already creaking under the weight of the gathered lesser nobility who would be permitted to watch the council but not to participate without direct invitation from the king. These nobles were primarily members of the Rhales court, but Prentice spotted Viscount Gullden there and suspected he sat with other Reachermen.

Down the middle of the hall was a long table of dark, ancient wood, at which were set high-backed chairs, almost all filled already with men of an age and rank similar to the king. The highest nobles of the kingdom sat together to speak of war. Maps were spread upon the table, along with other documents and books scattered about. Even in the early afternoon, the hall was dark enough that oil lamps were set to illuminate the writings and diagrams. Stewards attended the high table with drink and platters of fruit and cheese. Each noble seated was attended by at least one man who stood at his shoulder, usually in the same livery, and most of those were armed. Some were obviously sons and heirs, while others were knight captains or similar military advisers. The king himself was not seated on the throne on the dais but on a similar chair to all the others at the head of the table. It was an unusually modest position for the king to take, and Prentice wondered what it might signify.

Only two chairs at the table were unoccupied—one at the king's right hand and another in the farthest corner from the king. Without even looking at the nearest stewards and heralds, the duchess made her way to the far seat, the least position at the table, and Prentice admired her aplomb. The court was forced to accept her by dint of her military power, but they wanted her to realize she was present under sufferance. She made it obvious that she could not care less.

"I crave forgiveness for my lateness, Your Majesty, noble gentlemen," the duchess said almost casually before she sat.

Several of the seated men seemed ready to take offence, but just as Duchess Amelia sat, Lord Ironworth emerged from behind her to march up the hall and take his place just behind the king's right shoulder. All objections seemed to die unspoken. Any criticism for the woman's lateness would equally fall on the king's Knight Marshall, and that would be unconscionable. When she was seated, Prentice and Sir Gant took up similar posts behind the duchess, Gant at her right, Prentice at her left, as befitted his social status. It occurred to him that he was the only man in the room who was not a noble or a servant. It felt odd. Then he remembered that the duchess was the only woman, and it was all no less odd for her.

"There is no need to apologize, Lady," said the king. "We are yet awaiting our son's return as well. What does it say that a woman in her skirts can come in full dignity to a war council before he can change a doublet?" Many of the older nobles chuckled at the king's joke.

How deep does the bad blood run between king and prince? Prentice wondered, though he made sure to keep his face neutral.

The gathered assembly sat quietly then for a long time, noblemen occasionally sipping from their goblets or picking at some crumb. Everyone politely awaited Prince Daven Marcus. The quiet stretched on, with only the diffident movement of stewards when they were summoned or the occasional creak of the full benches to disturb the stillness.

"Good god," the king sighed in exasperation at last. "He didn't take this long being born!" He turned to a herald standing by. "Go now to the Prince of Rhales and say that the king has begun his council. His father advises that if he wishes any say in the prosecution of this war, he had best find a new doublet and get his posturing arse into that chair post haste!"

No one present laughed or even smiled at that. Prentice felt compassion for the herald, being given that message to deliver, though he imagined the king's exact words would not be repeated. As the messenger left, the monarch turned his attention to the documents on the table.

"Alright, good nobles, shall we to the business of war? Our chaplain ecclesiarch is holding a service for the success of our campaign, and we told him we would attend. The crown would rather not give Mother Church two reasons to be angry with us in the same afternoon." That drew some polite chuckles and smiles. The king nodded to Lord Ironworth. "Explain the plan as it stands, Knight Marshal, and let us see who can step into what role."

Carron Ironworth stepped around the king's chair and cleared away other documents to show a main map that took up more than half the table. From where he stood, Prentice could make out the details well enough, though several of the noblemen in the furthest chairs started to lift out of their seats to gain better views. For her part, Duchess Amelia remained seated in perfect dignity.

"Here is the Murr," Ironworth explained, pointing with his finger. "These are our encampments, and that there is the Vec town of Aubrey, currently occupied by the invaders from the west. All word is that this town is now the capital of their seized territory. They billet their soldiers in the houses and send out companies to raid along both sides of the Murr, as well as making forays farther south against other princedom territory.

"The plan is to seize the south end of the ancient bridge just north of Aubrey, currently in enemy hands, and then array in Cattlefields here to the east of this village called Three Roads. Our hope is that this will either draw him out of Aubrey to face us or else find himself bottled up in the town. Thus, we defeat them or else contain them in siege. Either way, the raids across the Murr onto Kingdom land cease."

Men nodded, watching the plan being explained.

"It seems straight forward enough," said one.

"Straight forward but not easy," countered another, and many nodded once more.

"If it was easy, milk maids could do it," said a solidly built older man in a doeskin doublet with slashed sleeves embroidered in gold thread. Then he looked to Duchess Amelia with a smirk. "No offence, My Lady."

"Milk maids or popinjays," the duchess returned without hesitation. "Iron work requires iron men."

Smirks went around the table once more, and the well-dressed noble scowled with narrowed eyes.

You brought that on yourself, fool, Prentice thought. He cast a glance at Sir Gant over the back of the duchess's chair, and when their eyes met, he could see the knight shared his assessment.

"When we array in Cattlefields, how do we dispose the line?" asked a noble closer to the king, one of the heirs standing behind his father only one chair down from the prince's empty place.

"Indeed," agreed another. "We do not even know the enemy's battle order. Every time we send heralds, they are slain or driven off. Like the animals they worship, they are base beasts. Will this be a battle or a hunt?"

Prentice had to work not to scoff out loud. Facing an enemy more potent and savage than any other, these noblemen were still worried about who would stand where in the line of battle, not because they feared for victory, but because they wanted the best chance at glory and honor. To these men war was like a game, an extension of tournament competitions. More than a year facing skin changers and sorcery and still they held to their genteel traditions.

"We have one here who knows firsthand how the enemy arrays in full battle," said the king, and he gestured to Lord Ironworth. "He commanded our brother's forces at the Battle of the Brook in the west. Surely, My Lords, you remember the tale."

Ironworth bowed his head, and many of the seated noblemen nodded approvingly. There was a grumble of quiet assent from the lesser nobles on their benches as well, showing that the tale was indeed well known amongst the Denay court. Lord Ironworth then gestured to the duchess's end of the table.

"Actually, we have three veterans of that battle here, Majesty," he said with his characteristic humility. "Thrice the experience to answer your concerns."

"Well, what do they say about the enemy's battle array?" asked one of the nobles, and all eyes turned to the table's far end. Most looked to Sir Gant, recognizable as a knight because of his longsword at his hip. Gant, though, politely demurred their eyes and looked to his liege lady, as was proper. Without any hesitation, Duchess Amelia turned her eyes onto Prentice, and he felt a sudden chill as he realized he had gone from the least corner of the room to the center of its attentions without so much as making a half-step. These were the highest born of the Grand Kingdom. One wrong word with them could humiliate his liege or even bring his own life to a swift, unpleasant end. He paused to think what the best observation would be to offer first and how to phrase it, but just as he opened his mouth to speak, a wizened old noble seated in the middle of the table cut him off.

"Before we go asking every village idiot to put his hand to the hilt," the man grumbled in a loud, croaking voice, "perhaps, young Ironworth, you could explain your reasons for foolishly giving up our best advantage. The river, lad, is better than any castle rampart. Why meet them in a field when holding them at the river is so much more to our advantage. You Ironworths always trust too much to heroism and not enough to good sense."

Prentice wondered what ancient grudge led to this elderly man's criticism. It had to be from a long while past if he was calling Lord Ironworth "young." But before the knight marshal could defend himself, the duchess's clear feminine voice cut the heavy masculine air.

"I can answer that, My Lord," she said.

CHAPTER 17

"I mean, surely it is obvious," Amelia said as every eye turned on her.

Even in the poor light, she could see their expressions, ranging from genuine surprise that a woman had spoken in this martial company through to undisguised contempt. The elderly noble who had been chastising Lord Ironworth, whom Amelia was almost certain was the ancient Earl Lastermune, openly scoffed at the interruption. Lastermune was over eighty years old and had ridden in tournaments with King Chrostmer's father. It was no wonder he thought of Ironworth as a younger man.

"The river," Earl Lastermune declared, slapping his hand on the table. He gave Amelia a contemptuous glance, which she was sure he meant as a dismissal. "We have held the Vec at the river for centuries. Let these new painted dandies see what a defense we can make of the Murr."

"You would have knights of the Grand Kingdom cower behind a watercourse, My Lord?" Amelia called loudly. "Does this suit our king? Is this the honor of the Grand Kingdom?"

An angry mutter swept through the room as her words stung their pride like a swarm of hornets.

Too bad, she thought. The Reach had not come to the river to sit in camp and discuss strategy. Perhaps it was having to face down Daven Marcus yet again, but Amelia found she no longer had patience for noblemen posturing and dragging up old grudges. Like everyone, she had been nervous to meet the king, but now that she was facing his courtiers and nobles over the business of protecting the land, all her nervousness was gone.

"Do you mean to insult my captains and champions, Lady Amelia?" asked the king mildly, but with a tone that warned caution.

"A year, Your Majesty," Amelia declared, pointing at the southern wall to indicate where the enemy was to be found. "More than a year, that fiendish, sorcerous filth has occupied the south side of the Murr. If they were inclined to meet us at the river, they would already have come." She turned to Earl Lastermune. "A battle strategy is only worth pursuing if it actually comes to battle. For now, the Murr defends the Redlanders as well as it protects us. Better, in fact, since we hear next to nothing from the lands across the river. The little we do know is that Aubrey is in their hands and life there is a nightmare to make a devil pale with fear. Bestial men prowl the streets, even in the day, devouring children in plain sight of their parents. Foul rituals are performed on altars of skulls. If even one tale in ten is true, then this army cannot be allowed to remain."

"That is the Vec," dismissed a nobleman's son, standing behind his father. "What do we care if they suffer?"

"Were they not ours once? Do we not want them back within the king's embrace?" Amelia asked, and she could see by their expressions they had not considered those questions. Young nobles like Prince Daven Marcus talked continuously about reclaiming the Vec for the kingdom, but they did not actually care about the people of the princedoms. Reconquering the Vec was just a game that noble boys wanted to play.

"And even if we dismiss the small folk of the Vec, abandon them to the misrule of the upstart princes, how long do we let the Redlanders beset the land beside us and raid along our watercourses? If a horse in the next stall to yours took ill, so infested with ticks that it sickened and died, would you wait? Would you stand at the entrance of your horse's stall and bat away the ticks? Could you drive them all back?"

Scanning the watching faces around the table, Amelia could see her words were penetrating their thinking. Their expressions were changing, the hostility draining away. But she knew she had to press her advantage carefully. She was making sense to them, but she was still a woman, an upstart made noble by marriage, and the ruler of an uncivilized, backwater province. Making sense was the only way to gain and hold their respect.

"You would remove your horse from its neighbor, would you not? And if you couldn't, or if the stables were yours by right, you would drive that pestilential animal out of your sight, digging out the vermin as it went. You'd burn them out if you had to. Would you not, gentlemen?"

There was a moment's silence in response to her words and Amelia let it sit. The nerves rose in her again and she had to work hard to hold her tongue, trying not to overcome the uncomfortable silence with too much talk. She had made her point well enough. They just needed a moment to grasp it. Of course, there were other reasons to push for battle, not the least of which was the cost of keeping an army in the field. Her militia was powerful, but it was draining her treasury. Keeping their forces "at arms" had to be doing the same to every nobleman present. Whole fiefdoms must already be in debt up to their eyeballs, Amelia was sure. But getting nobles like this to address matters of money publicly was like trying to nail a shadow to a wall. Every noble of the Grand Kingdom wanted to be wealthy, to enjoy the power and prestige wealth could afford them, but none of them wanted to admit to even thinking about it. Coin was supposed to be beneath them; profit was the concern of the greedy and grasping merchant and guild classes. That's why coins were called guilders, was it not?

It was crass hypocrisy, but no one in this room questioned it.

"Well, Lord Lastermune," asked the king eventually. "What say you? Do the duchess' words sway you?"

Earl Lastermune opened his mouth, then closed it with a frown that increased the already deeply wrinkled state of his face. He lowered his head and glowered at the table.

The king turned to his knight marshal. "And you Lord Ironworth? Does the lioness speak your thoughts?"

"I think, Your Majesty, that I may have to relinquish my name, or at the least share it with the duchess. Do any doubt the iron of her soul?"

"If there is iron in my soul, My Lord, it is the iron of the Reach." For the first time, Amelia looked over her shoulder at the benches behind her where every present Reacherman was seated together as a group. She nodded to them, and they bowed their heads in return. "I am a woman, a mere vessel of my people's will. We have not come south to watch a river drift past. We can do that in the north. The Dwelt is a pretty enough river. We have come south, Majesty, to dig out the infestation of ticks on our border with fire and sword."

Now the mutters were approving in tone, coming mainly from the Reachermen, though Amelia thought she heard some others. Looking to the end of the table, it appeared that King Chrostmer also approved, a smile on his face. He wanted to get to battle too, Amelia was sure of it, and he must welcome any goad to drive his nobles to the task.

"With your permission, Majesty," said Lord Ironworth before beginning to lay out his strategy. "My Lords, we must accept that this will not be war as we understand it. The Duchess of the Reach is correct when she observes that we have been here more than a year and this enemy has shown no interest in honorable battle. Heralds sent to treat with them are either rebuffed, imprisoned, or executed summarily. There will be no offers of parole on this battlefield, no taking of noble prisoners to be ransomed to their families. We must accept that the civilities of war will not be observed."

"So, like most battles against the Vec, we'll be fighting peasants and mercenaries," someone at the table observed.

Lord Ironworth shook his head grimly. Suddenly his hand went to the hilt of his sword, and he drew it forth with a flourish. He held it aloft over the table, and many near him flinched back in spite of themselves. Nonetheless, the knight marshal was not making a challenge.

"You see this blade, Nobles?" he declared.

Amelia looked at it and realized that although it had the typical cross hilt of a knight's longsword and was of a similar length, the blade itself was broader and slightly curved. With a single edge, it was made for heavy chopping rather than deft slashes and cuts. For a moment, the duchess wondered if it were harder to wield, since it seemed so much weightier.

"I know that some scoff at my new sword," Lord Ironworth continued. "But I assure you all, I have not forgotten my heritage or forsaken my knightly oaths. No, Gentles, I have faced this enemy—his beastmen, wolves, and stags, and worst of all, his bulls. They all have skin that turns a cut, and the heads of those mightiest are hard as steel. I've taken to this cleaver, My Lords, because I have no better choice. This is a new enemy that has come, and we must all make sacrifices. We can sacrifice a portion of our honor, the least portion, or we can sacrifice our lives. This enemy has come to slay."

While Lord Ironworth was making his speech, a man in royal livery rushed into the room, head down and plainly hoping to be discrete, but in full haste, nonetheless. He went down on one knee beside the king's chair and leaned in to speak quietly. In spite of herself, Amelia found she was distracted by the messenger, and she watched the king's face in hopes of discerning the meaning behind the intrusion.

For his part, King Chrostmer tried to wave the messenger away and concentrate on Lord Ironworth's words, but the man was persistent. He kept speaking until the king's features twisted in sudden rage.

"What?" he bellowed, launching himself to his feet so that he towered over the cowering messenger. Lord Ironworth stopped speaking, and every head turned to the king's chair. The man at the king's feet tried to continue his message quietly, but Chrostmer was having none of that. He seized the man by the collar. "Oh, for God's sake, cease your groveling, man!"

Pulling the man half to his feet, the king dragged the messenger from the room, leaving everyone else to look at each other, wondering what the matter could be.

CHAPTER 18

"The Redlanders?" Sir Gant speculated quietly, watching the king leave the hall.

Prentice clearly didn't agree with that. "There's no need for discretion in that case," he argued, his voice as low as Sir Gant's. "The army's commanders are all here. If they have crossed the Murr, then the king only needs send us to the field with that news. This is something else."

"Except that we've still no sense of Lord Ironworth's strategy. We're still at the speeches stage."

"Not reason for secrecy."

Amelia listened to her two retainers' discussion and found herself with a sudden intuition. "Not all the commanders are here."

"Pardon, Your Grace?" asked Sir Gant.

"Not every ranking noble is present. One is yet notable in his absence." Amelia looked to the empty chair next to the king's and knew she was right. Prentice and Sir Gant followed her gaze.

"The prince?" said Prentice, and by his tone Amelia was sure he understood her meaning.

Sir Gant was slower on the uptake. "He's changing his doublet. He'll be with us presently, surely..."

"No, Sir Gant," Amelia said, her eyes searching the faces of the other nobles at the table to see if they, too, had deduced the truth. "He's ridden off in a huff, I guarantee it, sir."

"Why? Where would he go?"

"To rebuke his father," Amelia explained. "It's precisely the kind of petty gesture he favors. As to where he has gone... he could well have ridden for Rhales, knowing him."

"Or Dweltford," said Prentice, and that sent a chill down Amelia's spine.

"He wouldn't dare!" she hissed.

"I would not put it past him, Your Grace. He is just fool enough to think he could snatch your capital while you are away. The king just put paid to his claim for your hand in marriage, but that does not just deny him your marital companionship, Your Grace. It also costs him the Western Reach. It is your land and your money the prince wants. He might try to exploit your absence."

"He'll get himself another bloody nose if he does," said Sir Gant confidently.

Amelia knew he and Prentice had gone to great lengths to make sure the capital of the Western Reach was strongly defended in their absence. They had all but forbidden her to march south until they had. Over five cohorts of militia remained behind in her town and castle, with stores and plans to hold the fortification for over a year should things become desperate. Amelia had expected any attack to come from the west, from a new Redlander force. She had not thought she still had to guard her lands from the crown prince.

"Should I send word to the camp, try to stop him there?" she asked.

"He won't go around the south, not through our men, Your Grace," Sir Gant assured her.

"If he goes north, it will be the Foothill Highway, Your Grace," Prentice added. "Then cross west through one of the passes, probably the Griffith Road."

Amelia listened intently and tried to sort her fears from her thoughts, but this unexpected news had set her mind bubbling and threatening to boil over.

"How many men does the prince command?" she asked, composing a list of questions in her mind and planning to go down them one at a time until she had a surer picture of the danger she and her people might be in.

"Several hundred," said an unexpected voice in reply to her question. Amelia looked up to see Viscount Gullden standing at a polite distance. "Not enough to cripple the Grand Kingdom's army with their absence, by no means, but inconvenient."

"Lord Gullden," Amelia nodded to acknowledge him, and he approached closer.

"With your permission, Your Grace," he said politely and bowed, "I had presumed to give you the news of the prince's departure, but I see the tale has already reached your ears."

"Her Grace deduced the prince's actions on her own," said Prentice, "from the evidence of the king's distemper."

The viscount's eyes widened in surprise, and his smile conveyed genuine admiration. "The wisdom of the Lioness," he said almost breathlessly.

"But what of the specifics, My Lord?" Amelia pressed. Already the council was breaking up, many of the nobles standing to withdraw. Had word come that the king had dismissed them? "Where has the prince gone? Do we know how long?"

"I am told that the crown prince has ridden for Rhales and taken his entire court with him. For how long, who could say."

"Is it possible he might turn west? Try to cross the mountains?"

"To what end?" asked the viscount. The notion of treachery took a moment to occur to him. "Ah, to press his claim with steel? It would be an ill-done thing if he did."

"Indeed," Amelia agreed. What else was there to say?

"If I might presume a little further, Your Grace," the viscount pressed. "There is someone who craves an audience and has asked me for an introduction."

"An audience?" Amelia looked about at the shuffling crowd clearing the hall. Who amongst these most ranked of men would need the viscount's introduction to meet with her? And what was the protocol for her to receive a petitioner at the king's council? Her mind was still trying to assess the threat to her lands in her absence. "Is this the time?"

"The man is in earnest need of discretion, Your Grace," said Lord Gullden, seeming to choose his words carefully. "He could come to you at another time, but it might be received differently. It could be impolitic."

God deliver me from politics, Amelia thought and then chastised herself inwardly. She was a duchess. Her cursing politics was like a carpenter cursing wood or a shepherd despising sheep. "Alright, My Lord, make your presentation."

"If you would accompany me, Your Grace."

Amelia cocked an eyebrow but stood and accepted the viscount's offered hand. He led her across the chamber toward a vestibule, away from the direction of most of the other nobility. Where was this supplicant? Could this be some kind of treachery? She looked over her shoulder and saw that Prentice and Sir Gant were right there. If the viscount planned something untoward, she at least had her best men present to defend her.

The vestibule was small, with several exits. One of these was covered by a curtain, and Amelia had to force herself to remain calm as the viscount ushered her through this one into a dark, closeted chamber lit by a pair of wax candles on a table. There were only two chairs in the tiny space, and one of those was already taken by a man in a sable clerical robe, with his hood pulled up.

"Who is this?" she asked, but the viscount only put his finger to his lips for silence until Prentice and Sir Gant were already in the room. Then he surprised her further by stepping back outside, leaving the three of them with this unnamed churchman.

"Viscount?" she asked after him.

"He will keep watch for us," said the cowled figure. "Please, Your Grace, take your seat."

"Who are you, sir?" Amelia asked, though she did as she was invited.

There was something about the man that spoke of authority, of a man used to giving orders and having them obeyed. When she was seated, the man pulled back his cowl, revealing someone of healthy middle age, with a neatly trimmed, dark beard and short-cut hair, greying at the temples. His cheeks showed some unhandsome pockmarks, but his tawny eyes were deep and penetrating, speaking of a fierce intelligence. As the cloak fell open, it was clear he was wearing a fine doublet of pale green linen. Whoever he was, this was no churchman.

"We have never met, Duchess Amelia," he said, "but I flatter myself that perhaps you might recognize me."

"I fear not, sir," Amelia replied, now too puzzled to feel any actual fear. "Should I know you?"

"I suppose not," said the man, and he smiled in amusement. "When you live your life known by all around you, it can be hard to imagine anonymity." He paused and then bowed in his seat. "I am Forsyte the Third of the Manry family. Lord of the South Bank of the Murr and rightful ruler of Aubrey, currently in exile."

Amelia felt her eyes go wide, and her inward breath hissed across her teeth.

"I am a prince of the Vec."

CHAPTER 19

A Vec prince? Here? Amelia felt as if she had just stepped beyond the natural world. It was like encountering a mythical beast, as if the closeted little room contained a unicorn. Of course, the Murr River was barely five leagues to the south, and the other side was the Vec. It was not so far in distance, but in politics, it was another existence entirely. Trade occurred across that single watercourse, as well as warfare, but to Amelia's knowledge no prince had crossed the Murr in person since King Kolber's failed invasion of the Western Reach over a decade ago. As for being somewhere like here, on Grand Kingdom land proper, she didn't think it had ever happened before, not since the secession of the princedoms centuries ago.

"My Lor...Your Highness," Amelia stammered, lifting herself from her chair so that she could curtsey. How did one address a Vec prince? What was the protocol? There was so little interaction between the nations that she had only the vaguest idea.

Would even Prentice or Dalflitch know? she wondered, and the distraction annoyed her.

She was in a private room, meeting secretly with a man still officially an enemy of the Grand Kingdom and the Denay throne. Every year, sacrists in parishes across the land preached sermons against the rebellion of the Vec princes. Just being in the man's presence could be interpreted as treason.

"Please, Your Grace," Prince Forsyte said, as if reading her thoughts, "I recognize the risk I ask you to take, meeting me here. If it is any consolation, my risk is even greater."

That had to be true. Even with the Redlander invasion, there wasn't a knight or noble in the king's camp who wouldn't give his left hand for the honor of capturing a Vec prince alive.

"Why?" Amelia forced herself to ask in a whisper.

The prince nodded and looked down at his own hands for a moment. *He's in torment*, Amelia thought, watching the man's movements.

The strong hands clenched and unclenched as if they wanted to pray or beg of their own volition, and he was forced to stop them by will alone. His jaw clenched visibly, and he stared into the space beside the candle. It was as if he expected some magic to occur there. Then he sucked in a breath and looked up, meeting Amelia's eyes directly. Even in the shadowy chamber, the earnestness of his expression was unmistakable.

"Since the Blood Sects came from the head of the Murr River, I have been in exile."

"Blood Sect?" asked Amelia. "Is that what you call them?"

The prince nodded. "Because of the ungodly rites they practice that give them their power. I hear that you Grand Kingdom folk merely call them invaders."

"Redlanders," Amelia corrected him, forgetting rank in the confusion of this strange meeting. "It is the translation into the common tongue of the name they call themselves."

"Then Gullden was correct. You do know things that we do not."

It was such a direct flattery that it took Amelia a moment to realize she was being complimented. She smiled and nodded.

"You are hiding with the viscount?" she asked, not sure how much the prince would be willing to tell but as eager to know anything he might reveal as he clearly was to hear from her.

"Only for the last few weeks of spring," Prince Forsyte explained. "He and I have distant relatives in common."

That surprised Amelia to hear, though it made sense when she thought about it. Aubrey and Griffith were not far from each other, and the lower born a noble, the more likely he would have a family relation low enough to cross the Murr.

"Before that, I have been a vagabond throughout the Vec," the prince went on, "wandering like the Israelites in the wilderness and seeking what allies might be found."

"The other princes? Will they come to your aid?"

Behind Amelia, Sir Gant gave an impolite snort and Prentice coughed quietly to cover the indiscretion. Clearly, neither man thought it likely that Prince Forsyte had won much support from his peers. The prince, however, only smiled sadly at their response.

"Your men are quite right in their skepticism," he said. "In the Vec, we sometimes hear tales of the rivalry between the Grand Kingdom nobility. We find them...quaint. We call our politics the great game, and it is played continually and to the death. Poison and assassination are but mundane gambits in the great game. Every prince is merely an opponent to his fellows, an enemy in all but name. Kolber managed to get the fraternity of crowns to unite under his leadership only by dint of the most extreme confluence of threats and promises. Even before his death, his son tore the alliance apart from under him. A madman herding cats is how he is remembered."

Amelia listened quietly to the prince's explanation. Her initial reaction was to scoff when he used the word "quaint." After the way she had suffered under Grand Kingdom politics, she was not persuaded the Vec were so much more dangerous. She kept her tongue, though, and focused her mind on the more important questions.

"So, you've come north to the ancient enemy in hopes of finding allies?" she asked. That had to be the man's plan in meeting her.

"I have," he admitted, shamefaced.

"It embarrasses you to seek the help of a woman?" she guessed. The prince seemed surprised at the question.

"Your sex, My Lady, is of little consequence. I am ashamed to have lost my land to an invader and to have to go cap-in-hand to anyone for help. Would it matter to you if it was from a baron or a baroness that you pleaded aid if you had to go abegging?"

Amelia noticed he'd picked the rank of baron, someone who would be beneath a duchess. He was subtly reminding her how much humiliation it was for him as a prince to beg aid from her, a mere duchess.

A fair enough objection for a prince, she thought.

She could not imagine Daven Marcus humbling himself this much to plead for aid, even if he were starving and being whipped to death.

"But this indignity is nothing compared to how my people suffer," Prince Forsyte went on. "Every day they are exploited, worked as slaves, and then at night plucked from their homes and sacrificed to false gods. We know the tales of conviction and of the harshness of the Inquisition, Your Grace. But even the meanest of your convicts does not suffer as my people do right this very moment. And word has come that even worse will be upon them soon."

Amelia wondered what Prentice might think about these claims, given his time on the chain. Could anyone suffer worse than a convict? Whatever his reactions to the prince's words however, Prentice diligently kept them to himself. The duchess respected that.

"Why come to me, Highness, if this is so urgent?" This was the part she didn't understand. The prince needed an army, and King Chrostmer had one here. He'd had one here for over a year. Why wait for the frontier duchess? "Do you think I have the ear of the king? You are deeply misinformed if you have heard that."

"No, I had not heard that," the prince conceded. "But I have heard tell of the lioness who defends her people, who has raised an army to defeat the Blood Sects and is driving them from her lands with noble diligence. We share a love for our respective people, I think, Duchess Amelia, and that is something I hope can bridge the river of mistrust that the Murr has caused between our peoples."

Amelia blinked at this second direct compliment, praise not couched in poetry or metaphor, and seemingly offered without expectation of return. It was a strikingly blunt honesty that caught her by surprise. Years ago, she had dealt with bankers from the Vec on behalf of her late husband. They, she remembered, had been similarly direct, but she had attributed it to their trade, their focus on hard coin, loans, and interest payments. Perhaps all Veckanders were more naturally direct folk. If so, Amelia thought it a factor in their favor.

"You think we are of a similar type, Highness?"

"In this fact, Your Grace."

"And that is enough for you to think that you might trust me?"

"That, and your White Lions," the prince answered and cast an eye at Prentice and Sir Gant.

"You want the use of my soldiers?" asked Amelia, wondering if all the conversation up until now had been only a prelude. Was this the man's true request coming forth?

"I hope they will help, but no Duchess, leastwise not at first."

"Then why do you mention them?"

"I heard the reports of them amongst the other princedoms, and I knew. I knew what kind of ruler you were."

"And what kind...?" Amelia began to press, but Prince Forsyte spoke over her.

"A modern one. A thinker," he said earnestly and surprised her by leaning forward to grasp her hands. She nearly flinched, and the two men behind her stirred defensively. But the prince meant her no harm. "The Grand Kingdom is mired in tradition. The same family has sat upon its throne for over a thousand years. Its knights fight as they have for centuries, though the rest of the world moves on without them. We Vec princes cast you out centuries ago and little more than a decade past almost snatched the west out of your loose grip."

"You insult us...?"

Again, the prince cut her off. "I judge the institutions of your nation as they deserve to be judged. As I know you, Duchess Amelia, must have judged them. You don't rely on knights with their own ambitions and petty traditions. You won't throw even the most worthless of men at your enemy's steel out of mere convenience. You have trained and equipped a professional army as large as any commanded by a Vec prince, and an army with the newest of weapons. Oh yes, Your Grace, we have heard of the lion's roar, the burst of steel shot from serpentine barrels.

"If any noble of the Grand Kingdom might be ready for the radical notion of allying with a Vec prince, for the unthinkable possibility of treating with the enemy across the Murr in the hope of driving away this new, worse enemy from the western headland, then it is you, Duchess Amelia, Lioness of the Reach. I risk my life coming to you. And with no etiquette between our lands, I know it would cost you no honor to have me killed right here. There is no decorum keeping me safe, but nothing is keeping my people safe either. I could not face God in the world to come if I hid to preserve my life while the men, women, and children I am charged to rule are accounted as lambs to the slaughter."

For a long time, the prince stared into Amelia's eyes, solemn in his need. He was truly begging, and not for himself—for his people. She felt his hands tremble slightly as they held hers. She could feel the calluses on his palms. These were a swordsman's hands, a warrior's hands, and the humility of his gesture in approaching her in this way touched her heart.

"What would you have me do, Prince Forsyte?" she whispered.

"Be my envoy to King Chrostmer..."

Amelia recoiled as if struck before the prince could complete his request. "I cannot. You must not ask me this. If the king learned of your presence here in the Kingdom, I would be obliged to reveal your whereabouts. You would be dead within the hour."

She tried to withdraw her hands, but the prince held them tightly for a moment.

"I swear I will be long gone from here and in a different disguise before you even found his majesty to report me. But that is not my intent. I want you to make this offer to the throne of the Grand Kingdom. Tell him that the Prince of Aubrey will cede his title and surrender the town to the king if the king will agree to spare his people from the sack of the town and to do all within his power to rescue my son, who is currently held by the Blood Sects within Aubrey's prison, the Ditch."

At last, he released Amelia's hands and immediately one went to her mouth. She swallowed heavily, her mind racing as it tried to comprehend what she had heard.

"Will you do this for me? Will you risk this for the sake of my people?"

Amelia hardly heard her own voice, but she knew she formed the words.

"Your Highness, I will."

CHAPTER 20

"He wants to give up his seat of power?" asked Lady Dalflitch as she sat on the bed opposite the duchess. Her tone made it clear how amazed she was by the news. As the two high-born women spoke together, Prentice went to the stair to make sure no one was coming up to the duchess's chamber. His wife went to the other and made sure none of the watch guards were coming down from the roof. Duchess Amelia had agreed immediately to Prentice's suggestion that they keep the closest watch possible to preserve the privacy of this meeting. The curtain that had been installed to guard the ladies' dignity was now drawn fully back so that no one could hide behind it, listening. Construction of the panel wall was still only barely begun.

"He surely does not want to give it up," the duchess said emphatically, "but he is desperate, and the tale he tells of his people's suffering makes it clear why."

"How bad is it?" asked Righteous.

"Like Fallenhill," said Prentice.

"For us or for the previous?"

"For Stopher and his family," he answered her, and she whistled. Prentice and Righteous had survived the bitter winter's siege in the ruins of Fallenhill, but the previous lord, Baron Stopher, and his family had been burned alive there by the Redlanders, along with all the original townsfolk. "And the prince seems to think something worse is coming."

"What's worse'n Fallenhill?" asked Spindle. Looking around the room, no one present wanted to know the answer, Prentice was sure.

After the duchess pledged to take Prince Forsyte's request to the king, she had left the tiny room and returned into the afternoon air of the garden to reunite with her entourage. By that point, the ladies-in-waiting had already heard of Daven Marcus's petulant departure. The council was dismissed amid rumors that the king had sent a contingent of houseguards to arrest the prince or had taken to his carriage to chase the royal heir down personally or something else entirely. Every next courtier had a different tale to tell, and the variety added up so swiftly that the duchess decided there was no point trying to sort the actuality from them. Most likely no one had the full truth of it. She ordered her own carriage brought and they began the return journey to the White Lions' camp and her tower residence.

Prentice urged swiftness and vigilance the whole way back since the chaos of the broken council was the perfect opportunity for anyone who sought to do violence to the duchess. The Vec princes might find Grand Kingdom politics quaint, but Prentice wasn't minded to trust that they would not attempt something murderous in the name of the Prince of Rhales or Mother Church. He still remembered vividly his brother's hate-filled tone when Pallas called the duchess a slut.

The carriage ride back had been a tense rush, passengers bouncing while the soldiers jogged and sweated in their armor. The ladies tried to speculate as to the Prince of Rhales's actions, but the duchess shushed them, for which Prentice was thankful. He gave the return escort his full attention then. He did not begin to feel confident until the carriage was in the camp proper, and he was unable to fully relax until the duchess stepped through the tower door, and only after he'd sent Sir Gant in ahead to guarantee it was safe. Now at last, Duchess Amelia and her household, including Sir Gant and steward Turley, were all gathered to discuss the day's events and help her grace plan her next moves.

"I suppose the most important question is what do you risk by doing what he asks?" said Dalflitch.

"You think that is the most important question?" asked the duchess. Prentice was sure she was seeing in her mind the horrors of Fallenhill and imagining that they were being repeated at this moment in Aubrey.

"Lady Dalflitch is right, Your Grace," he said quietly, returning from the stairs and letting Turley take up his duty as sentry. "There is nothing about this that does not involve risk for you and for the Reach. Just this morning, Daven Marcus was still calling you a wayward wife and the Church was accusing you of harboring heretics. The king might have dismissed those charges, but he could easily change his mind if he discovers you have been treating with the enemy across the river."

"I thought the *Redlanders* were the enemy across the river," the duchess retorted.

"For now, Your Grace," Prentice conceded. "But when they are driven back, the pendulum of hate will swiftly swing back to the Vec princes."

"You are doubtless correct, Captain," said the duchess. "But is what Prince Forsyte wants truly that much to ask of the king? Does what he offers not coincide with the knight marshal's plans, at least as much as we've heard?"

Prentice could see how that seemed a fair point, but he nodded as Sir Gant outlined the military perspective.

"Booty is the problem, Your Grace," the knight explained. "Every man-at-arms sworn to a noble will want to take something from the victory, a prize equal to his rank and participation in the battle. For dukes and earls and barons, that can be quite a sum, and a captured town represents a rich prize to divide amongst victors. Everyone will be expecting a pillage from captured Aubrey."

That was the sober reality of war, and its brutality depressed the mood of the room further.

"There is another possibility, Your Grace," Prentice ventured as an idea occurred to him. "What if the king were to see himself as the liberator of Aubrey?"

"Isn't that what we are planning, Captain Prentice?" Dalflitch objected, as if he were not keeping up with the conversation.

Prentice shook his head.

"Your pardon, My Lady. I mean not as liberator from the Redlanders. From the Vec entirely. Prince Forsyte has already agreed to surrender the town to the king's forces and thus effectively the entirety of the princedom. It returns to the Grand Kingdom at that point, but it need not be a conquest. It could be a liberation. King Chrostmer could be the first king since the secession of the Vec to legitimately reclaim the loyalty of a renegade prince. The town returns to the Grand Kingdom and cannot be utterly sacked by royal law."

"Reclaim the loyalty?" the duchess repeated thoughtfully.

"When the prince agrees to bend the knee to King Chrostmer."

The ranked people in the room all had eyes wide with shock at the notion. Sir Gant shook his head in disbelief, and Lady Dalflitch sighed heavily. Meanwhile, the commoners in the room stood puzzled and confused.

"And the prince becomes what?" Dalflitch demanded. "An earl again? Does his princedom turn back to a duchy? You think Forsyte would accept such a thing?"

"Right now, he's just a vagabond with a title, and the people he professes to love are accounted as lambs to the slaughter, his words. What are their lives worth to him?"

"Is it so big a thing, bending the knee to the king?" asked Spindle, her brows furrowed under her lace mask.

"For a Vec prince? It's unheard of," said Dalflitch.

"So what?" said Turley, shrugging. Dalflitch cast him a withering glance that Prentice noticed, but he was too focused on Turley's question to worry about the lady's disapproval.

"What do nobles want most?" he asked his friend. Turley opened his mouth, but Righteous got in her answer first.

"Gold and silver," she chirped. Sir Gant scoffed at that, and Amelia and Dalflitch both shook their heads. Righteous shook her head with them doubtfully. "Not gold and silver?"

"No, my lady wife," said Prentice, smiling at her. "Gold and silver are what they *need* to buy the tools to get them what they *want*."

"And that is?" she asked, eyes narrow, clearly suspicious that he was mocking her. He knew he'd answer for it later, and that only made him smile more.

"Honor," explained the duchess, catching Prentice's eyes with a knowing and approving look. "Honor and glory are the measure and the method of a nobleman. A wise man once told me that."

"A name," added Sir Gant firmly, agreeing with his liege. "A name is what matters to men of rank. The women, too."

"Not just men of rank," said Turley. "All men, when you think about it."

"Is that right?" asked Dalflitch archly.

"Surely 'tis, My Lady," the steward insisted. "Turley is just the name of any common man. But Turley, Chief Steward to the Duchess of the Western Reach, is head of a household staff, a man of influence and place worthy of some respect, even if he doesn't ride a horse or swing a longsword."

"I suppose that must be true to some degree," Dalflitch conceded, looking away from Turley disdainfully. "I must just not see it all that often."

Prentice blinked in surprise. He looked to the duchess, but her head was down once more, clearly thinking about the important political questions. Taking the opportunity, he moved back closer to Turley.

"What's all that about?" he whispered surreptitiously, nodding toward Lady Dalflitch.

"Never you mind," Turley hissed back, and when Prentice looked at him, his friend refused to meet his eye.

"Truly?" Prentice could not remember the last time his friend had so flatly dismissed him. Turley must have realized he had spoken out of turn because he then turned to Prentice, keeping one eye on the rest of the room.

"It's a private matter," he said more gently. Prentice nodded and turned back to the duchess. No more needed to be said between friends. If Turley wanted to share the story, he would when he was ready.

"Doesn't a king already have enough names?" asked Spindle. "It seems every time someone says his name, he's defender of this, unchallenged lord of that."

"Those aren't his, they're his ancestors' names," said Prentice. "Every time he hears them, he is reminded that he sits in a better man's chair. Every king lives in the shadow of his ancestors. He must add to his name for himself or else be dismissed as an empty robe, a thing for a crown to rest upon until a worthier man is born to wear it."

"Even the brat craves a reputation for the ages," said Dalflitch, referring to Daven Marcus. "He marched west for that purpose and the whole time constantly talked of reclaiming the Vec. He longs to outshine his ancestors."

"So, the gold and silver isn't for keepin' in coffers?" said Spindle. "It's to buy thread to sew more gold eagles and silver lions on their clothes. And they don't get to have those things until they make some form of honor for themselves, which costs them money to pay men-at-arms?"

"Not the worst way to understand it," said Prentice. He would have kept speaking, but the duchess looked up from her thoughts at that moment and gestured for quiet.

"Would this be a thing to get King Chrostmer a name?" she asked the room. "He's already led a successful crusade that drove back the Vec and civilized the Reach. Isn't that enough honor?"

"Defending land that was already his?" Sir Gant answered her. "Not insignificant, but not much more than any other king has done since the first Grand Kingdom folk crossed the Azures. Consider though, no king has received the fealty of a Vec prince. Ever. No one has brought one of the rebels back into the fold."

The duchess looked around the room. Dalflitch nodded her agreement with the knight's assessment, and when she looked to him, Prentice concurred as well.

"Even if Prince Daven Marcus achieves his fantasies to the fullest extent," Sir Gant went on, "he would still be only following his father's successes. Chrostmer the Fourth, Liberator of Aubrey, Unifier of the West and the Vec? That's a name that would stand out in the annals, have no doubt."

"For only one princedom? It's not as if the other Vec rulers will accept it and start bending their knees willy-nilly."

Sir Gant shrugged, accepting the duchess's reasoning. She scanned the rest of the room once more, inviting final comments. Turley nodded to his friends, Gant and Prentice, signaling he agreed with them. Spindle had nothing more to add, following the duchess's eyes to watch and hear what the others said.

"What of you, Righteous?" the duchess asked Prentice's wife. "No insights to offer from the realm of pit fighting and street crime?"

"Well, it's true enough what the steward said," Righteous replied thoughtfully. "Be sure, a name matters in the ring and the pit and the alley. Any gang leader needs to make it known what kind of blade he is, that he won't take guff from no one, else he has to fend off challengers all day and night. Can't imagine what'd be like if you had to fend off challenges from your own dead ancestors. Imagine how many ruffians you'd have to watch for if everyone was always saying how you weren't as bad as some swift-cutter who'd been dead for a hundred years. It's not like you could call 'im out and prove your steel. Can't call out a ghost."

"And the palace in Denay has stood for many centuries," Prentice added, supporting her point. "That's a lot of ghosts to haunt a king." Righteous regarded him through slitted eyes again, but this time seemed to accept he was speaking *with* her, not against her.

"It seems that the politics of all the world is much the same, from the highest to the lowest," the duchess observed.

"It merely differs by degrees, Your Grace," Prentice agreed. "A street thief might only put a knife in your back over a question of honor. A king will conquer your town and burn your land. Redlanders will do all that and butcher your people while they do it."

Silence fell as the duchess wrestled herself to a decision. Looking around the room, Prentice could see by their patient expressions that her household all understood this moment as he did. Once, Duchess Amelia had been an uncertain young widow, feeling out of her depth as she tried to defend her dead husband's lands. That girl was gone now, grown into a confident woman who needed no handholding. She knew her power and her limits, consulted the advisers she trusted as she chose, and made her own decisions.

"Come what may, I have to speak to the king about this," she said at last. "In fact, I have no choice. He might accept Prince Forsyte's offer of fealty or not. The prince might still balk at this whole plan. No matter what his people are going through, even his son, Forsyte might not want to go down in history as the first Vec prince to return to the Grand Kingdom." She paused for a breath. "But all of that is secondary. I've met with an enemy of the throne, denounced by the Holy Church. If I do not tell the king as soon as I may, then I make myself a conspirator, potentially even a traitor to the crown."

And we all with you, Your Grace, Prentice thought, but he said nothing.

"That will do for tonight, everyone," the duchess said, dismissing them. "My thanks."

Pausing only to give their respects, the duchess's household broke apart to their evening duties. The ladies began to put the curtain back in place and help her grace to ready for bed. Turley went downstairs, and Prentice joined Sir Gant to follow him, looking forward to removing his armor and stretching his tired limbs.

"Captain, a moment?" the duchess called, and Prentice waved Sir Gant on, waiting patiently behind the curtain. Duchess Amelia stuck her head through and waved him closer. "Do you think he was telling us the truth today? The prince? About what is happening in Aubrey?"

"You saw his face, Your Grace," said Prentice. "Do you think he was lying?"

"No. But I do wonder about his fears. What could be coming that is worse than is already happening in the town?"

Prentice couldn't even imagine and shook his head.

"But even if it is only as bad as we have already seen, we both remember Fallenhill, Your Grace. We know what Redlanders are like when they capture a town."

She nodded solemnly, and for a moment her eyes glistened, but she did not shed a tear. "I agree. But still, I find myself calculating the strategies and weighing the politics. Have I become the kind of noble I once despised, valuing the common folk only as much as they are useful to me?"

"You have your own common folk who must take precedence, Your Grace," Prentice answered. "And of course, all of this first depends upon us defeating the Redlanders."

"Are you not confident?"

"Confidence is not certainty, Your Grace."

"Is anything certain in this life, Captain Ash?"

Prentice frowned. "If nothing else, Your Grace, we can be certain of this: If we do not defeat these invaders, they will lay waste to everything they touch. They will slaughter and burn every man, woman, and child in the Vec and in the Grand Kingdom until we are all slain, or they are."

"Then we must win."

"Yes, Your Grace."

CHAPTER 21

"Don't you have someone to help you with that?" asked a feminine voice from behind.

Prentice was fumbling at the laces of his brigandine, trying awkwardly to untie them so he could remove the heavy armor. He turned to see his wife standing just inside the flap of his tent and smiled.

"No, I do not," he said, answering her question. "A knight has squires and pages to help him into his armor, but I am no knight. Maybe I could order one of my militiamen to assist me, make a manservant of him, but none of them want the duty."

"No?" said Righteous as she stepped into the tent. "Why is that?"

"Because my wife has said that she will kill outright anyone, man or woman, who dares to take this privilege from her."

"Is that right?" Righteous swatted away his fingers and began to untie the knots. "So how did you get into this armor this morning? Surely you didn't tie these yourself?"

"I refuse to answer that. It might cost a good man his life."

"Oh, can you not keep your lady wife under control?"

"I have not figured the trick of it yet, if there is one."

Righteous stopped what she was doing and stepped directly in front of him. "I've told you, husband," she said. "I will be content to sit at your feet and eat from your hand the rest of my days, if that would please you."

Prentice knew she meant every word. He reached out and put his hand through her hair, pulling her into a deep, passionate kiss that she returned.

"You are the queen of my heart," he told her when they broke apart. "The only place I want you is beside me, day and night."

She pushed away and went back to unlacing his armor, helping him pull it over his head once it was loose enough. The air felt suddenly cool on the sweat-damp doublet beneath.

"Are you sure that's all you want?" Righteous went back to teasing as he waved his arms and enjoyed the relief. "With the powerful duchess hanging on your every word? Or the wondrous beauty of Lady Dalflitch within your reach?"

"I have all the beauty I need here," he said, reaching for her, but she stepped out of his grasp deftly and began to unpin her hair and hood.

"Yes, well, you're too late in any case, if you dream of the former countess."

"I tell you, wife, I do not..." Prentice paused as he realized what his wife was saying. "Why too late? Does the lady have a suitor? Who?"

Righteous only nodded in reply, giving nothing away before standing and turning her back to her husband. "Time for you to do mine."

"You're staying the night?"

"No, but I'm not wasting this chance neither. You might tell me you're loyal, but I've been living with courtly ladies some while now. There are wolves less ravenous than a waiting-lady seeking a husband, I swear. When a court maid gets the scent, ain't no prey she won't run down. Hunting hounds'll give up before she does."

"And the Lady Dalflitch has someone in mind?" Prentice untied his wife's bodice laces and she let the garment slip to the floor, stepping from her skirt at the same time.

"She does indeed, and he's got the blood up for her, too, but neither of them knows how to take it to the duchess, which Dalflitch has got to do, being a lady-in-waiting. She needs the mistress' permission to wed." Righteous flopped down on Prentice's cot in her blouse, sitting to peel the stockings from her legs. "Hot bloody things for summer."

"So, who is it?" Prentice tried to sort through the nobles he knew of to guess who might be interested in Dalflitch's hand.

"Oh, surely you can figure it, old man," said Righteous, rolling onto her stomach and kicking her now naked legs in the air behind her. "It's not like they're doing much of a job keeping it a secret. It's practically gettin' embarrassing. Tonight especially, sniping like striplings with a crush."

"Tonight...?" Prentice's brow furrowed and then it hit him. "Turley? She wants Turley?"

Righteous winked and clicked her tongue. "That's the one. She's carried a torch for him since he rescued her in that ride from the prince. He's the one who snatched her onto his horse and took her to safety. Did you know that?"

"I have heard the story," Prentice admitted. "How do you know all this?"

"Because she told me, dearest husband. How do you think I got to sneak away for this evening? I keep her secret when she has a tryst with the chief steward, and she now has excuses ready for if the duchess calls for me."

"The duchess does not know you are here?"

Righteous shook her head mischievously.

"I do not approve, wife," Prentice said, and he meant it.

Righteous was not the least bit chastised. "Then stop wasting time talking about other women and come give your wife her marital entitlement. Then I'll be back, and you won't have to worry about disapproving no more."

Prentice finished undressing and stood at the edge of the cot. It was going to be an awkward place for two people to lie together. "Take that off," he ordered her with a nod.

All of Righteous's teasing and bravado evaporated, and she nervously gripped at the collar of her blouse. Before she had been convicted and transported, Righteous had been a pit fighter, and while she was proud to have no scars on her face, other than her brawler's brand, she was ashamed of those on her body, even with him.

Prentice was having none of that.

"You are queen of my heart," he told her again in a serious, authoritative tone. "Night and day, dressed or naked, you are the beauty that I long for. Every part of you. Now do as your husband commands, excellent wife, and remove your blouse."

She smiled up at him then, a small, shy expression, completely different from her usual mocking air. With slightly trembling hand, she pulled her blouse over her head. The cot creaked as he climbed on next to her and they took their moment together as husband and wife. Knowing the battle that was soon to come, Prentice tried not wonder if this would be the last time.

CHAPTER 22

"This is the only bridge?" Amelia asked as she looked down on the broad, stone-footed span that crossed the Murr River from north to south. In the distance, on the south side, the last of the winter green and the fresh spring colors of Cattlefields stretched off to the walled town of Aubrey in the far distance. The dark shapes of cows grazing could be seen in the new grass, but otherwise there were no living things.

"There is no other bridge this far west, Your Grace," Viscount Gullden answered her, standing at her shoulder. He pointed downriver, eastward. "Bridgetown is that way, fifty leagues. It is the main highway between the Grand Kingdom and the Vec. Almost all the wagon trade goes that way."

"Is it only riverboat trade this far west then?"

"In the main, Your Grace. I suppose some locals might walk the bridge if forced."

"And where are the Redlanders?"

"Your Grace?"

Amelia looked over her left shoulder. In that direction she could see the king's army camp, a virtual sea of canvass, a town in its own right, housing men and women, horses, and other animals, as well as all the goods and chattels needed for their living. Then she looked over her other shoulder and could see her tower on its ridge and the smoke rising beyond it from the cook fires of her own forces.

"Captain Prentice," she called, summoning him from where he stood nearby with other White Lions as her bodyguard. Prentice insisted these days that she never travel without a military escort. "Where are the Redlanders?"

"They are in that town there, Your Grace," Viscount Gullden explained, pointing south at Aubrey. His tone was polite but confused, as if she was asking a question too simple to need an answer.

He doesn't understand, she thought. She was sure Prentice would.

Her captain approached, picking his way over the tumbledown stones of the ruins where they stood. They were on a lonely hill, just north of the Murr River bridge to Aubrey. Once, this had been a watchtower, lesser sister to the tower where Duchess Amelia now slept, but King Kolber had destroyed them both as the first aggressive act of his invasion over a decade ago. Unlike Amelia's tower atop the spur, this one had never been rebuilt.

"What was your question, Your Grace?" asked Prentice as he bowed.

"Where are the Redlanders, Captain? Why can we not see them?"

Prentice looked across at Cattlefields, the little village of Three Roads almost hidden near trees at the edge of the sweep of meadows. "It is a mystery, Your Grace."

"The town," the viscount objected, his brows knitted. "They are in the town."

"My Lord Viscount," Amelia explained, "with the Reach's forces added to his own, the king has brought over twenty thousand men to the campaign, and signs of their presence can be seen for leagues in every direction. If not for the ridges and mounts blocking our sight, they would be seen even farther. Now look across the river."

The viscount did as she instructed, obedient even if confused.

"The Redlander army is at least as large, or that is what we have heard," she continued. "And they have taken Aubrey for themselves. Not just the town, but almost the entire princedom. Yet I see not a single tent. Not one. You tell me that they are all billeted in the town, but what town have you ever known that could absorb twenty thousand men-at-arms or more and give no sign?"

Realization dawned in Viscount Gullden's expression, and he looked from the duchess to the town and back. "I never," he muttered. "Where...where are they?"

"Your thoughts, Captain?" Amelia asked. It was Prentice's wisdom that she mostly wanted, but she hadn't wanted to insult the viscount by not asking his opinion first.

"They are on the river, Your Grace."

"Where?" the viscount scoffed. He looked down at the broad Murr. There were no boats in sight.

"There is a tributary in that direction," Prentice said, looking to the southwest. "It is out of sight here, because of the lay of the land, but it can be seen from the marshes on the west side of our camp, just. It curls around in the south and passes by Aubrey's walls on the far side. Almost all the river traffic into and out of the Vec from the Reach passes through there. It is the Aubrey princedom's own little River Dwelt."

"Is that what they call it?" Amelia asked, surprised.

Prentice shook his head. "I do not think so, Your Grace. I do not know what they call it, in all honesty. I just know that it serves the same function as the Dwelt serves your lands, allowing trade without needing a road."

Amelia nodded thoughtfully. She'd been pondering these questions since she'd first heard Lord Ironworth's plans. They had been pushed to the back of her mind by the political considerations of the king and Prince of Rhales, along with Prince Forsyte's request. But three days had passed, and King Chrostmer was still not seen abroad by the court. No one knew for sure where he was, it seemed, nor Daven Marcus's

whereabouts either. Every request she sent for a private audience
with King Chrostmer was answered with a polite refusal and a
statement that the king was "not available."

How bad are relations between king and prince? she wondered.
*And is there anyone's favor the prince couldn't sour with his
childish petulance?*

With the political situation stalled, the duchess felt she could
take a breath to consider their strategic position. That was why
she had come to the hilltop to look at the bridge and the town.
Also, she wanted to see if there was some sign of the "worse fate"
that Prince Forsyte feared the Redlanders were preparing for his
people. All she saw was a rural idyl, seemingly utterly peaceful.

"The Redlanders came from the west across the shallow sea,"
she mused out loud. "And they came down the Murr on the
same boats, we presume. Is that right gentlemen?"

"They certainly did not march here," Prentice agreed.

Viscount Gullden nodded blankly. An obviously loyal and
honorable man, it was becoming apparent the young noble
lacked any strong mind for strategy. That was alright as far as
Amelia was concerned. Her captain had proved equal to every
challenge so far.

"And they have no cavalry, no knights ahorse?"

"We have seen chariots, but few, Your Grace, which makes me
think they might have my aptitude for horsemanship."

Prentice's self-deprecating joke made her smile. She looked
south again.

"So, I am thinking, Viscount, Captain, if they can bring
whole armies across seas and down rivers by boat, then why
would they need a bridge?" The two men followed her gaze, and
all three regarded the stout stone footings. Viscount Gullden
started, as if the truth of her insight had physically slapped him
in the face. Prentice's eyes narrowed.

"I have personally seen the Redlander boats sail against the
wind," Amelia told them. "So powerful is the sorcery with
which they are imbued that wind and waves make no matter

to them. Would the flow of a river trouble them much, do you think?"

"They could cross the river to attack us without ever going near the bridge," the viscount said in horror. He looked back at the king's camp, positioned to be ready to intercept an invader force trying to cross the long span over the river. Now its strategic location was so obviously irrelevant. A light of hope brightened his expression. "But so many men, so many boats? Wouldn't they be seen sailing on the water? We would see them coming."

"Assuming the sorcery that propels them cannot also hide them from sight," Prentice observed flatly. Amelia had never seen or heard of such magic, but after all she *had* seen, she would not be surprised if the Redlander vessels had that power to add to all their other advantages.

"Perhaps we should prepare for such a possibility," she said, grimacing.

"Yes...yes, Your Grace," the viscount stammered.

"I am not sure that we can, Your Grace," Prentice answered, looking down at the river. The polite viscount looked at him, eyes wide in disbelief. Amelia cocked an eyebrow. When the captain noticed them both looking at him, he shrugged and bowed his head apologetically. "What could we do, Your Grace? An enemy who can move unseen by any scout? How would we prepare?"

It was a fair response but insufficient for a duchess.

"I expect you and Sir Gant to think of something, Captain," Amelia said to him imperiously. "And you, Viscount, if you or any noblemen have any thoughts, you must bring them to the captain's or the knight captain's attention immediately."

"Without hesitation, Your Grace." The viscount bowed formally.

"In the meantime, I would like you to go to Prince Forsyte and inform him that although my efforts on his behalf have been frustrated so far, I am still working to bring his petition to our king. I hope even to do so today. I have not forgotten him or his people's plight."

"I will inform him so, Your Grace."

"You may deliver that message immediately, if you please, Lord Gullden," Amelia said when it became clear the man hadn't recognized the implicit dismissal in her previous words.

The viscount bowed again and departed with a stricken look on his face, as if he feared he had insulted her. Amelia felt a moment's sympathetic affection for him, colored by the memory of his brother. The house of Griffith produced earnest, straightforward noblemen, it seemed. Honorable but not very cunning.

"Gant will be besieged by suggestions from the nobility before nightfall," said Prentice with a low smile once the viscount was out of earshot. "Every sworn man of a banner will have his own 'foolproof' plan."

"None will come to you, you don't think?" asked Amelia.

"Nobles answer to your knight captain, Your Grace. No earl or baron wants to consult with a mere captain of peasants."

"You don't think you've earned a better reputation than that?"

Prentice shook his head, but then it turned to a nod. "Perhaps a little, but they will all know the favor I enjoy with you. They will expect me to hear their plans and take the credit for them. Reputation or no, they will not fully trust me. I may be a reformed man, but I am still lowborn. Noble honor will not bind me; at least that will be their expectation."

"I should have you knighted," Amelia said without thinking and then remembered Prentice's past. She gave him a sharp glance and was thankful that he did not seem insulted.

"Not within your power, Your Grace," he said enigmatically, his face a mask.

"Forgive me, Prentice. That was insensitive."

"Think no more of it, Lady Amelia."

Amelia almost never used Prentice's name without his title these days, and his referring to her by name, even addressing her as lady, was so rudely informal that she could not ever remembering him doing it. But she knew why he'd done it. Prentice was her sworn man, her captain and loyal retainer, but somewhere under all of that, he was her friend. She liked that. Friends were too rare for folk of her rank. She looked at the river again.

"Is there anything we can do about those boats, Captain?"

"I have some ideas, Your Grace," he answered her soberly. "I have Sergeant Felix working on a gambit or two, as well as other duties about the camp."

"Indeed, the past few mornings we ladies have been awakened to the hammering of picks on rocks beneath our windows. Nearly a thousand men are carving the hillside these days it seems."

"They are building a second path to the tower, Your Grace, so that you may travel to and from your lodging without having to leave the camp," Prentice explained.

"Yes, that was the story Turley told me. It also occurred to me that it might be more convenient for other members of my household to make contact with the camp as well." Amelia looked at Prentice to see if he took her meaning.

"I had not thought of that, Your Grace," he said, then blinked when he realized what she was fully implying. He turned to her and bowed with a stern expression. "Certainly not, Your Grace. I did not set your army to building a new road just to make it easier to tryst with my wife of an evening."

"I am only teasing you, Captain," she said. "You know I trust to your loyal service implicitly. Although, I will tell you that your lady wife appreciates every moment she has with you. She speaks highly of your company in every respect."

"Does she, Your Grace?" he muttered, and his lips pursed in a sour frown. "I should command her not to be indiscreet."

"Do you think she would obey you?"

He shook his head and they both laughed honestly.

"She adores you, you know?"

"I adore her."

"And I envy you both." Amelia sighed, but there was no resentment in her. She missed her husband, that was all. "Do not be too concerned, Captain. We are all 'maids' in a tower. Gossip fills more hours than you could imagine. And when Righteous comes back in the morning, smiling sweetly and singing to herself, we all ply her with every question that we can, even me. But trust me, we do not violate the privacy of your marriage bed."

"Thank you, Your Grace," he said flatly, and Amelia wondered if he were actually embarrassed. It was such a rare emotion in him that she wasn't sure she would recognize it if he was. "My wife assured me you did not know she was gone of an evening."

"I didn't. I found out recently. Please remember, I say we're maids, but none of us truly is. We are widows or the like, one and all. Our minds turn to such matters readily, in private. I am sure you understand."

"In truth, Your Grace, I was never much of a one for wooing or understanding women," he said. "I was so completely aimed at Ashfield from my earliest days that I never had time to spare for indulging the flesh. Then, when I was convicted...well, what has a convict to offer a woman? Whatever I know of love, it is nothing to impress, I swear."

"Nevertheless, your wife tells tales of you enough to make us all jealous, I assure you."

"Can we please speak of something else, Your Grace?"

Now he really is embarrassed, Amelia thought and smiled affectionately. That was enough.

She sobered her thoughts and gestured toward her escort. "Let us depart."

"Your Grace." Prentice accepted her instruction and waved the escort to form up.

There was no drummer or standard-bearer with this group, but the White Lions were as disciplined as ever. As Amelia made her way to the path that led down off the hill, Prentice made a request.

"With your permission, I would like to cross the Murr this evening," he said.

"Truly?" Amelia asked, looking at him, mouth agape. She had no idea what he intended.

"I think we need to know what is going on up that tributary. And we need a better notion of this 'worse thing' that Prince Forsyte fears. Whatever the Redlanders are planning, odds are they are putting it together in that waterway. We have driven them south out of the Reach, at least between the mountains and the Dwelt, but they are still close across the river. That nobleman in the king's war council was wrong. We must not treat the Murr like a wall, especially not if it is one over which we cannot see. They are just there, supposedly, only a handful of leagues south of us, but we cannot even see them. We have to find out what their plans are, or we will never defeat them."

Amelia thought of her contact with Prince Forsyte. If it came out that she had had a secret conference with a Vec prince, then sent men south into Vec territory, it might look even more like treason. Nonetheless, Prentice's idea made sense, so much sense that she couldn't believe no one else had thought to try it. Perhaps they had, and the king had simply not thought to tell her about it.

"Will you go alone?" she asked and then thought that under no circumstances could she allow her captain to take a risk like that. Prentice shook his head.

"But no more than four or five of us," he said. "On foot and dressed for secrecy. No plated armor or heavy weapons."

How was four or five better than a man alone? The entire Redlander army was hiding across that river.

"What will you do if you are found out?" she demanded, liking the idea less and less.

"Run, Your Grace. Run like the hounds of hell are after us because they will be."

"And if you are caught?"

"Then we will die, Your Grace, brutally," Prentice told her, and he looked her straight in the eye. "And we will be neither the first nor the last in this war to do so."

"I do not like that prospect."

"Nor do I."

Amelia wanted to tell him no, to forbid him taking the risk, to command him to send someone else, but in her mind, she knew he was right. They needed a clear notion of what was happening in Aubrey and on the rivers, and Prentice was the best man she had to assess the situation. With a heavy sigh, she nodded her head to give him permission.

"You know, when she finds out, your lady wife will have some choice words to say about you risking your life like this," she said to him wryly.

He shrugged, and a roguish grin that reminded her of Turley lit his lips for a moment. "Well, Your Grace, you must breast that storm alone, I fear. I will be safe across the river by the time she finds out."

"Safe in the belly of the beast?"

"The tortures of the Redlanders or my wife's displeasure? The frying pan or the fire, Your Grace."

"I can see how you and Turley became friends, Captain," she said, noting the mocking gleam in his eye. "I promise I'll give Righteous extra free time with you when you return. I wouldn't want her to miss the chance to share her thoughts with you."

Amelia turned away and allowed herself to be escorted to her horse for the ride back to her camp.

CHAPTER 23

"Your name is Larriman?" Prentice asked the half-starved young scarecrow standing before him. "My sergeant tells me you know something of the south bank? Is that right?"

The youth looked back and forth between Prentice, Sir Gant, and Sergeant Felix. Eyes wide with fear, he kept his chin against his shoulder and did not answer Prentice's question.

"You're a local? What was it you did to find out about the Vec side? Were you involved with local smugglers?"

Larriman's head shot up in alarm at that. "No, master. No, sir," he insisted, shaking his head vehemently. "I'm an honest man, master sir, I swear it on my life, sir. I keep the sheep and I'm going to be a carder's 'pprentice once I 'ave the fee, master sir."

"His rank is Captain," Felix declared in the same stern tone he used for any new recruit who hadn't yet learned the right forms of address for White Lions.

"Sorry, Captain, master sir," Larriman said and ducked his head, tugging his forelock as he did so. Felix rolled his eyes in disgust, but Sir Gant smiled sympathetically.

"Carders are an honorable guild, lad," said Prentice. "Do you have a place waiting for you in Aubrey? A relative who can cover your pledge?"

Again, Larriman shook his head. "Nothing like that. I don't really know nothin' 'bout Aubrey, truth to tell. It was Vesta;

her plan was to go 'cross the river. She said the Vec princes were fighting the invaders and that we'd be safer there, away from the Kingdom knights what steal all the village food."

"Vesta's your betrothed? The maid you were caught with?"

Larriman nodded, still nervous in demeanor, but with a fiercer look in his eyes. Prentice took that to mean the girl was the heart of the boy's motivation.

Good for you, lad, Prentice thought. *Stick by her.* "How does Vesta know about Aubrey?" he asked.

"She knows lots of things, Captain master," Larriman answered. "More'n me at any rate. She said the prince's son was still fighting the invaders and we'd be safe, even though the prince hi'self had fled the town."

Prentice pointed to the ground, indicating that Larriman should stay standing where he was, then waved Sir Gant and Felix to him and they stepped away to speak out of the youth's hearing.

"We'd be better off getting this girl Vesta to act as guide," Prentice told them quietly. "Seems she is the one who knows something at least, even if her assessment of politics is right off."

"What peasant does know the truth of their prince's doings?" mused Sir Gant, though not critically. "And the girl is at least half right. Assuming Prince Forsyte is not lying, then his son is in Aubrey still, just not leading a defense."

"Sorry, Captain, but the girl's in no condition," said Felix, beating at river midges on his face with his hat in his hand. "Damned bugs."

"She's going to lose her arm?" asked Prentice.

"Healer's already taken it off," the sergeant confirmed, giving Larriman a sad look. It was the sergeant's first gesture of compassion toward the youth since he presented him as a possible aid in the scouting mission Prentice wanted to undertake across the river. "And she's still under the laud most of the day. Girl won't even be walking for another week. Be full summer before her pain's down enough for her to do just household chores, and that's if the rot don't get her."

"Miserable business," said Sir Gant, and he spat at the grass, waving away many of the same bugs that beset the sergeant. "And these bugs are only going to get worse now summer's coming on."

"And this Larriman's the best we can do? Is there no one else?"

Felix shook his head apologetically. "Between Redlanders killing 'em and the Kingdom pressing 'em to be bearers and servants, any free peasants in the area have gone to ground. There's two or three villages within a day's walk o' here, and they're truly empty. Nothing but ghosts and rats. There's sure to be some locals in service in the king's camp." He pointed eastward toward the Grand Kingdom's main encampment. The sky in that direction was already darkening, the Rampart starting to glow. "But you said that this had to all be done on the quiet. Can't go asking around in that camp without folk finding out. I just don't have the—what did you call 'em Captain?—connections."

Connections are Dalflitch's domain, Prentice thought.

But even Lady Dalflitch's connections, which incorporated a surprising number of the servant class, didn't stretch far enough east or far enough down the social order to include pressed peasant farmers in the Grand Kingdom camp.

"So, we go across blind."

"Perhaps Prince Forsyte could provide us some information," Sir Gant ventured. "Since we're doing so much on his behalf."

"The prince's whereabouts are a secret known only to a few. We cannot easily consult him," said Prentice.

"Damned inconvenient," muttered Felix.

"And a damned sight safer for everyone," said Prentice definitively. As he spoke, some of the river insects swarmed near his mouth, and it was his turn to wave at his face aggressively.

"You can see why we grow the long moustaches, Captain," said Felix wryly. "Keeps the flies and midges out."

"When I want your grooming advice, Sergeant, I will be sure to ask for it."

"Very good, sir." Felix snapped a crisp salute that struck his chest with an audible thud. Prentice looked back to Larriman.

"They tell me you are never far from your maid's side," he called to the youth.

Larriman rushed closer and tugged his forelock again.

"No, sir, Captain master, sir. The one time the healer lady said Vesta stirred from her sleep, I was away at the call of nature and getting some soup. I never even got to speak with her. Can't let that happen again."

"I like loyalty, Larriman, and I like to see it rewarded," said Prentice. "Stay by your betrothed's side until she wakes. Then we will get you work fetching and carrying. I will give orders that you are to be fed in the meantime. Up north, at the other end of the Dwelt, there is a town called Fallenhill. We have many sheep, shepherds, and wool carders up that way. When the duchess marches back north, if you and Vesta march with us, I will see about getting you back into your trade."

Larriman looked like a child just promised sugared fruit for dinner. "Oh, thank you, Captain master! Thank you. Thank you." He tugged his forelock repeatedly until Felix cuffed his shoulder and pushed him away.

"Some days you are a soft touch, Captain," said Felix, not seeming bitter exactly, but with a disapproving scowl. "You're crossing the Murr to sneak amongst the cutthroats, and he's going back to sleep beside his sweetheart."

Prentice clapped his hand on his sergeant's shoulder. "That barefoot lad, with just a tunic and pair of trews, is wearing everything he owns in all the world. All he's missing is the ankle fetters and he would be no different from a convicted man. You and I, with our blades, armor, and uniforms, are wearing more wealth than he will ever likely see in his lifetime, even if the

Carder's Guild accept his pledge. In a life like that, I am happy to bless him with a few days' food and help in his devotion to his beloved. I hope another lord might do the same for me in his place."

"Well, when you put it like that..."

"I do." Prentice released Felix. "In the meantime, what is the status with the wagons?"

"We've done about twenty so far. One side only for now, just like you said."

"You only want one reinforced side to the wagons?" asked Sir Gant. "Won't that make them a simple enough prospect to defeat? The enemy will only need to circle around their flanks and attack the undefended side."

"I wanted to speed up the conversions. When we put them together, it will only be one-sided, but the more we get done, the longer our portable curtain wall can be, and thus the harder it will be to flank."

Sir Gant's expression showed he wasn't fully convinced, and Prentice did not blame him. The wagons would always be safer if all sides could be reinforced, but he simply did not have time to wait, especially if the enemy really could cross the river with boats at any location. He needed to be able to reinforce anywhere he could, whenever the need arose.

"Have any of the cart owners resisted?" he asked.

"Two got it in their heads to turn around when they heard, tried to head back to Griffith," Felix reported. "They got taken down straight off. Turned out they had some unpaid guild dues on their goods, something about river trade versus road, and they thought we were after them for that. So those wagons became ours for free. After that, most wagon owners have accepted the new duty and surrendered their vehicles for service, with a proviso of compensation."

"The duchess will handle that," said Prentice. He could only wonder what complex interrelated web of taxes and dues the guilds had placed on merchants supplying the army, but he expected Duchess Amelia was at least aware, since any extra costs would ultimately be borne by her treasury. Her household seneschal was a competent man. Prentice turned his mind back to the military matters that were his purview. "The ones that are converted, get them into the camp proper ready for the men to train with. In fact, make that a priority for tonight."

"You don't want to leave it for daylight tomorrow?"

"I want men training on them tomorrow. Tonight, think up some practice drills, loading and firing from inside and underneath. Claws fighting over the top, repelling assault. Things like that. I'll go over it with you when I get back. In the meantime, have the wagons brought in and lined up near the river. Close as is safe, but not so close they'll be stuck in the mud if we get a late rain or the river floods."

Felix accepted the commands with a salute. He was moving off as Prentice gave him one last instruction.

"And set a sentry on them."

"You think the Redlanders might try and fire 'em, secret-like before they come ashore?" asked Felix.

"Aye, or some resourceful merchant might make off with one or two, take them up the Foothill Highway, cut back across the mountains to Griffith, strip the sides off and drive them back down south to resell to us."

"An enterprising notion," said Sir Gant, his lips under his moustache twisting in disgust at the thought of such treachery and corruption.

"There's plenty of smaller roads 'cross the Azures 'tween here and Griffith," Felix agreed. "They wouldn't even need to go that far north." Then he marched off to fulfill his orders.

Sir Gant waved at the bugs once more and looked up at the sky. "It'll be fully night soon," he said. "Are you sure you don't want me to go with you? Wasn't I good enough to sneak around Dweltford at your side?"

He pointed to a small silver pin in the shape of a rat which he wore on the embroidered collar of his tabard. Prentice owned a similar one, but he wore his on a chain around his neck, like a charm. They were a strange trophy, one that few recognized, but they marked apart the men who had liberated the duchess's capital when it had been captured years before. They had infiltrated the walled town through its sewers and earned the title Rats of Dweltford.

"You know I trust you, sir," said Prentice, showing his friend full deference for his knightly rank. "But if this little expedition goes sour, the duchess will need someone to take up the field command. Felix can give the Lions orders, but the bannermen are only going to follow a knight. It is hard enough to get them to accept my orders."

"All the more reason for me to go across the river and you to stay here."

Prentice shook his head. "I need to see for myself if I am to figure out something of their plans. Besides, I think we both know that the rogue I am taking with me is the best there is for this kind of guileful intrigue, even with only one good arm."

Sir Gant nodded his agreement at that. "No wilier rascal have ever I met. Excepting perhaps, if you'll forgive me, your good lady wife."

"Sir Gant?" said Prentice with a cocked eyebrow. He was surprised by his friend's bold snipe, but not truly offended. "How can you say such a thing to a woman's husband?"

"Do you disagree?"

Prentice paused dramatically, as if he had to think about the question, but he knew Gant was right. Righteous had once been named Cutter Sal, and she had not been convicted by mistake.

"I cannot pick between a weasel and a vixen," he said at last. "And I would rather have my vixen at my side than any other blade, even yours, sir, if you'll forgive *me*. But Righteous has her own duties to the duchess. Turley is the next best in cunning, more than either you or me. But do not fret, we will be back before dawn, and you can be sure you and I will have the chance to stand side by side in honorable battle before this campaign is done."

Sir Gant did not seem much mollified by Prentice's explanation, but he said nothing more.

CHAPTER 24

"You sent Turl...your chief steward across the Murr?" Lady Dalflitch was apparently so shocked at the news that she completely forgot her manners while addressing the duchess.

"Please lower your voice, My Lady," Amelia instructed flatly. Outside her new wooden door, she could hear the tromp of boots as the sentries on the roof changed shifts, going up and down the stairs. "And yes, I did."

"But his arm," Dalflitch protested in a quieter voice, before remembering to add, "Your Grace."

"Turley insists that his maimed arm gives him no pain any longer, and while he clearly cannot do with it what he once could, he is still quite competent. Since he has healed, he has been nothing short of an exemplary steward. I doubt I could find a better man with two good arms to trust my household staff to. If he says he is still useful to Captain Prentice, then I believe him."

"Your Grace..." Dalflitch began but fell silent. The lady clutched at the air, as if wanting to shake her fists in frustration but remembering her manners enough to know not to.

"Please, Lady Dalflitch," Amelia said, taking up her book from her sideboard once more and looking for the page she was up to, "retake your seat. Perhaps you might play with the cards? You know the solitaire."

Apparently unable to resist her own sense of decorum, Dalflitch curtseyed to her mistress and returned to sit on the bed next to Righteous, who was practicing needlework under Spindle's watchful eye. She did not take up the deck of playing cards Amelia suggested as a distraction.

"It's not a dirk," said the masked lady-in-waiting as she put her hand onto Righteous's, steadying the motion. "You don't have to stab it like you're trying to pierce a man's ribcage."

"I know how to sew," Righteous retorted, shrugging off her instructor's hand.

"Prove it then. It's just a kerchief, a 'little favor' you said, something you could give your husband to carry into battle like the fine ladies do."

"I know what I said," Righteous muttered. "I'd much rather give him a dirk, in any case."

"I thought he gave you his?" Spindle sniped back, but with a smile.

Amelia lifted an eyebrow at the unladylike jest but did not interfere with conversation. Talk lapsed for a time except for Righteous cursing under her breath as she worked her best to sew in the lion pattern Spindle had produced for her. Amelia felt her eyes tiring as she read in the flickering lamp light, and she lowered the book to her lap for a moment.

"What I don't understand is why you have such dislike for the man," she said, continuing her conversation with Dalflitch about Turley.

"Dislike, Your Grace?" the lady replied. "I don't..."

"I see the scowls and baleful glances the pair of you exchange. I sometimes half expect you to leap at him and claw his eyes out."

"She'd never get near him," Righteous muttered without looking up. "I seen him fight. Even one-handed, he'd have her in a trice."

Dalflitch hissed at Righteous, eyes narrowed in fury, then schooled her face before turning to Amelia.

"I do not hate him, Your Grace, I swear to you."

"Then what is this matter between you two?" Amelia insisted. "It must be something. The way he looks at you is just as hostile at times."

"Might be he's just defensive," said Righteous. "High and mighty former countess showering him with icy glares and steely glances. Such a lower-born man might feel intimidated, even if he's strong enough to take her any time she threw herself at him."

"Can you not mind your own business, Cutter?" Dalflitch demanded, her voice rising to a near shout as she whirled on the lady seated next to her. She might control her emotions with the duchess, but she wasn't affording the others the same courtesy.

"Have you ever known her to mind her own business?" asked Spindle lightly, as if the conversation was still concerned with needlework.

Righteous, though, had looked up from her work and fixed the Lady Dalflitch with a cold glare. Amelia wondered if they were about to come to blows, which of course meant that Dalflitch would be dead in a trice. Righteous's needle might not be a dagger, but there was no doubt she had one on her person somewhere.

The duchess was delighted and relieved with her third lady's aplomb. While the other two glared balefully at each other, Spindle merely reached over and took Righteous's hand, redirecting it back to the sewing on her lap. Amelia was about to round the entire conversation off by telling Dalflitch to make peace with Turley when Spindle spoke first.

"You shouldn't tease her so, Righteous," the masked maid said. "She can't help it. You know what it's like when such a spirited man looks at you, even when it's in a fury. You know how it flusters you when your husband catches you up in his passion."

"Oh, I do that, Lady Spindle," Righteous replied, and there was a mocking tone in her voice. "You're right. I shouldn't blame her for being breathless and provoked by his ways."

"I am not breathless or provoked!" Dalflitch insisted, her brow knitted and her mouth turned in an uncharacteristic scowl.

"No?" asked Spindle, eyes on her own needlework. "I know I would be. Such a strong man, those shoulders, and them dark eyes he's got. He's a—what's the word ladies use?—a prospect."

"A genuine prospect," Righteous agreed, now obviously warmed to Spindle's topic and mimicking her friend, eyes on her needlework but casting surreptitious glances at Dalflitch.

For her part, Dalflitch opened her mouth in shock. But again, apparently unable to think what to say, she sat back with a dismissive snort. "I don't know what you two are talking about," she said, tossing her head.

"No?" said Spindle. "Then maybe I should give him a whirl. I think I could saddle a buck like him, and I'm sure I'd enjoy the ride."

"Fat chance, seamstress!" Dalflitch slammed her palm down on the mattress. Righteous and Spindle were smirking now and shaking with the obvious effort of keeping from laughing.

Amelia found herself regarding the three women as if she was watching a performance, with three actresses playing gossips. "What is going on here?" she asked them.

"Honestly, Your Grace, I have no idea," Dalflitch answered readily but too sulkily to be as dignified as she was obviously hoping to be. Amelia was about to ask the other two when Righteous suddenly threw down her half-embroidered lion and fixed Dalflitch with an exasperated expression.

"Oh, for God's sake, tell her!" she all but commanded.

"Tell me what?" asked Amelia.

"I'm sure I don't know..." was all Dalflitch managed to get out before Righteous cut her off once more.

"She's sweet on him. Surely you can see it, Your Grace?"

"Sweet?"

"Deep sweet," Spindle concurred. "She writes poems 'bout him and everything."

"I do not," Dalflitch protested but half-heartedly.

"No?" Spindle challenged.

"You can't even read. You don't know what I write."

"Her Grace can," said Righteous. "Bring 'em to her. She'll read 'em fine. Then we'll know if they're poems or not."

Dalflitch looked stricken by the suggestion, eyes wide as she looked to her mistress.

"But all the hostility? The angry looks?" Amelia was still struggling to put everything together in her mind.

"She's sweet, but he's draggin' his feet, Your Grace," Spindle explained. "She wants him to ask your permission to marry."

"Marry? How long has this been going on?" Amelia looked to Dalflitch, but the former countess had hung her head in misery by this point, apparently shamed to have her secret out. Spindle was happy to answer for her.

"Since you all got back from the west, Your Grace. She sat by his bedside as he healed, tending his arm and mopping his brow. Any moment you let her free, she was there with him."

"Truly?"

Dalflitch looked up. Her eyes were becoming moist with shame. "He saved me Your Grace. I was sure I was going to die that day, and then he pulled me on that horse. He deflected Robant's blade with his bare hand. His bare hand, the fool. That stroke was meant to kill me. It's my fault Turley lost the use of his left arm."

"And he *is* easy on the eyes," Righteous added.

Dalflitch shot her another glance, but this one was much less hostile. When she looked back to Amelia, she merely shrugged and then nodded sadly. Suddenly all the unspoken communications between the two of them made sense to Amelia. Dalflitch didn't hate Turley. She was frustrated with him. She wanted him to step up to his duty and ask permission to marry.

"So why hasn't he asked me yet? Is he playing her false?"

Dalflitch shook her head, an even greater look of horror on her face. The notion clearly terrified her. Even Spindle looked serious as she answered Amelia's question.

"Might be, Your Grace," said Spindle. "He's been a rake in his time, we all know that."

Righteous didn't agree. "He's scared, Your Grace. He knows what he's supposed to do, but he doesn't know how it's done. It's like with Prentice. He knew he wanted me, and I promise you, I ain't never been loved like I am in that man's eyes. But I fair had to whip him to get him to speak with you."

"You spoke with me yourself, as I recall," said Amelia.

"You see? These men, they spent so many years on that damn chain. Fetters on their feet so long they got into their souls, leastwise a bit. That's why I prod Prentice so much, to remind him he's a bloody man, and one of the best ones too! Damn fool. He'll throw himself at a monster without a moment's thought, but he's scared of embarrassing you, Your Grace. I think they both are. They're free by your hand and they'll be in your debt to the day they die. They'd go back on the chain, I swear, before they shamed you by doing the wrong thing."

"Is that true?" Amelia asked softly.

Every other woman in the room shrugged, but they all knew it was true. The duchess could see that easily. It overawed her for a moment. She trusted Prentice and Turley utterly, almost without thinking, but to see this deep loyalty in such hard men spelled out so nakedly was a little shocking. She blinked and swallowed.

"You love him?" she asked Dalflitch.

"I think I do," came the answer. Then the lady shook her head. "No, I've been married to a count and lain with a prince, but this man? He is the first man I have ever loved, Your Grace."

"Then why not come to me yourself? Righteous did, back when she was nothing more than a corporal in the militia. You know I'd permit it and bless you for it."

"I wanted to, Your Grace. But Righteous is right. Turley's a man, maybe more of a man than all the courtiers I've ever known. More even than Daven Marcus imagines himself to be. Turley and I both have our sins, and he has admitted to me there might be one or more illegitimates in his past, but we wanted to do this the right way. I can't explain it, Your Grace. Perhaps the sermonizers have started to get through to me."

"I am happy for you," Amelia told her. "And as soon as he gets back, I will tell him it's time for him to ask my permission, manliness be damned." She smiled a moment, and then her hand flew to her mouth. "Oh god! I've sent him over the river. Oh, dear Dalflitch, I'm so sorry. You must be desperately afraid."

"I am, Your Grace," Dalflitch admitted, and she hung her head once more.

"We'll pray for their safety tonight," Amelia told her, and the lady nodded thankfully.

"Don't worry too much, m'lady," said Spindle comfortingly. "Whatever God made that man out of, it's strong enough to make steel envious. Even with only one arm, there's no one I'd bet on against him."

"Except my man," said Righteous, and she looked about the room defiantly. Dalflitch fetched a kerchief from her sleeve and used it to dab her eyes.

"We can't all be as lucky, or clever, in love as you are, Lady Righteous," she said, straightening herself upright. The two women met each other's gaze, and for the first time, Amelia felt she saw something like respect for each other in their expressions.

"I'll pray with you tonight too, Lady Dalflitch," said Righteous. Dalflitch nodded politely.

"You neither of you know how lucky you got it," said Spindle, eyes on her work. "I'll join you all at prayer, but know I'm still sparing a breath for me self and a husband of my own like I do every night."

"Fair enough," said Amelia, and she remembered her own widowed estate. She still missed her husband Marne at times, but mostly these days she was comforted by the fact that Daven Marcus wasn't going to replace him. She'd offer thanks to the Lord again for that tonight, in amongst praying for Prentice and Turley's safe return.

CHAPTER 25

"Why don't we just use the bridge?" whispered Turley as he and Prentice manhandled a tiny, wood-framed leather coracle through the riverside marsh. "Kingdom boys has got the thing under their hands. I seen 'em as we went past that day we took the duchess to the king."

"They only have control of the north end," said Prentice. "No one knows what forces the Redlanders have on the south side. You know how well their soldiers can hide."

"That's true."

"And what's happened to your accent?" Prentice asked him. "I thought you'd learned to speak like a proper houseman?"

"I have," said Turley, somewhat defensively. "But when it's all private like this, I like to remember to speak as I was raised."

"An important tradition to maintain, I am sure."

"Besides, there's some folk quite like a common turn o' phrase, leastwise in some moments." Turley's voice softened a moment as he spoke.

"Folk like pretty ladies, maybe?" Prentice needled.

Turley didn't answer the question. The mud sucked at the two men's feet as they shoved and scrambled toward the water's edge. The light of the Rampart was glittering gently on the surface of the water.

"When were you going to tell me?" Prentice asked.

"Tell you what?"

"About Dalflitch."

"How...?" Turley cursed under his breath. "Bloody Righteous. You should do something about your wife. She's a scold and a gossip."

"Is that right?"

"You know it is."

"And you think I am going to take your side against my wife?" There was a cold edge to Prentice's tone that made it clear what he thought about being told how to relate to his spouse.

"You think I should keep my nose out of your marriage?" Turley whispered, managing to sound defiant even while keeping quiet. "Maybe you could show me the same respect."

"I am not disrespecting you. Love the woman or do not. That's up to you. I just don't know why you didn't come to me for help. You know I would smooth the way for you if I could. Introductions and advocacy. I have some influence now, you know."

"Oh, so that's what this is about? I ain't given you enough chance to be lord of the castle over me. Forgive me, Captain, I didn't know I owed you so much fealty." Turley made to mockingly tug his forelock, but even while he was halfway through the gesture, Prentice whirled in place and furiously pointed a finger at Turley's face.

"Do not," he commanded with a voice like iron, even though still a whisper. "Not ever."

In the night dark the two men could only just see each other's silhouettes. They certainly couldn't see their eyes or make out expressions. Nonetheless, they understood each other.

"Sorry," said Turley. "I just. I get nervous is all and...dammit, this whole thing'd be easier if she was just some milkmaid."

"And even if it wasn't easier," said Prentice, "if it was just some farmer giving you grief because he didn't want you to sully his daughter's reputation with your convict past, I would still stand beside you then. And vouch with my whole honor."

"Course you would," Turley conceded.

Prentice turned back. He was surprised at the strength of the emotion inside himself. He really was insulted that his old friend had kept this secret from him. "What have I got to lord over you, anyway? It is because of you that we have a duchess still ruling over us at all, instead of that bastard, the Prince of Rhales."

"I didn't know you saw it like that," Turley whispered as they finally got close enough to the water for their feet to splash and the coracle to start floating of its own accord.

"How did you think I saw it?"

"Like I was...I don't know...just a servant, I guess. I only got one good arm, now. You're the hero captain of the White Lions. You do the fighting and get the glory and I'm holding silver trays and sayin' 'Yes, Your Grace' and 'No, Your Grace.'"

"Well, here is your chance for more glory," said Prentice, readying himself to jump into the little craft. He put both hands on the side and pushed up. "Let's go."

Turley made to leap in as well, but with only one strong arm, he missed his grip and slipped into the water with a quiet splash. He came up spluttering but obviously trying not to make too much sound.

"You alright?" asked Prentice.

"Just remembering what glory tastes like," Turley answered and spat out the taste of the river mud. "What did Gant call it? Ditchwater?"

"I remember."

Prentice sat still while his now sopping-wet friend clambered into the coracle. Neither of them were wearing armor. Even if they hadn't been trying to keep quiet, a river crossing in armor, in the dark, was a recipe for disaster. He wondered if the Redlanders, with their magical boats and waterman skills, would find a crossing like this such a challenge.

Once they were both set, they grabbed up little wooden paddles and began to push toward the opposite shore and then upstream.

"Where're we hoppin' out?" asked Turley.

"Not until we round the bank and are in that side stream," Prentice explained. "The farther we go on the water, the less chance we'll get noticed. I hope."

With gentle strokes of their oars, they pushed themselves upriver parallel with the south shore. Every limb was tight with the tension and even the slightest noise grated on their nerves. Frogs gulped and insect wings buzzed. A night bird cooed somewhere on the riverbank, answered by a similar call from farther south.

"Damn it," Turley cursed as they neared the corner where they would turn course onto the tributary.

"What is it?"

"Me oar's caught on something." They began to slip backward in the current, and Prentice fought to keep their position as Turley pulled his wet oar across his lap to figure out what was wrong. "It's an old net, I think," he said, working hard to free his oar with only one good hand.

"It's likely there are more of them in the water," said Prentice. "We will have to keep an eye out."

With so many local peasants having fled or been slain in the region, river fishers would have abandoned any number of nets in the shallows. At last, they reached the bend and turned. Almost immediately the water's flow increased, and they had to labor harder to make headway.

"This is taking too long," Prentice said when he realized they had been paddling for nearly a quarter of an hour and were still barely past the mouth of the tributary. "We will do better ashore now."

They steered toward the riverbank and found a stand of weeping willows there. Under the drooping branches, the dark was utterly impenetrable, and they slipped and staggered over roots as they dragged the coracle up out of the water. When they were confident their boat was well enough hidden, they checked their weapons. Prentice wore his basket-hilted Captain's sword, with its two-lion pattern, on a baldric. His buckler shield was held to it with a metal clip. The captain would have liked to bring his partisan, a long-hafted spear with a winged blade, but such a weapon was not conducive to stealth.

For his part, Turley was carrying a flanged steel mace. He had owned it since he returned with the duchess from the west, and it was becoming something of a symbol for him in the household. Normally, it hung from hooks on the wall of the Dweltford castle kitchens, but he'd packed it when the duchess marched south and seemed quite happy for this chance to pull it from his luggage. He hefted the heavy-headed weapon, one handed, onto his shoulder. Both men also had dirks sheathed at their belts. The ideal for this night's work was that they would not be seen or heard, but they'd come prepared for the less than ideal.

Stealing southward, the riverside grasses gave them excellent cover and they kept low the whole way. Nevertheless, with the darkness the going was slow, and they made much more noise than they would have liked.

"Where are their sentries?" Prentice asked as he looked up to their left.

Even with all their mystic powers, he had expected the Redlanders to maintain a basic watch. Had the south bank been this empty the whole time, or were they missing, especially this night? He and Turley had come far enough south now that they were almost level with the town itself. There were few torch lights in the streets behind the wall, and the shadows of the battlements were blotting out stars so that its silhouette could be easily made out. Soon, the little river would twist farther east toward the town, and still they had encountered no enemies.

Turley might have been about to offer an opinion, when, as if summoned by Prentice's question, they heard the sound of someone tromping through the long grasses and caught the glimmers of a candle lamp. Whoever was coming, they were moving reasonably fearlessly and muttering to themselves.

"Alive," Prentice whispered, leaning in so that his mouth was almost on his friend's ear.

He felt rather than saw Turley nod, and the two of them crouched to stalk the lone figure as it approached the river. Apparently, it was a night fisher, because he stopped at the water and began hauling in nets and checking the catch. He had his lamp on the ground by his feet. With the noise of his work, it was an easy matter for Prentice and Turley to sneak up and take him unawares. Turley aimed a gentle swing of the mace at the back of the man's knees, not to injure him, but to bring him down. Prentice seized the man by the shoulder, hoping to bring him to the ground quietly and get his dirk to the man's throat. The whole action went smoother than expected, and the fisherman ended up on his back, barely resisting. Prentice was still trying to bring his dagger up to threaten with when the man began tugging at the collar of his tunic, pulling it down to reveal some kind of scar or mark on his flesh.

"Supple'cant," the man protested. "Supple'cant."

Prentice looked at him. "Do you mean supplicant?" he asked.

"Aye, that's the word," answered the fisher, then something dawned on him and he visibly relaxed, his eyes rolling. "That's a kingdom accent? You from the north?"

"That's right," Turley hissed, thumping his mace into the mud beside the man's head. "So just you watch yourself."

"Or what?" the man scoffed. "Least you lot won't eat me."

"Eat you?" Turley blinked, and Prentice didn't blame him. There were rumors of cannibalism amongst the Redlanders, but he had always assumed they were just that—rumors.

"That's right," said the fisherman. "They took me brother and sliced him up like a ham."

"Well, that's a bloody horror," said Turley. "You here by yourself? And don't lie to me. I won't eat you, but one hit and I can make porridge out of your brains all the same."

The man nodded, looking a little cautious once more. "It's just me, kingdom man, I swear."

"What is that mark?" asked Prentice. "Why did you say you were a supplicant?" He pulled at the man's collar and then seized up the candle lamp for a better look. There was a circular tattoo there with a series of six sigils written around the circumference.

"It's the only way for sure to keep living," the fisherman explained. "They make you swear to their gods, you drink some foul muck they make in a cup. Then they put a mark on you and that's how they know to eat you last."

"Eat you last...?" Turley repeated, but Prentice cut him off.

"You joined their religion? You're a convert, an apostate?"

"I don't even know what that is," the man answered. "But it sounds like sacrist talk, an' what do I care 'bout that? Princes tax you and make you kneel. Sacrists tax you and make you kneel to God. Sect priests don't just tax, they take your flesh and blood. They're a damn sight more terrifying. If mumbling some words and getting their silly tattoo'll keep me and mine from ending up on a plate, then so be it."

"Tattoo? You're becoming one of their painted soldiers?" asked Turley, now sounding truly aghast.

"Don't be daft. They don't let Veckanders join their brotherhoods. It's hard enough to get them to let you keep a butter knife. If you get this mark, they let you stand at the back while the priests do their mumbo jumbo and cut some other poor fella or lass into chum. It's a touch bloodier than what the sacrists did, but not much different other'n that."

In spite of his own history with the Church, Prentice found himself appalled at the man's calculated change of religion, even for the sake of survival. But as he thought about it, he realized he was not truly shocked. A clergy who practiced their faith for themselves instead of for a love of truth or of God would only ever produce an oppressed, cynical congregation who would do as this man did, changing his religious conviction for survival or convenience. Prentice would have liked the chance to question the man at length. There were so many things about the Redlanders that he just did not know. But they didn't have time for that.

"Cut some of the rope off those nets," he told Turley, who went immediately to the task.

"Oh, not me brother's nets," the fisherman whined. "I needs them to live. The sect folk don't eat our foods so much, but they like fish."

"Shut up," Prentice ordered, slapping the man with the hilt of his dagger. "The rope's to tie you up. The better you behave and the more clearly you answer my questions, the kinder the knots will be. Make trouble and we'll just slit your throat and throw you in the river. Not eaten but just as dead. Understand?"

The man nodded, and Prentice was glad he looked suitably fearful.

"Now, you work the riverside, so you can tell me. How many boats do the Redlanders have?"

"The what?"

"The invaders. How many boats are in the port in Aubrey?"

"I don't know, but a lot. Must be 'least half what they come down the Murr in."

"Half?"

"That's what I figure. Last year they had their brotherhoods out on the boats, animal folk and skin mark'd. They were sailing up and down the river to raid. Even through winter. They even stopped killing Aubrey folk, 'cause they were bringing in so many prisoners. Then the spring come, and they started keeping the boats in port. That's why I'm doing so fine a trade with fish and why they let me out here from the town to catch 'em. So many brotherhood men in town needin' to feed. They don't feed their prisoners so good, but who does?"

"Only the men?" Prentice asked, wondering about the serpent-woman that had attacked his camp before.

"Brotherhood's only the men," the fisherman said. "The women's are all in the sect priests, except for the snake maids.

And where'n ever *they* are, there ain't many in town, thank God."

Thank God? Prentice thought. *Does this fool not know what faith he believes?* A dark thought occurred to Prentice about the man under his knife, and his lips pursed tight.

"Is that good enough answers? You gonna let me go now?" the fisherman asked, eager but not truly desperate.

"One more thing. Are they doing anything with their boats? Something big? Something special?"

"Like what? They sleep on 'em, if that's what you mean?"

"Sleep on them? They're not billeted in the town?"

"Oh, there's a load in the houses what have been emptied, 'cause those families's already gone to the altars, but those're sect folk. The magical ones, mostly. One of 'em lives on my street now. Used to be screams in that house every night, but it's been quiet since winter."

"And the rest sleep on their boats?"

"It's like they're afraid of the land or something."

That explains the lack of an encampment, thought Prentice. The "brotherhoods," as this man called them, must be close with each other. It would also account for their battlefield discipline if they were all crews of the same craft and slept together every night. Soldiers who lived and trained so close to each other always had a definite advantage. It was part of what worked so well with the White Lions.

"And all their boats are intact?"

"I don't know."

"Come on, man," Prentice pushed. "Have you seen them break any apart or make changes. Say, tying some together?"

"Oh sure, some. They use a lot of the prisoners for that work, too. Fetch and carry. Why, kingdom man? You runnin' out of convicts to do your labor?"

Prentice sucked on his teeth angrily at the man's taunt, but Turley returned with rope cut from the nets before he could say anything about it. Prentice pointed at their prisoner's feet.

"Ankles and then wrists, behind his back," he ordered, and Turley set to work.

"You're tying me up, so you ain't gonna kill me, right?" the man pressed, not resisting as Turley trussed him up. Prentice scowled and raised his dirk in front of the man's face, grey-blue eyes narrowed until they were angry slits.

"You say these are your brother's nets and there's an occupied house on your street. Your brother's already been sacrificed and you're a supplicant. How did they choose your brother?"

"What?" The man's expression became truly fearful for the first time. "What do you mean?"

"I am willing to bet it's not your street you live on, but your brother's, isn't it?" said Prentice. It was the man's comfortable demeanor that made him suspicious. Attacked by two men in the middle of the night and this fisherman had barely seemed perturbed. This was a man used to playing all the angles and talking himself out of almost any trouble, Prentice was sure of it. "You offered your brother up, didn't you? That is how you became a supplicant, how you proved your loyalty to their dark gods? Is it not?"

"Bastard," Turley breathed as he tied the man's wrists. The fisherman turned away, a sour frown on his lips. He looked more churlish than guilty.

"It's not like that," was all he said.

"Why do I not believe you?" said Prentice, and he felt the weight of the dagger in his hand. This vile man had sold out his own brother and taken his home and trade to appease the Redlanders and save his own skin. Prentice wanted to kill the man. He deserved it.

Vengeance is mine, the words of scripture sounded in Prentice's mind. *I will repay.*

"Little sod deserves to die," hissed Turley.

"No, I don't," the man objected. "I only done what was needed. To survive."

"You turned on your brother and your God," said Turley more vehemently, turning the man over to look him directly in the face. "You deserve to die."

"Maybe," Prentice said. "But not today and not by our hand." Using his dirk, he quickly cut a strip of the man's tunic and stuffed it into his mouth as a gag. The fisherman tried to fight against that, but to no avail. Prentice slapped Turley on the shoulder. "I think I've seen enough. Let's head back to the bridge."

"The bridge?" Turley asked as Prentice led them inland away from the treacherous fisher and his guttering candle lamp. "Why are we going to the bridge?"

"We aren't. I just said that so that if anyone finds him before we are done, he'll send them looking for us somewhere we definitely won't be."

"I thought I was supposed to be the cunning one."

"I thought so, too."

Prentice gave his friend a wink, then realized he wouldn't be able to see it in the dark. After heading inland a short distance, they turned southward once more. Prentice wanted to get as close as he could to the docks. He was developing a strong idea what the Redlanders might be planning, but he had to see for himself. He had to be sure.

"You know, now that I think of it," Turley whispered a little while later, "if they do find that fisher, and he gives 'em your bum steer, his new pagan masters won't be too happy with him."

"I would not expect so," said Prentice.

"How do you think they'll punish him?"

"There is a good chance he will end up as a sacrifice himself, I would guess."

"That's what you're hoping for, ain't it?" asked Turley. Prentice did not answer him, but Turley took the silence for an admission. "Oh ho, I might be supposed to be the cunning one, but you are an iron cold son of a bitch, Captain Prentice Ash."

They were silent then for the rest of the short journey around the corner of Aubrey and towards its docks, sometimes so close that they had to watch out for garden fences of the outskirt houses.

CHAPTER 26

Amelia and her ladies finished their prayers and dressed for bed. She had just settled onto her mattress and pulled the sheets around her when an insistent hand began to knock on the partition door. From the next bed where Spindle and Righteous slept, one of the two went to the door and slid back the wooden bolt. A hurried, whispered conversation was held, and presently Spindle was at her bedside.

"If it please, Your Grace, the servant must speak with you."

"Very well," said the duchess.

By the time she had thrown back her cover, Spindle had already laid out slippers for her feet and Dalflitch was bringing a robe to put about her shoulders. Meanwhile, Righteous was at the door, making sure the messenger didn't presume to enter her grace's chamber. A candle was lit, and Amelia went to the door to speak with the messenger.

"Begging your pardon, Your Grace," said the man, tugging his forelock. "I don't mean to overstep, but the chief steward is out of the household and the messenger insisted the matter was in haste."

Amelia wondered what message could have come in haste at this time. Were the Redlanders attacking? And if they were, what did that mean for Turley and Prentice across the river? She held out her hand for the message, but the man in the doorway only looked at her, uncomprehending.

"Well," Dalflitch urged on her mistress's behalf. "Where is the message?"

"Oh, 'tweren't nothing written on paper, Lady." The man tugged his forelock again. "Your Grace, 'tis a herald come from the king to escort you to an audience, he says."

"Now?"

"So 'says, Your Grace. He's waiting downstairs right now."

An urgent summons in the night? That was not something she expected and had no idea what it might mean. She cocked an eyebrow to Dalflitch across the candle glow.

"You suspect an arrest, Your Grace?" the lady asked in a whisper.

"Bailiffs don't ask politely," Righteous countered just as quietly.

"Kings don't send bailiffs to arrest duchesses," said Dalflitch. "They send heralds. Or men-at-arms if they expect danger."

Amelia worked her mind to think as swiftly as she could. It was possible that the king had learned of her contact with Prince Forsyte, but she was sure she could explain herself if she got the chance. She'd been hammering at the king's door for days to speak with him; if she was challenged for her meeting with Forsyte, she could always argue that she had been trying to inform the king the whole time and thus been keeping no secrets. It wasn't even that far from the truth. The only people who knew for certain she had agreed to act on the prince's behalf were men she counted on for absolute loyalty. Any accusation would come down to the prince's word against hers, and she was confident nationality would trump rank in this case. A Reacherman duchess would beat a Vec prince in any Grand Kingdom court.

So, what does the king want?

Had Daven Marcus won his father over? That could bring the whole marriage issue back into play. In fact, knowing the Prince of Rhales's fondness for rushed actions without warning, it was possible she was being summoned for a nocturnal wedding.

"I need time to send for an escort, some men from Sir Gant," she said to herself as the servant stood by attentively. "Offer the herald victuals and some of the fine beer. Give him reason to be delayed while we surreptitiously get some extra lions up here."

"Pardon, Your Grace," said the servant, "but we already offered 'freshment and the herald, he turned it down. He said he would wait ready for you ladies to dress, and then he was to take you straight to the king. He said he's even brought a carriage for you."

No time for an escort. But a carriage? That gave her some options.

"Go now and tell the herald we are dressing. We will join him presently."

The servant accepted the command and withdrew. Amelia turned to see that Spindle had already lit rushlights from the banked night fire and was in the process of laying out a gown for her. "Good woman. Once you've set that out, look to your own dress. All of you."

"All of us, Your Grace?" asked Dalflitch.

"I will not attend the king alone," Amelia answered. "It would not be seemly. Oh, and Spindle? Righteous? When you dress, why don't you see how much cutlery you can fit under your skirts, hmm?"

All three ladies-in-waiting looked up sharply at that command.

"You thinking it'll be trouble, Your Grace?" asked Righteous.

Amelia nodded and swallowed. "I hope not, but I don't like leaving at night without an escort. And your husband would not approve either. If all goes well, you both will just have some extra weight to carry tonight. But if it goes poorly, you'll not only be our last line of defense, you'll be our only line."

Both women seemed more than happy with that notion as they set about readying themselves. Even in the dim light, Amelia caught at least one flash of steel in amongst their garments. It wasn't as comforting as she would have liked.

"You know that if the king plans our arrest, two ladies with daggers won't be enough," whispered Dalflitch as she laced Amelia's bodice. "Not against men-at-arms with mail coats and swords."

"Perhaps not, but I'm not going unequipped into any battle ever again. Maybe we aren't up to the skirmish, but I'll be damned if I go meekly under the shadow of the axe. Are you with me, Lady Dalflitch?"

"It cost a man his hand and arm to save me last time, Your Grace. A man I hold in great esteem. Let's at least make it cost them something too, this time."

"Lord willing it won't come to that, My Lady," said Amelia, but she was pleased to hear her resolve echoed in her companion's words.

It took nearly half an hour for the four women to dress to a minimum standard for an audience with the sovereign of the Grand Kingdom. Amelia descended the tower with her ladies-in-waiting to find a man of middling age standing respectfully in full regalia, wearing a royal red surcoat that hung to mid-thigh, edged in gold thread, with the royal eagle on the front. He had a broad-brimmed leather hat trimmed with dyed feathers in crimson and gold, which he snatched from his head at Amelia's arrival, then bowed low with a broad sweep of his arm.

"Your Grace, Duchess Amelia of the Western Reach," he intoned ritualistically but with a professional smoothness that spoke of a long career as a royal herald. "His sovereign majesty, King Chrostmer the Fourth, bids me come to you and escort you unto an audience. A carriage awaits outside."

"Thank you," Amelia answered him with a polite nod.

How else did one respond to an invitation that had the full force of law, no matter how polite? She gestured for the herald to escort her to the waiting carriage, and as he turned, she followed. When they reached the tower door, the herald turned back and noted the other three women close with them.

"Your ladies...?" he began to ask, but Amelia was ready for his objection.

"Will be coming with me," she told him.

He looked momentarily embarrassed, and his poise slipped as he obviously reached for the polite way to refuse. Amelia allowed him no chance to do so. "You surely do not expect me to wait upon the king without my necessary attendants?"

The herald blinked twice and then smiled a perfectly polite, if somewhat unctuous, smile. "Of course not, Your Grace."

My words can have the force of law as well, Amelia thought to herself smugly as she followed the man out to the waiting carriage. *Or very nearly.*

She seated herself with her three ladies, and as the carriage was driven away into the night, she wondered just how much "cutlery" Righteous and Spindle had managed to secret on their person while inwardly praying they wouldn't need one bit of it.

CHAPTER 27

Keeping to the shadows, Prentice and Turley managed to track back to the river right at the point where it became a dockside, fired-brick walls giving the water's edge an orderly structure. Where the little tributary turned along the south side of Aubrey, it was more like a walled canal than a river. One bank had long wooden wharfs that extended south into the flow. On the opposite bank, the waterway spread narrow canals southward, like fingers of a hand, and down each canal, on either side, were pier works for loading and offloading boats of many sizes. Even in the dark, the two men marveled, for although Aubrey was only about the same size as the Reach capital Dweltford, the Vec town had at least three times the docklands. Its trade must have been vast, at least once. Now, the entire waterway, every dock and wharf, had a Redlander boat tied to it, and on the water in between the two banks, the many craft were so tightly packed together that it would be possible to walk from the north bank to the south without touching the water once.

"One wagon load of black powder and we could halve their force," whispered Turley as they looked at the myriad glimmering torchlights bobbing on the river flow.

"We'd need to get it on a boat," Prentice responded. His friend's idea wasn't a bad one, just not an easy one to execute. "And we'd want it in the middle of them."

"True enough. What about some oil? We could float it on the water at night and start a fire."

Another reasonable idea, but Prentice's mind gave him immediate objections once again. "We'd need a barge load, and we'd need to dump it into the water up stream. That's the other side of the town. Otherwise, it'd all just wash the wrong way and do nothing."

"Well, I don't hear you making any suggestions."

Prentice slapped him on the shoulder. "Let's see if we can get closer before we decide on a strategy."

They crept forward and came to a pile of bales stacked higher than a man, which made a perfect hiding place. They clambered up the bound cloth sides of the bales. When they got to the top, Turley pointed to an emblem printed in faded ink on the canvass of one of them.

"That's Reach wool," he whispered. "All the way down from Dweltford, by the merchant's mark." He sniffed the air as they crawled like stalking cats across the top of the enormous mound. "Ugh, mildew. This stuff's ruined. How long have they left it out here?"

"All through the winter, by the smell of it," Prentice agreed. "Be careful; if it's well-rotted, we might slip into it and end up trapped."

"Or make enough ruckus to draw their guards down on us."

"Most likely."

The two men became even more cautious, spreading their bodyweight as flat as they could, slithering across the stinking wool bales and watching for any sign that they might not support their mass. At last, they were at the edge of the spongy edifice and looked down on the docks proper.

"Well, this ain't the only bit o' trade gone to rot," said Turley.

Looking across the once prosperous economic center, it was obvious how true his words were. Even with only torchlight, the wreckage on the docks was unmistakable. Crates and barrels lay broken and scattered in every direction, their contents

spilled upon the brick harborside. Mostly it was goods that lay
discarded, making Prentice think that the Redlanders were only
plundering food, but even there, it seemed the invaders were
particular in their tastes. Mounds of grain—wheat, oats, and
rye—were piled up here and there, and in the sparse light, it was
clear they'd been there long enough for the seed to sprout, so
that the mounds resembled little hummocks of grass growing
on the dock.

"What is it these bastards want?" Turley asked, surveying
the wasteful destruction. "They don't take gold, treasure, or
prisoners. Not even food."

"Revenge," Prentice said without thinking, but as soon as the
words were out of his mouth, he knew it was true.

"For what?"

"I have no idea." But Prentice was reminded of the scholar
Solft's animals again, the subtle, seemingly passing reference
to a grudge so ancient that no one in the Grand Kingdom
remembered it and even the written histories didn't understand
it.

"Have we seen enough yet?" asked Turley as he nervously
shifted his weight on the bales beneath him.

"Almost."

Prentice scanned the boats on the water and across the docks,
straining his eyes to pierce the ill-lit darkness. What were they
planning? He had only a vague idea what to look for, but after
a long moment of silence, he thought he'd spotted it.

"Down there," he said, pointing to the far end of the docks.
"Does that look like construction to you?"

"It all looks like rubbish, if you ask me," Turley said without
thinking but then followed his friend's pointing finger. "Looks
like, I guess...maybe a tower? No, it's like a bridge, but pointing
in the air. A drawbridge, maybe...?" He looked a little while
longer. "For a very narrow moat? And there's another one. And
another."

"I count six at least," said Prentice. "And they're moving them."

The two men watched as the short, broad, bridge-like constructs, held upright, were being maneuvered to the edge of the docks and then somehow out in amongst the boats.

"They're floating 'em on the water," Turley muttered.

"We have to go now," said Prentice realizing what was happening. "We have to get word to the army."

"Why? What's the hurry?"

"That is a bridge," he told his friend. "I thought they would come on their boats, two or three crews at a time. But if they line those six up across the Murr, they can march an army straight over, fast and safe as the bridge we've already got."

"And they're coming now. Where're they going to line it up though?"

"Well, if it was me, I would go straight at the White Lions before anyone in the king's camp had a chance to respond."

"You think they fear us that much?" Turley sounded almost pleased at the prospect.

"It isn't about fear; it's strategy," Prentice corrected him. "Why fight your enemy in one big, tough battle, when you can fight a smaller part of his army in an easier battle first? Destroy him piecemeal."

"Like setting the hounds on a bear before you face it yourself?"

"Similar. And if they are fast and strong enough, they could smash the Lions with their full force and then retreat across the river and take their bridge with them."

"Well, that's a pack o' mongrels," said Turley, expressing his disgust at the prospect.

"It will take them time to get the whole thing into place. If we go now, we will be able to raise the alarm in time, I think," said Prentice. He began to slither backwards.

"What the hell's that?"

Turley's question caused him to stop and look to the other end of the dock once more. Behind the six bridge boats, a seventh construct was bobbing out among the Redlander fleet. It was even taller than the bridge pieces, heavier and sturdier looking. It must have been built on multiple boats lashed together—a wooden frame almost as tall as the walls of Aubrey. There were lanterns hanging at various points around it, so they could make out its shape.

"What's on its sides?" asked Turley as the two of them stopped their escape to figure out what exactly they were looking at.

So, this is the worse thing? Prentice thought. What was it and what was it for?

The towering wooden frame floated out into the tributary, and there were shouts echoing across the water as a way was made amongst the moored boats for it to pass. The Redlanders' water skill was apparent as the whole fleet made sail and left a channel for the tower and six bridge pieces. Prentice knew he had to return with warning of this coming invasion, but he felt himself frozen in place as the tower came closer. Somehow, he knew he must see it. He must understand it. A horrible, twisting need in his gut held him in place, even as painted boat crews came ashore nearby on the dock to use ropes to maneuver their craft out of the way of the processional seven.

"It's getting a bit chancy 'round here," Turley muttered nervously.

Prentice knew he was right, but neither of them moved. They were transfixed by the approaching craft. Eventually, even the six bridge boats moved aside for the tower. As it drew close, a new sound could be heard, an agonized moaning. It rose and fell over the water, and combined with growing torchlight, suddenly the two friends understood what they were looking at. All about the wooden frame, their arms spread wide, were people nailed in place and drenched in something that had to be oil or pitch.

This was a floating altar, crucifixion, and funeral pyre all in one. And they were witnessing its ritual sacrifice.

Prentice felt himself trembling and he began to rise involuntarily, swaying on the unstable rot beneath him. So many emotions roared through him that it felt like a tempestuous flood that would sweep him away. His heart broke for the dying, their mournful suffering making him want to weep. His stomach twisted at the unspeakable wrongness of this pagan insanity. But more than all these, he felt the rage, the burning, angelic fury that screamed for judgement and wrath to fall on this scene. It took all his will not to draw his sword and throw himself at the river to slay as many of these fiends as he could before they ripped him to pieces with their animalistic power.

"Who's the poor bastard on top, d'you think?" whispered Turley in a horrified tone, and Prentice cast his eyes upward.

Standing on the bales, Prentice was still a long way from the height of the pyre's top, but it let him see clearly as the construct floated closer. At the peak of the frame was a cross, two simple pieces of wood, like might be seen in any church in a thousand village parishes. And nailed to the cross was a man, stripped to the waist and painted with tattooed sigils. His body was also soaked with the oil, but his face was strangely visible. Prentice wondered if he was having another religious vision, so clear was the man's identity to him.

"It's Prince Forsyte."

"What?" asked Turley. "That's the prince Veckander who met with the duchess? What's he doing here?"

"His son was in prison in the city," Prentice answered. "Maybe he grew impatient waiting for our king, and he tried to sneak him out himself."

"And they caught him? Poor bastard."

They watched aghast, barely giving a thought for stealth anymore. The horror of what they were witnessing overrode their minds. Soon, the towering pyre was at the very front of the fleet, nearly even with where Prentice and Turley stood, with not more than fifty paces between them and it. The intervening space was so empty that they could see figures moving about on the boats at the structure's footings, guiding it into place. These figures moved with the inhuman nature of the Redlander beastmen, and it was easy enough to pick out some types by their movement, especially serpent figures, and one with an enormous pair of bull's horns sprouting from his skull.

Some signal must have been given because the guides on the craft quickly stepped away onto other boats and the pyre floated free on the current. It wasn't even ten paces ahead of the fleet when the first flames began to lick up its sides. The oil-soaked wood caught so fast that it was like a rising storm that rushed upward. The lowest victims screamed almost immediately from pain and the ones above from terror. Already in agony, they yet had more to fear. Only Prince Forsyte kept his mouth resolutely closed and his face was lost to Prentice as the smoke from below rushed past him in a column. Then the flames reached the top and burned the smoke away. In the moment before the inferno engulfed the prince, Prentice thought he saw the man looking up into the sky.

"Take him home, Lord," Prentice muttered a prayer, almost without thinking. He did not count himself as a man of strong faith, but if this was how God's enemies worshipped...?

As the screams began to be engulfed in the roar of the inferno, yet another noise arose—a bestial ululation that rang out from every boat and all along the dockside. The Redlanders were worshipping their demonic gods. The sound melded with the crackling roar of the flames and the pyre leaped upward into the sky. The ferocious heat that bathed the river grew and then suddenly withdrew, as if the flames were sucking their power back into themselves. The column burned even higher into the sky, until it seemed to reach all the way to the Rampart itself. This wasn't just paganism; it was sorcery more powerful than Prentice had even imagined was possible.

Had this ever been seen on the earth before?

"Let us make a tower for ourselves, whose top is in heaven," he recited from the scripture, remembering the hubris of Babel. Was this a tower like that? God had struck that arrogance with confusion. What would the creator do in response to this abomination?

Still the flames burned, and as they did, a dim ruby light began to spread across the sky, growing in intensity. The white of the Rampart was stained pink, then crimson. Soon the sky in every direction, almost to the horizon, was lit with the brutish glow. There was no night anymore. The whole of the land was stained with its light.

"The red land?" Turley muttered, and he sounded as disgusted as Prentice felt.

But something else in this madness drew his attention. "The river," he said and pointed to the water. It was hard to see, but the ruddy light revealed the full power at these Blood Sects' command. The water had stopped flowing. Slowly, but all at once, the crews of the boats moved into action. The ones in the middle of the river began to sail forward on the still water, their sails full of a sorcerous wind that nothing else could feel. The ones near the shore began to disembark and head northward into the city, doubtless planning to go through and on to the Murr to cross the bridge they were floating into place. It seemed that the ritual needed participants in their boats, but the invasion did not.

"We gotta go now! Prentice! Now!"

Turley was near to panic, and in some inner part of himself, Prentice understood why. Already the dock was swarming with close to a thousand enemy, and any moment some of those nearby would certainly see the two men on top of the mound of bales. But Prentice was still struggling to restrain the fury inside himself. He wanted these vile men stopped, ended, purged from the world. It was a need in him so deep it consumed him, so much that it was all he could do not to throw himself at them in a rage. It took all his will to remember that it would take an army. They had to get back across the river and warn the Lions. And the duchess and the king.

And they had to move faster than the enemy.

Prentice nodded to Turley who looked ready to bolt on his own. They both turned to retreat and the rotten wool under them collapsed.

CHAPTER 28

"Your Majesty," Amelia said as clearly as she could, curtseying deeply before King Chrostmer who sat upon his throne in the same audience hall the war council had been held in. She swallowed and hoped she did not seem as nervous as she felt. Behind her, several paces back, her three ladies likewise made their obeisance.

The carriage journey to the king's domicile had been much swifter than the previous one, but if anything, it was more unsettling for its speed. The path through the king's camp seemed shorter somehow and, with the majority of folk already in their beds, much quieter.

"Not so many crowds about," Dalflitch had noted, putting words to at least one of the duchess's worries—fewer witnesses.

When the carriage arrived, they had been escorted through the manor house directly, not through the gardens as before, and Amelia felt virtually whisked into the royal presence. There were torches in sconces on the walls and candles set on stands beside the king. Around the tapestry-hung room she could make out a few men-at-arms, but no more than a king might typically have as bodyguards.

"You have been petitioning for our attention, Duchess Amelia," said the king, using the royal plural, and his voice seemed a little hoarse. Amelia looked up, and in the poor light, the king did seem less vigorous than he had only days ago.

Perhaps he was tired. If he had had to chase Daven Marcus on the way back to Rhales, then he could well have ridden most of the last few nights, depending on how far north the prince had managed to get.

"I have, Your Majesty," she said. "I have an urgent matter to bring before you."

Before Amelia could say anything further, the king held out his signet ring for her to kiss. It was such an ancient formality that it caught her by surprise. The last time she had had to do this had been for the late Prince Mercad. Daven Marcus had never bothered with the ritual. She bobbed again and lowered her head to kiss the signet. When it was done, the king caught her by the chin, preventing her from rising again. He looked into her eyes and studied her face. She swallowed and tried to relax in the uncomfortable position.

"You are not so plain," the king said frankly. "He could at least have made an effort to woo you properly."

Amelia blinked but said nothing and schooled her face to her neutral, courtly expression. King Chrostmer was obviously talking about his son, but there was nothing she could say that would not risk offence. The king sighed and looked past Amelia at her ladies.

"And you would have let him still take some turns with the divorcee, I'm sure."

Amelia knew then that he was looking at Dalflitch. The prince must have told his father about his affair with the former countess, the affair that had cost Dalflitch her rank.

"I would never deny a loving husband anything," Amelia said through gritted teeth. She tried to keep the disgust and resentment out of her voice but was certain she was not succeeding. The king looked back to her, and he had a kindly, world-weary look in his eyes. He released his grip and Amelia bobbed again before stepping back.

"A loving husband?" the king repeated as he sat back. The shadows from the candles masked his face, and Amelia could not read his expression so well anymore. She wondered if she had offended him. "That's the rub, is it not, Duchess?" he said at last.

"Majesty?"

"Did you know he is our fourth child?"

"No, Majesty." Amelia said, surprised, though not by the idea that the king would have other children. A high noble siring a bastard was like a sheep bleating or a cow giving milk. It was almost expected, no matter the sin it implied. What surprised her was that the king was admitting it so readily, or even discussing it with her at all. She held her face in as tight a mask as she could.

"He was the only one that lived," the king went on. "We had two sons who breached the womb but never breathed and a daughter who wailed for but an hour, then passed as well. And then this one. His mother gave her life in his stead, I am sure of it."

Amelia had heard that the queen had died in childbirth with the crown prince, but of only one miscarriage. The queen had been known as a private person, not often seen during her marriage years. Now Amelia knew why. Her pregnancies were being kept secret.

"It took her the rest of the day to die," the king continued, "and we held her hand that last hour. Her damned confessor tried to keep us out of the room, can you believe it? He was in there amongst the maids and ladies and midwives, but her husband and king was to wait outside while she bled away. Oh no! We would not have it!" His face twisted in fury, and Amelia could only imagine what that memory felt like.

Still, she had no idea what to think or how to react. This rambling tale was a prelude to something, but what? Was he about to order the marriage to Daven Marcus after all?

"We were so grief-stricken we refused to look at him for three days," said King Chrostmer. "We didn't hate him; we just had nothing in our heart. No joy. No love. Our darling had taken

that all away with her. Then one of her ladies came to us and..."
He paused in the story, apparently thinking what to say next.
"And gave us comfort. Then she took us to him, and we were
happy to see him. He was so golden and perfect."

*You slept with your wife's handmaid within three days of her
death?* Amelia thought, and her lips nearly revealed her distaste.
She managed to halt the frown, turning her lips into a line and
blinking to keep her brows from knotting. *Like son, like father,
I suppose.*

The king was nearing the end of his story. "We thought he
would be our connection with his mother, a living memory
of her, and we doted on him." The king looked away into the
shadows. "Too much. Much too much."

Amelia risked a glance over her shoulder at her ladies. All
three were watching, fascinated by the king's tale. Amelia met
Dalflitch's eyes, and the lady raised her eyebrows. Both of them
recognized how significant this audience was becoming but not
yet why.

"Our son did not go to Rhales. He is meeting with the full
Conclave of Ecclesiarchs. He claims to have witnesses who will
testify that they saw you say your marriage vows. That you are
his wife gone wayward."

"Your Majesty resolved this," said Amelia. It was like a pain in
her chest to have to face this all over again.

"We did, but he has that reverend master's backing,
apparently. He means to retract your man's absolution as well,
claiming that we extracted it under duress."

What? The duress of having to act honorably in public? Amelia
thought. "I swear, Majesty, I never pledged or vowed to your
son."

"We know," Chrostmer conceded with a sigh. "He's doing
this to get back at us."

So glad I could be a thrown toy in your son's temper tantrum,
she thought.

It was all she could do to not demand the king do his duty as a father and punish the brat. Despite her annoyance, Amelia sensed an opening. The king's relationship with the Church was still in flux, and to have his word overturned by the Conclave would humiliate him. Perhaps this was the time to offer him a chance to make history. The Conclave would likely not want to offend the king who brought a Vec prince to heel.

"Majesty, this news is troubling," she began, working to convey the right emotions and hide her true ones. "And I am sorry for my part in this conflict with your son. But with your indulgence, I must speak with you of the matter that caused me to seek your audience in the first place."

The king blinked and his brows furrowed as he looked at her. "This is not what you wanted to discuss, Duchess?"

"Forgive me, Majesty, but no."

"I had assumed you had heard of my son's actions and were coming to plead with me to stop him."

"No, My King," Amelia said. Before she could stop herself, she added, "I would not pester you so diligently just to discuss the vagaries of my marital condition."

The king cocked another eyebrow.

"Your Majesty, I have been approached by Prince Forsyte of Aubrey. He wishes me to petition you on his behalf." In spite of herself, Amelia felt she rushed those simple sentences. Rushed or not, she knew the king heard her clearly, because he immediately began to shake his head, then rose from his chair and towered over her.

"You have been treating with the Vec?" The furious disbelief in his voice was matched by an angry sneer that caused Amelia to duck her head immediately after a single glance. "And you confess it so readily? Are you the heretical rebel they all say you are after all?"

Amelia did her best not to cringe and tried not to hear the sound of men in armor moving as they readied to respond to their sovereign's offence. She kept her head down and her voice respectfully low. "No, Majesty," she said, shaking her head. "I would never betray the throne or the Grand Kingdom, I swear. The prince came to me in secret, but only the once. Then he withdrew to hide once more. He asked me to beg your royal assistance. His people are being horribly mistreated by the invaders and his need on their behalf is great. He has asked me to plead in his name."

"Plead for what?" demanded the king contemptuously. "His town is in the hands of an enemy, and soon it will be in our hands."

"He fears for the sack of the city, Your Majesty. A second sack."

"Well he should. Our nobles will take the Kingdom's share and then some. He should blame his ancestors, not our army. They brought this fate upon him."

"I think he might be ready to acknowledge exactly that, Your Majesty. Publicly, and before God," Amelia said quietly. For a long moment there was silence, and finally she dared to look directly at the king. On his face she read his thoughts and knew he understood what she and her advisors did also; the chance to make history. But there were other notions there as well. Chrostmer IV had ruled too long and too well not to be at least a little pragmatic.

"I will have the town in my grip, returned to the Grand Kingdom in fact," he mused, sitting back upon his throne. Amelia was so relieved to see his anger abate that she almost didn't notice he had switched from the royal 'we' to the singular 'I,' "What could this renegade prince offer to add to that?"

"He will bend the knee, Majesty."

"No Vec rebel has repented since the rebellion centuries ago."

"Exactly so, Your Majesty."

Amelia was sure the king was coming around to her way of thinking. She just had to resist the temptation to try to push him. He had to get there by himself. Of course, there was still the question of whether Prince Forsyte was willing to give up his sovereignty and return his family line to being mere nobles of the Grand Kingdom, subjects of the Denay throne. If the prince balked, Amelia would be lucky if she came away from this only looking like a fool. But that was a problem for later.

"If he pledges to us," the king thought out loud, "then the town cannot be sacked. Pillage will have to be curtailed. The great houses will not be pleased with that. They've waited more than a year for their share of plunder."

"I am sure you are right, Majesty," Amelia agreed. She'd been considering this objection since Sir Gant had raised it that night in her tower. She hoped her solution would be sufficient. "A new crusade, Your Majesty, declared by you from Aubrey and paid for by taxes on the town."

The king nodded as he considered the possibility—a new crusade against the Vec, with a beachhead already established over the Murr River and not funded by the crown but by new lands. The frustrated army, ready for battle, would be let loose to either fight or return home as they chose. As well, there would be any remnants of the Redlander army to hunt down in order to pacify the province. The re-submission of Aubrey could begin a new golden age for the Grand Kingdom, and all on King Chrostmer IV's account.

"You say the prince moves by stealth, Duchess? How will you contact him?" asked the king.

"He is distantly related by marriage to one of my nobles," Amelia explained. The king's eyebrows rose. "I know, Majesty. I was astonished to discover it, too. But through their family links, I can send a message to him."

"We note that you do not reveal the noble's name," said Chrostmer. "Do you think to hide his identity? We could compel you to reveal it."

"I would not hesitate to do so, at your command, Majesty," Amelia curtseyed again. The longer she kept her cards in her hand, the more negotiating power she had. But the king always held the highest trump; he was the king. One order from him, and she would obey. She had no other choice.

"Very well, Duchess," said the king at last. "Send to your noble and let us bring Aubrey back into..."

The king stopped speaking as a dull red glow began to filter through the windows of the hall. It grew in intensity, and soon everyone present, from the king himself to the lowliest guard, was looking about in wonder and uncertainty. A small clutch of household staff burst into the hall, accompanied by the king's personal chaplain. All had faces stricken with fear.

"What is it?" King Chrostmer demanded.

"The sky, Majesty," said a steward, leading the entire contingent in going down on one knee, all except the chaplain.

"What about the sky?"

"It is as blood, Majesty," said the churchman. "The night sky filled with blood. It is an omen, Majesty. A dreadful omen. We will all soon die."

CHAPTER 29

"Where've them willows gone?" Prentice heard Turley gasp breathlessly behind him. The two were pelting though the long grass at the edge of Cattlefields where the pasture met the tributary water. On their left they intermittently passed stands of riverbank trees. With the glowing crimson sky, they could see each tree reasonably clearly, but their headlong flight gave them little chance to search for the exact willows that concealed their leather coracle.

"We haven't time for the boat," Prentice called over his shoulder.

"So, what we gonna do?"

"Swim."

"You're joking."

Prentice devoutly wished he was. But they had no other choice. Even if they risked stopping to find their boat, they would have to row out amongst the Redlander craft sailing down the tributary to the attack. There was no possible escape that way.

"Running from the hounds of hell," he muttered, remembering his last conversation with the duchess. It was exactly as he had predicted to her; they were running for their lives. He looked at the bloodied sky a moment and then gritted his teeth. Running from hell hounds was one thing, but how far could you run from the devils when you were already in hell?

From his right, Prentice heard the tell-tale clicking of another approaching enemy.

"Mantis-man," he hissed and whirled to let Turley pass him while he drew his sword and looked for the approaching hunter.

When the bales had collapsed from under them, both Turley and Prentice had flailed about to save themselves from the fall, and that had accelerated the bales' destruction, the rotten wool breaking apart in clouds of mildewed fiber. The whole short process had drawn the immediate attention of the nearest Redlanders, and by the time the pair had regained their feet, at least a hundred enraged warriors were stalking their way.

"Where's me damned mace?" Turley cursed.

"Leave it!" Prentice pulled at his friend's shoulder, shoving him away from the docks.

The sorcerous twilight served them strangely well in this moment. There was more light for them to choose their paths by, but the crimson leached the other colors from the world and in many ways only deepened the shadows of the houses and yards they ran past. Even though the maddened enemy was never far behind, and Prentice was sure the beastmen would hunt them well enough by smell even if they never laid eyes on their prey, nonetheless, the two Reachermen kept ahead of their pursuit. Only once were they overrun when a pair of wild spearmen burst through a rotting chicken shed at the side of a naked insectoid figure with the face of a man but with limbs chitinous and serrated like a grasshopper. That was how Prentice learned to listen for the clicking of a mantis-man, like the chirrup of a cricket but enlarged and deepened in pitch.

When the hen house burst apart, it threw half rotted feathers and guano up in a cloud that confused the Redlander's vision, and that was what had saved Prentice and Turley. While the attackers flailed about, half blinded, Prentice drove straight between the two spearmen, with cold, calculated thrusts of his drawn sword. Turley, with only his dirk to hand, slashed the bug man's unprotected torso, tearing him from belly to throat. The slain man tried to cry out, but it came out as only another form of clicking, mixed with a buzz like a bee's wings. Then Prentice and Turley were running again, leaving the chaos behind them.

"We cannot wait, and we cannot hide," said Prentice when they reached the edge of Cattlefields. They said nothing more as they burst from cover and began the desperate sprint north across the meadows. Behind them, the hunter's cries seemed to dissipate a little and then merge with the deeper roar of a growing host. Risking the time to look over his shoulder, Prentice saw the main of the army beginning to emerge from Aubrey's gate, a vast crowd of warriors. The one advantage was that having to travel through the town from the docks meant the main of the army was still some way back. Sucking in a burning breath, Prentice set his resolve and started running for the Murr once more.

So it was that he and Turley were almost to the north shore when the distinctive clicking sound gave warning of a second mantis-man about to attack. He pushed Turley forward and turned, scanning the unholy grassland, transformed from healthy green to venomous scarlet and shadows, impossibly deep. Cows were lowing in panic and then there was an animal scream, followed by the wretched sound of bones and flesh rending.

They're killing everything they find alive, Prentice thought. He saw the mantis as it burst from the grass in a swift leap that carried it easily fifteen paces. This one was barely a man anymore, more a man-sized insect, and it fell straight at Prentice, razor-edged forearms leading. Setting himself, Prentice dodged at the last moment, deflecting the insectoid limbs with his buckler. The mantis-man fell sideways but rolled comfortably across the ground, barely seeming to notice as Prentice slashed away with his sword. The chitin on the beastman's body turned every edge. Prentice was reckless and he hammered away, hoping to keep the foul creature off balance long enough to find a weakness. He realized his mistake when the mantis twisted suddenly and was facing him, catching his sword edge in the serrations of one arm. It turned the weapon deftly and brought its second serrated arm over to lock the blade in place. It was such a perfect disarm position that the cool part of Prentice's mind knew he should relinquish his sword and go to his dagger while he had the chance. But the astonishment that the creature's skin was so hard to cut made him hesitate, and he found himself in a fruitless tug-o-war over his blade. It was the kind of mistake every skilled swordsman knew not to make because the insect man now controlled him through his blade as much as he threatened it. Prentice cursed his error as the mantis switched its footing and pulled him so far off balance that he tumbled into the grass, losing his sword as he went. He tried to roll away, as the mantis had, but the beastman was so much faster, and he found himself pinned, face down.

Something wet dripped on his neck, and he remembered the reports of poisonous ichor that drooled from the mantis-men's mandibles. He was struggling to reach under himself, to pull his dagger, sure that at any moment the fell jaws would snap around his exposed neck and kill him. Then there was a loud thump and the weight fell off his back. Rolling over, he saw Turley standing there with a heavy rock in his hand. On the ground beside him, the mantis-man emitted an inhuman, buzzing groan, apparently dazed by Turley's stone strike. Turley raised the stone again and dropped on the creature. Prentice drew his dirk and joined his friend, driving the dagger at the hard, chitin skin until he found a seam between two pieces and wedged the blade fully in as far as it would go. The thing died with a sighing breath and Prentice pushed himself upright.

"I'm not right for this kind o' work no more," Turley said, gasping for breath. "I'm a house man now, a steward. I'm not for running through the night no more."

"Not far; we're near the Murr," Prentice encouraged him, feeling as weary and overwhelmed as his friend sounded.

"You lost your sword?" asked Turley as they trotted off, the ground under their feet starting to squelch with moisture. They were close to the river.

"I am not going back for it," said Prentice.

"Well, I don't feel so bad about me mace now."

They began to labor through the mud, and then the grass was gone and they were staring at the ruddy-black water of a river held in place by blood sacrifice. Across the Murr they could see torchlights from the White Lions' camp, and the natural yellowish light was like a balm to the soul, something mundane in this aberrant night. From what he could see, the crimson sky had stirred his soldiers in their camp. He hoped Sir Gant and Felix had everyone getting ready. They had only minutes before the artificial bridge pieces would round the corner of the riverbank.

"Our boys look like they might be close to ready," said Turley and he sounded relieved.

"I hope so."

"Course, if the Redlanders see that, they might float down past our camp to look for some folks less ready."

Prentice wasn't worried about that. "If they are stupid enough to put themselves in the middle of two armies, then they deserve to break. We will be the hammer and the king's men the anvil. And the Roar'll harry every boat that floats past. They will eat so much shot getting there."

"That'd be mighty convenient."

"It would be," Prentice agreed, but he shook his head. "When have you ever known the Redlanders to be convenient?"

"Ay, you're right 'bout that."

Prentice nodded at the still, dark water in front of them. "Just one more obstacle and we're home."

Turley's shadowed face looked horrified, the whites of his eyes looking almost bloodshot in the fell light. "You truly want me to throw myself into a stopped river full of pagan magic?"

"You can go back and ask them to make it run again, if you like."

"Bugger that!" Then he slapped his maimed arm with his good one. "You know I wasn't never a good swimmer, even before."

"I will not let you drown," Prentice told him. "And I am not leaving you here, even if I have to drag you across like a lump."

From somewhere in the grass behind them they heard a sudden hissing noise and a scream that sounded all too human. Someone unseen in their retreat was dying now, and they both had a sense of what was killing them.

"Snake-woman," said Turley and he began to wade out into the still water.

"You did not think you would get to hell and not meet a serpent?" Prentice joked in a whisper beside him. He pulled his buckler off his hand and dropped it. It would only be dead weight now. "The serpent's been waiting here since Adam and Eve in the garden."

"How'd they get away from that one?" Turley whispered back, his words labored with the effort of keeping himself afloat and moving forward with only one good arm.

"They didn't. God cursed the serpent and drove the man and the woman out of the garden. He set an angel with a flaming sword at the gate so that they could never return."

"We could do with one of them now—an angel with a flaming sword."

"We've got hundreds of them," Prentice said, "just over there on the other shore."

I just hope they're all awake, he thought, *with their flames loaded and ready to roar.*

The two men said nothing more, saving their strength for the short swim that was the distance between life and death. Prentice never had to pull Turley, but he made sure to swim slower and stay close for his friend's safety. He would never abandon him, not even in the face of hell itself.

CHAPTER 30

"Hold and name yourselves!" commanded a sentry voice, and Prentice had never been so happy to be challenged by a guardsman.

"Prentice Ash and Steward Turley," he gasped as he helped his friend wade up the shallows. The two men were soaked and bone weary, mud and river grass dripping from every part of them. They panted with the effort of their frantic swim, and their heads hung low. The focused light of a bullseye lanthorn shone on them both.

"Prove it," came the challenge. Turley groaned and slumped against Prentice, who took the weight readily, peering into the lamplight and blinking. Half bent under his friend, he awkwardly brought his right hand to his chest in salute.

"I am Captain Prentice Ash," he declared as loudly as he could, after spitting mud and water from his lips. "Sworn servant of the Duchess Amelia, Lioness of the Reach. Commander of the Claws, the Fangs, and the Roars."

"It's him," shouted another voice, one that apparently recognized Prentice now. "It's both of them. Run to the knight captain; tell him they've been found and are safe."

Figures slopped forward over the mud and took Turley's weight, then helped Prentice fully out of the shallows.

"I need to see the knight captain right now," Prentice ordered, not resisting the assistance, but not letting them take full charge of him either.

"And I need a bloody drink," said Turley. "Every time you get me out at night I end up with nightmares."

"What are friends for?" Prentice turned to the men helping Turley. "Take him up to the duchess's tower. He needs his rest."

"Where are you going?" Turley demanded.

"I am needed here. We have an enemy coming."

"Then I'm staying with you."

"No, you are not, Chief Steward," Prentice ordered, aware of the men around him—the men who must see him as an undeniable force of command. "I have my duties and you have yours. The duchess must be told what is happening, and she must send warning to the king as soon as possible. That all falls to you. We are all depending on you."

Turley looked at him, and in the weird mix of lantern light and crimson sky, Prentice saw his friend's expression firm up and acquire a dignity he had never seen in it before.

"Of course, Captain," Turley said. He tugged his forelock, and there was not a moment's mockery in it. "We aren't wild convict men anymore, are we?"

"No steward, we are not," Prentice agreed, and he smiled grimly.

He watched as Turley took his own full weight again and told the men helping him to escort him straight to the duchess's tower.

Let my family cast me off and Pallas hate me enough to draw blood, Prentice thought. *That man is still my brother.* He looked about himself at the sentries and other White Lions coming to his aid. *And so are these men.*

There was a splashing at the edge of the river and a challenge call from sentries. Prentice turned and watched his soldiers respond.

"What's that?" came one call.

"Get a light on it," said another.

"Snake-woman! There! Hiding in the shadows."

"Shoot the bitch 'fore she spits her muck!"

A serpentine fired, and another—smoke and flame flaring in the night. The serpent-woman tried to flee, but more weapons fired, and the iron shot brought her down. Prentice nodded in satisfaction as men began to diligently scour the river's edge for more swimmers coming across. They were all plainly unnerved by the sorcerous sky, but as he hoped, they were defaulting to their training. It pleased Prentice to see because it was exactly what he wanted. When in doubt, they remembered they were Lions, and clung to that first.

"Sir Gant and Sergeant Felix," he told the men closest to him. "I need to speak with them immediately."

Dripping and feeling disgustingly filthy, Prentice followed his men's guidance to find his two subordinates coordinating a full muster of the entire company. Over five thousand men were deploying in their cohorts, armed and ready to march. Drums beat and weapons and armor jingled at every corner of the camp. Line-firsts were keeping discipline while corporals ran back and forth with orders.

"Well done, Sir Gant, Sergeant Felix," Prentice said loudly as he approached. "Nice to see you did not need me to interpret the omens for you." The two officers were attended by a small crowd of corporals and a number of drummers. Clearly everyone was trying to make sense of the strange cosmological event and what it might purport.

"Good Lord, Captain Ash?" Sir Gant replied, eyes wide. "It's good to see you back safely. Is Steward Turley with you, too?" The corporals stood respectfully back and saluted at Prentice's approach.

"Safely returned, thank you," Prentice answered Sir Gant's question, and returned the salutes. "I have sent him to the duchess to report."

"Very good, Captain."

"That report going to explain this devil light?" asked Sergeant Felix. There were uncomfortable murmurs. Prentice's men were turning to their duty, but they were still unsettled.

"Some," Prentice answered. "But we do not have much time for that now. They are coming."

"The Redlanders?" asked Sir Gant. He looked south and then eastward. "By boat or the bridge?"

"Both. They have used this magic to stop the Murr from flowing, and they have a floating bridge of pieces made up on rafts to link up straight across."

"They won't attack the Aubrey bridge at all?"

"They might still," Prentice admitted, "just to keep some forces tied up there. But I am almost certain they mean to come straight across the river at our camp."

"How many?"

"All of them."

The two men nodded grimly, as did some of the corporals, and Prentice was glad to see they understood his import. The crimson sky was only the beginning of this terrifying night's grim work.

"What are your orders, Captain?"

Prentice drew in a breath and sneezed as his nose sucked in little bits of mud and water still lurking on his lip. He could feel his heart hammering in his chest from the long retreat. Any moment now he knew he would feel the fatigue come on him, and he would want to sleep more desperately than he wanted to breathe. But there was no time for that. He rubbed at his temple for a moment, head down. Then, he looked up at his waiting officers.

"Send the Roar straight to those wagons. Get them on board and loaded, waiting for the enemy." As the orders began to flow, he felt his resolution overcome the lurking exhaustion, at least for a moment, and he rode that feeling forward. "Send word to our sentries that the minute they see pieces of the bridge, they're to cry it out. Set five cohorts to the wagons. We don't have time for horses, so men'll have to do the labor. When they know where the bridge will line up on our shore, they are to make a wagon wall right in front of it, just past the mud. Then have the Claws on top of the wagons like we said. Put the Fangs on the flanks, along with any other Roars that aren't fitted to the wagons."

"You want us to try pushing the bridge back into the river?" Felix suggested, but Prentice rebuked that idea harshly.

"Absolutely not! No man is to go to the river's edge. Look at me! It's a bloody bog down there. Our men in armor would be swimming and drowning even before they saw the water. The Redlanders don't wear heavy armor. They will have all the advantage in that ground."

"And their beastmen will barely notice it," Sir Gant said, agreeing. "They'll dance across it like fillies in a pasture."

"Not quite, but near enough," Prentice said. "So, we stay out of it. And we make it our killing ground."

"And our banner nobles?" asked Gant, looking to his own duty as knight captain of the Reach's heavy horsemen.

"Have them mounted and ready. If a mass of Redlanders break clear of our wooden wall, you are to ride them down. Do not let them form up. We both know they can hold against a charge if they are given the chance."

"We'll make them leaves before our storm wind."

"I know you will, sir," Prentice said as he felt his shoulders slump. He forced himself to stand tall once more. "Also, one of you corporals send to fetch me my armor and a cloth to clean myself with. I am not going to face the enemy looking like a gong farmer."

"You've done it before, Captain, so I've heard," joked Sergeant Felix.

"And never again!" said Sir Gant, sharing the soldier's humor but defending his commander's honor.

Smiles and nods all around.

"Go swiftly, Lions," Prentice ordered. "The enemy is on his way, and he is coming apace. His first blades will be here before I even get my brigandine buckled, I promise you. I need you to keep him entertained while I dress for the dance."

"We'll try and leave some for you, Captain," said Felix, and he turned to his nearest corporals and drummers, barking orders that were soon beating out over the camp.

Sir Gant strode away, drawing only one corporal with him to arrange the Reach banner knights to their task.

As Prentice watched the organized chaos flow around himself, he drew a breath and noticed one of the drummers standing nearby. Barely a boy of ten or eleven, it was clear he had been assigned to Prentice to be the carrier of the captain's orders. The lad was perfectly turned out in a bleached buff coat. He had a serious, resolute expression on his young face.

"You know the standard-bearer, Markas, lad?" Prentice asked him. "The one who marches with the first cohort and carries the duchess' colors."

"I do, sir," the lad said earnestly, snapping out a perfect salute, his drumsticks rattling in his hand as they slapped against his shoulder. Prentice wondered how many times the boy had practiced that one gesture, hoping for this day when he would give it to his captain.

"Run now and find him," he ordered. "Tell him to attend me here with the colors."

The boy saluted again and then made to head off. Prentice called him back.

"Leave the drum, son," he said gently. "It will be here when you come back. But I need you to go fast as you can."

The drummer boy looked a little confused as he lifted his main tool from his shoulders by its strap and laid it on the ground.

"Swift like the wind," Prentice urged him. "Time is the one thing we have none of to spare. Men's lives depend on your fast feet."

The boy bolted off just as another man handed the captain a cloth to towel himself with. By the time Prentice had wiped his face and removed his filthy jerkin, his armor had arrived, and he was not even fully dressed when the drummer boy returned at the standard-bearer's side. A drumbeat rang out and was picked up from the south, the warning beat of an enemy sighting.

The night's true work was about to begin.

CHAPTER 31

T he garden courtyard was a nightmare of garish, crimson-lit shadows. Amelia watched the king staring at the sky while servants buzzed around him like angry bees and the chaplain harangued him intermittently between bouts of loud, pleading prayers. It reminded the duchess of the cowardly sacrist who had ridden out with Prince Mercad at the Battle of the Brook. When the Redlanders had sprung their trap that day, the fat, wealthy cleric had managed to bleat out a single "God save me" before he fled the battlefield. Appointment as a royal chaplain was probably a highly sought and lucrative position, she imagined, and most likely, these men won their status through clever politicking rather than religious devotion. This chaplain seemed about as much use as the other in the face of the enemy's sorcerous power.

"What do you think it means, Your Grace?" Dalflitch asked quietly.

"Nothing good," was all Amelia could think to say. She looked over her three ladies' expressions and was pleased to see none of the panic that was infecting the royal household, only resolve and watchfulness. The four stood slightly apart, and Amelia felt like an audience member again, watching a morality play about the end of the world.

"Apocalypse, King Chrostmer," the chaplain cried aloud, as if to fulfil Amelia's impression of the scene. "Hell has conquered the Rampart, and the devils will soon come for our souls. Confess your sins against God and Mother Church lest Satan claim you for himself!" The chaplain clutched at the king's hand, as if to lead him in prayer. The panicked churchman was halfway to his knees when the king threw off his grip, causing the man to roll sideways on the ground and become entangled in his heavy silk robe.

"Unhand us, you mewling twit!" the king commanded. "We've known yapping dogs that pestered less than this!"

"His majesty is not inclined to a religious interpretation of events," Dalflitch observed.

"He seems quite...dour," Spindle said carefully. Amelia and the other ladies looked at her with raised eyebrows. She shrugged apologetically. "Is dour not the right word?"

"No, it seems quite apt," Dalflitch conceded, blinking and looking back to the king.

Spindle smiled, seeming satisfied with herself. She noticed Righteous still looking at her. "I've been learning," she said by way of explanation.

A servant carrying a sack of something unspecified close to his chest pushed through the gathered ladies with barely an apology. Righteous and Spindle both hissed, ready to rebuke him, but he was already gone across the courtyard and lost in the scarlet twilight shadows.

It could well be hell, Amelia thought and suppressed a shudder.

"You do not think to run, Duchess Amelia?" the king said loudly as he cuffed yet another servant who was on his knees, pleading for the king to flee.

To where? Amelia thought. She curtseyed to the king across the courtyard. "You are here, Majesty. Where would I go?"

"See that, fool?" King Chrostmer shouted, sneering at the man at his feet. He did not spare a glance for the chaplain who was still on his knees, clutching his heavy, gilded cross and weeping loudly. "There are four women, most lowborn, who hold more courage and devotion to the throne in their skirts than the entire royal household can manage. If you have no iron in your soul, just mimic them, at least."

Amelia wondered if the king was including her in the "mostly lowborn." It irked her that even in the midst of a supernatural crisis, the Grand Kingdom did not forget that the Duchess of the Western Reach had not been born to a noble sire. What did she have to do to finally get them to forget? Or would they never?

"Go, rouse our heralds, damn you," the king continued, almost bellowing. "Send to the lot of them."

"Many are still riding with the prince, Majesty," the servant stammered. "At your command."

"I know what I commanded!" King Chrostmer shouted, forgetting his royal person again. "Send to the heralds you can find and then summon them to the court. My son has all his silly puppy nobles with *him*, so *my* court better find its stomach and attend me, ready for battle."

"For battle, Majesty?"

"Of course, for battle, cur!" The king turned to Amelia once again. "What say you, Duchess Lioness? Are we being attacked?"

"The Redlanders use sorcery in battle, Majesty," Amelia replied loudly. "Your expectation is pure wisdom."

"See, she can read the omens. See that word goes about our camp. The king rides to battle and the woman from the west rides with him. Every moment their sovereign is forced to await their pale livered presence, she rises further above them in his esteem."

"I would not like to have to deliver that message," said Dalflitch, and truly the servant did seem unhappy with the duty the king had given him, but he bowed and then rushed from the garden.

"I wonder if he's going to do it?" muttered Righteous.

"We'll know soon enough," said Amelia. She noticed that the groveling sacrist had pushed himself up on his knees.

"You cannot trust her, Majesty," he protested. "She is a heretic. Her house is full of ungodliness and debauchery." The man's voice was pitched so high in his rising panic that he almost squeaked.

"Oh, shut up!" shouted the king, and he kicked the man. "You sound more like a woman than they do!" He held out his hand in Amelia's direction and waved toward the garden gate. "Come, Duchess, attend us." He strode away, bellowing more orders. "Squires? Fetch our armor!"

"Do we go with him?" asked Righteous.

"The king commands," said Dalflitch, but she cast a nervous glance at the sky.

"We go with him," Amelia confirmed. "Things are chaotic, but assuming doomsday is not upon us, we must maintain our place. When all this is done, if we live, how we conducted ourselves will be an important consideration."

They followed the king, moving close to the sacrist who held his cross out between them, as if warding away evil.

"He don't like us much, does he?" muttered Righteous, eyes narrowed.

"He is likely not the only one in this crowd, Your Grace," said Dalflitch.

Amelia recognized how right her ladies were. This would be the perfect time for an overzealous noble to try an assassination, and the sacrist on the ground made it clear how the Church would respond to such an outcome.

"Perhaps you should go first, Righteous," she instructed. "And you come last, Spindle." Amelia was sure they would understand her reasoning, but she couldn't help herself when she added. "Best to have your cutlery ready, too."

The two women reached down in awkward, unladylike gestures, to fetch long fighting daggers from under their skirts.

Then they took up sentry duty ahead and behind as their duchess followed the sovereign.

King Chrostmer led the way through a war camp in the grip of wonder and on the verge of panic. Nobles and servants, sworn men and pressed peasants, all swarmed about like an anthill poked with a stick. Amelia watched men rush to their horses and then not mount up. Squires charged about with weapons and armor, but some, not finding their knights, only threw the equipment on the ground and waited to see what would happen next.

"Where's the king going?" Dalflitch all but shouted over the din.

"I do not know," Amelia answered. Armed men charged past, buffeting her little group, but where they were headed was anyone's guess. "This is as bad as the day the Redlanders attacked the prince's camp at the salt sea tower."

"It was like this?" asked Righteous, looking over her shoulder at her mistress. "I'm impressed you both survived, Your Grace."

"We had many to thank for that," Amelia answered, though her words were almost swallowed by the sound of shouts as a melee erupted on the other side of a large tent.

Wild cries and the clash of steel echoed as crazed firelight shadows played through the tent canvas. Then, as swiftly as it had broken out, it was over.

Hoofbeats announced the arrival of a small company of horsemen made up of king's heralds and squires. They brought Chrostmer his fine armor and weapons, as well as his war mount, a monstrous brute of a late-gelded stallion that jingled and rang under the weight of its gold-trimmed plate barding.

"Here, Halamond, good lad," called the king to his chief squire. The "lad" was forty if he was a day, and Amelia wondered how long he had been the king's squire—probably since he had been a lad. Never knighted, he'd likely live his whole life as a squire, never doing the deeds needed to win his spurs.

"He might get his chance tonight," she muttered under her breath.

Jostled by the newly arrived horses as their riders did their best to keep the unnerved animals under control, Amelia and her ladies stayed as close to the king as they could. Aided by his cadre of squires and pages who continued to arrive with pieces of his panoply, Chrostmer stripped his fine clothes from his body so that his pale belly flopped out, and he waited for his arming doublet to be pulled over his head. His gorget was fitted around his neck, then his chest and back plates were buckled together, squeezing his mature stomach into place like the most ruthless corset. Other plates and sleeves of mail were tied into place so that with impressive rapidity the king became a colossus of white polished steel.

In spite of the speed with which the king was armored for battle, Amelia still felt unnerved by being forced to wait. She was impressed, though, when the aging monarch, weighted by his equipment, still levered himself into his saddle without assistance.

"Now we can ride to war as God intended," he declared proudly, and the squires and heralds about him shouted a huzzah. The king looked down upon Amelia as his men all mounted up to ride with him. "Will you yet accompany us, Duchess? Or is this where we part?"

"I was with Your Majesty's brother at the Brook," Amelia cried to be heard over the noise.

"Very good. Well, I suggest you find yourself a horse."

Amelia looked about herself, eyes wide. Where in this madness did his majesty expect her to acquire a horse? Another herald rode up and bowed in the saddle to the king.

"Majesty, I bring word from the Prince of Rhales," the man shouted.

"That word better be that he is mounted and ready to ride with us to victory," the king responded.

"No, Majesty," the herald said, bowing his head again apologetically. "The prince sends to say that he has secured the road to the Foothill Highway and is ready to defend your withdrawal."

"Our withdrawal?" Even in the noise and chaos, King Chrostmer's disgust was obvious.

"Many nobles have already begun to retreat, Majesty. This sorcery bodes so ill..."

"Shut up, fool!" Chrostmer bellowed. "Go tell my son it's his choice if he wants to cower at the back of the field, but if he doesn't ride with his king, I will ascribe him a coward myself. See what his damned princedom is worth to him then." He turned to his heralds. "Sound the muster, all of you. Let those who can ride with us to victory or else damn them to hell. Let the devil take the hindmost!"

Trumpeters put their instruments to their lips and blew the blast. Forgetting everything else, including the women who had loyally accompanied him to this point, the king drew his sword and brandished it over his head.

"The bridge! To the bridge! Let us bottle the devil men there and show them what Kingdom steel can do!" His mount surged away beneath him and he rode off, squires and heralds with him. Trumpeters continued blowing their call to battle, and many knights and nobles, with no better plan, rode or jogged after the royal party. Amelia and her ladies found themselves in a sudden moment of relative calm.

"What should we do now?" asked Righteous.

"We could look for some horses," Spindle offered unenthusiastically.

"You suddenly learned how to ride?" Righteous joked, but her tone was bitter.

"For Her Grace," Spindle spat back. The tension was getting to them.

"Ladies, do not forget yourselves," Dalflitch rebuked them, but her own tone made Amelia think that even her noblest attendant was on the verge of losing her nerve.

The duchess knew that there was no place for ladies on a battlefield, not in dresses and hoods. On horseback they might be able to join the king's party, at least until he rode into the fray itself. Amelia could feel herself shaking and knew that while some of it was fear, mostly it was tension. She wanted to join the king; that was where the greatest chance for advantage lay. The king himself had already said it. She could raise herself and the Western Reach to the peak of his affections through such a show of loyalty. But she also wanted to be safe, and she wanted to keep her ladies safe. They could not follow on foot. Battle moved too swiftly for slippered feet to run under skirts. But where would be safe? Now that the king was gone, where was security for them?

The duchess was sorting the array of bad options in her thoughts when a new fracas burst into her thinking and a train of four horses pulling her carriage rattled down the rutted mud track between two tents. The rear wheels caught one tent's guy lines, pulling the shelter down as it passed, but the vehicle did not even slow. On the side were armed men, holding on for dear life while the driver held the reins loose and free and steered the nearly panicked team like a madman. And standing next to him with a heavy lantern lifted high in his one good hand was Turley.

"There she is!" he bellowed, and the driver heaved back on the reins with his full strength.

The carriage wheels sprayed mud, and even before it had come to a halt the men on the sides were dropping off and drawing their swords. As fast as she could realize it was happening, the duchess found herself surrounded by an escort of six Lion Fangs, weapons ready and cordoning the ladies off from danger. Turley jumped down, too, after securing the lantern. No sooner had his feet touched the mud than Dalflitch rushed to him, holding herself against his chest. His one good arm circled her waist and he hugged her to himself ferociously.

"You're alive," she said softly.

"Ah now, could you ever doubt it...?" he began with his typical charm, but suddenly all roguishness fell away. He lifted her chin to look into her eyes. "I'm sorry, my sweet. Sorry I made you wait. As soon as Her Grace allows, we'll pledge and be together for life."

He kissed her and Amelia waited, ready to tell him that she would give her permission for marriage. Turley's face grew deadly serious. He pushed past his lady love to the duchess and tugged his forelock.

"Obviously, Your Grace, I have some private-like matters to bring to you. But that'll have to wait. I come with word from Captain Prentice. Urgent word."

"In the carriage, steward," Amelia said, relieved to hear that Prentice was alive as well but not forgetting that the newly arrived carriage gave her a chance to catch up with the king. "Tell me in the carriage."

"Very good, Your Grace," Turley answered. "We'll have you going in a trice."

"To the bridge, steward," she insisted to Turley's obvious surprise. "The king is there and has bid all the nobles of the kingdom attend him for the battle."

"As you say." The chief steward turned to the men standing by. "You heard Her Grace. We're heading south. Get the ladies aboard and you'll run escort!" Turley handed Dalflitch up into the carriage first, breaking rank slightly, but Amelia refused to care amid the chaos.

Then they were all aboard and she was sitting with Righteous next to her, fighting knife ready on the slender woman's lap. Spindle was similarly armed and watchful, sitting next to Dalflitch. Turley clambered up onto the board next to the driver again.

"There's more than a handful I need to tell you, Your Grace," he said as he slapped the driver to get them moving.

"I can imagine," said Amelia, and she drew in a relieved sigh for a moment before casting a glance skyward. Being in the open-topped carriage made her feel a little safer, but the night's dangers were far from settled. Turley caught her looking up.

"That?" he said and flashed her a smile. "That's not even the half of it, Your Grace."

CHAPTER 32

T he crackle of the muskets seemed continuous now, and Prentice watched from a vantage atop one of the war wagons, staying half crouched behind a pavis shield that he'd had hefted-up for cover. Beside him men thrust long pikes down at the Redlanders who were trying to hammer at the wagons' reinforced wooden sides. Already their bodies were beginning to pile up, but still they came on. Everywhere smelled of fire and hot steel and blood and filth. The clouds of serpentine smoke were stained red by the arcane light as they drifted over the field.

The battle was going as he'd hoped. The wagons ringed the ground where the floating bridge came ashore, leaving the beachhead a churned, boggy killing ground. Lightly armed, the Redlander spearmen slipped and scrambled over the muddy surface, driven by their bloodlust, even as the Roars ripped them to pieces. Ordered volley fire had broken down now as every gunman fired as swiftly as his weapon could be loaded. Even before he'd climbed to his observation point, Prentice noticed that the Roars had begun to share duties. Either they shot through the special fire ports in the wagons' sides and then withdrew to load while another man took their place, or they held their position and passed their spent weapon back for another to load while a fresh one was handed to them. Either way made for speedier fire than a man trying to load while cramped in the close quarters of the wagon itself. Prentice wished he'd thought of that himself but was happy enough to pass the word that every wagon should be run that way.

With the weight of fire the Roar was pouring forth, even the powerful beastmen were struggling to reach the wagon line before falling. But still, many did. Only three wagons to his left, Prentice saw a wolf leap from the mire to the wooden rampart. Inside the range of the pike heads, the creature made short work of two defenders, but instead of fully clearing the wagon, it leaped down, perhaps thinking to range behind the lines like the hunting beast it resembled. But his Lions were ready for that. Prentice didn't need to even call an order before a squadron of six Reach banner knights thundered over the field and ran the beast down, driving through it with multiple lance strikes. The black-furred monster perished with a wail, and the knights cried a victorious huzzah. This was faintly answered from somewhere else much farther behind the line, which would be where Sir Gant held his command. The sound made Prentice smile as he turned his attention back to the ground in front of him.

"Do we have enough powder?" he asked the nearest Roar.

"No idea, Captain," was the reply.

Prentice turned to his drummer boy, standing diligently by on the ground behind the wagon. It occurred to him that in the rush, he had not learned the lad's name. The poor child looked pale and wide-eyed, even in the crimson light, and he was clinging to his drum like it was a floating barrel in the midst of a storming ocean.

"What is your name lad?" Prentice shouted at him.

"Solomon," the boy called back.

"A biblical name? That's good. You know that Solomon was a king and the wisest man who ever lived?"

The boy shook his head. There were tears on his cheeks.

"Well, he was," Prentice continued. "And God protected him and made him rich all his days. So, tell me Solomon, can you be wise like a great king? I'll bet you can."

Solomon the drummer boy nodded, but it was clear he did not really understand what Prentice was saying. That didn't matter. Prentice just wanted the lad to concentrate on something other than his fear and the horrors around him.

"Solomon, I need you to be wise and really clever," he said. "I need you to run to the corporal in charge of the powder wagons. I do not know his name and I don't know where he is, but he is back somewhere with the reserves. You will have to be clever to find him. Do you think you can do that?"

The boy nodded and began immediately to lift his drum strap over his head once more.

"Good lad," Prentice urged. "You run and find him and tell him exactly this: The captain wants to know how many barrels of black powder we still have left. The exact count. Can you do that?"

"Yes, Captain," the boy said and saluted. Then he dashed off.

"Brave little beggar," Prentice said affectionately, watching him go. Then there was a crash and a wild bellow, like the trumpeting of a savage animal. Prentice looked to his right and saw one of the wagons rocking backward before righting itself. The bellow sounded again and as the wagon bounced around, it was rocked backward even farther. Men cried out in fear as the heavy structure finally toppled over in a slow, creaking arc. Prentice had his long partisan in hand, and he used it to balance himself as he jumped up onto his wagon's ramparts to see what was happening. Men next to him shouted warnings that he was exposing himself to danger, but he ignored them. Looking toward the toppled wagon he could see a brutish figure, bigger than any mortal could be, with two vast, curved horns, each the thickness of a man's arm, sprouting from its skull. This was one of the infamous bull-men he had been hearing about. Even as he watched, the enormous slab of muscle and bone slammed a heavy iron mace upon the toppled wagon's side and the wooden planks cracked audibly. Prentice leaped from his wagon to the next one and began clambering like a river-boatman, using his spear as a balance pole and crossing the distance to the raging bestial warrior.

In the cold, calm part of his mind, Prentice knew this was the wrong thing to do. He was a captain now. He should be sending men to the gap. It was others' job to do the frontline fighting, but he had sent his drummer away and he could not send any orders. Even as he scrambled up the far side of the next wagon, almost spoiling his own men as he pushed past them, he knew the missing drummer was an excuse. This thing—this horror—was a champion, a captain of the enemy. By its own might, it had toppled one of his wagons and its horns were already stained with blood where it must have gored his soldiers. Prentice had to face this thing. He knew it in his soul, just as he'd known the moment he threw himself at the Horned Man at the Brook all those years ago.

"Roars and Fangs," he shouted 'til his voice cracked, hoping his soldiers would understand what he wanted as he leapt from the last wagon rampart onto the fallen vehicle's side. He thrust straight at the bull-man's head, but the twist of the horns deflected the shaft so that the winged blade barely cut the thing's scalp. The beastman swung his mace in a wide arc and Prentice was forced to retreat, almost falling off the wagon. He had good reach with his long spear, but the bull's height and long, hafted mace gave it a nearly equal range. The iron-ball head arced up and over, forcing Prentice to dodge to one side as he made a return thrust that again did little more than scratch the creature's skin. Just as Lord Ironworth had said, the bullmen's hide was like armor itself.

"Roar," Prentice called out his order again, but his hoarse voice sounded weak in his ears in the din of battle. In reply, the bullman bellowed, and being so close this time, Prentice's ears rang with the boom. He tried a twisting thrust, hoping to find a more vulnerable point on the creature's body, but the brute caught the haft with its own weapon and pushed downward heavily. For all their animalism, the beastmen were expert warriors, and Prentice found himself disarmed for the second time this night. His partisan was trapped under the creature's weapon hand as it raised one foot and made to clamber up finally onto the upturned wagon.

Prentice reached for his dagger and remembered that it was still embedded in the body of a mantis-man on the other side of the river. With no weapon and the monster closing on him, he made to jump back when suddenly three serpentine shots cracked from behind him and the bull hesitated, blood dripping from two wounds in its chest. It slipped but kept its footing. Prentice seized his spear back from under its weakening grasp and thrust straight at the stomach as two Fangs leaped up beside him and began to thrust again and again at the beast. Prentice twisted the blade buried in the guts, but even as it died, the bullman seized one of the swordsmen by his leg and threw him like a doll. The militiaman crashed headfirst into one of the nearby wagon's sides and perished without a cry.

The other Fang found his opening and his sword point went through the monster's left eye. It toppled backward in the mud as Prentice and the swordsman beside him pushed it away from them. Redlander spearmen who had been scrambling toward the toppled wagon, sensing an opening in the enemy line, hesitated as they saw one of their mightiest champions fall, and into that gap, more Fangs and Roars seized the moment to clamber up and renew the defense. Iron shot ripped into the skirmishers, and they began to fall back.

"Looks like we might win this, Captain," said the Fang beside him. There was blood running down the inside of the man's helmet, but he saluted and smiled. Prentice returned the salute.

"You can hold here?" he asked. The soldier nodded resolutely. "Good man. I will see you get reinforced."

He climbed down and walked away a handful of paces, looking for his drummer. When he saw the lad Solomon returning with a Roar corporal, he was about to order more serpentines to protect the damaged wagon, but around him swordsmen and serpentines were already running into the gap. Other men who had been trapped when the wagon was overturned began to scramble out, either to seek help for their injuries or to return to the fight. Prentice watched his men serve and strive exactly as they had been trained. He smiled, hung his head, and leaned on his partisan for a moment.

He was so damned tired.

CHAPTER 33

"Prince Forsyte is dead?" Amelia asked as the carriage bounced toward the rise where the king and his entourage had stopped to take in the state of the battle.

"Sorry to say, Your Grace," Turley said over his shoulder. "Captain Ash and I saw him go up in the 'ferno that lit this whole devil sky. There were dozens of folks crucified to a wooden tower pyre, and Prentice said for sure he knew the man at the top was the Veckander prince."

"God ha'mercy," said Spindle.

"How did they capture him?" Dalflitch wondered.

"I think I can guess," said Amelia.

She was sure that the prince must have grown frustrated waiting for word of her meeting with the king and tried to liberate his son by his own means. She shook her head sadly.

I did what I could, she thought but wasn't sure she believed it.

"How does this affect us, Your Grace?" asked Righteous.

Amelia felt her head snap up and she glared at her lady-in-waiting, but as she met her gaze, she realized that Righteous was trying to help her keep focused. Blade in hand and grim expression on her face, Righteous waited expectantly for her liege lady's answer, and that attention turned Amelia away from the indulgence of self-pity. This wild night was not the time for such emotions.

"Right now, it doesn't affect us at all," Amelia said, sitting back and straightening her shoulders.

She looked out of the carriage and watched as they began to mount the rise beside ranking noblemen of the Denay Court. Many were dressed in armor but as many were not. Ahead to her left, she saw contingents of banner knights forming up as the sworn men of the gathering nobles joined the army proper. Marshals under the command of Lord Ironworth were riding up and down along the line, establishing the order of battle. It was disordered, but it lacked the confusion that she had seen during Prince Daven Marcus's crusade west. These men knew their place, and if they did not, they knew to look to the knight marshal for their orders. King Chrostmer was every bit the war leader his son dreamed of being yet failed to become. The veteran Ironworth, who Daven Marcus had dismissed as old and worthless, was ordering the king's army with swift and efficient precision. Seeing them, the array of the Grand Kingdom's great might, Amelia found her flagging resolve refreshed. She was sure now that they had a genuine chance of victory.

"If and when we retake the city, though," she said, returning to the question of Prince Forsyte's imprisoned heir, "we need to make straight for this prison—the Ditch it is called—and see that the prince's son is safe."

"You feel you owe that to the prince, Your Grace?" asked Dalflitch.

"Yes," she said, and Amelia felt a slight sting of shame inside herself. Her actual motive was less honorable. "Also, with his father slain he will be the one who can actually bow the knee to the king. If both prince and his heir are dead, King Chrostmer might feel my plan is redundant, and I don't want to give away any advantage. Especially if Daven Marcus is coming back with some High Church edict to have me brought to heel."

"Of course, Your Grace." Dalflitch nodded thoughtfully, and from her expression, Amelia wondered if she were embarrassed that she hadn't seen such a possibility herself.

"In the meantime, we will join the king's entourage and be watchful," the duchess went on. "We are here for advantage, but battle is risk. We need to be ready to withdraw if the circumstances call for it." She lifted her voice to address Turley directly. "Did you hear that, steward?"

"I did, Your Grace. We will have hands on the reins continual-like until you are safe back in your tower."

"Good man. Now drive me closer that I may address the king."

The carriage driver brought the vehicle around in a wide swing to approach King Chrostmer, but many of the mounted nobles were in the way and reluctant to move for the more awkward carriage.

"Make way there! The Duchess of the Western Reach! Make way for the duchess," Turley shouted as if he were trying to clear a flock of sheep on market day, and he cracked the driver's whip over his head. Many nobles turned, furious expressions on their red-stained faces, but before any could object, the king himself also turned to look.

"Lioness," he shouted, his words echoing over the battle array like joyous thunder. With his army gathering and battle likely soon, the king's spirits were fully lifted, and the weakened croak that he'd been developing in private was gone from his voice. He seemed to be genuinely enjoying himself now. "By God, woman. You surprise us."

"The king rides to war," Amelia shouted back, trying to sound as happy as he was, though she felt her knuckles twisting with tension as she gripped the carriage's open-topped side. She forced herself to stand and curtsey, making her vehicle rock on its wheels. "The Reach would not miss this for the world."

King Chrostmer laughed heartily. "You see, gentlemen?" he asked the worthies jostling around him. "While you struggled to find your swords and your saddles, this woman sent for men and a carriage and still joined us here in time for the fight! Duchess, we think we see now what your husband Marne saw in you. If we were twenty years younger, we'd marry you ourselves."

"I fear I was just a suckling babe twenty years ago, Your Majesty. You would not have enjoyed my company so much back then," Amelia joked back, and the king laughed again. So did many of the men around him.

"Women should be at home," croaked Earl Lastermune. The elderly noble was mounted and wearing a coat of mail with a surcoat, his house colors stained by the abysmal light. Amelia gave the man credit; he had not let his age slow him from answering the king's summons to war. Nevertheless, she wasn't about to bow to his criticisms now.

"A wife and a woman should be at home, My Lord Earl," she called to him. "But a duchess rides at her king's command." She snatched up Righteous's knife, and leaning out slightly from the carriage, used the flat of the blade to rap on the helmet of one of her guards. "And she brings steel with her!"

Several of the nobles nearby laughed or cheered softly at that, though Earl Lastermune only scowled and turned away. Amelia sat down and carefully handed Righteous back her knife, giving a nod of thanks. When she looked back, she realized that the king was riding toward her carriage to continue their conversation. More than publicly joking with her, more than saying he might have once liked to have married her, this gesture declared the king's respect for her. People came to kings; kings did not come to anyone, not even duchesses.

"There's word of Redlanders on the river, Duchess," Chrostmer said as he approached. "Many of their boats, in fact. What say you? Will they come by the bridge or by boat, do you think?"

All around the king, other nobles moved closer as well, perhaps hoping to be a part of the conversation. Amelia had been at the center of such conversations like this before, and as she looked about, she recognized the situation. These men who wanted to disdain her as a mere woman were just like her.

They watched every other court member for any threat or hope of advantage. They were suddenly no different in her eyes than the merchants that traded horseflesh or other stock on market day, or the fishwives trying to outshout their competitors and sell their husbands' catch first. Despite herself, she smiled. They would see how this mere woman from the frontier could hawk and haggle with the best of them.

"I have word from scouts, Majesty," she said loudly. "The Redlanders have a set of boats they have made into pieces of a bridge. They are crossing the Murr to the west, just past the ridge, as we speak." Turley had outlined everything that he and Prentice had learned as he drove her here, and Amelia was thankful once again to her captain and steward for their excellent service.

"Why would they come ashore there?" asked someone Amelia did not know.

"Because they are assaulting my camp," she answered readily, and she felt her smile fade. She had made great strides politically this night, and that was cause for satisfaction. But there was still the military situation, and according to Turley's report, her militia was in a fight for its life. She swallowed her fear and forced a light smile onto her face again.

War is a game to these men, she told herself. *But I must never forget it is a game in which men die. Men are dying now.*

"But the king is here," the unknown noble protested gently. Amelia nearly scoffed out loud. It was such an obvious little barb. Whoever this man was, he wanted Amelia to boast that her low-born soldiers were worthy of the enemy's attention, which by implication would insult the king. After all, the king was the most important man on the battlefield. This noble, whoever he was, wanted to lure her into a prideful boast that would take some of her sheen off in King Chrostmer's eyes. Amelia had won too many word battles to fall for such a basic ploy.

"The king *is* here, My Lord," she offered the gentleman and hoped she guessed his rank about right. "But in this...dour twilight, perhaps the enemy does not see our ranks aright. In truth, I cannot guess the thoughts of madmen who paint their bodies and worship pagan gods. If you have more experience with the minds of lunatics, please share it, if it please, Your Majesty."

Amelia met the king's eye for a moment, then looked down to not be rude.

"Dour twilight?" she heard him repeat in a light-hearted tone. "You say the battle is already joined, Duchess, to the west?"

"So I am told, Majesty."

"We should see for ourselves."

Amelia looked to the west. Even with the eldritch light, it was hard to make out anything but blackness in the distance. And the ridge was blocking a direct line of sight in any case. "If we go to the ruined watchtower, Majesty," she offered, pointing in that direction, "it is not too far and would give us a good view west along the river."

"Seems fair enough." The king turned to the unnamed noble. "But you think they'll attack across the bridge yet to get to us?"

"You are the king," the nobleman said, as if it were a self-evident explanation. After a moment he added. "If you fall Majesty, the battle is lost. Surely even these heathens understand that, madmen or not." He gave Amelia a cold scowl, his eyes dark shadows.

"We think we should see for ourselves," the king repeated. He turned to a herald. "Go tell Lord Ironworth to keep mustering the army to order. Also, tell him to send word to the Bronze Dragons. The king rides to the ruin to see the west of the river. We will return in a chop of the candle or else send for the rest of the army to join us. Come, Duchess, let us lead the way and see this bridge of boats your scouts tell of."

"At your command, Majesty."

My men are fighting and dying under this hellish sky, but let's make sure we don't rush to their aid too soon.

Amelia forced herself to sit straight-backed and dignified as the carriage jostled away again, keeping up with the invigorated king.

CHAPTER 34

"That's most of what we got left, Captain," said the corporal, showing Prentice the remains of the White Lion's powder stores. "There's more coming from the north on the river, but that's mostly still up at Griffith. The Roar's chewin' through it faster than we ever thought, beggin' your pardon."

"That is because they are doing the main of the killing," Prentice muttered. He had originally conceived of the Roar with their gunpowder weapons as a support for the main hand-to-hand fighters of his White Lions. With the enemy struggling over muddy river shallows and his forces behind a line of fortified wagons, there was much less hand-to-hand than he ever imagined possible in a battle. He looked at the small pile of powder barrels. It wasn't much, and even if it was more, it could take an hour to disperse it to the men, doling it out to their individual powder horns, not to mention replenishing their supplies of shot and wadding that they also needed to keep fighting.

It was time for a different tactic. He turned to his drummer, Solomon.

"Beat the summons for the company standard and the knight captain," he ordered. "And keep pace with me. We are the rally point."

The lad saluted and began to hammer out the correct patterns on his drum. At least these were orders he could use his training for. Prentice smiled wearily at him and turned back to the corporal.

"Fetch runners to bring these barrels to the wagon line. I will give you orders when you get there."

The man saluted and dashed away. Prentice turned and began to walk back to the riverside. It had to have been at least two hours, possibly three, since the invaders had started rushing over their bridge, and still the serpentines cracked, and men and monsters fought and died. But it seemed that the tempo was diminished. Even the ferocious Redlanders had a limit to their bloodlust.

It must be dawn soon, Prentice thought, looking up. *Lord God, let your sun banish this vile witchlight.*

He stopped a handful of paces back from the wagons and assessed his situation. There was a lull in the fighting in front of him as men were swapping posts, wounded stepping back and water being brought for others to drink. Even in the dull red light, the Roar were distinctive by the powder burns on their faces. Some men looked like they'd buried their heads in a charcoal burner's mound, so soot-stained were they. Expressions were grim but resolute, and any man who met his eyes saluted.

"We might be getting towards the end of this, Captain," Sir Gant called as he rode up and dismounted. There was a spray of blood down the front of his surcoat and his hair was disheveled from being under his helmet, but otherwise he seemed quite fresh.

"How has your night been?" Prentice asked, having to shout over the rattle of his drummer.

"Mostly it's been like the old days for us," he said, managing to seem both light-hearted and remorseful at once. "We've been hunting down beastmen that manage to crest our wagon wall. There was a flock of boats that sailed up from the west and landed their crew to try and flank you, but they were slowed by the marsh, just as in front, so we rode them down without too much trouble. Hundreds of Reacher nobles eager for honor are still a force to be reckoned with."

"I do not doubt it." Prentice heard something on the wind, under the drums, and he put his hand on his Solomon's shoulder to stop him a moment.

"Boats. More boats. Coming on the river." The shout was being passed along the front line and Prentice sighed to hear it.

"I was afraid of that," he muttered and headed toward the nearest wagon to climb up and see.

"What is it?" asked Sir Gant as he climbed up beside him.

"The other half of their forces."

The two men peered westward. The red light wasn't much good for seeing long distances, but the square cut of Redlander sails slowly emerged against the black of the river water.

"It's still not flowing," Sir Gant observed. "They'd make better time if they got the river going again."

"Who knows if they can," Prentice said, realizing how little he understood the magic being used against them. What kind of power could hold a river's flow in place for hours, and what would be needed to dispel it? Would the Murr ever flow again?

"Well, if they try and land here, they'll still have the mud to deal with. We'll just run them down like before." Sir Gant's confidence seemed undimmed.

Prentice shook his head. "We're almost out of powder," he said flatly. "We have done alright up to now, but without the Roar to disrupt their charge, they will be able come across that bridge with full force and start pushing us back. Have you seen that ground out there? So many dead and dying that there is no more mud to be seen. The next waves will mount up over their slain comrades. The corpses are halfway up the wagons in some places."

"You have the right of that, Captain," said Sergeant Felix, approaching from the east flank. He clambered up next to them and saluted.

"How goes your end of the line?" Prentice asked, peering over the sergeant's shoulder.

"Secure, for now. Looks like they had none of their boats downriver so their bridge blocks them getting any river crews up to us. We've only had to hold against the beachhead, and we've done that with mostly Roar fire, but we're out of powder now." Felix looked to the rear of the camp, waving in the direction of the powder store. "I sent a corporal for more, but he came back saying there's none to go around. Your orders, Captain. I had to see for myself."

"There is only a meagre amount left," Prentice confirmed. "What is the butcher's bill?"

"Not too bad, actually," said the sergeant. "Had a pair of them snake-women spitting poison at us for a while, and we kept our heads down. That was easy enough. Stings your eyes and nose, but most of it landed on the wood. What'd we care. That was until it got touched by the flash of a Roar shot and took fire. Nearly lost the whole wagon before we got the flames done with."

"Their venom is flammable?" Prentice asked, wondering how many more horrors the Redlanders had at their disposal.

"Like straw soaked in lamp oil."

"Serpentines and serpent-women. Yet another thing we must watch for," Sir Gant said, and the three men nodded at the grim but practical sentiment.

"Course, that's not the only mad story I've heard, if you'll permit me, Captain," Felix went on.

"What do you mean?"

"Well, there's a tale being shared among the men of how some dunderhead with a winged spear was acting the hero." Prentice blinked as he started to understand what Felix was getting at. "Bloody fool apparently threw himself at a giant with bull's horns," the sergeant continued. "Went all honor duel at one of those monsters with a partisan, like that haft there in your hands, Captain. I only ask because I know your legend, how you once took down a horned man with just a dagger, and I'd hate for the men to think you hadn't learned your lesson from that experience, you being a captain and all and far too important to risk on childish heroics, not when there are hale men ready to do the bloody duty."

Prentice felt himself scowling, and there was a savage rebuke rising within him, ready to remind the sergeant of his place in the scheme of things. But just before he spoke, he looked at Sir Gant and saw disapproval on the knight's face, which caught the fury on his lips. Sir Gant agreed with Felix, and in truth, the sergeant was right. Prentice had known that, even when he'd been racing toward the bull-man. He nodded, and his wry smile flashed again.

"I would not worry, Sergeant," he said and clapped his gauntleted hand on Felix's shoulder. "If you ask about, you will find that that man was not as alone as you feared. And he certainly will not make a habit of it."

"Glad to hear it, Captain," said Felix with a salute. "Because your place is not on the front rank. You do know that, don't you?"

"I know, Sergeant, thank you." Prentice accepted his underling's rebuke, but he gave his thanks through gritted teeth. Felix cast a further meaningful look at Sir Gant, and Prentice thought his knight captain was about to join in telling him off, but the nobleman cocked his head

"Are you out of powder here as well?" he asked.

Prentice shook his head and then listened and realized that the sound of firing had died away. The Redlanders had completely stopped their assault. Some still crouched on their bridge, taking cover, but no attacks were coming across, at least for the moment. Farther west, he could see the approaching boats all turning south to land on the other side of the river.

"It seems the enemy's captains share your assessment of the landing situation, Sir Gant," Prentice said as he watched. "They are going to marshal on the south and come across the bridge again."

He chewed his lip as he strained his eyes to pick out the shapes of beastmen in the shadowy crowd. The distance was too great, but he was sure they were there. If even two or three bullmen were among them, the White Lions were in deep trouble. One had turned a wagon by himself. A trio of them acting together would be worse than a battering ram on a castle gate. And the rest of the force coming looked at least as large as the one that had already been turned back. If anything, the first assault was looking more like a vanguard. Perhaps the crimson witchlight was more than just to stop the river flow. Maybe it was also a banner, summoning all the invaders from their secret camps and raids up and down the river to the west.

"Dawn's coming," called Solomon.

Prentice looked to the east to see the horizon lightening. At first it looked red like the rest of the sky above, but even as he watched, the red-black of the night, right where the dome rested on the land, was fading to purple and towards blue, just as it did on every natural morning. The glowing band of the Rampart met the horizon, and where they touched, the stellar feature was losing its crimson stain. It was daylight faded, but it was coming clean. There was a limit to the Redlanders' magic, and the dawn was washing the power away.

Still looking east, Prentice thought he saw movement, and the flash of dawn light reflected on the hilltop ruin. If the rest of the Grand Kingdom was assembled for battle, that would be where they were watching. Lord Ironworth was marshalling the king's forces, and *he* knew what Redlanders were like in battle. He would see the value of the plan that was birthing in Prentice's mind, even if no one else around the king did. There was a point in every battle where everything was won or lost, and Prentice was sure this was theirs. He looked back to where the Lions' first cohort was standing, waiting. His reserves—five cohorts, fresh and ready for their chance to prove themselves. Their Roar had a full supply of powder and shot too, but that wasn't enough to hold the entire wagon line. Behind them was the camp where the wounded were being taken and servants and camp-followers were watching to find out what the outcome would be.

"We cannot hold against another assault like that," he told his men, and no one muttered the least sound of disagreement. Even Sir Gant, flush with a knight's joy at successful battle, accepted his captain's assessment with a nod. "We cannot hold. And we dare not retreat. So, what does that leave us, gentlemen?"

His officers looked at each other and then shook their heads.

"Attack," Prentice told them, and he smiled in spite of himself. "Remember how I said I never wanted a single man out on that patch of mud, Sergeant?"

"I do sir."

"Well, I'm revoking that order." He looked down to his faithful drummer. "Beat the summons for the standard and first cohort to rally on me."

Immediately the complex rhythm rattled out.

"We're taking the bridge?" asked Felix, but Prentice raised a hand to hold his question while he turned to Sir Gant.

"Two riders," he commanded. "The fastest two Reacher knights we have. Send them straight downriver to Lord Ironworth. Tell him this, exactly this: The Lions are going to breast the river and engage the enemy reinforcements on the south bank. If it pleases him to cross the Aubrey Bridge and cut off the Redlanders' access to the town, I'm sure the Kingdom will have the joy of riding the trapped enemy into the dirt all morning."

The orders were ten times more poetic than Prentice would normally have bothered, but he wanted Sir Gant to understand and impress it upon his messengers. He was a commoner sending an order to the highest military noble in the Grand

Kingdom. It had better sound like a groveling request or the Denay and Rhales Court forces were just as likely to turn their noses up and snub him. And then they would all die. Lions could defeat wild dogs, but not if they threw themselves all alone into a pack as large as the one gathering across the river.

"A pincer," said Sir Gant appreciatively. He turned away to send his orders, but Prentice called after him.

"And then tell any of your bannermen that if they will consent to dismount their horses, they will be welcome to join us in the fray."

"I'll pass along your invitation, Captain," Sir Gant said with a salute, but as he jumped down off the wagon wall, Felix jumped with him. The sergeant clapped the knight on his shoulder, and they spoke together quietly. Sir Gant looked up at their captain, his gaze pregnant with meaning. Prentice was trying to assess the ground to the bridge and did not fully notice what was happening until Felix was climbing back up next to him.

"Something I need to know, Sergeant?"

"Just a private moment between soldiers, Captain."

Prentice trusted his men and gave the incident no more thought. Behind him, he heard the sound of the reserves forming up according to the drumbeat.

"Alright, you lazy sods," he shouted. "That bridge belongs to us now! The knights and fancy noblemen have the other bridge, but that one is ours. We have suffered for it; we have paid for it. I want you up and over to take it off these preening, painted floosies."

Calling the Redlander warriors floosies was like calling a hurricane a light breeze, but Prentice didn't want his men thinking about how difficult this next part would be. They had to be fearless. He turned to the company standard-bearer, Markas, with his distinctive white-woven noose around his neck, and signaled his order to advance. The drums beat, and as fast as they could, the ready reserves clambered over wagons and out onto the charnel ground to the bridge.

"We could have moved some o' the wagons," observed Sergeant Felix.

"I know," said Prentice. "But the enemy would have seen us doing that and likely come at us. Could have been a mess. We have to hit before they have a chance to get organized. Tell the Roar to stay to the sides of the bridge. They can rake the enemy flanks with their fire while the Claws hold the end."

"I'll pass the word, Captain."

"And one more thing," Prentice added. "Get two men to bring a barrel of powder each out to the middle of the bridge."

"You mean to blast it?"

"If we cannot hold it. This night has cost us bloody and I want to punish those bastards for our pain, but I will not lose what we have gained by being too greedy."

CHAPTER 35

F or the second time in one day, Amelia found herself amongst the hilltop ruins overlooking the Aubrey Bridge and the Murr River. The circumstances of her second visit could not have been more different from the first, though. It was not merely the company, with her ladies-in-waiting, her carriage and attendants, the king and his entourage of the highest nobles of the Grand Kingdom and all their hangers-on. The magically afflicted sky casting scarlet light made everything otherworldly, but even that was becoming normal to everyone's eyes, it seemed to the duchess. No one was rushing about in panic any longer, and there were no sacrists about, prophesying doom either.

All of these things made the hilltop a vastly different place, but the thing that caught Amelia's attention most was the presence of four vast bronze bombards, cannons of the Royal Dragons, also called the Bronze Dragons, with muzzles so large that a man could clamber into them. The enormous firearms were carved to resemble their namesakes, with dragon's heads and teeth at one end. Squads of men, ten to a cannon, clambered about the terrible devices, or drove bullock teams to maneuver the broad-wheeled wagons on which they were mounted. Amelia had seen weapons like these before. Prince Daven Marcus had marched west with five of them, entrusted to him by his father, and all five had been lost by the end of the crusade. Nonetheless, the duchess had no doubt as to the awesome power each weapon dispensed with every shot. Her Lions might roar, but the king's Bronze Dragons breathed horror upon his enemies, scouring the earth with their might.

"These weren't here yesterday," she muttered, recalling her visit with Viscount Gullden and Prentice Ash. It seemed like so long ago, now that she thought about it, but still it was less than one full day. She was looking around in wonder when the king rode nearer to her.

"You seem confused, Duchess," he said benignly.

"I was only here last morning, Your Majesty, and none of this was here then." She pointed at sacks of powder, double sewn and stacked ready to load the cannons, and beside them massive stone balls that could shatter buildings and earthworks. Men would be nothing but grass for such might to mow down.

"When we arrived from fetching the prince yesterday morning, we told Lord Ironworth to begin preparations for the attack," King Chrostmer explained. "We suggested he should put our dragons to use from this height and he prepared well according to our orders. The invaders thought to catch us out, and we are ready for them."

"Indeed, Majesty." Amelia had no doubt the placement of the cannons was Ironworth's idea, and he had only waited for the king's permission to put them into place. That would explain the swift deployment. Nonetheless she smiled and bowed to acknowledge the king's self-proclaimed prescience.

"What's happening down there?" asked a nobleman, and heads craned to the west.

On the river shore in front of her encampment, a melee of men and wagons, barely distinct in the distance, swarmed with torchlight and tiny flashes of fire. A pall of red-stained smoke hung over the long stretch of muddy ground, and by that same light, the definition of the floating bridge Turley had reported to her became easy enough to pick out against the river water.

"How does it not float away?" asked someone.

"Clearly it is anchored at this side with hooks or something," declared another nobleman.

"So why don't they just cut the ties?"

"Because they're fool peasants playing at war without proper leadership," growled Earl Lastermune. "We should send the women back with some simple orders, something peasants and duchesses can't get wrong."

"Likely every boat in the line has its own anchor to hold it in place. That's not a small number of ties to cut, My Lords," Amelia declared as loudly as she could, not bothering to conceal her annoyance. "But even if they have not, it would not matter. The river has ceased to run. The boats will not float away."

Earl Lastermune scoffed openly at her declaration, and muttering swept among the other nobles. Some were curious, but most were dismissive until the captain of the Bronze Dragons spoke to the king.

"It's true, Your Majesty," he said, and there was a tremulous tone in his voice. It might have seemed cowardly in such a large man, dressed in a gilded coat of plates and royal livery, but under the ruddy sky, an unnerved tone did not seem out of place. "We've had scouts on the riverside since before sundown in case invaders might try to fire the powder. Soon as that scarlet burst lit the sky, men started to come back, saying the river has stopped in its flow. All my men are stout, Majesty, stout and true, but we have never seen the likes."

More murmurs, much more troubled, swirled about.

"You didn't think to inform us?" the king demanded of his cannoneer.

"I sent runners, Majesty," the man answered, bowing his head, "to report the river and to say we've arranged the guns in place."

"We received no report," the king said sternly, but then his expression softened. "But we suppose this night has been confused enough."

Amelia looked from the king to the waiting noblemen, and she could see by their expressions they were, if anything, even more suspicious.

"They wonder why you knew what the king did not," Dalflitch whispered to her. "Keep ready to explain, Your Grace. Any minute now there'll be an accusation of witchcraft."

Of course, there will, Amelia thought. *I'm ready while they run about like chickens fleeing a fox and that could only be explained by witchcraft. The wayward duchess and her heretical household.*

The accusation never had a chance to come though. Instead, in the quiet, a new sound drifted to them from the west, a crackling, like a fire burning through twigs.

"What is that?" asked someone.

As the collected nobility watched the west, Amelia noticed that the light was changing. She looked east and saw the dawn beginning to brighten the night. She smiled. Then her attention was drawn by the sound of two horses galloping up the hill. Looking back the way they had come, she saw two men-at-arms in Reach blue and cream coming at full pelt. They pulled up a short distance from the crowd and the cannons, but before one of the king's heralds could detach himself to challenge them, they noticed the duchess's carriage and rode straight for it. The two men bowed formally in their saddles. They were flush from their headlong ride, but Amelia noticed they also had sprays of blood on parts of them, as well as the dirt and other signs of having been in battle.

"A message from Knight Captain Sir Gant," said one of the two men. Amelia had a momentary stab of panic. Sir Gant was sending a message? Did that mean something had happened to Prentice? Had he survived his scouting mission to Aubrey only to fall in the later battle? She waved the man closer to receive his message quietly, fearing ill news.

"What is the knight captain's message?"

"Well, it is really for Knight Marshal Lord Ironworth," the knight said apologetically. He looked surreptitiously toward the king who had ridden a little closer to the edge of the hilltop to get a better view of the battle in the west.

"Then why did you stop here?" Amelia demanded through gritted teeth. This night seemed to go on and on, and she found herself at the limit of her patience.

"Well, the king is here," the armored man said with a shrug and looked at his comrade, who nodded with him. Amelia did not bother to suppress her sigh of frustration. The message was sent to Ironworth as knight marshal, but these two young noblemen had seen the king's banner on the hilltop and thought to present the message to him themselves, like heroic heralds in an inspiring saga. Kings were known to handsomely reward timely couriers. Of course, they might also have assumed that wherever the king was, the knight marshal would also be.

"Tell me the message, and then ride west," Amelia told them. "Lord Ironworth is with the arrayed horsemen in front of the bridge. You will find him there."

Doing a poor job of covering their surprise, the two gave her the message from Sir Gant, and she was relieved to learn it was in fact from Prentice Ash. Even as the knights finished their speech, she turned and put her hand on Righteous's shoulder.

"He lives," she said, and Righteous smiled thankfully. Then her eyes narrowed, and her expression turned cunning.

"Course he's alive, Your Grace," she said. "Take more than an army of beasts and heathens to stop my man."

It was all Amelia could do not to burst out laughing. She looked back to the two knights who were waiting to be dismissed. "You have your duty, gentlemen," she said. "Go to, and with haste."

The men bowed in the saddle again and wheeled their horses. Amelia looked to the king and realized that in the short time since they had last spoken, the crowd of mounted nobles had pressed around him at the hilltop's edge. There was no way she could have her carriage driven through that. She thought to shout for King Chrostmer's attention, but she was too sick of this whole nonsense to be yet more undignified. Without another pause, she pushed open the carriage door and stepped down into the mud. Before anyone could object, she slapped one of her guards on his armored shoulder.

"You, and your companion, I need an escort to the king," she commanded. "Make me a way, and with haste."

The two men saluted, and they took up a place each, one ahead and one behind, using their sheathed swords like shepherd's rods to gently but forcefully push a safe space through the crowded mounts for their mistress. There was a call from the carriage behind her, but Amelia didn't pause or look back. A rough jostling caught her attention, and she noticed that Righteous had jumped down to join her, fighting knife in hand but concealed under the sleeve of her gown. The little party made an uncomfortable but rapid journey through the press of horseflesh. As she emerged, Amelia was at the king's stirrup, looking west. The tiny flashes of light that marked gunfire were now seen on the sides of the bridge. Prentice's men were assaulting across the river already.

"Ah, Duchess, perhaps you might enlighten us," said the king when he noticed her. "What is that sound? That popping, like grains in a hot pan?"

Everyone was quiet so that Amelia could hear what he meant, but she already knew what the sound was. "That is my men's handguns, Your Majesty," she told him proudly. "The Roar of the White Lions."

"Roar? Sounds more like the crackle of a warm winter fire," scoffed a nobleman on the other side of the king.

"I invite you to stand in front of them when they shoot, My Lord," Amelia snapped, not bothering to hide the contempt she felt. She had had enough. "I assure you; you would find it very warm fire indeed." The entourage laughed or scowled as the mood took them, but Amelia ignored them for fools. Men were dying heroically, and the king's court thought it high sport. To hell with the lot of them.

"I've received word from my captain, Majesty," she told the king. "He says that they have repelled the invaders and are taking the bridge before a second wave might try an attack. He expects to engage them on the south bank and invites the knights of the Grand Kingdom to assault their flank and rear across the Aubrey Bridge. In a pincer." She hoped she conveyed Prentice's meaning correctly.

"Does he indeed?" said the king.

"Yes, Majesty. He thinks that he can keep the Redlanders occupied so that you might cut off their retreat to the town. They would be trapped."

"Without the bridge they will be trapped regardless," said the king enigmatically and the men around him chuckled. Amelia felt her stomach twist with ominous fear.

"I do not understand."

"However hot your lion's roaring might be, Duchess, my dragons thunder to the heavens. And my captain tells me they can comfortably range to that false bridge."

"The Dragons, Majesty?" Amelia looked to the west where the heavy conflict had reached the other shore, and the coming dawn revealed the massive crowd of enemies still ready to fight. Her little militia seemed dwarfed and ready to be overwhelmed, despite their taking the assault to the enemy.

"We will destroy their bridge from here, Duchess," said the king, and he turned to wave to the crew of the nearest cannon. The men there all bowed and set about loading their monstrous weapon, which was already turned to face west along the river. How had Amelia not noticed that two of the four had been ready to fire in that direction all night? And how had the king waited this long to support her men?

"If they might fire that far, Majesty," she asked, feeling the emotion shaking in her voice. "Could they not fire upon the enemy directly across the river?"

"They could, Duchess, but that is not how war is fought."

"But my men are upon the bridge. And on the opposite shore. They'll drown or else be trapped and slaughtered by that horde."

The king looked down on her and gave her the condescending look she had grown so accustomed to from members of the royal family. "Your rogues are very pretty in their armor, Duchess," he said pityingly. "And your lioness nature is bracing. But this is why men afoot are convicts. It is the unavoidable fate of an unmounted man on a battlefield."

Amelia knew how Prentice would respond to this outmoded philosophy of war, how he would describe it as foolish and intractable, not to mention a vile and callous disregard for human life, but she shook with fury being confronted with this arrogance so completely. No wonder Prentice hated noblemen. They threw lives like his away for mere convenience.

"Let me send a warning, Majesty," she begged. "Please. To give my men a chance to withdraw."

Even before the king could answer, the first dragon fired. The air shook and battered everyone gathered about. Amelia's ears rang from the cacophonous explosion. She looked west and saw the first cannonball land short, throwing up a waterspout where it struck the river. There was a disappointed groan in the crowd that made Amelia want to rage at them, but she clenched her fists and huffed her breaths through flared nostrils.

"Don't fear, Duchess," the king said grandly as he wheeled his mount about, almost knocking her over. "Your man's plan was sound, though of course it is not so much different from the one we made with Ironworth from the beginning. And once that bridge is kindling, we'll cross the other one, cut them all off from the town, and run them down like so many spring flowers. The invasion from the west is over. I realize the loss of men will cost you, but your duchy will receive its share of the spoils. Or else, perhaps from a new tax."

Was the king trying to console her by agreeing to her plan for the dead Prince Forsyte and offering her tax revenue while he butchered her soldiers with his damnable cannons?

"See, dawn is coming," the king said, pointing east where the sun had crested the horizon at last. He looked upward. "And it dispels the wicked false light of the enemy. No devils have come for our souls this night. We ride to glorious victory. Today will be a good day for the Grand Kingdom and the Denay throne. Your part in it will be remembered." Then he spurred his horse, and the mighty brute forced its way through the herd while the other nobles moved as rapidly as they could out of the way, turning to follow him. Soon, Amelia was alone with her ladies and guards on the hilltop, while a short distance away, the Bronze Dragons roared at the enemy bridge. Her body shook with the explosion of every shot, and tears streamed down her face.

Righteous hugged her with one arm while she cried, and Amelia made no effort to put her off.

CHAPTER 36

"They don't much like the iron shot, Captain!" declared a Roar corporal as he rested the butt of his serpentine on the bridge boards and began the complex process of reloading his weapon.

"Just keep a watch on your ammunition," Prentice urged the man.

The corporal paused to salute, and Prentice returned it. Standing in the middle of the bridge, he felt himself in a strange pocket of calm, safe and yet only one step in any direction from the battle chaos. Under him, the boards of the floating bridge were firm and steady, so that he might as well have been standing on stone footings in a mere stream, not a floating arrangement of boats across one of the broadest and most powerful rivers in the world. Each boat, acting as a pontoon, was anchored in its place, and each bridge piece was tied to the next so that everything was locked. Under other circumstances, Prentice would have admired the engineering feat that the bridge represented, but the Redlanders already had so much power in their hands and so many advantages. To respect their skills at boat building and similar craftsmanship felt like ceding them too much honor, like it was one too many strengths to admire.

But they don't like our iron shot, he thought and smiled to himself.

Along both sides of the bridge, the Roars were firing straight into the crowded enemy who were pressing toward the southern end with the same reckless abandon as the first assault. Down there, the White Lions' Claws were earning their pay and then some. Tight packed ranks of pike and halberd made the bridge end a hedge of sharp steel, and no matter how hard they pushed, for now the horde had not found a way through. Some bolder Redlanders tried to leap onto the parts of the boats that jutted out from the sides of the bridge in order to attack the Lions' ranks from the side. But pike and polearms farther back protected the lines in front, thrusting at the leaping flankers and easily pushing them into the water. Once there, if they swam, pikes were still long enough to harry them, or iron shot found them, and they almost all drowned. The melee was tight and hard fought, but for now the Lions held their own.

A knight staggered past Prentice, his tabard slashed to ribbons and one hand clutched in the other, blood running through his fingers. Still the noble man-at-arms smiled and ducked his head respectfully as he passed. "Cursed wolf thought he had my measure," the man declared, as if he was describing a successful hunt. "Took a devil of a time for me to put him down, though, and the sod still took my sword and one of my fingers with him to the bottom of the river."

"The duchess values your service, sir," Prentice said, ducking his head. The man blinked and smiled even more broadly.

"Oh, I'm not done yet, Captain, have no fear," he declared. "I'm just nipping off to get a rag around this hand and fetch my mace and axe. I fancy stoving in some painted skulls before this night's work is done."

"Well, let me not keep you, good sir," Prentice said, and the knight managed an awkward half salute before trotting off down the bridge.

His blood's up, Prentice couldn't help thinking. *His hand'll hurt like the devil once the battle joy fades.*

"I'm done," shouted one of the Roars on Prentice's left, holding his firearm up to signal that he had fired all his ammunition.

"Powder or shot?" shouted his corporal.

"Both," the gunner declared, confirming that he had no mismatched scraps, extra iron, or unspent powder to hand off before he quit his duty.

"Hand your weapon to a runner and head down there to carry out the wounded."

"Aye, Corporal."

Prentice watched the man hand over his firearm and then trot down behind the massed phalanx of fighters to be ready to help carry the injured off the bridge. Sir Gant was coordinating there, and the whole process was running smoothly, as smoothly as any battle had a right to.

"We can hold this some while yet," Prentice said and looked down at the two powder barrels he had set in the middle boat and the smoldering long-match that was ready to fire their fuses if necessary. If the king and his knights were already on their way, then they might only have to hold here another half of an hour. Victory was in sight.

There was a dull rumble of thunder in the east, and Prentice wondered if God was planning to wash the sky clean of the Redlanders' blood magic. It would be a fitting end to the night. Rain would spoil his Roar's usefulness, dousing their trigger fuses and dampening their powder, but at least half of the gunners had already spent their shot and were now doing fetch and carry. Prentice wasn't worried about a rain shower, and when water fell on him, he welcomed its coolness. Then he heard a second burst of thunder and realized it wasn't rain that was falling on him; it was splash from a gout of river water. He looked east just as a second geyser erupted from the water's surface.

"Oh God, no," he muttered. He had hoped to hear the trumpets of the knights riding over the bridge, to see lance tips and helmets flashing in the dawn light. Instead, he saw a puff of smoke above the hilltop ruin and a lightning-fast streak of black through the intervening air, then a massive crack that set the entire bridge shaking as if in an earthquake.

"What the hell was that?" cried one of the corporals.

"Has the river started running again?" another man asked. Prentice saw another puff of smoke, and though he couldn't see this cannonball's flight, he saw it hit home, tearing the prow off one of the pontoon boats. It was sheer chance the shot was glancing. If it had hit head on, Prentice was sure the boat would have been matchwood.

We only have moments, he thought and found himself in motion before he realized he had made a decision.

"Withdrawal!" he shouted over his shoulder at Solomon while he rushed toward the front of the bridge. "Beat withdrawal and get off this bridge, boy! Do it now!"

The signal began to sound from the loyal boy's drum while Prentice rushed to where Sir Gant and Sergeant Felix were directing the sharp end of the battle. Another dull thud and a moment later the bridge shook again, almost knocking Prentice's feet out from under him.

"Sir Gant," he shouted as he arrived. "We are withdrawing."

"Withdrawing?" The knight was clearly so focused on the battle front he had not noticed the cannon fire assaulting the bridge.

"The cannons!" Prentice said, and as he did, another shot skipped on the water and ripped through the air over the bridge, two pontoons back.

"The bastards could have at least tried hitting the enemy first," said Felix hammering his halberd furiously on the decking. "Those big stones could kill fifty at a time in that crowd."

"I have sounded the withdrawal," said Prentice. "Start pulling the men back in good order, but as fast as a rout, if you can." He knew how ridiculous the order was, but there was nothing else for it. Sir Gant looked at the hard-pressed front, and Prentice saw what his knight captain could see. These were the cream of the White Lions, the best trained and bravest, first cohort. If the bridge held, they might even have lasted hours more of this fighting. Sir Gant turned back, and the sad pride in his eyes told Prentice what he thought even before he spoke.

"It cannot be done, Captain," he said with grim resolution. "If we move too swiftly, that press will overrun us. You know it. We could make a fighting withdrawal, but it will take too long." The bridge shook again, as if to emphasize his point with the danger. Prentice knew the wisdom of Sir Gant's assessment. Retreats from the line of combat were brutally dangerous. Prentice had already seen how savagely the Redlanders punished enemies who broke and ran. His own first encounter with the invaders had been a rout that he had barely survived.

"We have no other choice," Prentice ordered. "Set the rear line to a one-step withdrawal. Pass the orders. We'll take a third of the men each and guide them as we can. I'll see you on the far shore."

Sir Gant and Sergeant Felix exchanged a knowing look, and then the knight looked his captain straight in the eye.

"No, Captain," he said respectfully.

Before Prentice knew what was happening, Felix had stepped up, and using his halberd as a bar, he shoved his captain backward.

"You need to go, Captain Ash," he said in his parade ground voice. "To the other end of the bridge. Now."

Prentice could not understand what was happening, and he resisted his sergeant's pushing reflexively. Felix was resolute, though, and he shoved with his full weight, causing Prentice to fall backward on the planks. Felix pointed over Prentice's head at Markas, who was standing a pace back.

"Take the captain back to shore," he ordered.

"This is mutiny," Prentice muttered as he fought against the arms trying to seize him by the shoulders.

"No, Captain," said Felix. "This is the duty a sergeant owes to his commander. We'll get the men off as best we can, but you go now."

Prentice was already scrambling back to his feet to tell the sergeant he was being a fool when the world erupted in a storm of splinters and water that tossed him back against the bridge once more. It took a moment for his hearing to return, and in that time, he wondered if he had died. But his face stung where shards of wood had embedded themselves in his skin, and he blinked his eyes to try and clear the water and detritus from them. He struggled to his feet and nearly retched from the effort, coughing out more splinters. He was alive.

A direct hit from a cannonball had severed the bridge as neatly as a giant's sword swipe. A section of the structure ten paces long was simply missing. As he regained his feet, Prentice could see the other side where men who, like him, had survived the shot and were regaining their feet. He was happy to see Sir Gant amongst them, seeming as uninjured as Prentice. The shocking impact had the additional benefit of stunning the assaulting enemy so that the fight on the other section of bridge had momentarily ceased while Lions and Redlanders got back to their feet and recovered their wits.

But Sergeant Felix was gone.

As he watched, Prentice felt his end of the cut bridge begin to move, and he realized that the Murr had begun to flow once more. It was a good sign that came at the worst moment, causing his part of the bridge to flex away in its flow.

"Fetch ropes," he shouted, not even knowing if there was anyone still around to obey his orders. Sir Gant looked at him sadly.

"Go with the standard-bearer, Captain," he shouted over the growing space between the two bridges. "While you still can."

"No!" Prentice shouted as he felt hands grabbing him again and dragging him away from the shattered edge. As he watched, the Redlanders started to shout cries of bloodthirsty frustration as they saw the bridge being taken from them. The White Lions still on the rump of the other side bellowed back in kind, knowing now they were fighting to the death because there was nothing else left to do. Sir Gant raised his sword and hammered his fist to his chest in a last salute to his captain.

"It has been my greatest honor, Prentice Ash, my captain," he shouted.

"God welcome you into heaven, sir," Prentice shouted back, his voice cracking with emotion.

"I will wait for you at the gates." Then Sir Gant turned his back and dove into the collapsing ranks of his men, clearly determined to die with as many enemies on his account as he could.

"Swim, sir," Prentice muttered as he let himself be dragged. "They should all have dived straight into the water." It was a vain hope. Swimming in armor might be possible, but it was not a task to be attempted at the end of a long night of battle.

Prentice let loyal hands drag him in a ragged dash for the north shore, but as soon as he felt the slip of mud under his feet, he began to fight them off like a drunk in a bar brawl. Men backed away as their exhausted commander raged out the last of his emotion, staggering until his feet nearly went out from under him. Then he stopped, his breath heaving and his head hanging down. For a long moment, they circled him like men trying to hem in a wild animal. Then, when he had not moved for some time, one soldier came gingerly forward and pushed the captain's partisan, symbol of his authority, into his hand.

He looked up to see his standard-bearer next to him, the White Lions colors flying still from their pole in his other hand.

"Thank you, Markas," Prentice said to him. He leaned on his weapon, trying to lever himself upright, and then let himself bow in exhaustion once more.

"Captain," asked Markas quietly, "what are your orders?"

"My orders?" Prentice repeated. Who would he give the orders to? Sergeant Felix and Sir Gant were both gone. Yet around him stood his men, waiting for his commands. Across the river, to the east, he heard the blast of trumpets. The Kingdom knights had engaged the enemy at last.

"Oh God," he moaned. He tried to form another thought, to devise the orders his soldiers needed, but for a long time he could think of nothing to say.

CHAPTER 37

"D o I look as poorly as I feel?" asked Lady Dalflitch, apparently of no one in particular as Amelia's carriage rattled into the White Lions' camp at mid-morning. The duchess looked her lady over to see if the question was serious.

"You look more beautiful than most women ever dream of being," she told the ex-countess.

"Only most women, Your Grace? I suppose that will have to do," said Dalflitch, and Amelia realized the woman was feigning vanity as a jest, probably to cover the disquiet she felt. The duchess was sure they all felt much the same. But, however worn they felt from the night's horrors, the men-at-arms around them were so much the worse.

"Straight up to the tower, Your Grace?" asked Turley with the team's reigns in his one good hand. Amelia cocked a surprised eyebrow. When did he take over driving the carriage? And where was the man who'd been driving before that? "You and your ladies can refresh yourselves. I'll set your staff to heat water for a bath as soon as you wish."

A bath sounded like a wonderful idea, and looking from Dalflitch to Spindle to Righteous, Amelia was sure all four of them would want the chance to clean and dress themselves afresh. The clothing they had hurriedly outfitted themselves in the night before could now be charitably described as shabby. But whenever she looked beyond the confines of her carriage,

her own aches and needs seemed small and superficial. Men sat
staring at fires, their armor plates dented, their buff coats torn
and dirty. It seemed every second man had a cut or other injury.
Many were bandaged by rags or were receiving some treatment.
When they saw her carriage approach, all made an effort to
stand, and some even cheered, though it was a heavy sound
made soft by fatigue. All saluted, though, and many smiled,
which helped her. These were victors, though the price had been
great, and they were now counting the cost.

"There will be time to reset our hair and retie our ribbons
later, steward," she told Turley. "First take us to our captain. He
and his men deserve congratulations."

"Very good, Your Grace. With your permission, I'll dismiss
the escort."

Amelia looked to the six men who had marched beside her
carriage through the night. They looked as weary as the rest of
the company, though their armor still seemed clean and neat in
comparison. She wondered if they were glad to have missed the
battle or disappointed to have lost the chance to serve as their
comrades had. She gave Turley a nod, and after he waved them
off, he took directions from a line-first and drove the carriage to
the company standard where Captain Prentice was to be found.

The banner colors, the broad blue field with its rampant
white lion, fluttered from its pole, which was planted in the
churned earth about thirty paces back from the line of wagons
that had been the night's defenses. Several of the vehicles had
been damaged, and one toward the eastern end of the line
looked as if it had been burned to uselessness. Others had been
pulled out of the line, and in the gaps, militiamen moved back
and forth, hauling the corpses from the boggy ground between
the wagons and the river. Redlander dead were stripped of
anything of value and thrown into a burning pyre that was
sending a column of foul-smelling black smoke into the air.
Piles of metal, mounds of spears and other weapons, and every
piece of usable clothing were being sorted by half a dozen older

women under the watchful eye of another line-first who seemed completely fixated on seeing all the spoils scrupulously sorted. Slain Reachermen, most in militia uniform but some in knights' tabards and surcoats, were brought out with more dignity and laid in a row while three sacrists walked up and down, seeking to identify each dead man-at-arms and offer benediction when they could.

Overseeing the entire ghastly business, they found Captain Ash seated on a simple wooden chair directly in front of the company standard. He was still in his armor, as dirty and blood-stained as any of his men's, and he had his long partisan upright in his hand, as if he needed to lean on it to support himself. His face was covered in a mass of little cuts that left thin trails of blood in all directions. As the carriage approached and she got down from her seat, he looked to Amelia less like a captain of an orderly militia and more like a barbarous warlord, overseeing the enslaving and despoiling of his conquest.

"Captain Ash," Amelia called as she approached, Turley at her side as an escort. She was astonished when he only glowered at her in response. In her time, she had seen him furiously angry and hatefully violent, but he had never been this disrespectful to her face before. And he had never frightened her as he did in this moment. Slowly, as if hurrying was beneath him, he reached down and took up a clay jug, taking a long swig before lazily rising to his feet. He spat the fluid all out to one side, and with a heavy sigh, drew himself fully upright. Then he snapped himself taught, his fist slapping against his armored chest, head bowed in complete formality.

"I am at your disposal, Your Grace," he said, his voice sounding like a barrelful of gravel rolling over cobblestones. "When it suits you, I will be happy to give you a report of the night's engagements and what we know of this new day."

This was the respectful Prentice that Amelia knew, but it was a respect that weighed on him, heavier even it seemed than the convict chains he once had worn. In some of the books he had set her to read so that she could better understand war and warriors as a leader should, Amelia remembered there was talk of some soldiers losing parts of their souls on the battlefield. They returned with injuries that healed but not fully the men they had been. Even righteous knights, showered with glory in victory, could return with hearts crippled beyond repair. Amelia had wondered about this first when she had seen Prentice the day after the Battle of the Brook. But he had recovered then, and she realized that she had assumed he was armored against any further such wounds, like a child who has had the cowpox and then could not ever get it again. Perhaps she was wrong. Perhaps he left a little bit of himself on each battlefield, another slice of his soul discarded, and this was the last one. She looked about herself and wondered how many of the other men around her were similarly injured in their inner characters.

Next to her, Amelia noticed Righteous almost twitching with nerves. The duchess leaned close to her lady and whispered, "Go to him. He needs you."

Righteous bobbed a little curtsey and then almost rushed at her husband. She came to a halt right in front of him and cocked a hip, projecting her usual self-assurance.

"You have a bit of rough night, old man?" she asked loudly. "What'd you do, tie one on?"

Prentice stared at his wife for a moment, and it seemed to Amelia as if he was looking straight through her. Then he tugged one of his gauntlets from his hand and reached out to stroke her face. "Wife," was all he said, and the playful belligerence drained out of her like a sail that loses all its wind in a moment.

"Husband," she whispered to him and bent down to fetch the jug at his feet. She offered him another drink and then pulled a small cloth from her sleeve. It was the unfinished token she had been sewing the night before. Righteous dipped it in the jug after Prentice had drunk from it, and using the moist corner of the cloth, began to clean the blood from his face. And he let her. Amelia doubted anyone present had ever seen these two as intimate as this with each other before; they were normally so private.

"I know you need your rest, Captain," Amelia said gently. "But if you can give your report soon, that would be best."

Prentice looked like a man halfway to restored when he turned from his wife's care for a moment.

"I'll give you the word now, Your Grace," he said, sounding more like himself with every breath. "The good news is that we held the bank and repulsed the enemy assault. With the bridge now destroyed, the enemy is trapped on the south side and the king's knights are enjoying their chance to destroy the enemy at their leisure." The resentment in his tone was unmistakable.

"And what has the king's leisure cost us, Captain?" Amelia felt the same emotion rise in herself, and while it would not do to be critical of the throne publicly, she could not find it in her to hide all her feelings from her soldiers. She wanted them to know what she thought of their sacrifice and of the men who had made it so much worse than it should have been.

"We think it's near to a thousand, Your Grace," Prentice said, and Amelia felt herself suck in a breath. One man in five? "I've got men scouring the banks. Every slain lion gets a funeral, Your Grace, but we have to find them. Many will have sunk and drowned in their armor."

Amelia swallowed at the thought of a thousand graves and involuntarily looked at the sacrists beginning the wretched duty. "And the enemy?" she asked.

Prentice looked to a burly man in a buff coat with a white steel pauldron on his shoulder who was supervising the burning of the Redlander bodies.

"What's the count, Franken?" he shouted. The man jogged over and saluted readily.

"Got the sticks here, Captain," he said, but then it seemed he realized he was standing next to a lady. His eyes went wide, and he clutched his forelock, bowing his head and holding it down.

"Your Grace," said Prentice, smiling. "This man is Franken. Last night he was a corporal of your Claws. As of this morning he is, if you so approve, a sergeant."

Prentice had never asked her permission to promote a man before, but Amelia realized he had also never done it in her presence. He had to defer to her authority if she was actually there when it happened.

"If he meets your standard, Captain," she said, forcing her voice to have a noble tone. "Then by all means I approve."

"There you are, Franken," said Prentice. "You have a full promotion. When we get back north, we'll have Yentow Sent fit you up personally for a sergeant's brigandine."

Franken looked up and locked his heels to give another salute. Then he seemed to remember a bag he was carrying and handed it over to Prentice. It rattled like a bundle of firewood, which it seemed like it was when Prentice opened it and looked inside.

"I did as you said, Captain," Franken explained. "Each mark on the side is ten bodies and no stick gets more than ten marks, to make a hundred. I ain't never counted so high in my life, beggin' your pardon."

Prentice fished out one length of wood and showed it to Amelia. Down one side was a series of ten cuts, carved in a row on the surface of the wood. She nodded and looked past, into the bag. There were dozens in there, and each one represented a hundred enemy dead. Amelia looked toward the river and then farther over at Cattlefields, where the battle still seemed to be going on.

"These are the ones we can find, Your Grace," Prentice reported, and he dismissed Franken back to supervise the burning bodies. "Many of the enemy will be lost in the river or blown apart by the king's cannons. My estimate is that we've taken five of theirs for every one of ours, at least. Maybe more."

Five thousand enemy casualties? That was good news. How much better news would it have been if King Chrostmer hadn't fired on her men?

"You've had to promote a number like this Franken, I take it?" she asked as she still looked across the river.

"I needed a new master sergeant," said Prentice. "And a new knight captain."

Amelia turned on him, jolted out of her resentful thoughts by that grim news. "Sir Gant?"

"He and Felix both," Prentice confirmed and blinked his eyes as some of the water from Righteous's cloth got in them. His face was mostly clean now and so she stopped. "They were both on the far end of the bridge when a cannonball ripped it apart, Your Grace, along with the entire first cohort. Hundreds of good men slain in one..." He paused, and Amelia knew he was considering his words. It was right he should not curse the king's decisions, but she found herself wishing that he would, as if it would free her to do the same somehow. In the end, he met her eyes and they both knew there was no point completing the sentence.

"When the battle is done, we will send men to the south bank and fetch any bodies washed ashore there," she told him. "With God's grace we will find the sergeant and the knight captain there for burial."

"Perhaps Sir Gant," Prentice said. "But whatever the cannonball left of Felix is at the bottom of the Murr."

"The cannon struck him fully on?"

"Right in front of my eyes, Your Grace."

"God have mercy," breathed Dalflitch behind her, and Amelia was reminded that her other ladies were still there. For a moment she wondered if she should dismiss them rather than force them to endure hearing these horror stories. Then she almost laughed at herself. Not one of her ladies was unaccustomed to the dreadfulness of this war. Her soldiers were men of iron, clad in steel, but that did not mean her ladies were made of fluff.

"There is another loss I must report, Your Grace," Prentice said, drawing her attention once more. "The prince of Aubrey, Forsyte, is dead."

Amelia nodded solemnly. "Turley informed me," she said. "He said you only saw the man at a distance, but you were sure?"

"I saw him clearly, Your Grace. And the little I learned at Ashfield of deviltry and the dangers of magic makes me think that it would have had to be the prince."

"Have to be?"

"A sacrifice of royal blood to invoke such a dread power," Prentice explained.

Amelia shivered in spite of herself, then sighed at the reality of the slain prince. She still had her commitment to Forsyte to rescue his son. Across the river, the battle continued to rage, but soon the king's forces would break the Redlanders. Everyone around her seemed confident of that now, even Prentice. The night river battle had been the hard part. Now the Grand Kingdom was fighting the way it loved to and at which it was the best. She would let her men rest a bit and perhaps take a nap herself. Then they could form a plan...

"With your permission, Your Grace, I'll take ten or twenty men now to Aubrey while the battle is still in Cattlefields," Prentice said, and Amelia found herself so surprised that it took her a moment to understand what he was saying.

"Why now?" she finally managed to stammer, thinking of how exhausted he looked and how much she wanted to give him the rest he needed.

"The Reach needs the young prince, the heir, Your Grace," he explained, and as he spoke, his expression took on his characteristically shrewd cast. "You need him. You need him brought to you so he can bend the knee to King Chrostmer and fulfil your plan. He needs to be in your hands and as soon as possible."

"Can it not wait until you've had your rest?" she asked.

Prentice shook his head. "While the battle is still joined, there will be few if any Redlanders in the town. If they sense themselves beginning to break, they might retreat to Aubrey's walls and make it a siege. We will never get the prince out then. And if the king breaks them and takes the town, which he might easily do at any moment, then he will have the prince, and your advantage will be lost."

"But you are hurt…" Amelia began to protest, and she looked to Righteous, imagining how much the woman would object to her husband being thrown back into danger. "I could send a stronger force under the command of a fresher man. Five hundred, with knights to support, perhaps."

Prentice shook his head, and next to him Righteous bristled, apparently offended on her husband's behalf. Amelia had not wanted to insult her captain's honor or capacity, only to allow him a chance to recuperate.

"Five hundred is too many, Your Grace," Prentice said. "It will look like you are trying to take the town for yourself, or else draw other attention, and your men might rescue the prince only to be forced to surrender him to a more ranking noble. If the Prince of Rhales sees us, he will move to intervene, do not doubt it, Your Grace. He's a bloody fool at times, but his instinct for advantage is well honed. I have had word he is back from his temper tantrum, and we will do well to watch out for him."

"He refused to join his father on the field," Amelia said, and it was Prentice's turn to be surprised.

"The Prince of Rhales seemed convinced that the bloodening of the sky was a portent of doom," Lady Dalflitch explained. "He and a contingent of the Church's high clergy remained at the rear near the Foothill Highway to cover his father's *inevitable* retreat."

Prentice smiled in genuine amusement, and it was so infectious that Amelia felt her own lips turn upward.

"Forgive me, Your Grace, I misspoke," he said, shaking his head. "The Prince Daven Marcus's instinct for advantage has failed him this once at least, it seems."

"The prince has an instinct for stealing other, better men's advantage," Dalflitch declared. "He has little taste for forging his own. Too much like hard work." Then she curtseyed to Amelia, apologizing wordlessly for talking out of turn. Amelia nodded her forgiveness, her own smile broadening further.

"You are our expert on the prince, Lady," she told her.

Dalflitch's features screwed up in mock disgust. "To my everlasting regret," she said and looked sidelong at Turley. He seemed to realize and turned to her, smiling openly.

"Well, Captain," said the duchess, "if you think you can achieve this task with haste and stealth, then you have my permission and full trust."

"I'll go with him, Your Grace," said Turley suddenly. "If you'll allow."

"No," Dalflitch all but shouted. "I mean, please, Your Grace, no."

Before Amelia could answer her lady-in-waiting's fears, Prentice was shaking his head.

"Not on this one, old friend. You have a new love to look to. A man in your position is spared the duty of warfare."

"I swam the river with you," Turley protested.

"I dragged you the last part," Prentice retorted. "I have not the strength left to carry you this time."

"So, I'm not good enough for you?"

Amelia watched the exchange between the two old comrades, unsure if they were genuine. There was a lack of enthusiasm to the argument, as if it were being done out of obligation rather than emotion. Perhaps Turley felt a responsibility to offer his friend his service no matter what.

"You have other duties today," Prentice said. "We discussed this last night."

"Is that what you learned types call it? A discussion?" said Turley. "I remember getting told off by a pompous militia captain who needed me to thump a bug-man in the head with a rock to save his life."

Thump a bug-man in the head with a rock? That was a part of the past night's tale that Amelia hadn't heard yet. She was about to intervene when Prentice stepped up to his friend and put a hand on his shoulder.

"This is going to be fast, cruel, and bloody," the captain told the chief steward. "Last night I took the second canniest blade I know with me. Today, I am not as sharp myself, so I need the best."

"Second canniest?" Turley repeated, but Prentice was already looking over his shoulder at his wife.

"What do you say, sweetheart? Want to come rescue a prince with me?"

Righteous's eyes flared with delight.

"You always take me to the best revels," she said, sounding and acting exactly like a child being invited to a carnival.

"There's your trousers and doublet in my tent. You can go change."

Righteous seemed ready to dash straight off but caught herself and turned to give her duchess a perfect curtsey. "With your permission, Your Grace?"

It was such a sudden transformation from eager urchin to refined lady that Amelia scoffed reflexively. She looked at Dalflitch, who was smiling with marked respect. Before she knew what she was doing, Amelia nodded her permission, and Righteous hiked her skirt and scrambled over the churned ground to her husband's tent.

"She's your *wife*, Prentice," Amelia marveled. "How can you put her in danger so readily?"

"She has seen as much danger as any of us, Your Grace. Any respect I have won by my steel, she is due as well. If Turley had no other duties, I would take him in a flash, and he knows it, which is why he is so surly about being left behind."

"Surly Turley," Dalflitch repeated quietly, but with a happy expression. The chief steward groaned loudly and turned to his friend with an exasperated tone.

"She's going to call me that every day now, thanks to you."

"Every wife needs at least one good switch to goad her husband with," Prentice said with a cunning smile. "You have seen what mine does for me."

"Your wife is a hunting cat with claws to match," said Turley.

"And that is why I am taking her with me."

"Well, that makes sense, I suppose."

"She is your wife, Prentice," Amelia said, "but she is also one of my ladies."

At these words, Captain Prentice turned from Amelia to look over her shoulder at Spindle, standing loyally behind and silently discrete.

"Righteous will be with me, Spindle," he told her in a firm voice, as if giving orders to one of his soldiers. "That means the whole of the watch of the duchess will be on your shoulders for a while. You know you are up to the task, don't you?"

"I do, Captain Ash," Spindle answered readily, and she curtseyed. "I will carry the duty to the full."

"I know you will, Lady. But be utterly ruthless in your performance of this duty. Any man, and I mean *any* man—king or prince, yeoman or convict—who so much as looks askance at the duchess, or Lady Dalflitch or yourself, I expect to return to find his innards spilled at the edge of your blade!"

"I'll make a pie from their offal," Spindle said in a tone that let everyone around her know she might well do exactly that.

"Prentice," Amelia breathed, a little shocked at the brutality of the talk, even standing in the remains of the previous night's battle. "These are my ladies-in-waiting you are speaking to."

She was astonished when he held up a hand to quiet her.

"With respect, Your Grace," he said, bowing his head formally, "Righteous and Spindle are not just your ladies. They are the secret claws of the lion, charged with the protection of your person, and in that duty, they answer to the Captain of the White Lions first."

He's fully restored to himself, Amelia thought, but a part of her worried that the lost heart of him was still hidden under the adherence to duty. Nevertheless, he had a plan to rescue the imprisoned young prince of Aubrey in order to allow her to honor the debt she owed to the man's slain father.

"Go to, Captain," she said, forcing herself to sound more confident than she felt. "Take whatever of my forces you see fit and accomplish your plan. I will await your success in the tower."

Prentice saluted her once more, and as they saw it, the men moving around stopped and joined him, until, as far as Amelia could see, every man in armor or uniform was saluting her. She offered Turley her hand and let him escort her back to her carriage. As she stepped up, she looked over the bloodied, victorious scene and smiled at them all.

"The White Lions have done the Grand Kingdom and the Western Reach great service this day, Captain," she shouted in the morning air. "Men will hear the tale and learn to fear us. The lioness pays homage to the pride, one and all. These are the true kings of the battlefield."

She lifted her hand over her head to wave to them, and men began to cheer her. This time the shouts were not muted, and they followed her as she rode back to her tower to change her clothes and wait for news of a rescued Veckander prince.

CHAPTER 38

"How are you still walking, husband, not collapsed on a bed somewhere?" Righteous asked Prentice as the pair of them led the small column of hand-picked Claws across the Aubrey bridge.

"I fetched down a bowl of porridge oats and a pot of small beer while you took your time getting ready, wife," Prentice snapped at his beloved. He could feel the warmth of the late morning sun, but his thoughts were still overshadowed by the deaths of his friends and comrades. His body ached so that every move was an effort, and the skin on his face stung from all the splinter cuts of the explosion.

"So, you can go all night through a battle but can't do me the same service? Is loving your wife so much worse a duty?"

Prentice cocked an eyebrow at his wife and then looked over his shoulder at the men marching behind them, scowling. "I am not going to discuss the practices of our nights abed in the presence of others."

Righteous gave him an impish grin and winked, then took a tearing bite from the hunk of brown bread she'd brought from camp to break her own fast. Prentice knew that look. She was telling him that she wasn't afraid, that she still loved him and wanted to play. It was her way of escaping the horrors just past. She made fun—of him, of the world around her—to drive away fear and hold pain at bay. That was who she was, the street fighter within her, the spirit of the knife—a short, bright edge that cut any and all who made the mistake of mishandling her.

Prentice loved her for it.

Somewhere inside of him, his last words with Felix—that strange moment of loyalty that had felt like mutiny, cut short by pointless brutality—were eating away at him. His sergeant had died saving his life. If Felix had not shoved him backwards, Prentice would likely have been caught in the blast and killed. But if Felix hadn't needed to make his captain stop being a hero, then...?

"Make way dogs, the prince's business! Make way!"

Prentice broke from his reverie as he and his men were forced aside by five horsemen riding single file at a canter. Their armor jingled and their livery was bright in the sunlight. The men rode proudly past, lances held high, with royal red and gold pennants flying beneath.

"Better hurry, boys, can't be much battle left, you know," Righteous called after them, and several of Prentice's soldiers chuckled. Without thinking, Prentice cuffed his wife's shoulder.

"What was that for?" she demanded.

"What are we going to do when they turn around all offended at your cheekiness?" he demanded of her.

"What? This cheek?" she pointed to the scar on her face, the brawler's mark she was branded with before being transported across the mountains.

"You know what I mean."

"I don't know," she said, feigning uncertainty, with the knowing glint still in her expression. "I'd likely do what I always do. Curtsey and beg for forgiveness so that the big, bad knights don't hurt poor, little me."

"And you think that would work?" Prentice could hear the sour tone in his voice, but he couldn't stop it. It was like a venomous spring bubbling up from deep in his soul. He knew he wasn't angry with Righteous, but he couldn't stop himself chastising her. "Knights and nobles kill folk like us out of mere convenience. Hell, even out of boredom. Why provoke them?"

Righteous looked at him for a moment until he looked away, and then she leaned in to whisper in his ear, "You know why."

Not knowing how to answer that and not trusting himself not to be needlessly cruel, Prentice said nothing but continued the march across the bridge. They were just about to step off the bridge when Righteous called the men to halt.

"What for?" he asked, but she ignored him and looked to the two lines of five swordsmen who'd come to an obedient stop.

On their shoulders some carried ropes and other tools. One of them had a small keg of black powder tied to his back. Their captain had tried to equip them for every problem they might encounter, since he had only a vague idea what getting into the Ditch prison would entail. Each man was stern, looking as grim as Prentice felt.

"I' been talking with the captain," Righteous told them, "and he says this is like to be a bloody little escapade. Big risk and maybe no reward. He don't feel it's fair for blokes what have just fought all night to be forced to face another day's brawling and affray. So, he's agreed, anyone who wants to drop out, go right ahead. No shame. But if anyone steps a foot off this bridge, he's in this to the end. 'Til we get this Vec prince back or die trying."

Prentice wanted to rebuke her. If she'd raised such an idea with him privately, he'd have been angry with her. To do it like this made him nearly explode in fury. But even as he was trying to keep the emotions inside him under control, he realized that every man had marched forward until they were off the bridge. The entire grim parade had not even hesitated or needed to so much as look at one another.

"You see," Righteous whispered in his ear, "they don't blame you. They know you're looking out for them and won't ask them to risk what you won't. If you don't trust yourself, trust them. They trust you."

Prentice wanted to kiss her. "How are you so fearless?" he asked, shaking his head.

"'Cause I'm wild at heart. Isn't that what they say?" said Righteous. "Too wild to be a lady-in-waiting."

"I have heard it said," Prentice agreed.

"Well, they're all wrong. I'm fearless 'cause I got a man that knows me all the way to the bottom. He knows all the bad and all the nasty, and he isn't afraid of none of it. My man slays monsters in the night and then comes to my bed with kisses. Woe betide any man who crosses me 'cause they'll have to face me and him together, and we're the sharpest, hardest pair o' blades any kingdom's ever seen. I'm not afraid, because I'm the safest little minx in a thousand leagues."

That did make Prentice smile. "Alright, Corporal Minx," he said. "How about we set our minds to our duty and stop this lollygagging."

"As you order, Captain."

Now that the little squad had crossed the bridge, the sounds of battle seemed somehow closer, even though the actual fighting was no nearer. It was a trick of the mind, Prentice knew. With the river in the way, the fighting had seemed farther and the safety greater. Now, any force could detach from the main fray and charge them down. Looking over his shoulder, he guessed that his little troop also felt the increased tension.

"Double time, Fangs," he called, and everyone lifted their pace. "We're in bad country now."

They jogged past the village of Three Roads, its daub cottages shadowed and silent in the noon sun, thatched roofs fallen in with neglect. There were no sounds of animals from pens, and the yards were overgrown with unmown grass. Likely the whole village had been deserted since the invasion, the people either fled or enslaved by the Redlanders. Prentice wondered if any of them had turned their neighbors over to the mercy of sacrificial altars like the treacherous river fisherman.

"Oh damn, riders comin' in, Captain," called someone in the lines, and every head turned to look. A handful of men-at-arms and squires had detached themselves from the back of the king's army and ridden the league or so to investigate this small band of armed folk creeping around behind them.

"Steady," said Prentice, assessing the incoming men on horseback.

"Just keep quiet and trust the captain," said Righteous, happily acting the corporal. "Let him do the talking, and be ready to bend the knee if they get all hoity-toity. We got a job to do for the duchess and don't need no trouble."

His wife's orders were perfect and her anticipation sound, but as he watched the riders coming closer, Prentice found himself wishing for trouble. He had chastised her for cheek and disrespect on the bridge, but now he felt the same temptation in himself. His time in this war had begun something like this, on a hot summer's afternoon with kingdom knights riding up after a battle with Redlanders. Then, he had been a convict on the chain, forced on his knees with his fellows. This time he was a sworn man, well-armed and bloodied, while clean-cut squires and lesser knights, who'd enjoyed a pleasant morning's exercise hunting the remnants of an army he and his men had broken for them, rode up to confront him. Prentice felt in no mood to show the least bit of deference.

"Ho there," called the lead knight as he reined in his horse, his armor and tack jangling musically. "Stand and name yourselves."

"Lions of the Reach," Prentice answered. He saluted and his soldiers followed his example. The man in the saddle blinked and looked to his fellows, plainly bemused at the unfamiliar gesture of respect.

"Rolan?" he called over his shoulder to a squire dressed in Prince of Rhales livery. "You rode west with the Rhales court. What say you? Do these look like Reachermen to you?"

Rolan was lucky to be sixteen if he was a day, which meant that he must have been a mere page if he'd ridden west with the prince's failed crusade, a lucky youth to have survived that march. The squire trotted up on his horse and imperiously looked them over.

"They're wearing the bitch's colors, Sir Micah," he declared. "And sure that calling themselves lions while skulking about like rats is the way of all Reachermen. I say they're like to be deserters, fleeing into the Vec."

"Seems right to me," agreed Sir Micah. Prentice felt his men behind him bristle at the insult, though to their credit, they uttered no sound.

"We are under the duchess' direct orders," Prentice told the man, his eyes slitted. He felt his hand drifting toward the borrowed sword hilt at his hip. His own sword was lost somewhere on the riverbank, and he'd left his partisan behind because it was the wrong sort of weapon for close-in fighting in a prison or the alleyways of an enemy town. He wished now that he had brought it. With the long-hafted weapon's reach, he was confident he could have both Sir Micah and Rolan out of their saddles before either snobby noble drew their own blades. Sir Micah walked his horse closer to Prentice and then raised his hand as if to slap the captain.

He tries to cuff me and I'm taking his cursed hand home with me, Prentice thought, and his hand quietly gripped his sword hilt. But Sir Micah was pointing.

"What's in the barrel?" he demanded. "Wine? Whiskey? Thinking to have a tipple to celebrate your escape?"

"Black powder," said Righteous. "Duchess wants us to blow out the Aubrey gate so there's no retreat from the king's victory. We win the battle today and they ain't gettin' to hide in no walled town after."

Several of the riders blanched at the mention of black powder.

"We need to go. I've seen what that alchemy can do," said Rolan, and Prentice believed him. A powder explosion had done savage damage to the Prince of Rhales's army during a battle in the west, so the story went.

"What, a little keg like that?" Sir Micah asked, eyebrows raised, but even as he did so, Rolan was wheeling his horse about and trotting away, followed by another of the party. "Come, gentlemen," the knight called after them. "Is it so powerful?"

"Let the fools have it," called Rolan, riding away. "Like as not they'll kill themselves."

"But the king's dragons use..."

"The king's dragons are brave fools who are welcome to risk their lives on that black sand. I am brave but no fool."

Young Rolan's certainty seemed to unnerve the rest of the mounted warriors, and in a moment, Sir Micah found himself alone while his comrades were all riding to a "safe" distance.

"Count yourselves lucky, *lions*," he sneered at the two lines of soldiers. "No one will call your bluff today. But if I lay eyes upon you again, I'll give you all a taste of my steel. I don't forget faces." He spurred his horse after his fellows.

"If you lay eyes on me again," Righteous muttered loudly when he was out of hearing, "it'll only be after I've cut both your haunches and your throat like a slaughterhouse calf, you high and mighty twit."

"That's my girl," said Prentice, and the soldiers chuckled to hear it.

He waved them on, and they all resumed their jog toward the gates of Aubrey.

CHAPTER 39

As it turned out, the gates of Aubrey were lying wide open, as if it were any other trading day for the town. When they charged out, the Redlanders either had not thought or hadn't cared to worry about the town's defense in their absence.

"They never imagine they will lose," Prentice said to himself as he led them under the stone arch of the gatehouse. There were three gates, each anchored to stone pillars so thick it would take a half dozen folk to wrap their arms around them. All three gates were open and, though Prentice went first with watchful caution, not a single armed man held the strong point. There were no guards—not on the walls, not in the towers, nowhere.

"Well, this is nice and convenient," said Righteous, but Prentice could hear the uncertainty in her tone. It was unnerving to walk so easily into the enemy stronghold; too much like a trap. For a long moment they stood in the middle of the road just inside the walls, waiting for the sound of the gate closing behind them and ready to dash to freedom, but time moved on and the town remained silent, the open gates unmoving.

"Alright, so where's this Ditch place we're looking for?" asked Righteous.

Prentice shook his head. "I was planning on asking a local for directions," he said, looking up and down the deserted street. "So, it looks like we need to find a local to ask."

With any direction likely to be as profitable as any other, Prentice pointed the way down the main street leading from the gate. He drew his sword, and everyone followed his example, fitting their small shields on their left hands.

With every footstep into the town, its emptiness became more oppressive, as if they were advancing into an accursed ghost town. Prentice sneered at the idea inside himself, but he felt the uneasiness, nonetheless—a feeling made all the worse as the farther into the town they ventured, the more signs of the Redlanders' cruel sorcery became evident. At the first corner there were several skeletons chained to the eaves of a building, hanging and clanking in the wind. That wasn't so shocking. Crow's cages were known throughout the Grand Kingdom, reserved for the worst criminals like traitors and heretics. A man hung from the walls to starve was not unknown. It would likely have been Prentice's fate, once he'd been convicted of gross heresy. It was only King Kolber's invasion and the calling of a crusade to oppose it that had saved him from such punishment. A crusade meant every convict that could walk was summoned to serve as a rogue in battle, and that had kept Prentice from being hung on a wall like these. What made this trio of skeletons so bitter a sight was that from the size, two were obviously children, and from the scorch marks on the masonry behind them, they had been hung in the chains and then set alight.

A little farther on they began to find walls and doors daubed with Redlander symbols and arcane writings. It might well have only been graffiti, the self-indulgence of conquerors expressing themselves on the conquered, but something about the daubings sat uneasy in the mind. Looking at them was strangely sickening, even more so than the hanging dead. One house had a string of words on both doorposts and the lintel, written in blood, now dried and flaked like a perverse mockery of the first Passover of long-lost Egypt. A closer examination showed that the door itself was nailed shut, and the fate of those inside could only be guessed at.

Two more streets into the town and they came upon a mound of stones and the first signs of life. On top of the mound were the remains of some animal, or a person perhaps, ripped apart and left to rot, and it became clear that the stones were an altar. Prentice wondered if this was the altar where the fisherman's brother had been killed, or were there a number like this about the town? Among the body parts, fat healthy rats gnawed at the remains.

"Something's alive at least," muttered one of the Fangs behind him, but Righteous held a finger to her lips for quiet.

Something was moving on the other side of the altar. They all watched as a filthy, hairy figure rose ever so slowly above the level of the stones. Pale eyes showed in a muck-stained face that seemed not quite human, but those eyes were not focused on Prentice and his squad. The creature was stalking the feeding rats. With a sudden leap, it dove forward and seized one of the fat vermin. The prey squealed and bit to win its freedom, but the hunter barely paused before raising its two hands and hammering the rat onto the stones, stunning it. The creature then held its target up and danced gleefully for a moment, singing to itself. By its voice, its true nature was revealed.

"Just a little girl," said Prentice. From the size of her, the child was likely between six and eight. "Ho there, child."

The little urchin propped herself up to look over the altar stones, revealing the wretched state of the rags that covered her body. She shrieked in fright and bolted away down a side street.

"You startled her," Righteous chided.

"Well, we better get after her then," Prentice snapped back, and the whole force started after the runaway child.

Around the corner, it took a moment to pick the girl from the detritus on the streets. Prentice had seen towns looted after a battle, and they typically looked like this. Houses were ransacked, their goods dragged into the streets, broken or destroyed as the victors searched for valuables. But that was the destruction of a handful of days and military leaders. Even the most disdainful Grand Kingdom noblemen brought their plundering forces to heel quickly, lest a town be utterly consumed. This was like a plundering that never ceased but ground on and on over the months of the Redlander occupation. This was rapine governance, pillage as a form of rule. No wonder Prince Forsyte was so desperate for his people.

No wonder little girls hunted rats in the streets.

The urchin dashed over a mound of shattered, half-burned furniture and used it as a launching point to throw herself at an overhanging eave. As adroit as a monkey, she scrambled up onto the tiled overhang, still gripping the rat in one hand, and began to run along the gutters from building to building. The high path put her out of reach of Prentice's people, but it also slowed her down as she had to leap gaps or watch for loose tiles. The White Lions followed her easily enough until they almost reached the end of the street. Then she ducked away down an unexpected alley, narrow and shadowed by an overhanging higher floor. She clambered along the side of that overhang, holding onto the bracing beams by her fingertips and never dropping to ground level.

Prentice, Righteous, and the men had to kick their way through rubbish and ruin to pursue her down the dimly lit passage. They nearly lost her in a maze of back ways between closely built houses when suddenly they burst into another open thoroughfare. At one end of this road, the detritus was piled higher than a tall man on either side—so high that it formed a kind of wall with an open "gateway" through the middle of the street. The little girl skittered across tiles and beams to drop down behind one of the piles of rubbish, out of sight.

"We'll get her now," muttered one of the men as the squad emerged into the road and watched the urchin jump down. He took a step to resume the chase, but Prentice seized him by the shoulder, pulling him up short.

"Captain?" the man asked, confused.

"There is a reason she goes by the roofs," Prentice told his man and pointed to the gap in the rubbish "barricade." There on the roadway was a handful of dead rats, flea-bitten and rotted. As the group stalked carefully forward, following their captain's lead, they saw a line of arcane writing across the cobblestones like that they'd seen on the doorframe earlier, though if this was written in blood, it had faded in the weather to be little more than a dim stain on the already dark stones.

"Invader magic, you think?" asked Righteous. "You got sharp eyes, Captain Ash."

"I saw the vermin," Prentice replied. "It made me think."

"Good thing you think quick."

The other men crowded around, looking down at the barely visible line of arcana.

"That magic kills 'em, does it, Captain?" one of the men asked.

Before Prentice could answer the question, another, unexpected voice spoke for him.

"Kills everything—rats and men, dogs, cats, horses, and cattle."

They looked up to see the wizened figure of a nun in a habit of filthy homespun, patched and torn in many places. Crouching at the woman's feet, half hiding behind the dirty linen skirts, was the urchin, prize rat still in hand. The elderly woman's lined face was pinched and drawn with hunger. She had a rag tied around one eye, suggesting the orb underneath was gone, and her other eye watched the gathered Kingdom soldiers warily.

"It'll even kill a bird," she finished her explanation, "if the thing's unlucky enough to land on the writing directly. And no, you can't poke it with a stick. Now tell me, who are you who come into our town to frighten little orphans?"

"We meant the child no harm, I promise you," Prentice answered her. "We are from the Grand Kingdom. White Lions, militia of the Duchess of the Western Reach."

The nun nodded solemnly, her expression dull, almost unfeeling.

"I have seen a white lion in my dreams," she said, and that caused Prentice to start with surprise. "He hunts in the night beyond the walls of Aubrey. I wait for him to come into the town, but he never does."

"I have seen him in my dreams, too," said Prentice, uncomfortably aware of the people standing around him. For years, on and off, he had had dreams and waking visions of an angel in the form of a massive white lion. It had prophesied warnings and victories in battle, as well as inspiring him to form the structure of the White Lions militia in the way he had. But he did not like discussing these auguries with others. It worried him what folk might think. One man's visionary was another man's lunatic. And for a convicted heretic as he was, the notion that he might see angels was likely to offend the clergy of the Church, at the very least.

"What does he do in your dreams?" asked the nun.

"He fights a multi-headed serpent," Prentice told her, and that seemed to penetrate her fugue, because her good eye widened in surprise.

She nodded. "Does he win?" she asked.

Prentice shook his head. "Not yet, but I have hope."

"We have little hope left."

"I can imagine."

"The king's thumping the invaders good, just out front o' your town," said Righteous, looking over her shoulder toward the town gate. "You could go watch if you like. We're going to win, I promise you. My man and his army bloodied the Redlanders up but good last night, and now the king's riding 'em down to finish off."

The old woman looked at Righteous, then at Prentice, then back to the young woman in armor. "We cannot leave."

"Sure, you can," Righteous urged happily. "The Redlanders is broken. They ain't coming back."

The nun shook her head and looked down at the sorcerous writing on the road. "We cannot leave," she repeated.

"These are everywhere?" asked Prentice, eyes narrowing. If the Redlanders had painted these death spells on many roads around the town, then the entire of Aubrey could be a maze. There might be no way through to the prison.

"Around Bridles," the nun explained, indicating the neighborhood about her by her gestures, "all the lanes west of High Street, down as far as the Tilted Crown Tavern, or what is left of it. To the east, they have painted every lane that lets onto Wall Road. We are trapped in our homes, or the homes we have taken when their owners were murdered."

The little urchin at her feet whimpered at that, and the nun leaned down to stroke her hair gently.

"They're keeping you as slaves? Convict labor?" Prentice asked. He felt the men around him bristle with anger at that prospect, but the old woman shook her head once more.

"They have the lowest caste of their religion for labor. They build so little that they need few workers."

"The lowest caste? The one's that swear to their sorceresses and take the brand to become supplicants?"

The nun nodded.

"So why all the magic to lock you in?" asked one of the other Fangs, who then turned and saluted to Prentice, nodding his head to apologize for speaking out of turn.

"It's a good question," said Prentice, turning back to the aged woman.

"It is their gospel, a gospel of blood offered to demons," she explained and there was a broken-hearted sadness in her eyes. Her voice, though, showed no emotion. "They pushed us here to force us to submit."

Prentice remembered the fisherman he'd met last night. His eyes met the woman's and he nodded to show he understood. "You starve until you sacrifice a family member to their gods."

"It doesn't even have to a be family member anymore. One only has to point to another person and speak their name to the serpents. That's all they require. Then, painted guards seize the victim and drag them to the altar. The serpent priestess takes your hand and tells you the words that bind your soul into hell, you get the brand over your heart, and it is finished. They let you leave their magic prison and go back to your life, such as it is without a soul."

"So the magic can be crossed?" Prentice seized on that.

"Only by the serpents and those they are touching or have cast their spells on, it seems," the nun said.

"And of course, they've put their spells around the Ditch prison."

The nun cocked an eyebrow. "You've come to free the prince's son?"

"Then he is in there?" asked Prentice.

"There are rumors," was all the nun confirmed. "As to the magic there, who could say? The invaders are not like Vec princes. They have not needed prisons to hold criminals or to torture their enemies. All the world are their enemies, and those they do not slaughter at first they can herd into their homes and make that into a prison. Whatever you find in the Ditch, it will either be nothing or worse than everything you've already seen."

Prentice suppressed a shiver at that prospect. He'd been brutalized for over ten years as a convict on the chain and had seen so many of the horrors the Redlanders inflicted on the world around them. He could not imagine what might be worse. "How do we find the Ditch?"

"Go back to the High Street," the nun told him. "Then turn south and go toward the prince's palace—the tall mansion made to look like a castle keep. Then, to the east of that is a low stone block of a building, surrounded by an old moat. That's the Ditch. It used to be the original castle, so they say, but the bridge can't be drawn anymore, and there's no gate, just a door. The bar is thick though. If the beam is shot, your little posse won't be enough."

"We got something special in that case," said Righteous happily, and Prentice realized the men around him were grinning as well. Some of them, at least.

Why not? he thought. *In the face of this nightmare, a keg of black powder seems positively wholesome. Let them enjoy their feeling of power for a moment.*

"Is she the only one that can get over and around the spells?" Righteous asked, looking down at the urchin.

"She is not the only one, but few are left," said the nun. "They could find the gaps to sneak through, and for a while they smuggled in food. But hungry folks become readier to make harsh sacrifices, and another parent's child can seem like easier pickings."

"Bastards," hissed Righteous, but Prentice put his hand on her arm.

"I'm guessing the ones left are too weak to sneak the urchins' ways?" he said. The nun nodded.

"We last remaining few have meagre strength, and as you can see, there is no easy game for the urchins to hunt. The end is drawing near. We are resolved not to convert to their slaughterhouse faith, but the invaders allow no other escape. Some would sacrifice themselves for the others. Sacrist Jonathan said that their altars were just stones and their knives just steel. They could kill his body, but a devout soul would go to God. He took a boy to the priests and offered himself as the sacrifice if they would let the boy go."

Prentice nodded again sadly.

Righteous was slower on the uptake. "Did they let him go?" she asked.

"They killed him," said Prentice.

"Right in front of Sacrist Jonathan's eyes," the nun said, closing hers. There was a flicker of a bitter smile at the corner of her mouth. Perhaps it was the last emotion her brutalized soul could feel. She opened her eye again. "Then they dragged Sacrist Jonathan to their altar and cut him apart anyway. Perhaps his soul went to God, and not to their demons, but he went screaming and weeping."

"When we come back, we'll take her and any others that can get around the spells with us," offered Righteous. Prentice looked at her sharply, but she refused to withdraw her offer. "We will, or you won't sleep sound another night in your life."

As they glared at each other, the nun snorted with fatigued derision and then turned away, taking the little girl with her.

"She doesn't trust us," said Righteous, giving her husband an angry, accusatory glance.

Prentice shook his head. "She doesn't think we're coming back."

Chapter 40

The Ditch was exactly as the nun had described it—a flat slab built of stone blocks next to the prince's palace. It was only two or two and-a-half stories high, and the only windows were right near the top, cross-barred with iron. The moat that gave the prison its name was about ten feet deep but empty of water. Instead, long grass grew on the bottom, some of the fronds reaching halfway to the bridge that ran across to the entry gate.

"Be ready to use the powder," Prentice said as they crossed the bridge slowly, eyes scanning the boards for signs of a painted killing spell. At the heavy, ironbound door he hesitated and listened for a moment, but there was only the sound of insects in the grasses of the ditch beneath them. The prison was quiet, and so was the town in every direction. Even the sounds of the distant battle at Cattlefields were too faded to hear. Prentice pushed the door, and to his relief, it swung open smoothly, as if it were any other well-maintained portal. The flagstones on the floor held no obvious enchantments, but Prentice looked all around the door frame and even at the ceiling to make absolutely certain. Then, with a raised eyebrow for his wife, he took the first step inside.

Not dying brought a sigh of relief unbidden to his lips, but he did not relax; no spell on the threshold didn't mean none at all.

The cursed writing could be anywhere in here. Every unturned corner could be deadly.

Inside, the vestibule led ahead in nearly total darkness. Prentice heard his men file in behind him slowly, and there was a scraping sound as one of them pulled a brass lantern out of its sconce and shook the oil reservoir. "Empty."

"Maybe no one's here, Captain," one of his men said with an optimistic shrug.

"Or maybe they just don't need light to see," said Righteous. Several of the men turned to look at her, and Prentice glared at her, eyes wide. "I'm just saying," she went on. "They got snake folk and wolf folk and other folk like that. None of them creatures need firelight to see in the dark."

"Thanks for that," said Prentice.

She was right, but it was far from a comforting thought. A short way into the stone-walled room there was an upturned table and several broken chairs. Among the wreckage were rush torches, scattered on the floor. It made sense. The table was likely a guard sergeant's post, a place from which other guards would be sent around the prison. Escorts would need light to go wherever they were sent. He set the men to lighting the torches and then contemplated their next move.

"Alright, where do you keep an imprisoned prince?" he asked them as they looked about with the new light, getting a better sense of their surroundings.

"In a tower, like a princess?" suggested one, but almost immediately another one disagreed.

"The worse the prison, the deeper you go," he said. "Dungeons go down, not up."

"You speak like an expert, Reton," Righteous teased him.

"I bet I seen the inside o' more prisons than you have," flat-faced Reton shot back.

Righteous leaned closer to him with a cold look on her face. "I'll take that bet," she whispered with a wintery smile. "And when we get back to camp tonight, you'll owe me the finest cup of something sweet you can find."

"We'll see," said Reton, but Prentice cut him off.

"Bet or not, Reton's most likely correct. We'll find stairs and head downward." All the men nodded their acceptance and turned, ready to follow the captain as he led them out of the vestibule. Before he turned down a large corridor, Prentice looked back over his shoulder. "Oh, and Reton? My wife prefers white wines over reds, or a lager over an ale."

"What?" asked Reton.

"For when you pay her winnings. Inside more prisons than she has? As if."

The little squad moved through the prison, and while they remained on the ground floor, it seemed the nun's prediction that they would find nothing would prove true. They found cells, some locked, some not, but all empty, straw and rushes mildewing on their floors. Whenever they found other torches—some burned out in sconces, others discarded—they scooped them up, and in one cell they found manacles torn from the wall and a discarded crowbar on the floor.

"Someone got busted out," said Righteous.

Prentice took up the crowbar and handed it to one of his men. They'd already come with one, along with rope and hooks, but another would not go amiss. A little while later, they found a spiraling stair going down into the earth, and they followed that. Beneath were dungeons, and it swiftly became clear that the Redlanders had found a use for Vec prisons every bit as brutal as all the other dire things they did. Bodies and parts of bodies were scattered about in cells and in the corridors so that the Fangs choked and spat at the charnel stench. Most of the flesh had rotted or gone to feed rats, but every footstep stirred a cloud of decay so powerful that even before they had reached the end of the first corridor, two of the men were pulling their helmets up to vomit.

Prentice led the way, and in the paltry light shed by the torches, he found himself straining to study every patch of wall, floor, and ceiling he could see, certain that they must find some arcanum somewhere. Sergeant Felix would not have approved, and Sir Gant would have lectured him about the role of a commander, that he should send a less "valuable" man first. But they were dead, and Prentice would not let any man face this hazard before him. He could not make them do it; his conscience would not let him. He was so focused on his immediate surroundings and the threat of magic that as he crept forward, he didn't notice the flicker of light farther along the corridor they were walking.

"Down there," Righteous hissed, pointing, and Prentice looked to realize there was a dim torchlight ahead.

As he was watching, there was an echoing thud, the light dimmed, and a metallic clang tolled in the dark. Someone ahead had closed a door and locked it. Prentice could sense his men's eagerness, poised behind him to rush forward, but he held them back with his slow advance. Anyone who let them hear a door closing was likely baiting a trap.

Methodical steps brought he and his men to a simple square room with a single cell door on the other side. It was solid wood, ironbound, with a cross-barred viewing window. A small amount of light flickered through that window. Gesturing for his men to wait on the other side of the room, Prentice crept to the door, and pressing himself to the side in case a weapon might suddenly be thrust through the opening, he peered inside. No blade of ambush waited, and he made a bolder examination. The chamber on the other side was curved and deep, with what looked like a winding stair going from the door around the wall to the lower floor. There were empty manacles and chains in the stones of the stair and a burning torch in a sconce. Someone had to have lit that, and there looked to be more light farther down. He tried the door latch and found it bolted on the other side.

"Well, this might be it," he said to his men. "But it's locked."

"That's why we brought tools, Captain," said Reton. They set about rigging ropes and hooks through the viewing window while Reton and another Fang put crowbars to the door hinges. When they were set, they all put hands to the rope to pull.

"Right, heave with all your might, you mongrels," said Righteous, standing apart from the rest of them. Prentice, his own hands on the rope, raised an eyebrow. "I'm just a lady-in-waiting," Righteous protested. "You don't expect mild little me to haul on a rope, do you?" Then she poked her tongue out at him.

Prentice shook his head, and with a nod, he and eight other men began to heave upon the cables. The cables creaked with the strain and the door almost immediately began to rattle in its frame. Men slipped on the muck-riddled floor, and now and again a metallic clink sounded as their armor banged against a stone wall. The two on the crowbars dug them around the hinges, sometimes striking stone, sometimes the wood of the door, until they were able to get them wedged in and begin to lever the structure apart. At first, everyone tried to maintain a modicum of quiet, but as the strain of the task went on, they began to grunt and labor more openly. For himself, Prentice felt his exhausted body crying for relief, muscles burning with fatigue, but he gritted his teeth and kept to the task. Reton's crow slipped in his hands suddenly and the man swore loudly as the clawed end tore the leather palm of his glove and the flesh underneath.

"Shh," hissed Righteous, but Reton only gave her a rude gesture with his injured hand. He put himself back to the task and suddenly there was a loud crack. The iron of the hinges had started to tear away from its fixtures. All the men smiled, and they redoubled their efforts. Soon, the door was loose, and with a weighty last heave that sent several of the men on the ropes sprawling, the door's top hinge and locking bolt ripped free. The door tumbled backward at an angle, still attached by the lower hinge.

"Right," said Reton with determination as he threw away his crowbar and drew his sword again. The broken door had half collapsed on the other man wielding a crow, knocking him to the ground. But Reton wasn't waiting, and the other man had to pull his legs out fast as his partner clambered over the splintered wood, ready to put his blade into the first thing he found alive inside.

"No, wait!" Prentice shouted, one hand helping up a fallen man next to him.

But it was too late. Reton stepped through the ruined doorway and fell, face forward. His steel helmet rang like a bell as it struck the stone steps beyond, and the sword in his hand clattered away. It was so swift that everyone blinked for a moment, even though none of them could have any doubt what had just happened.

Redlander magic had just killed Reton.

CHAPTER 41

A coughing, hissing laugh echoed through the doorway from the depths of the chamber beyond, and then a sibilant female voice called up in mock pity.

"Oh, he came so far and fell so hard."

"Bitch!" spat one of the men, but a comrade put a hand to him to hold him back from doing anything foolish.

"Maybe we could rush through," whispered another. "Like overwhelming a guard."

"Or just as likely all fall dead faster," Righteous said, tutting in disgust.

Prentice held up a hand for quiet and crept back to the doorway, looking down at the man who had fallen under the broken door and was now scrambling away. Righteous hissed at her husband nervously, but he ignored her and raised a torch in his hand to see the doorframe without entering it. Sure enough, there was the enspelled writing inside the jamb. As soon as Reton crossed the threshold, it took him. Prentice stepped back with a frown.

"What? No more brave men? Are all the feskanners cowards?" hissed the voice.

"What's she saying?" asked a man.

"She means Veckanders," whispered Righteous. "Her voice is strange. Remember, she's a snake and a foreigner."

Prentice could hear them, but he wasn't listening. He was trying to puzzle out the spell on the door. The nun had warned them not to touch it, not even with a stick, she'd said. That made him think there was no way to wash it or wipe it away without triggering the magic. But the girl had clambered around it, and she'd been keeping herself up on the sides of the walls pretty fearlessly.

"You can get close," he muttered, coming to conclusions, "as long as you don't touch or cross the line of the script."

"You sure, Captain?"

"I think so."

"They show you what to do with these things at the academy, did they husband?" asked Righteous.

Prentice looked back over his shoulder at her in the flickering torchlight. "If anyone at Ashfield knows anything about this, they never shared it with me," he said.

"If we can't cross the writing, then we can't go through that door. Do we even know this prince's son is down there?"

"He's down there." Prentice was sure of it. "And we cannot go around the doorway, can we?"

"No!"

"So...?"

"So? So what?"

Prentice could hear the rising tension in his wife's voice. Yet somehow, he felt calmer now that he had a problem and an enemy in reach, even though the solution he was about to propose was far from practical.

"So, we need to make a new doorway."

"How do we make a new doorway?" she demanded. "We going to turn miners now? I thought we left those fellas up north in Fallenhill."

"We don't need miners. We have the next best thing."

He stepped back to his last man, the one carrying the little keg of black powder. As they realized his plan, most of his men looked grim, and one or two of them cast glances at

Righteous. In the quiet, inner part of himself where his thinking was clearest, Prentice was pleased to see that. That was how it should be; a soldier should look to the corporal or sergeant to tell the commander when he was about to do a damn fool thing. That had been Felix's point the previous night. But these thoughts were not in Prentice's mind for long. He was too busy calculating. Whoever was down there was the only enemy they'd encountered the whole way here. That meant they were likely not out with the rest of the Redlander army for a reason and they were probably alone, or few in number, because they were hiding and using the trap, not trying to win by force of arms. And they weren't trying to escape, at least not yet, so whatever they had down there was something they hadn't finished with.

It had to be Prince Forsyte's son.

And over all this thinking, driving Prentice forward, was the clear certainty that they had to rescue this lad and get themselves out of Aubrey with him before King Chrostmer crushed the Redlanders and took the town for himself. He grabbed the little barrel and pushed it under the broken door, right up against the remaining hinge. He reached a hand behind himself, holding the palm open to his men.

"Longmatch," he ordered.

The coil of fuse was handed to him, and as he began to unwind it, Righteous snuck up beside him.

"You know, darling husband, that I would never think to question you," she whispered in his ear. He knew what she was leading up to and planned to ignore her until he was ready to explain himself, but this statement was too much.

"Is that right, wife?" he asked her, incredulous. All pretense of girlishness or playful trouble fell away from Righteous, and she fixed him with a serious eye.

"It's been a long night, husband," she whispered, leaning in so close that none of the other men could hear. "You've not slept, hardly eaten, and you've lost friends. Good friends. Are you sure your thinking's as straight as it should be? Tell me you know what you're doing."

"I know," he said without hesitation. He looked back at the door, still calculating, and pulled his sword part way from its sheath, using the edge to cut the cord to the length he wanted. Righteous reached out and took him by the chin, turning him to face her once again.

"Prentice, truly?"

He didn't want to stop. He wanted to finish this horrific task for the duchess and bring the whole brutal night to an end. It was still not even a full day since he and Turley rowed the Murr to simply scout the enemy. Through the morning he had been burning with fury, but now he was tired. He knew that, and though he wanted to dismiss his wife's concerns, he also knew she could be right. He forced himself to draw in a taught breath.

"Is there some other way? Can you think of anything else?"

"I...this is..." she said. She was reaching, hoping to think of something, anything other than this hazardous plan. Prentice could see it in her eyes.

"We did not come all this way, through all of that, just to turn back now," he told her.

"You never back down from nothing, husband."

"Trust me."

"I do, but..." she wanted to say more, but Prentice put his gloved finger to her lips. It was an odd gesture, the gentle intimacy of his finger's touch mixed with the military practicality of the gauntlet he was wearing.

"Take the men back down the corridor and into one of the open cells. That should protect us from the blast," he told her. "I'll light this and join you presently."

Righteous nodded reluctantly, then turned and gestured for the others to follow her. "Captain'll blast the magic away and then we get that Veckander prince-whelp out o' there. Righto?"

They nodded and she led them out of the chamber. Prentice was alone with a single torch and the end of the fuse in his other hand. He held them a moment to allow his people to reach their refuge, then shouted through the accursed doorway.

"One chance. Dismiss the spell and surrender, and I will spare your life."

The hissing voice laughed and scoffed. "I do not fear death like you, lesser mortal. And I know you are lying."

Prentice realized that he wasn't sure if he had been or not. It was a fair offer of reprieve, but he also felt the anger inside himself, colder now, but still there like a frozen sea, black and deep, only awaiting a winter squall to whip it into a murderous fury once more. He might well take prisoners and march them out of here, hands bound, but then, as soon as he saw the wild, starved eyes of another tormented orphan, he would take out his sword and cut the throat of every captive and not feel the least twinge of mercy. It was a grim thought, but he shrugged it off. He'd offered them the chance to surrender, and it was more than he'd wanted to do.

Taking the end of the fuel-soaked twine, he put it into the torch flame. The fuse smoldered a moment, then began to spark and spit as it burned rapidly. He dropped it to the ground and turned, torch ahead, to run down the corridor. Finding the cell they had all hidden in, he rounded through the doorway and saw Righteous crouching in a corner. He threw himself over top of her, covering her body, and leaned close, pushing her head down to be safer under him.

"This is nice and all, but how long--" Righteous had begun to ask when there was a boom like a thunderclap impossibly close overhead. The stones around them heaved and groaned, and dust fell from the ceiling. All but one of their torches guttered, and the air was so clouded with particles that it was like standing in a mist. Someone coughed and slowly they all rose back to their feet.

"Everyone hale and healthy?" Prentice asked, and they nodded or saluted as they tried to get their breaths back. The force of the explosion had knocked the air from their lungs.

Righteous stood up and recovered one of the extinguished torches, struggling to get it relit from the other through the dusty air.

"Was that enough?" she asked. "I mean, did that do it, do you think?"

"Only one way to find out," Prentice answered her. He drew his sword and put his buckler in place. He was already heading out of the cell when Righteous caught his belt. "What are you doing?" he demanded.

"You plan on going first, don't you?" she said levelly.

"Yes."

"Make sure it's safe?"

"Exactly," he agreed.

"But if it ain't, then you'll be dead on the other side," she said.

"Yes. If that happens, there's nothing else for you to do but go back and report to the duchess."

"Sure, all fair and good," Righteous agreed. "Except I'm going with you. You fall, I fall too."

"No!" Prentice all but shouted, but his wife only shook her head.

"I got a pit-fighter's scars, a brawler's mark, and a list o' sins so long a sacrist would go grey tryin' to read them all out to absolve me," she told him. "You ain't going nowhere without me. Not even the afterlife."

"Fine," he said at last. He looked at the other men. One of them shrugged at him through the settling dust.

"You married her, Captain," he said, and everyone chuckled.

"That's enough out of you," Prentice replied, but with a wry smile. He gave the rest of them orders. "If you see us fall, you go straight back to the duchess and tell her everything that's happened here, understand?"

They saluted him. He turned to his wife.

"Do or die time."

They left the cell, Righteous pressed up against his back every step of the way.

CHAPTER 42

Amelia was exhausted enough to try napping in her chambers, but after a fitful hour filled with crimson-colored nightmares, she abandoned the notion. She contemplated calling for brandy or something similarly strong and drinking herself into a stupor but dismissed that idea as well. It might work, but it might also force her into nightmares she would be too drunk to awaken from. That prospect did not appeal. With rest so elusive, she dressed and sent for an escort to go back to the camp and watch the cleanup after the battle. It would be a grim business, but she still preferred it to fretting in her tower like a useless damsel.

She allowed Lady Dalflitch to remain behind to watch over affairs there and to have a moment with her betrothed. Both Turley and Dalflitch made an effort to object, but it was half-hearted, and it was clear both chief steward and lady-in-waiting longed for nothing more than time in each other's company.

So it was that Amelia was amongst the tents of the encampment with two Claws and Lady Spindle when a runner found her with the message that the king was victorious.

"A herald has come?" she asked.

"Don't know nothing 'bout that, Your Grace," the lad said. "But sentries on the riverside is watching, and they've reported to the new sergeant, Corporal Franken."

Amelia smiled at the muddle of title and name, and then realized that with so many injured and slain, Prentice would have to do a deal of reorganizing of the remaining militiamen. She wondered how she could help him with that as the messenger led her party to the river.

The misery of the morning seemed now to have settled into an orderly gloom. Soldiers were still grim, and bodies were yet lined in heartbreaking ranks. Sacrists still performed rites while the enormous pyre of Redlander dead continued to burn. It would likely smolder for days.

Nonetheless, the men who were working were more upright now and cleaner, for the most part. None were badly injured, and those that showed any harm were neatly bandaged, their wounds cleaned. The militia was recovering quickly—the injured taken somewhere to heal while the remainder rested in shifts and then returned to duty. Newly promoted Sergeant Franken saluted Amelia's approach and then bowed his head.

"Your Grace," he said nervously but with a good approximation of courtly form. He was standing on a rise with two drummers and a corporal, wearing a woven white lanyard around his neck, now stained with dirt and sweat.

"You're watching across the river?" she asked as she looked south.

"Aye, Your Grace, and there's sentries up and down the riverside in case some of the retreaters come across the river. Captain Ash's orders, Your Grace."

"Do not fear, Sergeant," she said to him, noting his nervousness but not looking at him. "I will not second guess you in your duty. If I disapprove of something you do, I'll set Captain Ash to address it. He'll know better than I how to punish you, I'm sure." She turned then and gave the man a knowing smile, which Franken returned and then coughed, remembering his place.

They're almost all former convicts, she reminded herself. *Rogues in spirit, if no longer in name. No point expecting them to behave like courtiers.*

She looked across the river and saw that the Kingdom army had clearly broken the remaining Redlanders' resolve. The invaders were retreating westward where trees and riverside shallows gave them shelter from the charging destriers. She wondered if any of the knights would dismount and pursue on foot? A quick look at the churned bog where the Redlanders had been pinned by Prentice's men in the night told her what the men-at-arms would think of that prospect. Looking farther west, she realized that an increasing number of Redlander sails were heading out into the river. Soon, there was a crowd of them, heading up the Murr, away from the Grand Kingdom but toward the mouth of the river Dwelt.

"They're escaping," she said through gritted teeth. This was why Prentice had wanted his men to attack across the river by the bridge—to pin the enemy down on the riverbank and prevent exactly this retreat. Now the raiders would be able to harass her people in the southern Reach for another season. Her militia could end up hunting them for years, and she doubted any of the Rhales or Denay nobles would offer her any support.

"I've got men trying to keep a count, Your Grace," said Franken, "of boats and any who swim ashore. You know, I'm not so strong with counting, but I got some men more learned than me. We'll know how many got away."

"Small comfort," she said out loud, then realized how bitter she sounded. "But that is not your fault, Sergeant. You've done well. Make sure Captain Ash gets that count as soon as you see him. Knowing him, he'll already have some ideas about hunting down these stragglers."

"Yes, Your Grace."

A cannon shot sounded from the Bronze Dragons, and a splash in the river showed that the cannoneers at least were not willing to let the enemy craft escape easily. A second shot hammered west and dismasted one of the boats. Men on the riverside cheered.

"Should we send the Roar down there?" Amelia asked Franken, pointing west. "Our shot could harry them as well, could it not?"

Franken looked genuinely embarrassed by her question, and she wondered if she'd shamed him by thinking of something he had not. She was not sympathetic.

He shouldn't need me to tell him, she thought. But Franken's explanation showed the issue was something altogether different.

"Captain Ash gave opposite orders, Your Grace," he told her, and Amelia immediately understood the man's trouble.

"Why?"

"We haven't got so much powder left," he said, pointing to the wagons and the killing ground still slowly being cleared of victims. "The night took almost all we got. Captain said he wanted the rest kept back for what he called a reserve."

"I'd not heard that," Amelia said, looking over her shoulder at Spindle to see if there had been a message she'd missed. Spindle shrugged and shook her head. As she thought about it though, Amelia wasn't surprised. She was learning much about military matters, but her captain was still a long way ahead of her.

"Do as the captain ordered," she told Franken, and the man seemed immediately relieved. The sound of a trumpet across the river drew her attention, and she looked to see riders breaking into smaller groups and beginning to range freely over the ruin of Cattlefields. The battle proper was over, and the taking of trophies and plunder had begun. That meant that the king was most likely riding to Aubrey at this very moment to claim the town for himself. She wondered if Prentice had found Prince Forsyte's son yet. If not, her captain's mission to the town was about to fail. She hissed to herself at that thought.

"Something troubles you, Your Grace?" asked Spindle attentively, stepping close to be discrete.

"No more than the usual, Lady," Amelia responded. "The king will be on his way to Aubrey now. He'll liberate it, and if Prentice is unsuccessful, or if the king finds the prince's son first, then my plans will have failed. This night's battle will be such a waste."

"Except that the invaders are broken and driven off, Your Grace," Spindle countered.

"That should be enough."

"But it's not, is it Your Grace?"

"The Redlanders were never our only enemies." Amelia started to bow her head, but then realized what she was doing and squared her shoulders, lifting her eyes and fixing a stern expression on her face. She was the Lioness, the Duchess of the Reach. Regret and self-pity were for when she was in her bed at night.

For another hour she watched as the Bronze Dragons took fewer and fewer shots at the retreating boats. The cannoneers doubtless knew their business, but they only struck one time in four or five. Those strikes were usually fatal, but as the sun began to sink, the canons ceased to fire and the last few boats on the river escaped unscathed. There was a small melee on the riverside to the west when a handful of Redlander painted soldiers swam ashore after their boat was sunk. Lion patrols were ready for them, and it was a swiftly one-sided combat. Amelia was about to retire when a knight in a yellow and white tabard with no armor rode up at a pelt and all but threw himself from the saddle to kneel at her feet.

"I come with word from the battle, Your Grace," he said, head bowed.

"Victory, I trust," Amelia said, more coldly than she wanted. She was still so tired, and the sight of the enemy fleeing had wearied her further, it seemed.

"Yes, Your Grace," the man answered, looking up. His expression was not a happy one. "But it is a victory tinged with sorrow. Your captain has been slain."

"Oh God no!" Amelia gasped, putting her hand to her mouth. Beside her, Spindle hissed and Sergeant Franken swore under his breath. The standard-bearer also muttered something sad but guttural that Amelia did not understand.

"Do they have his body?" she asked.

"Lord Ironworth is bringing it, Your Grace. He insisted upon the honor. He is not far behind me."

Of course, he did, Amelia thought. The knight marshal would not hesitate to show Prentice that respect. She blinked her moist eyes to keep from crying as she looked east and saw a company of several knights on horseback, all dirty from battle, but riding proudly, high in the saddle. Lord Carron Ironworth would have insisted on no less than the greatest dignity for a fallen comrade, no matter the differences in status. Between two of the horses was a cloak in which was wrapped the dread burden. Soon enough the little cortege reached the duchess, and Lord Ironworth stood high in his stirrups to salute her. There were sprays of blood dried on his tabard and his horse.

"Your Grace, I have the mournful duty to present your faithful retainer, slain in noble battle. He has given his last breath in your service, and as a comrade of the field, I beg you to receive his body with all due honor." It was a traditional greeting for a slain man's escort, and Amelia was thankful for it. Tradition and ritual were about the only things that could help her keep her nerve at this point.

"You have my thanks and the thanks of the entire Western Reach," she told the knight marshal. "I shall see his remains bestowed with all the honor befitting the glory he won for himself in life."

Lord Ironworth bowed in the saddle again and waved his men with the cloak to bring it forward. Amelia watched it coming, dreading the moment she had to receive it.

"Was he alone when you found him?"

"No, Your Grace," said Ironworth.

No, they'd have all stayed and died beside him, thought Amelia. The lord's next words caught her by surprise, though.

"The riverbank was littered with the slain, I fear, Your Grace. Many were yours, in your livery. It was by sheer luck that I happened upon him to pick his face from the many."

By the riverside? What would Prentice and his squad be doing at the river? Amelia stepped up between the two mounts carrying the cloak and, in the late afternoon light, stared into it.

"Show me," she commanded the knights bearing the makeshift stretcher, and one of them pulled back the hem of the cloak. There was the Reach blue of his attire, the steel of the armor looking more watery than shining in the dimmer light. The face was a mass of bruises, as if he had died from a beating to the head, and above that was a water-plastered matt of red hair. Amelia couldn't stifle a gasp of shock.

Red hair? It wasn't Prentice. For a moment elation thrilled through her. He was still alive, or at least he could be. Then the reality of what she was seeing hit home.

This was Sir Gant, former hedgeknight and sworn bannerman, slain in her service and now brought home in his cloak. Suddenly she wanted to weep again.

CHAPTER 43

"You have my devout thanks, Lord Ironworth," Amelia told the knight marshal again.

"I have done only my duty, Your Grace," he answered looking down from the saddle.

"Nevertheless." The duchess turned to the sergeant standing by, "Have men come to escort the knight captain's body."

Franken saluted and immediately sent orders. Amelia looked back down into the cloak. "Tell your men to have a care. He is to be buried in his harness. He has earned the right."

"Yes, Your Grace."

Amelia reached in to touch her dead knight's face and noticed the silver rat pin on his collar. She took it in her fingers and began to work it free from the coarse fabric. Knowing the significance of the pin, she was sure Prentice would want it kept safe. As she pulled it out, it tore the fabric some, but not badly. It only left a small hole in the cloth, and Amelia was sure Sir Gant would not resent the small damage. She remembered the threadbare surcoat he had been wearing when they met, the clear sign of a noble man-at-arms without means. He had not been ashamed of that coat of near rags, and he would not resent a small tear. The thought made her smile sadly. She wrapped the pin in a kerchief and stored it in her sleeve.

"You and your men have served the Grand Kingdom faithfully this day, My Lord," Amelia told Lord Ironworth as her own soldiers took custody of the body. "Will you dismount and receive refreshment? It would do me honor to take wine and food with you."

"Your offer is sweet and generous," Lord Ironworth replied politely. "And we will, if it please you, accept some small refreshment for ourselves and our horses. But to dine with you would be a dereliction of my duties to the king, Your Grace. I have other tasks yet tonight."

"Of course, My Lord."

Ironworth looked about himself with the air of a professional assessing the quality of another craftsman's work. Amelia wondered what he thought of what he saw.

"It was a hard-fought conflict here last night, My Lord," she told him. "Many died, Reachermen and Redlanders."

"So t'would seem, Your Grace," he replied in a noncommittal tone. He stared past the pyre to the killing ground where the wagons were still mostly in place.

"The wagons made a battlement, and the mud slowed their assault, I assume," he said. "Looks effective."

"Captain Ash's stratagem," Amelia told him proudly. She wanted Lord Ironworth to see her soldiers' worth, especially Prentice's. The Church disdained him as a heretic that they couldn't bring themselves to absolve, and the court thought he was just her fancy man, winning favor between her sheets because that's what so many of their own debauched ladies allowed. But he was her captain and worthier of respect than all of them. If he had been listened to, there wouldn't be a fleet of raiders escaping to the west.

"A goodly enough tactic indeed. Make for a much easier battle, I would think."

Amelia wondered if the man was being deliberately provocative. "I do not know about easier, Lord Ironworth. It cost the Reach many, many men, as well as all our powder, or near enough."

Lord Ironworth looked at her suddenly and then blinked, as if he hadn't really been seeing her. Perhaps he had been lost in thought. "Forgive me, Your Grace. I am being rude. We accept your offer of refreshment and are thankful."

"No forgiveness is needed," Amelia replied, and she was suddenly glad she didn't have to host these knights herself by their own request. Lord Ironworth was an honorable man, but he still saw the world from a knight's perspective, and she had no heart to endure any more of that cold contempt for the common man. Common men and convicts had just saved her lands. The knights were just cleaning up after them. Amelia gave orders that refreshment be brought and, after offering the minimum farewell that courtesy allowed, started back for her tower as swiftly as she could. She had had enough of this day.

She was leading the way purposefully through the rows of tents when two men rushed from between the shelters by another way. One was slender and the other burlier, but both were wearing clerical garb. They emerged so suddenly that the two guards escorting Amelia stepped forward reflexively, holding the men at bay with their halberds. Both men recoiled and tugged their forelocks apologetically.

"Forgive me, Your Grace," said the slender one. "We did not mean to startle you."

Amelia recognized that voice. "Sacrist Fostermae?"

"We heard that Captain Ash had been slain, but others said it was not so," said Fostermae. "When I saw you, I guessed that you would know the right of it."

"Knight Captain Sir Gant, was killed last night," Amelia told the pair, who had the decency to look more sad than relieved. "Some confused him with Captain Ash."

"A sad outcome," said Fostermae. "A great loss to us all. Sir Gant was well loved and rightly so. Is there someone to conduct his funeral rites?"

"Do you wish to do it?" Amelia asked.

"I will, if you ask, but I would not presume to put myself forward."

"Ever the humble servant, sacrist." Amelia nodded approvingly. She looked to the other man standing respectfully behind Fostermae. "We have not met, master."

"My name is Solft, Your Grace," he said with a courtly bow. "I am a...traveling scholar, seeking to document the king's victory."

"A worthy task, I would think." *And something Chrostmer would heartily approve of,* she thought. The sooner someone laid the victory and return of Aubrey at his feet, the better for the king's legacy. It was all a part of her plan as well, but having spent the day surrounded by the human wreckage of the king's pride, Amelia would just as soon have the ruler cast as history's greatest villain. She sighed.

"Might I crave your indulgence, Your Grace?" Solft asked formally.

"If you must."

"My researches have pointed to some important sources in libraries and collections held across the river."

"What do you need across the river?" asked Spindle, and Amelia found herself surprised and curious as well.

"A codex," the scholar explained. "Well, two or three, actually. Possibly a folio as well."

"What could they possibly have to do with King Chrostmer's victory?"

"Master Solft wants to record both the breakaway and the return of Aubrey," Fostermae answered quickly. "A history of both fall and restoration. Some of the texts the master seeks date from the original rebellion of the Vec princes, or even before. If they are still there and not lost in the invasion, it would be essential to rescue them from possible looters."

Something about Fostermae's explanation sounded rehearsed to Amelia's ear, but it did not seem false especially. It made her think that they were not telling her everything. It was certainly an unexpected request. The town had not even been officially taken yet, as far as she knew, although it surely must have been with so many of the Redlanders driven away. But there might yet be pockets of enemy holding out in the town, not to mention that the locals would likely not welcome a Grand Kingdom army coming inside their walls. The Vec and the Kingdom were still enemies, after all.

"Can this not wait?" she asked. "It would be very dangerous."

Both men were earnest as they shook their heads.

"You cannot imagine, Your Grace, how many great works are lost to history during sieges like this," said Solft.

Can I not, indeed? Amelia thought archly, but she knew the lower-born man meant no insult; he was only being sincere. In fact, that earnestness persuaded her that, whatever facts these men were concealing—and she had no doubt they were—they meant her no harm. They truly believed that their purpose needed them to go to Aubrey this very night.

"If you are resolved, gentlemen," she said. "What is it you wish from me?"

Fostermae had a ready response. "An escort, if we may, Your Grace, and a letter of marque from your hand, allowing us to cross the bridge. I know that it is much to ask."

"You ask for more than you know, sacrist." Amelia pinched the bridge of her nose to relieve the tension she felt in her skull. When had she last slept? Not twelve hours ago, the sky had been the color of blood and the night lit up in sanguine twilight. It seemed like an age past. She wanted to rest, to sleep and forget the world for a night. Such was not her privilege.

"I have already sent Captain Ash and a contingent into the city," she told them, looking at both directly and frowning with the strain of focusing her weary mind. "As far as I know, he is still there. Now that the king has won the battle and taken Aubrey, I cannot send more men, not without his express permission. Nor can I give you a letter that would mean anything to any authority you found there. They would all answer to the king, not to my word."

"Then there is nothing we can do," said Fostermae, shaking his head sadly.

"I fear not, sacrist, other than speak the words for the knight captain's funeral."

Fostermae looked to Solft, an apologetic expression on his face, but the heavy-set scholar was not satisfied.

"I must go," he insisted.

"But the duchess has given her decision," said Fostermae. "It is too dangerous."

"Then God will protect me."

"Do not put the Lord your God to the test."

The scholar's soft features hardened suddenly, and the gentle-seeming man exuded a strong-willed commitment that seemed out of place in his comfortable form.

"I do not need an angel to lift my foot," he said vehemently. "I do not fear to dash it against a stone. I need only a covering against the murder in men's hearts."

"Many men hoped for that covering today, old friend," Fostermae responded firmly but gently. "You saw how many of them found their graves."

"And did we not pray to God to be delivered from the crimson sky?" Solft retorted. "You and I, side by side, on our knees before our maker. Look at the sky. Do you see demon red there?" The sun had almost completely set by this time, and the Rampart and the stars were coming out, glowing in the dark as they had on every previous night of Amelia's life. It was as if the witchlight had never been. The duchess shivered as she remembered the previous night, its sorcery and its bloodshed.

"Master scholar," she said to Solft who was still deep in his rhetorical debate with Fostermae, arguing the theological wisdom behind his desire to go immediately. They both stopped and looked at her. "I cannot send my authority with you, but I cannot and will not stop you. You must do as your conscience directs you."

Suddenly, she remembered the silver rat pin in her sleeve. She fished out the kerchief and unwrapped it.

"Captain Ash is still in the town, as far as I know," she explained, holding the pin out to Solft. "Like as not, even if he is there, and safe, you will not find him. But if you do, show him this and tell him you have it by my hand from Sir Gant's uniform. He will know what it means and give you any help you require."

Solft accepted the pin reverently. "My full thanks, Your Grace."

He and Fostermae exchanged one last look in the failing light, and then the sacrist tugged his forelock, making his thin tonsure hair flip about like a bird's wing. "With your permission, Your Grace?"

Amelia nodded to dismiss them, but just as they turned to go, one final question occurred to her. "Tell me, gentlemen, why did you not go to Mother Church with your request? Surely ordained and educated men such as yourself could summon some sort of support from the knights of the Church."

"The Church's martial arm is still with the Prince of Rhales," Fostermae explained readily. "They remain north of the king's camp."

"Daven Marcus never joined the battle?" Amelia asked, astonished. The prince was a venal failure of a man, but she hadn't ever thought of him as a coward. Not joining the battle meant no share of the glory for him at all and likely no plunder or tax rights for the Rhales courtiers. He would look an utter fool, as well as a coward.

"That is the word, Your Grace," said Fostermae, and then he and Solft withdrew, heading away through the camp. As she watched them go, she looked about herself. Smells of cooking and wood smoke reached her nose, and she realized the White Lions had settled in for dinner. There were lights amongst the tents, but there were many quarters where the shelters were still dark, no campfires or candles amongst them.

Too many, she thought.

"Truly, churchmen can't half talk," exclaimed Spindle next to her, and Amelia turned to see her lady had fetched an oil lamp from somewhere. With a gesture, she sought permission to lead the way back to the tower on the ridge, and Amelia accepted.

"That is true, Lady Spindle," the duchess said. "But at least those two wished to talk matters of faith and scripture, not doctrine as a tool for political advantage."

"Is there a difference, Your Grace?" Spindle asked, and it was clear from her tone that it was an honest question with no disdain behind it.

"I believe there is, but I think too many in the Church have forgotten it."

CHAPTER 44

Torch forward, Prentice pressed along the dust-shrouded corridor. He could barely see a pace or two in front of himself, and despite the urge to hurry, his boots kept slipping and tripping over rubble on the ground. Only once did he almost actually fall, but Righteous's hand on his belt steadied him. A couple of times it felt like he did her the same service as she pulled harder for a moment and cursed over her feet. He felt rather than saw when they had reached the door chamber. The dust cloud was thinner, but the air smelled of powder smoke now as well, and the room's boundaries were farther away. The chamber's squared shape had collapsed so that it more resembled a cave than a built dungeon. Overhead, the remaining ceiling stones groaned, and husband and wife shrank away involuntarily.

"That gonna fall in on us?" she asked, trying to peer upward through the smoke and dust.

"I hope not," Prentice replied.

"You know, husband, you usually have better ideas than this."

Prentice didn't say anything to that. His wife was right. What else was there to say? Finally, his torch lit upon what had to be the remains of the doorway, now shattered open like a mouth with its teeth knocked out. Beyond, he could see a downward slope scattered with broken rock that he realized must be the top of the stairs, and farther down still, he thought he could make out some surviving steps.

Of the door and its jamb, no clear evidence remained except a few splinters smoldering here and there amongst the rubble. Prentice searched but couldn't find any piece of the sorcerous writing. It seemed to be destroyed, but he had no idea if that meant it actually *had* been. He hoped that detonating the writing banished the spell, but he had no reason to assume that the curse didn't remain, floating in the air for all eternity, writing or no, until a serpent priest dispelled it.

"I love you," he told his wife over his shoulder as he prepared to test his theory with her.

"Oh shut up and..." Righteous paused and the testiness left her voice. "I love you too, husband."

Together they crept forward, Prentice holding both hands out in front of himself, one with his sword, the other with the torch. The stones under them slid and shook, and even though he tried to go slowly, maybe even save his wife in spite of her intention to live or die with him, he felt himself falling forward, and he had no choice but to rush down the slope until his feet found the security of a flat step. He managed to stop and realized that the lighter dust here in the deeper chamber let him see that there was still a good five-foot fall to the floor. If he slipped off here, he wouldn't die but could easily hurt himself, not to mention dragging Righteous with him.

"It's safe lads," Righteous shouted behind him, and the elation in her voice was unmistakable. "Captain's done it for us."

From the blasted chamber and corridor behind there came cheers and the sound of men clambering forward. Prentice was glad to hear them coming, but there was still the issue of the enemy that had been lurking in this circular pit. Even as the other Lions came on, he heard a strange, choking sound through the smoke.

"Watch out!" he bellowed and threw himself forward as there was a spluttering noise and something wet struck the wall just above where he'd been standing. It hissed as it ran down the stones. There was at least one serpent-woman down here, hiding somewhere in the smoke and dust.

Prentice tried to listen for her, but any sound was drowned out by Righteous's cursing as she was thrown over the edge of the stairs. Prentice's dive to safety had caused her to lose balance, and instead of fighting it, she chose to make a virtue of necessity and released his belt to drop into the space beside the stairway. From the sound of her unhappiness, she had landed poorly but not been badly hurt.

"Warn a girl next time," she muttered.

"There's a serpent here with us," he told her, and there was a hissing chuckle from somewhere deeper in the room.

"I kenned that much for myself, thanks husband, but where is she?"

The creature hawked and spat again, and Righteous cursed. "That was close."

"Did she get you?"

"No," answered his wife. "But I felt it go past my face."

The serpent laughed again. "Are you hunting me, or am I hunting you?"

Prentice didn't answer, and he trusted Righteous was canny enough to do the same. In the cloud, the serpent only had their voices to target them by. Eventually the dust would settle and then it would be up to God whether they were close enough to her to strike before she spat with a clear shot.

"We can find her, Captain," shouted one of the Lions on the stairs. "And we'll keep this entrance blocked. She won't escape."

"No, don't..." Prentice started to shout, but it was too late. The serpent-woman might have trouble finding individual targets in the haze, but she knew where the stairs were. There was another splattering impact, and at least two men cried out in pain. One fell from the stairs and must have dropped near to

Righteous, because she shouted with surprise. The room had become chaos, and envenomed men could not contain their groans of pain. Prentice knew that his other soldiers would seek to help their comrades, and he was certain the serpent would expect that as well. They were easy targets now.

"Hey, you witch!" Prentice shouted suddenly, his voice so loud that it echoed around the damaged pit, and the roof seemingly groaned in response. "Over here, if you're such a damned good huntress! I've faced you scaly harlots many times, and not one of you has been more than a waste of breath." He waved his torch in the air, holding it apart from his body, while trying to feel his way away from the stairs.

Another gobbet emerged through the haze, sizzling past his torch so close that he heard some of the droplets blistering on his gauntlet. He tried to pinpoint the direction from which it had come, peering.

"Is that it?" he mocked. "I've hurt myself worse lighting a candle." He waved the torch again, but for a moment there was no more poison. "What? Out of your vomit? Do you need a moment to go fill your belly? We can wait for you." There was no answer.

From above, on the stairs, he heard the painful whimpering of his wounded men retreating. They would soon be safe from the venom, but that meant he and Righteous were alone in the pit chamber with the enemy. Prentice found one wall, and he flinched as something resolved itself out of the haze until he realized it was an iron rack, bolted to the stones for interrogating prisoners. He decided to follow the wall around and was peering past the rack as the dust continued to clear when he saw something hiding just beyond the torture device. In that instant he realized it was not something but someone, crouched and waiting.

Their eyes locked and then the hiding foe launched itself forward, screaming a battle cry that echoed like an angry animal's in the confines of the chamber. Prentice had his sword held ready in a low guard, and the assailant must not have seen it properly through the haze, for they ran straight onto the point. The shout transformed to a howl of furious agony, but still the creature came on at him. Prentice absorbed the force of the charge, taking a step back. He felt the weight of the body trap his blade, pierced through as it was. With nothing else available, he rammed his forehead down on the attacker's face, the brow ridge of his helmet slamming into flesh and bone, sending the enemy tumbling to the ground. With the body groaning its last at his feet, Prentice struggled to pull his sword free.

"D'you get her?" he heard Righteous ask him.

"Yes. Run right through," he told her, and she chuckled. He knelt down to get a better angle on his trapped blade and the dead figure became clearer in his vision, revealing the tattooed body of a Redlander, a typical raider. "Wait no, it's another one!" he shouted as a warning. "The serpent's still down here!"

Over his shoulder Prentice heard the tell-tale hawking of a serpent-priest about to spit. With his sword trapped, he had no choice but to swing his torch around and thrust it in that direction, desperately. The light revealed the second enemy, the priestess, standing over him. The fiery end struck her on the corner of her jaw and deflected her face at exactly the moment when she opened to spit. The gout of venom flew straight through the flame and ignited, splashing liquid fire on the wall, the beastwoman's face, and Prentice's gloved hand. He recoiled, dropping torch and sword hilt, tripping over the man he'd just killed and scrabbling to get safe from the flames. The serpent screamed and raged in fury as she burned, reminding him of the sorcerous pyre that had consumed the prince and so many Aubrey-folk the night before. The pagan priestess perished in the same agony. Then there was another on top of him, beating at him. Prentice tried to fight them off until he realized it was Righteous, come to help him stamp out the flames.

The burning added black smoke to the room, but it rose quickly, and most of the dust settled. Soon, it was easy to see almost the whole of the narrow chamber's floor.

"Trust you to hog all the iron work," Righteous told him as Prentice got back to his feet and pulled his burned gauntlet from his left hand. The armored glove had saved his flesh, but the fire had ruined it otherwise. He threw it away and finished retrieving his trapped sword.

"Over here, Captain," Righteous called him, and through the haze he saw her standing beside another wall-bound rack. There was a person strapped into this one. "You reckon this is our prince's son?"

With only torchlight in the hazy air, Prentice couldn't be sure of any resemblance the figure had to Prince Forsyte. Also, this was a man, not a boy. He looked around the chamber. There were no other bodies he could see, though they'd do well to check all the shadows to be certain. If a child heir had been killed down here, the body could have been tossed into a corner, easily missed in the poor visibility,.

"Get the men down here," Prentice told her. "We'll do a quick search."

"And what about him?" Righteous asked, lifting the man's head by his hair. Both of them blinked when the man groaned, though he was clearly still unconscious.

"We'll get him down and then we'll take him with us as we get the hell out of here."

CHAPTER 45

"**P**rince Forsyte's son is a grown man?"

The idea astonished Amelia, though as she thought about it, she couldn't think why it should. The prince had been a man of forty or more years. He could easily have had an adult child. More than one, in fact. After another moment's consideration, she realized she had judged the man by her own experiences. Grand Kingdom noblemen rarely married in their youth; taking maidenheads was a sport almost as prized as hunting and jousting amongst them. Only later in life did they settle to marriage and children once the appropriate political match had been made. Her own marriage to Duke Marne, as well as the king's and Prince Daven Marcus's, all followed this pattern, or at least the prince's would once he finally got to marrying. Whoever that turned out to be to, Amelia was resolved that it would not be her.

"He looks to be about seventeen or eighteen, Your Grace," Prentice told her from where he sat on his wife's bed in the duchess's tower chamber.

Amelia had been overjoyed to hear that he and Righteous had returned when word came at near midnight. She and Spindle had been sitting together, half-heartedly playing cards to distract their sleep-deprived minds, when Lady Dalflitch entered with the news and then Turley escorted husband and wife into her presence. They were filthy with dust, blood, mud, and soot, but thankfully no more injured, it seemed.

"Were you two in a fight with a blacksmith's forge?" asked Spindle, putting her hand down.

"Yea," answered Righteous, wincing in discomfort as she pulled her gauntlets off. "Him and his three biggest mates."

"We must see to your comfort immediately," said Amelia. "Turley, have water fetched for a bath for both of them."

"Lady Dalflitch already gave the instruction, Your Grace," Turley said, nodding to his betrothed. "First lot'll be ready right quick. Only thing is, there's not but one tub, so they can't both wash at the same time, begging your pardon."

"Can we not find another?"

"I have folk looking, Your Grace, but no success yet."

"I'm a married woman," said Righteous, looking up at her husband. "I don't mind sharing."

"You just want to make the rest of us jealous," quipped Dalflitch, but there was no malice in it. Righteous gave her an impish grin. It warmed Amelia's heart to see her people together and safe after all the recent horrors. She was about to tell Prentice to take the first bath when he pre-empted her.

"You go first, wife," Prentice told Righteous. "I have to make my report to the duchess, and Her Grace needs you cleaned and attired as a proper lady."

Righteous stepped back from him and put her hands on her hips. "Oh, I'm not good enough like this? You want me back in a skirt, is that it?"

"You're filthy," he told her.

"And you want me washed and primped and put back in my costume?"

Prentice stepped up to his wife and looked at her sternly. "I want you to wash away the filth of this cursed night so that the world can see your proper beauty again. See you the way you deserve to be seen."

Righteous's eyes narrowed. She was clearly trying and failing to keep a disapproving look on her face. "You're a rogue, devious charmer, you know that?"

"*Your* devious rogue," Prentice told her in a low voice, and his eyes were focused on her as if she were the only person in the room.

"That's right!" Righteous stood on her toes and kissed her husband's filthy cheek, then flounced from the room to go to her bath, managing to seem girlish in spite of the dirty arming doublet and pieces of armor she was wearing.

"You can talk to me like that, if you want," Dalflitch told Turley.

Amelia understood what she meant.

"Like what?" asked Turley, clearly not understanding.

"Like he talks to her."

"I'm not an educated man like he is."

"That's not what I mean," Dalflitch told him. Amelia couldn't see her face, but she was sure Dalflitch was smiling at Turley. For his part, the chief steward returned the smile at first and then looked past his betrothed to Prentice.

"See the trouble you cause me?" he demanded of his old friend.

"Lady Spindle, am I not still liege over my own lands and my own chamber?" Amelia demanded loudly, getting everyone's attention.

"I would say so, Your Grace," answered Spindle.

"I only ask since everyone seems to be treating my bedchamber like the taproom of a drinking house."

Everyone in the room bowed to her.

"Apologies, Your Grace," said Prentice. "We do not mean to be rude."

"I know, Captain," Amelia told him with a smile. Prentice smiled back, but as he straightened from his bow, his eyes blinked a moment and he lost his balance, nearly collapsing against the wooden partition.

"Heavens, man," said Amelia as Turley helped her captain retain his feet. "You're exhausted. Come, sit here on the bed."

Turley walked Prentice over, helped him sit, and then withdrew to oversee the water for baths. And so, sitting on her own bed, with Prentice sitting on her ladies' bed opposite her, Amelia received the final report of the day and night that soon would be known as the Battle of Red Sky.

"And the prince's son hasn't awoken yet?"

"He stirs some, Your Grace, but he still sleeps."

"Will he ever wake?" Amelia asked the question and hated herself, because she knew she wasn't asking for the young man's good but her own.

"The healer says he thinks so," Prentice said. "Time and rest for his mind seems to be what he needs."

"So do we all."

Prentice nodded.

"And the town is a ruin you say?" Amelia pressed.

"Near to it, Your Grace. Not the pyre that Fallenhill was but drawing close. Half are dead and the rest are starving."

"And all of it in service of their pagan gods?"

"That's how it seems," Prentice told her.

Amelia nodded. She knew Prentice had to have spared her much of the details of the horror he and his soldiers had witnessed, but what he had told her made her shudder.

"To what end?" she wondered out loud. "Is it simply their way, or do they have some greater purpose? Have they merely slain every person in their own homelands and now come to us looking for fresh victims? Are they nothing more than locusts of men?"

"I cannot say, Your Grace," said Prentice. His voice was beginning to slur with fatigue and Amelia was sure that he would fall asleep soon. Strangely, it made her happy to think so. He had been exerting himself to the limit of his strength for days on end now. "Sacrist Fostermae introduced me to a man with some odd ideas that might tell us more."

"Sacrist Fostermae?" asked Amelia. "Do you mean the scholar Solft?"

"You've heard of him, Your Grace?" Prentice blinked, obviously surprised, even through the heavy weariness weighing on him.

"Fostermae brought him to me to ask my warrant to enter Aubrey."

"Why did he want to go to Aubrey?"

"They said there were books, folios there, that contained important history," Amelia told him. "The man Solft seemed in peculiar haste, but if he had heard something of the horrors you encountered, his urgency would make sense."

Prentice was nodding thoughtfully now.

"Do you know something of his purpose, Prentice?" Amelia asked him.

He shook his head slowly. "Some I think, but I would rather not say too much yet, if you'll permit me, Your Grace. When I know for certain, I will unfold it all to you."

"Very good." Amelia had no problem trusting Prentice. Then she remembered the silver pin she had given the scholar. "If you did not find him, or Fostermae, in the town, then you should know that I gave the man one of your silver rats."

"You did?" Prentice cocked an eyebrow.

"Sir Gant's body was recovered from the riverside. I had his from his tabard, and the scholar came to me straight after I had paid my respects. I gave it to him then. I hope you are not offended."

"The rats serve you, Your Grace. Dispose of the pin however you wish."

Amelia knew that Prentice meant what he said, but she also knew how important the respect conveyed in the simple pins was to the ones who carried them. If she were to show the least disregard to the bearer of one, she was sure it would wound Prentice more deeply than he might care to admit.

"At any rate," she said. "I thought you should know there was another pin out in the world."

"Thank you, Your Grace." With a heavy groan, he forced himself to his feet. "With your permission?"

"Where are you going?" she demanded. "You have not even bathed yet."

"You are kind, Your Grace, but I must pay my own respects to Sir Gant before he is buried."

"Can that not wait until morning? You are dead on your feet."

"Some duties should not be made to wait," he told her. His eyes were bloodshot, and his normally straight back was slightly bent, his shoulders hunched. "Please do not stop me, Your Grace."

Amelia wanted to command him, insist he wash and then take a night's rest. Sir Gant's body could wait until morning, surely. Then she remembered the day she had returned to Dweltford after being attacked by the first Redlander raiders. Tired and filthy, she had still insisted on going first to her dead husband's grave to mourn and pray for his soul as a dutiful widow. Suddenly she could not deny Prentice this service to his comrade.

"Very well, Captain," she said and turned to Dalflitch. "My Lady, see that an escort is brought to take the captain to Sir Gant's body directly."

"Yes, Your Grace." Dalflitch bobbed a perfect curtsey.

"Then tell them that my order is that the captain be marched directly to his tent. Men are to help him strip his armor and to clean it for him. Water will be fetched, and his body will be bathed. Then he will be put into his bed. They will set a guard over his tent, and if he rises before the midday tomorrow, they are under my orders to put him back there."

"Yes, Your Grace." The lady left the room.

"Do these orders suit you, Captain?" Amelia asked him.

"Well enough, Your Grace."

"He'd never tell you if they didn't," Spindle said quietly, and Amelia knew it was true.

Prentice bowed gingerly and made his way out of the room. Once he was gone, Amelia looked at her own bed and realized she was also deeply tired and finally ready for sleep. Prentice and Righteous's return had released much of the tension in her mind. And they had brought Forsyte's son with them. They'd been successful. As ugly a thought as it was, the news of the wreckage of Aubrey likely played into her favor as well. If the town was so abused that there would be little plunder, then taxes and future crusades would be the king's only option to keep his nobles happy. The prince's heir was a key to that. And Amelia had the young man in her care. There were more complex rounds of politicking coming in the near future, but she was now well placed and could afford to take a night's sleep. The rest of her plans and problems could wait until morning.

CHAPTER 46

Prentice did as the duchess commanded and slept until late morning. He awoke a little before her strict noon limit but compromised by quietly stretching his stiffened muscles in his tent and contemplating Solft's charcoal illumination copies. He'd seen to Sir Gant's body before bed and managed to choke out a prayer for his friend's passing. At one level it was so strange to lose such a comrade. Prentice had suffered at the hands of so many petty and venal noblemen in his life that it was all he could do not to hate them all without reason. But not all were like that, and Gant was the prefect proof—a man for whom honor and truth mattered so much more than success or status. Prentice was glad they had met and had the chance to serve together. Men-at-arms died in warfare. That was an unavoidable truth that Prentice had accepted long ago. Nonetheless, he shed a tear over his friend and felt no shame for it.

The noon beat echoed from the drums around the camp, announcing the change of watch, and Prentice stood to leave his tent. Before he could, Markas's head poked through the flap.

"You up, Captain?" he asked. "It's noontime."

"What? Were you waiting just outside?" Prentice asked him with a smile.

Markas nodded and grinned. "Corporal...sorry, Sergeant Franken, told me to get you soon as you were up."

"Has he made you his runner?"

"Nothin' like that, Captain," Markas explained as Prentice pushed past him into the sunlight. "It's just that Franken ain't been in the center o' things like Felix was, and he don't know how things work so much. He wanted someone who knew what was what 'til he got it under his hand, like."

That made sense to Prentice. Strictly, Markas had a unique place as the White Lions' standard-bearer, roughly equivalent to a corporal but with no soldiers directly under him. He was always close to Prentice and had had years now of watching how the company was run. In the captain's enforced absence, Markas was a good source to consult.

A waiting soldier fetched Prentice a pewter mug that turned out to be full of watered wine. He took it with thanks and downed a swig. Almost immediately he had to stop, his still aching body threatening to throw it straight back out of his stomach. Taking the hint from his own flesh, he proceeded to consume the fluid in small sips and waved Markas to lead him to his newly promoted master sergeant.

"Oh, thought you should know, Captain," said Markas as they walked, "a sacrist and some churchmen took the knight captain away this morning. I know you was close, but they said you paid your respects last night, so we didn't wake you for it."

"They took him away?" asked Prentice having difficulty concentrating on Markas's words. He'd just had a long sleep and was hungry and thirsty, but the bright, warm sun was making him sleepy again.

"Him and all those of noble birth, so they said," Markas went on. "To send 'em back to their families for proper burial. In crypts and whatnot."

"Of course."

It was typical for members of the Church to take charge of nobles' bodies if they were to be transported a long distance before burial. Ranking nobles slain in battle were often escorted by their high-born comrades, but Church knights might give that service to a lower-ranked nobleman if he had no comrades left. Realizing that, Prentice had a moment's concern.

"These churchmen, were they martial?"

"Captain?"

"Were they men-at-arms? Church knights?" Prentice insisted, wondering if Pallas might have been part of the escort.

"I think some were, but they were being led by a pair a sacrists, and Sacrist Fostermae was the one that showed 'em through the camp to start with."

That was comforting for Prentice, at least, but it did not mean one of the Church knights in the escort hadn't been his brother, Pallas. If he had been there, Prentice had missed him, and the captain wasn't sure if he was disappointed or glad. When he looked inside himself, he didn't know if he wanted to reconcile with his brother or not, to explain himself or just abandon the younger man to the harshness of the doctrine he embraced.

I almost was *him,* Prentice thought. But he didn't know what that meant, or what was right to do about it. He did know that his brother sided wholeheartedly with his enemies, and he expected that meant his father and the rest of his family did as well.

Sergeant Franken was down at the edge of the camp, still overseeing the cleanup. He saluted as Prentice approached.

"Glad to see you, Captain," he said earnestly.

"You seem to have things under control here, Sergeant," Prentice told him.

"Well, cleaning, burning, and burying isn't much of a challenge, even for the dumbest dog of a convict. Line-firsts have it under control, mostly. It's the still living that bother me, if you pardon me saying so, Captain."

"You're worried about the wounded?" Prentice guessed. Franken nodded. "Do we have any healers with us?"

Healers were mysterious figures. Academies and collegiates all over the world taught chirurgeons who performed the science of medicine. They studied the movement and organs of the body, and prescribed treatments of varying effectiveness. Medicines themselves were produced by herbalists, apothecaries, and the endless variations of pharmacopeia brewers that could be found across the Grand Kingdom. But healers could be any or none of these things. Healing happened by touch and prayer, and it was a gift from God. Who or how it was wielded was a counsel the Lord did not share with mortals. Even Mother Church was unable to force or constrain the gift. In times past, the Church had tried to draft true healers into the clergy, but they found the act like trying to grasp water in their hand. Those with the gift went where they wanted, and because of the gift they were welcome everywhere. Some gave their service freely, most charged whatever they wished, and yet somehow few of their patients felt exploited. Sacrist Fostermae could heal some and never asked a shaving of silver for it. During Prince Mercad's campaign against the first Redlander invasion, Prentice had been healed after a savage flogging that should have killed him. In less than a day, he'd gone from dying of his wounds to being strong enough to rejoin the march. That healer had charged a hefty weight of gold for her service. No matter their ways, battles and wars always drew healers forth, and one or more were always found amongst the wounded in the days after a conflict.

"We have a number, Captain," Franken confirmed. "They've mainly done what they can, so I'm told. Whoever isn't on the mend by now, though, isn't like to recover, I'd say."

"Let's not second guess the Lord, Sergeant. Healing is his prerogative," Prentice rebuked Franken quietly. He knew the man was right; it wasn't too hard to tell who'd survive their injuries and who would not. But there was always the possibility someone would surprise them. The girl who'd lost her arm trying to cross the river was healing well, for example, despite the brutality of her injury. Given what he had seen across the Murr in Aubrey, Prentice wondered if perhaps losing her arm wasn't the lesser of two evils.

"How are we with our wagons?" he asked, changing the topic.

"Two are wrecked, Captain. One's lost both axles and the other one's all burned out. I got the men hacking them up for pieces."

"As long as they do not just use them for firewood."

"I'll make sure we keep the bits for other wagons."

"And the rest can be moved?" The prospect of salvaging most of his mobile battlement pleased Prentice. In this one conflict they had proved almost impossibly useful, but he was fairly confident they could be used in a number of battle situations. He smiled for a moment.

"We've got to dig most of 'em out," Franken was explaining. "Some of 'em is up to their sides in the mud, even after we pulled away all the invader bodies. Hell, when you look at it like that, Captain, it looks like it was a real close-run thing. If they'd kept on at us a little while more, they could'a just used their own dead as a ramp to run over us, if you don't mind me saying so."

"I would not have put it past them, Franken," Prentice agreed. "Set double parties to digging out the wagons today. Cancel any drill or weapons practice. No one's going to want to train hard so soon after battle anyway. It looks like we'll have to march soon to start hunting down the ones that got away on boats. And even if not, we can use the wagons to take the wounded back north, at least as far as Griffith."

"I'll see to it, Captain," said Franken, and he walked off, barking for a corporal to attend him.

"D'you still need me, Captain?" asked Markas, who was standing attentively nearby.

"No, Markas, you can return to your duties," Prentice told him, but before the standard-bearer could go, he called after him. "Wait, there was a drummer with us on the bridge, a lad named Solomon. What became of him?" Prentice remembered that the last time he had seen Solomon, the boy had been bravely beating an orderly withdrawal as the Redlander bridge was smashed to kindling by the Bronze Dragons.

"He lived through, Captain," Markas reported. "Last I seen, he was in amongst the wounded, running errands for 'urgeons and healers. Him and the farm boy with the one-armed sweetheart. The pair of them is thick as thieves, last I seen. I figure the boys are keeping each other steady, you know, first nights after a battle and all."

Prentice knew alright. Battle wounded the soul as often as the body. The first nights after a bad combat, what sleep might come often brought dire nightmares with it. And the Red Sky battle had been a particularly bad one, for all that it was ultimately one sided. The Redlander's savagery made sure of that. Prentice fully expected to meet his fallen comrades again in his dreams when he next tried to sleep. He only hoped they did not hate him for living when they had died. He was glad Solomon had found a comrade to stand by him through this next, difficult period. The lad had been impressively brave.

"While I think of it, Markas," Prentice added, "what's the word from the Reachermen nobles? Sir Gant is dead, and the duchess needs a new knight captain. Have we not received any polite suggestions yet?"

"Not that I heard, Captain," Markas reported. "Course I'm just a lowly standard-bearer. I doubt knights and lords even know I'm there if the flag's all furled."

"True enough, Markas. Likely they have gone straight past us to the duchess directly. She will love that."

Prentice had won a good deal of respect for himself amongst the nobles of the Reach, but they still only saw him as a successful commoner. Sir Gant had acted as Prentice's subordinate because of the personal relationship and respect the two men shared. Whoever replaced him as knight captain of the Reach would likely assert a good deal more independence.

Another piece of Sir Gant's passing that's going to cost me, Prentice thought, and then he felt a catch in his chest that brought him up short. Sir Gant was his friend, and he was dead. They would never spar again, never poke fun at each other or compare tales of hardship over a brandy by a nighttime fire. The two men had strangely different heritages and yet both knew what it was to train for war and be brought low, not by enemies on a battlefield but by the vagaries of fate. Thinking of it, Prentice blinked and almost swayed for a moment. He felt no tears, but there was an unexpected pain in his heart. If he'd thought about it, he might have said that he had suffered so much loss in his life that he was beyond feeling anymore. To hurt so for Sir Gant, if only for a moment, was strangely comforting. He was not so dead inside that he could not mourn for his comrades.

That in itself must be proof of the miraculous power of God, he thought, and that brought a wry smile to his lips. Gant would have laughed at that thought.

"Alright, Markas," he forced himself to say, his face becoming a stern mask once more. "Go to your duties and I will head to the duchess' tower. No doubt she has fresh requirements of me."

Markas saluted and marched away.

CHAPTER 47

"The young prince will live, Captain Ash," Duchess Amelia told him as he was admitted to her presence. She had decided it was time to begin referring to the man as 'the young prince' to cover over any objections to the fact that no legal transfer of power had occurred. By rights, of course, he was due to inherit everything from his father, including the title of prince. But if someone in the courts of the Grand Kingdom wanted to raise an objection, they'd have a fair case that the recaptured town was no longer a princedom but a returned province that had been in rebellion for centuries and therefore there was no prince—Forsyte or his son.

"Has he awoken, Your Grace?" Prentice asked.

"Once," the duchess confirmed. "Long enough to tell his name and learn that his father is dead, though he already believed that, apparently."

"What is his name, if I may, Your Grace?"

"Farringdon, so he says."

"The serpents likely told him of his father's death deliberately to break his spirit," said Prentice, and Amelia nodded. She'd concluded the same thing herself. "Did they succeed, do you think, Your Grace?"

"I could not say, Prentice," Amelia told him. "Would it matter much at this point?"

"The Redlanders use cruelty to make converts, Your Grace, and horrors to break the mind and twist it to their ends. Their supplicants become willing participants in their cult of murder. If the young prince is broken in his mind, then he may be their servant in his heart, or worse yet, a servant of their demon gods. Bring him into the presence of the king and he might be zealot enough to martyr himself for a chance to kill the crown."

Amelia felt her hand go to her mouth in shock. Every time she thought she had understood the limits of the invaders' evil, a new, worse possibility made itself known.

"You think he has converted to their apostasy?" asked Lady Dalflitch standing attentively behind the duchess's chair. "I would not think you, of all people, would rush to accuse another of heresy, Captain Ash."

"I am not rushing to anything, My Lady," Prentice answered politely, though his cold attention remained fixed on Amelia. "What I saw in Aubrey tells me that this is the kind of thing the Redlanders do as a matter of course. They turned brothers on brothers, mothers on children. We found the new prince bound to a rack in the bottom of a prison in the hands of demon worshippers. Who knows what happened down there?"

"You do not want to be merciful to him, Prentice?" Amelia asked, saddened by the thought that Prentice might be a hypocrite toward other victims of the religions of this conflict. Having obtained mercy and forgiveness, was he now as hardhearted as the Church that had condemned him?

"It is not my place to be merciful to him, Your Grace," Prentice said without emotion. "Nor to condemn him. I do not know him. Perhaps, if we spoke together, he and I might reach an understanding. But in the meantime, his disposition is in your hands. In my hands is the duty to protect you and your domain and to advise you as to what dangers might yet lurk in the shadows around you."

Amelia frowned and then nodded. She should have known Prentice better. His duty would always be at the forefront of his dealings with her.

"Of course, Captain," she said. "I apologize."

"No need, Your Grace."

Amelia took a moment to think through the implications of Prentice's words and came to a quick conclusion. "The Redlanders use markings to make their magic, do they not?"

"I could not say for sure," Prentice answered her with a shrug. Then he paused and she watched him think about her question more deeply. "It does seem that markings are needed, somehow, almost always. The converts and raiders all take brands and tattoos."

"They are the painted men, after all," Amelia agreed.

"And even their beastmen seem to have some sense of having been marked, either before or after becoming monsters. The Horned Man was covered in their symbols, if you'll recall, Your Grace."

"I do remember. So, would you say, Prentice, that it would be fair to assume that if the prince had converted, he would have some marks in his flesh to confirm it? Some paint or brand?"

Prentice nodded, frowning thoughtfully. "I think that's fair, Your Grace. The man is covered in bruises and injuries. One of them might cover a more significant marker. Of course, if you will forgive my suspicious thinking, he might also have been deliberately left unmarked as a ploy to let him sneak harmlessly into a place where he might do most harm."

"But if that was the case, then he would have none of their magic in his flesh, no bestial ferocity," Amelia countered. "An injured, half-starved young man who threw himself at King Chrostmer would not survive two heartbeats, even if the king's own guards did nothing."

"A likely assessment, Your Grace."

Amelia took up a cup from a table beside her and sipped at the watered wine. She ran her fingers along the grooves in the table's rude wooden surface as she considered Prince Farringdon's condition. It was good for him that he was resting, but she needed him awake and capable of understanding his surroundings enough to bend the knee formally to the king sooner rather than later.

"I hate that I must be so cold," she said to no one in particular, though she expected both Dalflitch and Prentice would understand her meaning. She had already sent word to the king that she had the prince in her care and expected to be summoned into his presence at any moment. Putting the cup back down, she offered Prentice a thin smile. "What were the other matters you wanted to address?"

"Now that the Redlanders have fled into the western rivers, do you want me to ready the army to march back?" he asked her. "We'll have to hunt them through the summer or they'll make hell all through the Reach."

Amelia thought a moment about his question. "The battle was barely two days ago," she told him. "Do you need to think so soon about this? The king has not yet made known what his next step is. We may be called to join a crusade into the Vec."

"Assuming the ecclesiarchs allow him to call a crusade," Prentice said cynically, and behind her, Amelia heard Dalflitch snort derisively—not at Prentice, but in agreement with his opinion.

"It seems you two are of one mind on this matter," the duchess said with an arched brow. Prentice made to speak again, but it was Dalflitch who talked first, and the captain nodded, yielding the floor to her.

"The prince's tantrums and refusal to relinquish his betrothal to you, Your Grace, have revived the division between the king and the Church leadership," Lady Dalflitch explained. "The stories coming from the Denay courtiers all say that Church knights sat with the prince on the day of the battle, expecting King Chrostmer to be driven away in retreat. They were waiting to be his heroic rear-guard, saving him from inevitable defeat. Instead, he has delivered a near miraculous victory. The Redlanders are broken, and while the horrors of Aubrey dominate the rumors, the king is the hero overall, with some allowances for Lord Ironworth and, to a smaller degree, yourself, Your Grace."

"Nice to be remembered." Amelia rolled her eyes and her advisers smiled with her.

"A woman on the battlefield, Your Grace?" said Prentice. "I'm sure they'd much rather forget you were there at all."

"Fat chance of that," said Lady Dalflitch vehemently. "Every Reach nobleman knows that the Lioness stood by the king under the blood red sky while the rest of Denay's court ran about like chickens with their heads cut off."

"The battle at the floating bridge was still going on," Amelia protested. "Every Reach nobleman was there, fighting with the Lions against that bridge. How could they know what *I* was doing?"

"The courts tell all the rumors," Dalflitch answered. "But the Reach knows the story it wants to hear, and the tale of your loyal bravery has not been questioned."

"The truth, in other words," Prentice agreed.

Amelia rolled her eyes a second time. "My deeds were significantly less heroic than all that. Certainly less than the Reachermen and militia who shed their blood to save the Grand Kingdom."

"Your humility does you credit, Your Grace," said Prentice, presuming upon their relationship to encourage her. "But the Reach knows your character. If you were not with them exactly, none of them doubts where you were."

"The Denay court might imagine that the battle didn't begin until the king reached the field," Dalflitch added. "But the Reach nobility were right there, riding, fighting, and dying before the first dragon fired and the first Grand Kingdom knight crossed the bridge. They will not let any part of our battle that night be forgotten, including the fact that the king cursed his courtiers as cowards compared to your own bravery."

"Still, I'm surprised they even heard the tale," was all Amelia could think to say.

"Oh, I made sure they heard, Your Grace," Dalflitch said, and her lips twitched in a cunning smile. "I gather rumors for you, but I also know how to spread them."

Amelia returned her lady's smile and noticed an appreciative respect in Prentice's expression as well. Then she nodded and composed herself again. "That is all well and good," she said. "But as to the main question of whether you should set the militia to be ready for the march, Captain, it is clear I must say no at this point."

"Yes, Your Grace."

Amelia took another sip from her cup and thought for a moment, staring at the small fire burning in an iron brazier in a corner of the room away from curtains and wooden walls. For all its converted comforts, her tower chamber had no fireplace. Nonetheless, the weather was quite balmy day and night. Even that little fire seemed to make the room stuffy and too warm. She realized the heat was making her feel tired.

"Open the shutters, My Lady," she told Dalflitch, who moved immediately to obey. She looked back to Prentice. "Was there anything else, Captain?"

"We lack powder for the Roar," he reported. "I would like to send word for more from the north."

"How great a lack?"

"We have just enough for every serpentine to fire once, with a little left over. Personally, I would rather put several rounds into the hands of a chosen fifty or a hundred and let the rest of the Roar fill out the ranks of the Claws. We've plenty of spare pike and halberd now."

Amelia nodded. It was grim news but better than she expected. She'd told Lord Ironworth they had no powder at all.

"Do as seems right to you. And speaking of spare weapons and the reason we have them, what of our dead and wounded?"

"The dead are still being buried, and the wounded have received the treatments available. About a hundred are in dire straits and may or may not survive, Your Grace. If we have time when we march, I would like to send them to Griffith, carried in the wagons."

Amelia sighed as she felt a breath of air from the window Lady Dalflitch had just opened. "It sounds to me, Captain, as if you have everything under your control," she told him. "You hardly need my oversight at all."

"It is *your* army, Your Grace. I need your permission, if nothing else."

"Quite so. Is there anything else for which you require my...permission?"

"No, Your Grace, but there is an issue you will be forced to confront soon, if it hasn't already been brought to your attention."

"A replacement for Sir Gant as knight captain?" Amelia asked, knowing that must be what Prentice was speaking of. She'd not been approached directly, but over the afternoon, three letters had been sent to her by Reach nobles, each praising her victory and begging an opportunity to pay homage in person. No doubt the heroic but tragic loss of the loyal and skillful Sir Gant would feature prominently somewhere in their words of congratulations. Amelia had told Turley to refuse all direct requests until the following morning when she would be able to delay them no longer. In truth, she was waiting for her own chance to do just the same thing with the king—offer her own homage while weaving young Prince Farringdon into the conversation.

"*You* don't want the role, do you, Prentice?" she asked him wryly, and he shook his head with a smile.

"I fear I am unworthy, Your Grace," he said.

Amelia was surprised when she heard Lady Dalflitch snort with amusement behind her.

"You have something to say, My Lady?" Amelia asked her.

"Forgive me, Your Grace. I thought the captain was making a joke."

"Indeed, how so?"

Dalflitch looked to Prentice for a moment as if she thought he might rescue her in a moment of embarrassment. He simply shrugged.

"I'm sorry, My Lady," he said. "Tradition is clear, I think, on this. Only a knighted man or his superior could be made a knight captain of the duchess. I am simply unworthy."

This time Dalflitch scoffed openly. "Captain, if you were any worthier, they'd have to make you a saint, not a knight captain," she said.

"How is that for praise, Captain Ash?" Amelia asked him.

He ducked his head, and it seemed as if he might even have been blushing, though it was hard to see in the dim candlelight.

"I am both flattered and embarrassed," he said simply. "But I would remind the lady that I am quite married and happily so."

"Yes, perhaps you should not flirt so readily, now that you are betrothed to another man," Amelia chastised Dalflitch but spared a knowing glance for Prentice. She was sure he was teasing the duchess as well.

"I meant nothing...I simply..." Dalflitch stammered a moment, and Amelia was pleased to see the normally unflappable courtier at a loss for words for once. Then Dalflitch's eyes narrowed, and she frowned but without anger. "Hmph! It seems your good favor is a rose that has some thorns, Your Grace."

"Do not think too little of us, Dalflitch," Amelia said with a smile, waving her hand in apology. "For a while Prentice and I had only each other to trust and tease. We cannot help it now that we have a third whose mind works as ours does."

"Now *you* flatter *me*," said Prentice. He might have said something more, but Dalflitch had a quick retort ready.

"Perhaps we should tell your good lady wife that you're up here trading compliments with two beautiful ladies, unchaperoned," she said.

Prentice's eyes went wide with mock fear. "My Lady, you go too far!" Then he looked away and his lip curled mischievously. "Besides, if you did try to tell her, I wouldn't favor your chances of reaching the end of the first sentence alive."

"I think you are right, Captain," Dalflitch said. "But I would die content in the knowledge that the fate which awaited *you* would be far worse."

"Truer words were never spoken," Amelia said, and she and Dalflitch both laughed.

Prentice smiled and bowed his agreement.

A knock upon the door preceded Righteous's return to the room, carrying a three-stick candelabra. She headed straight to the duchess and then stopped when she saw that all three were looking at her.

"What?" she demanded, brows knotted, looking from one to the other and forgetting her decorum in the process.

"We were just talking about you, Lady Righteous," Amelia said. The truth was nothing shameful, so there was no point hiding it.

"Oh, ay? And what was being said?"

"Only that I do not show you as much care and love as you deserve," said Prentice, but his wife was not convinced.

"The duchess and her most beauty-praised lady took time out of their night to give you marital counsel, did they husband?"

"Do you doubt me, wife?" he asked her, stepping closer.

"Doubt you? I should put you on a leash, that's what I should do."

"His leash is quite tight and secure," Dalflitch reassured her.

"And how does she know?" Righteous demanded of her husband, showing she had enough suspicion to go around.

Prentice wrapped his arms around her waist suddenly, so that she was forced to lift the candle holder away from her or get wax on both of them. "Here, watch yourself," she chided him.

He leaned in closer and whispered something in her ear.

"Stop that," she said to him, but as he continued to whisper, her expression softened and her scowl became a smile. "Stop it," she said more gently and slapped his shoulder with a paper in her free hand. "Not in front of people. I've got a message for Her Grace."

She waved the paper, which Amelia could now clearly see was a letter. Not, she hoped, another hopeful noble's tribute and request for audience.

"I love you, wife," the duchess heard Prentice whisper as he stepped back and allowed Righteous to curtsey before her.

"A letter, Your Grace," said the lady, handing over the folded paper parcel and holding the candelabra up for Amelia to read. Turning it over, Amelia could see by the seal that it was not what she feared.

"It's from the king," she told them and cracked the wax. It was a short message, so much so that the list of the king's titles at the top almost took up more space on the page than the text of the missive itself. "He summons me to another private audience tomorrow just after dawn."

"An odd hour," said Dalflitch. "I wonder why."

"I'll find out on the morrow."

CHAPTER 48

"And you can assure us that you have the prince in your custody, Duchess?"

"I can, Your Majesty," Amelia told the king in a perfectly deferential tone. She could see that King Chrostmer was a man entangled in the conflict of his emotions, and she wanted to make sure not to offer him any excuse to turn his distemper upon her.

"That at least is something to take from this pile of dung we are forced to call a victory," the king muttered as he sat back in his throne. He was wearing a sleeveless robe of embroidered velvet that looked far too warm for late spring, even this early in the morning. Amelia wondered if his majesty was feeling his age at last. She was sure he would have joined the charges against the Redlanders across Cattlefields. Perhaps it overtaxed him.

"We know your people were in the town on the day of the battle," the king went on. "So, you know the state of the place."

"I have heard, Your Majesty."

"Have you seen it yourself?"

"No."

Amelia knew that many of the ranking nobles had gone to Aubrey after the battle to assess it for plunder. Rumors of the horrors there were spreading throughout the courts of the Grand Kingdom. As duchess, she had released the Reach nobility to seek whatever loot they saw as right to take, but

Righteous and Prentice's report had been enough for her. She
had no desire to visit the accursed community. Besides which,
she already had the prince, and he was the only plunder she
needed to take from Aubrey.

"Nearly two years they sat there," the king declared, his
voice rising in fury, "while our courts dithered and primped
themselves. Our damnable son strutted about with his tales of
mighty victories in the west, stolen by a wayward shrew who
preferred to lay with the lowborn than take the suit of the prince
of the realm."

Amelia sucked in a breath, unable to conceal her shock. She
had no doubt that Daven Marcus had said exactly those things,
and much worse, but to hear the king repeat them so baldly was
offensive, even given his preeminence. Was he trying to insult
her? If he noticed her discomfort, King Chrostmer gave no
indication.

"Then you finally arrive," the king went on, "with the
prettiest militia any of us has ever seen. By God, Duchess,
you should have heard them laugh at you over dinner in this
very hall." The king pointed to the long table running down
the middle of the audience chamber, still strewn with maps
and documents from the battle planning. She wondered if
there were any fresh maps there or any reports yet of where
the surviving Redlanders had fled. "Laughing at you while
they drank our fine wines and best whiskeys. We should have
rebuked the beggars then. The woman has the nickname
Lioness from her own people, and she's held Marne's legacy
for years now while prince and invader tried to take it away. It
wouldn't have mattered if she was born in a dung heap or the
back of a stable or laid in a manger like our humble Lord; the
woman's not to be underestimated."

He's talking about me like I'm not even here, Amelia thought.
Is he drunk?

The king had no cup and there was no steward or stand with
drink nearby. Perhaps the king was truly overwearied.

"And now they come, knees bent in false homage, to wring their hands at us and declare how little there is for them to take from Aubrey. As if it is our fault!"

The king's fist hammered on the arm of his throne, the dull thud resounding in the quiet. Amelia kept her eyes down and resisted any temptation to say something on her own initiative. This was not the King Chrostmer she had last seen. That vital, older man had been thrilled at the prospect of battle, even if it was the apocalypse itself against the forces of hell under a sky of blood. This was an old man frustrated and beset with troubles. For a long moment there was quiet as the king brooded. Amelia wished she had been able to bring someone with her to this audience—Dalflitch or even Prentice. Just their presence would have been helpful. But the king's instructions had specified that she would be received alone.

"We thought your plan with the prince of Aubrey to be an excess of cunning," the king said at last, much more quietly. "We have hated sitting over this nest of beggars and vipers, watching every twist and turn. Put a longsword in our hand and let us face our opponent. That is our preference. And the Lord delivers us exactly that at last, a battle with obvious sides and inevitable victory, only to have the devil snatch the prize away afterward. Our champion's medallion is gone, and we must accept the mere flowers of a participant. And we only have that possibility by your hand, Duchess. Your cunning foresaw a need we did not. How do you come by such insight? Are you the witch my son says you are?"

"I have no witchcraft and little enough insight, Majesty," Amelia protested.

The power I have is the courage of my men, she thought to add, but did not say. *The ones who struggled and died to give you your "inevitable" victory.*

"Of course not, My Lady," the king said, and his features softened with a weary smile. "We are fatigued. Day and night our courtiers come with some new request. "'Let us plunder the countryside.' 'Let us seize all the river trade.' Last night I had the Earl of Norassa demanding a letter of marque to take miners into Aubrey's castle and tear the cellars apart, hoping to find secret vaults full of gold and jewels. He generously offers to provide our throne with a half share of all he finds."

"Are there rumors of hidden vaults majesty?" Amelia hadn't heard anything of the like. She wondered if Dalflitch might have.

"We know only what the earl told us. The man is obsessed, and he is not the first or last. They'll tear the walls down looking for valuables before long. There's no plunder and they can't face it. Damned sheep, bleating about how much this campaign has cost them. How much has it cost their king?"

You need me more than ever, oh King. It was all Amelia could do to keep her face from breaking into a triumphant smile. "It may yet yield a better prize than you fear, Majesty."

Before the king could respond to that suggestion, he was distracted by a single figure entering from the back of the hall. Amelia turned to see Daven Marcus striding toward the throne. The prince seemed freshly rested and had a spring in his step. As he approached, his eyes met Amelia's for a moment and she nearly flinched, expecting to see hatred there, but he simply smiled enigmatically and proceeded to stand in front of his father's throne, bowing formally.

"You were summoned to attend us at dawn, Prince," said the king, his voice full of menace.

"And here I am, Father," Daven Marcus replied with a light tone. The king made a show of looking out the nearest window where the light outside made it clear that dawn was some time past. Daven Marcus followed his gaze and then shrugged unapologetically. "My tent is some distance away. It took some time to get here."

"The duchess came from the other side of the Azures, and she still arrived in time to honor her king."

"Well..." the prince began, but King Chrostmer cut him off.

"But since you mention your camp, there is another matter to attend to, my son."

"Oh?"

"You fled our presence. You left our court without permission. And when your king called you to battle beside him, you sat on your arse and did nothing."

"We were ready to protect your retreat," Daven Marcus objected smoothly, and Amelia was amazed that the prince still spoke with such disrespect. Could he not see how angry his father was becoming?

"There was no retreat," the king ground out through gritted teeth. "You sat out the greatest victory the Grand Kingdom has seen since its unification."

"Well, I'd hardly have called it..."

"Kneel, boy!" The king's voice was not loud, but the tone of command was so firm that the words seem to echo around the hall. It caught Daven Marcus so off guard that he simply blinked at his father.

"What?" he stammered.

"You have put yourself outside honor and the favor of the throne," the king pronounced. "You will kneel and beg our forgiveness before another moment passes. We will see you crave reconciliation with the throne before this hour is done."

"Now, Father, can we not let this conflict between us be in the past?" Daven Marcus asked, resuming his relaxed stance.

It was barely a week ago, Amelia thought, astonished the prince would call it "the past." The king was more than astonished, it seemed. Chrostmer surged from his throne, the bear-like strength he had shown on the night of battle unmistakable in his movement. He seized Daven Marcus by the front of his doublet and hauled him almost off his feet with one hand.

"You. Will. Kneel!" he commanded his son.

Shock took the mask away from the prince's expression, and for a moment he looked from his father to Amelia. His eyes narrowed to slits, and his lips twisted into a snarl. "In front of her? Never!"

Amelia wasn't surprised by the depth of venom in the prince's declaration, but the king's response made her step back and bite her lip to keep from crying out. The king cuffed his son straight across his face. It was an open-handed strike, but the older man's meaty palm crashed so heavily into Daven Marcus that the prince gave a momentary yelp of pain and shock. That first blow was followed by another and then another. Daven Marcus made no effort to resist, though what effort could he make? His father was monarch. There were half a dozen armed men within earshot who would not hesitate to kill even a prince who raised a hand against the king.

Nevertheless, Daven Marcus's limpness under his father's fury seemed to have an element of weakness to it. He made no effort to resist or even hold to his dignity, and it was only King Chrostmer's grip that kept him up. At last, the king stopped and pulled his beaten son closer, eyes locked.

"They call her the Lioness," the king growled. "They call you a coward. You're a prince. You had a future throne and kingdom to dangle in front of her. How could you make a such a pig's breakfast of that? She married a frontier baron twice her age for less than you have to offer. You're of an age and you're fair to look on. Your mother's blood in you saw to that!"

A part of Amelia was offended to hear her marriage so cruelly described, not to mention her husband Duke Marne described as a "frontier baron," but she kept her tongue. There was a satisfaction in seeing Daven Marcus finally taken to task, but this was the king's moment with his son. Chrostmer hardly knew she was there, and that was probably the safest for her.

"You shamed yourself and humiliated me!" the king said, forgetting his royal status again. "You will kneel and beg my forgiveness, boy. You will politely beg the duchess' pardon for all your wretched misbehaviors. Then you will begin your courtship again, properly. You'll take the gentlest of paths, publish poems to her beauty and honor. Have minstrels sing of your troth."

"Never!" the prince gasped, and his father slapped him again, this time releasing his other hand and letting his son fall to the floor.

"You will, and I will command her to accept your petition."

Now Amelia did gasp. This was everything she had worked to prevent. She wanted to object, to plead with the king not to do this, but what could she say? He was already enraged. How did you calm a wild beast and oppose it at the same time?

"Tomorrow evening we will host the two courts in a feast," the king told his cringing son. "There, the surviving prince of Aubrey will bend his knee and return the rebel princedom to us. We will be the first to reconcile a Vec rebel to the throne. You will be so touched by the duchess' role in this miraculous event that you will repent all your previous accusations toward her and declare your intent to woo her afresh. You will also publicly beseech your new friends in Mother Church to declare a new crusade, which you will lead, to bring more of the Vec back into the Grand Kingdom. Thus, you will prove yourself worthy to share the throne with such a lioness. People will forget that you're a pillow-hearted failure and her iron will stiffen your children's spines, giving you heirs worthy of the title."

"I will never do any of that!" Daven Marcus said vehemently, though he raised a hand to protect himself in case his father thought to strike him again.

"You will, my son, or I will have you gelded and locked in a chamber in my palace. I'll tell everyone you went mad and then recognize that bastard you sired with Lady Wradonger as my heir."

"You know about him?"

"Boy, I know about all of your foolishness and failures. The days of me indulging you and hoping a man would somehow sprout out of the dung heap of your youth are passed. And to that end..." The king looked up from his son to the two nearest guards in the hall. "The prince must attend tomorrow's feast, but he has a poor sense of direction and timing. Take him to a chamber where he can be kept safe until the appointed time."

The guards stepped up to the prince and lifted him up by his arms. He tried to shrug them off, but they stoutly refused to be rebuffed.

"Unhand me! I am the Prince of Rhales!"

"And we are the king and throne of the Grand Kingdom," Chrostmer said in a loud voice just short of a shout. "Whatever rank or authority you have, you have from us. Our word is law, even to you!"

The king waved the two guards away and turned his back on them, returning to his throne. By the time he sat down again, the prince was already almost out of the hall, shouting his objections the entire way.

Amelia watched the scene, eyes wide and scarcely able to breathe. When the prince was gone, she returned her gaze to the king who sat, head down, staring at the table full of plans.

"You may leave now, Duchess," he said at last, not deigning to look at her. "We will welcome your company at the feast tomorrow evening. Make sure the prince of Aubrey knows his role in proceedings."

And with that, Amelia was dismissed to contemplate her own poisoned victory and its worthless prize.

CHAPTER 49

"Do you really have no choice, Your Grace?" asked Spindle.

"The king has played his trump card," said Dalflitch, answering the question for Amelia. It was all the duchess could do not to throw her book across the room in disgust. A codex of King's Law covering noble marriage and treaties, Amelia had spent hours scouring it for any possible exception that might allow her to weasel out of the king's command. She had found none.

"And the prince is so foul a prospect for a husband?" the masked lady persisted.

"The prince's last attempt at wooing included throwing Her Grace into a cold stable to sleep on the straw on the ground while she starved," Dalflitch explained. "It took a concerted effort of Reach nobles just to get her a blanket."

"I hate stables," Righteous muttered, and the ladies present all knew she had her own reasons.

The four women then fell to silence for a long moment, contemplating the bitter twist of fate.

"Did the king truly cuff his son?" Spindle asked at last. It seemed the very notion fascinated her.

"Like a rabid mongrel," Amelia told her.

"Well, I'm sad I missed that," said Dalflitch, and Righteous nodded too.

"It was...somewhat satisfying," Amelia conceded. When she thought about it, it was a victory of sorts, but like the Red Sky, it was a battle that cost almost more than the victory was worth. Whatever discipline the king was seeking to impose upon his son, Amelia was certain it was too little, too late. The prince would bow to his father's wishes; he had no choice. But when Chrostmer was gone and Daven Marcus acceded to the throne, she was certain the resentful royal would punish her for every embarrassment and slight. If he did not have her executed outright, he would make her future as miserable as he could. Her marriage would make her a princess, future queen, and accursed all in one fell swoop. And there was nothing she could do to stop it.

"Some fairy-tale maiden I make," she said to herself. "Working to *not* become a princess."

"It isn't the usual fable, Your Grace," Dalflitch agreed.

"I sure wouldn't have liked it as a little'un," said Righteous.

Amelia looked down at the book in her lap again and then closed it with a clap. There were no answers for her there, and she had had enough of this self-pity. She looked her ladies over from one to the next.

"It seems I have only two courses available to me," she said. "Would you agree?"

She waited while the three women looked to each other, wordlessly sharing their thoughts by glances and nods.

"Tell me then," she told them.

"Marry the prince and one day become queen," said Spindle. The other two ladies agreed.

Amelia looked to Dalflitch. "That was your ambition," she said, but Dalflitch shook her head vehemently.

"Once, Your Grace. I've left that far behind now."

"I've never wanted it, but could I endure it?"

"You could," said Righteous. "But it wouldn't be no joy. You'd be best off saying the vows and going to him as many times as it takes for him to get an heir off you—maybe two, to be safe. Then you could stay out of his way as best you can. Two, maybe three years of suffering his attentions, then you can hope he forgets about you."

As brutal an assessment of her prospective marriage as it was, Amelia knew Righteous was also being wildly optimistic. Daven Marcus could just as easily make her a figure of torment, turning her continuing misery into a royal hobby.

"It is a grim prospect, but it brings with it the power and influence of the queen," Amelia mused with a cold scowl. "Could that not be used to moderate his...excesses?"

"I don't see how, Your Grace," said Dalflitch, lifting her empty hands in an apologetic gesture. "It is the king's power to act without concession that has placed you in this position in the first place. When Daven Marcus takes the throne, what chance he would be less high-handed?"

"Mother Church can restrain the king's hand you said, Your Grace," Spindle suggested but without enthusiasm.

"Only at the most extreme ends of doctrine," Amelia countered, knowing she was only going over something every woman in the room already understood but unable to stop herself. "They will likely not ever intervene in a king's marriage because he acted 'somewhat callously' to his queen. Especially when that queen has already embarrassed them, been declared a witch and a wayward wife once, and forced them to publicly absolve a heretic in her service who should have died exiled in the west."

Righteous scowled, her brows knotted in fury.

"I speak only what the Church hierarchy will say, Righteous," Amelia apologized to her.

"I know that Your Grace," the lady-in-waiting conceded with a polite nod, though her grim expression lost none of its fury. "I'm angry on my man's behalf, but not at you."

Amelia accepted her words as an apology. "So, this leads us around to the second path."

"Which is, Your Grace?"

"I thought you all agreed there were two paths."

"We agree, Your Grace," said Dalflitch. "It is merely that we cannot see the second path as readily as you. Please forgive us."

Amelia smiled, and a moment of wan amusement passed between them all. With a sigh, the duchess outlined her forlorn hope. "The second path is to find a way to make it impossible for the prince to marry me."

"Is that all?" Lady Dalflitch said with a feigned casual air. "What have we been worrying about all this time?"

"He couldn't marry you if you were already married, Your Grace," said Spindle.

Amelia felt her eyebrows rise, but Righteous's response captured her true emotion.

"Oh, if that's all it takes," the combative woman scoffed. "We've got a prince right here in the camp and a few good sacrists going spare. We can get you two hitched 'afore dawn."

Righteous was joking, but Amelia found herself looking at Dalflitch as both women considered the possibility. A prince was exactly the right kind of rank for a duchess to marry. It was part of what made Daven Marcus's claim so strong in the first place. Would it work?

"A rushed marriage won't look good to anyone," said Dalflitch. "Even your most loyal Reachermen would resent hearing about it after the fact. And most of them would still see Farringdon as a Veckander and an enemy."

"And he won't be a prince much longer," Amelia continued the line of reasoning. "Once he bows the knee, Farringdon becomes an earl."

"Still sufficient rank for a duchess to marry."

"But the king will want to give that marriage to an ally."

"Wait, can you actually marry the Vec prince, Your Grace?" Righteous asked, her face showing how astonished she was to have her joke taken seriously. Amelia found the possibility tantalizing, but ultimately, she shook her head.

"Even if we did marry, there's nothing to keep the king from ordering the match annulled. Do not doubt the Church would agree, even if the young prince and I managed to consummate the marriage. In the poor man's current state, I doubt that would even be possible. Prince Farringdon has lost his father, his inheritance, and in one more day, his title and sovereignty. I've made him enough of a pawn in our machinations. I could not add that indignity to all the others."

"So, no pitchfork wedding then?" said Spindle.

"Pitchfork wedding?" asked Dalflitch. "What on earth is that?"

"You know," explained Righteous, "When some buck's gone and got a lass pregnant but don't want to do right by her, so her farmer pa's got to force him to the altar. With a pitchfork. Usually at night, 'cause you got to surprise the bugger, or he'll get away. A pitchfork wedding."

"I've never heard the phrase before. Have you, Your Grace?"

Amelia nodded. She knew the expression, but it was one she had not heard for many years.

"The things you learn," said Dalflitch, and everyone shared a small laugh.

"Alright, marrying Prince Farringdon is not the solution we want," Amelia said, bringing the conversation back to the point. "And even if it could be, I wouldn't put the man through it, not so soon after everything else he's suffered."

"And there's not anyone else," said Dalflitch.

"Not without all the same problems. So, where does that leave us?"

"Without a second path after all, Your Grace," said Spindle. "Sorry to say."

"I do not accept that," Amelia declared. "I have not endured everything I have, everything *we* have, just to go meekly to the prince and offer my hand. The king has commanded, and Daven Marcus wants the match, but he doesn't want *me*."

"He wants the Reach and its money."

"Can we persuade him that it's not worth it?"

Fat chance, Amelia thought. With silver, iron, wool, wheat and cattle, the Reach was truly wealthy, and growing wealthier now that she had an army capable of protecting it properly. That army in and of itself was part of the problem. The strength she had built only made her dowry more inviting to a prince and a king, not less.

"The Reach might rise in rebellion," offered Righteous. "Nobles of the west hate the prince. That's well known."

"More reason for the king to put his son over them, not less," Dalflitch countered immediately. "Bring them to heel."

"And so, there are my two paths—acquiescence or open rebellion. I do not like either of them."

All of her ladies returned her frown but had no further ideas to offer. Amelia's head ached and she longed for sleep, though she was sure she would struggle to take any rest this night. She indicated that Spindle and Righteous should help her dress for bed and rose, her mind still chewing over the specifics of the challenge that faced her. Somehow, before the feast on the next evening, she had to devise a way to stop the king from forcing Daven Marcus to renew his suit for her hand in marriage. The question dominated her thoughts as she settled into her bed for the night, and it was still churning there when dawn broke hours later.

CHAPTER 50

P rentice watched as stewards and a squire provided by a Reacher baron named Tillervex worked to dress Prince Farringdon in appropriate attire to meet King Chrostmer. Every now and then the servants looked Prentice's way, and from their expressions, he realized he must seem very grim indeed. Their eyes flicked to him regularly, like men forced to work under the eye of a feral-looking guard dog.

Or fresh convicts on their first day under the overseers, Prentice thought.

The new ones always kept their eyes on the whips, as if to avoid a lashing when it came. Overseers were lazy but not that lazy. If they meant to lash you, they made sure you did not get away. The memory of his own first days on a convict chain soured Prentice's mood further and he turned from watching so closely. Nothing would be gained by intimidating the poor men.

Prince Farringdon could not be dressed in Reach colors, the cream and blue of Duchess Amelia's house. That would be too provocative to the two courts, especially Denay. It would make it seem as if the duchess was making a first claim on the captured Vec province. The proposal had then been to dress the prince in Aubrey's colors, assuming his and his fallen nation's were the same. But no one knew the Aubrey colors with any certainty. An attempt was made to consult the prince, but the man's mind was still not recovered from his ordeal in the Ditch. It took several attempts to make him hear every word spoken to him, and what he ultimately described was some strange mix of circles, stripes, and a symbol he called a farring, which no one could identify. The only thing anyone could determine for certain was that one of the colors was bright green and there should be a fur trim.

Word was sent to the Reach noble camp, and after a morning of searching, a single garment that drew close to the description—a dyed woolen cloak with a rabbit fur collar belonging to Baron Tillervex—was discovered. Then the baron had been summoned and the complex dance of asking him to give something up without insulting him by offering to pay for it began. The baron had been more than willing to give it up, as it turned out, once he learned the reason, and had nearly fallen over himself in gratitude when the duchess offered to reward him by bringing him along to king's feast that night. Now the fallen prince stood in a tent in the White Lions camp, staring into space as skilled hands worked to turn a cloak into a doublet that at least looked passable for a court appearance.

"He hardly seems to notice anything around him," the duchess had observed of the prince before she returned to her tower. "Will he even know he's standing in front of the throne of the Grand Kingdom?"

"He'll know, Your Grace," Prentice assured her. "We'll make sure."

"And what will he say? The king won't want anything that might embarrass him. The whole point of this night is to set things back in order, with his majesty at the top."

"Your need is just as great," Prentice added as he agreed with her. "Prince Farringdon, soon to be Earl Farringdon, is your best piece in tonight's game. You want to turn him on the choicest play."

"True enough," was all the duchess said to that.

Together, they agreed that the best plan was to have an escort at Farringdon's elbow the whole night. The young man could barely feed or dress himself, but he could be prompted. When the king asked if he surrendered his family's rebellion against the Grand Kingdom and once again bowed the knee to the throne, all someone should have to do is put their hand on the prince's shoulder and push him to his knees. It would be better if he said it, but Farringdon's kneeling would be enough.

"It should be quite simple then," said the duchess.

"Unless the man is deceiving us," said Prentice.

"Do you think he is?" His liege cocked an eyebrow at him doubtfully.

"No, I do not believe so, Your Grace," he conceded. "But better to be sure. It is always the things you are not watching for that cause the most trouble."

And so Prentice stood and watched as the near-catatonic prince was fitted for the last royal duty he would ever perform. After tonight he would have no princedom. Would that be the realization that finally pierced the veil over his thoughts? Prentice could imagine the man doing anything from raging to weeping when that light shone through.

And then there was the question of the duchess's marriage, which was now apparently most definitely going to happen. Prentice stepped to the tent flap and looked out at the camp in the afternoon light. He had spent years building this army to keep the prince's power at bay, to make the Reach independent. He'd followed divine visions to do it. And now it seemed it would all come to nothing. A clutch of desperate rats had been raised to become lions at the prompting of an angelic prophecy. He felt his jaw ache as he gritted his teeth, thinking about the injustice of it. For long years as a convict on a chain he had accepted injustice with bitter resignation, but since being freed, he had come to hope, to believe, a better day was coming. Now he felt bound to a woman who would be chained to a fate almost as vile as a convict's. And her chain would be his chain because of it.

"King and pauper all return to the same earth."

"What are you muttering to yerself about, husband?" asked his wife as she emerged around the side of the tent.

As he turned to see her, his scowl gave way to a broad smile. Dressed for the evening's feast in a cream gown, with her strawberry-blonde hair plaited under a net of gold thread, her beauty delighted him. In the afternoon light, something odd flashed, dangling from her left ear, and he recognized it as a silver rat. The only woman who'd earned her own, Righteous had had her rat pin recrafted into an earring. It was such an unusual, unladylike piece of jewelry, and it made him smile even more. It was so in keeping with her.

"You are as fine to look upon as any woman ever was," he told her.

"I hope not," she replied. "It wouldn't do for me to show up Her Grace." She kissed him happily for the compliment, nonetheless. "She's sent me to see how things progress."

"Well enough," Prentice said, looking back at the dressing going on in the tent behind him. "The prince will be ready on time, I think."

"Who knew how much effort went into being royal, eh? I used to think they just sat around, stuffing themselves and stealing from the lowborn."

"You are thinking of the other prince," Prentice told her, and she nodded more soberly.

"What happens to us, when the duchess marries the brat?" Righteous asked in a serious tone. "I mean, word is he hates you, and I doubt he's going to think much of me. Sure enough, Her Grace is going to be the worst off, but we aren't looking at a festival day either."

Prentice chewed over her words. She was right, of course.

"He will take away my captaincy first," he said, starting with the most obvious. "Daven Marcus would never suffer the indignity of having an army commanded by a heretic convict, absolved or not. And it will be a way for him to hurt Her Grace."

"Aye, Dalflitch thinks he'll give *her* some special attention as well," Righteous agreed. "Did you know they used to sleep together?"

"I did."

"She's a pretty bundle o' ribbons, but there's got to be some steel under there somewhere to put up with his rubbish, if the stories are true."

"They are true enough," said Prentice. The entire of the duchess's household had an unpleasant future ahead of them it seemed.

"I been thinking 'bout maybe taking to a mask like Spindle does," Righteous said out of the blue.

Prentice blinked with surprise as he looked at her. "Why?"

"Cause of this," she said and pointed to the brand on her cheek, the brawler's mark she was given when she was convicted.

"I thought you were proud that was the only mark on your face," he said, looking her in the eye. "All those pit fights and not a single scar to the face?"

"Well, 'course, but that's the old me. That was Cutter Sal. I'm Lady Righteous now, lady-in-waiting to Her Grace, the Duchess of the Western Reach. A brawler's mark ain't 'decorous'—that's what Dalflitch says it's called. Besides, Spindle's got her mask all lace and silk and it makes her look so mysterious. There's men who know she's all scarred underneath, and a ruthless little razor into the bargain, and they still look at her like a prize. I thought we could make like a matched pair. The duchess' mystery women."

"So, I'd be the only man who saw your full beauty, the glory behind the mask?" Prentice said, taking her hand and lifting it to his lips to kiss. "I like that, wife."

"Keep my secrets for yourself, would ya?" she asked, rising on the balls of her feet.

"Like treasures kings would kill to possess."

"Well, they can't because I've given them to you!"

They stared into each other's eyes for a moment and then Righteous stepped back, aghast. "Ah, you'll get me filthy, all that dried muck on your brigandine. Why haven't you washed it yet?"

"I have," said Prentice. "It's not getting any cleaner than this before tonight."

"You can't go into the king's presence like that," she declared. "The battle was days ago. You should have changed into something more suitable after you washed."

"I will find an arming doublet, or something in Reach colors."

"See that you do, husband. I'll not have you shaming me in front of the two courts."

"Shaming you?" Prentice folded his arms in disbelief. "Were you not a street-fighting gutter rat not so many years ago?"

She shook her head and put her hand to her breast in mock offense. Her voice mimicked Lady Dalflitch's rich, courtly tones. "That was another creature entirely. She was named Cutter Sal. I am Lady Righteous."

"And what is that, My Lady?" Prentice asked her, pointing at the dangling silver rat at her ear.

"That is one of the secrets of the mysterious ladies who wait upon the Lioness, Duchess of the Western Reach." She cocked an eyebrow. "And a true gentleman would ask no more about it."

"Then I shall ask no more." Prentice bowed to her formally. "And I will seek out more suitable attire."

"See that you do." She flounced away, enjoying playing the pampered lady, but she paused to look over her shoulder and blow him a kiss before disappearing between the tents.

Prentice chuckled and then returned his attention to the last phases of the prince's fitting. There would be time for him to find cleaner clothes yet.

CHAPTER 51

"I used to like evenings like this," Amelia heard Dalflitch say beside her as their carriage rattled once more to the king's manor.

The path they followed was lit by camp wardens with torches, and once again lesser nobles and camp folk were watching their progress. This time, though, there was an air of festivity, with spring flowers and ribbons woven through the women's hair or tied to men's garments. These lower-born folk would never see the inside of the king's feast, but they were permitted to share in the sense of rejoicing. After all, were they not a part of the victorious army of King Chrostmer?

Nevertheless, Amelia understood her lady's reluctance. This was as much a funeral for her hopes as it was a celebration of victory. Even as the carriage rolled calmly forward, she wracked her brain to try and devise some last-minute plan to scuttle the king's plan for her to marry. She looked from one companion to another as she had the entire journey, hoping for inspiration and finding none. Dalflitch returned her sad smile politely, while Spindle and Righteous only gave her courteous nods, their eyes so much more watchful. They were remembering the last time the duchess's household had visited the king, Amelia was sure, and the chaos that had ensued that night. Both ladies had 'cutlery' secreted about their persons, no doubt.

This journey was at least somewhat different, though, because there was a fourth companion accompanying the Lioness: Prince Farringdon. Dressed in a bright green jerkin with a rabbit-fur collar that looked too hot for the warm evening, he reminded Amelia of the Rhales courtiers dressed for her "wedding."

Daven Marcus'll likely say something about that, she thought. *Best be ready for it.*

Farringdon had spent the entire ride in silence, staring into nothing, and after a few half-hearted attempts to engage him in conversation, Amelia and her ladies had essentially ignored him. Prentice assured her that the prince would be made to play his part, but the man's mute presence was another irritant to her calm. He should be left to mourn and heal, yet here he was, a piece in a game that he could only lose. And at her hands. It disgusted her that she could be so calculating, and she swore to herself that she would seek to become his friend and ally in the years to come to make up for this wretched misuse.

The carriage rolled to a halt, and Amelia realized they had reached their destination. Behind them, a long column of riders, all ranking nobles of the Reach—this time including their wives and daughters as well as sons—began to dismount and process into the feast. Amelia and her entourage were not coming late now to an audience, as they had the first time. Now they were arriving on time to be welcomed as equals, bringing the captured Vec prince, the king's greatest plunder.

Turley jumped down swiftly and spoke with the herald in royal red just as he had the previous times, though this time the honor of escorting the duchess herself had been given to Baron Tillervex. Amelia turned to prompt the prince to get down first, since he ranked more highly than she for one more hour at least. Farringdon was compliant, and Baron Tillervex happily caught the man by his arm, as if he feared he might fall. He turned to give the prince off to Prentice, but the captain of the White Lions was not there. He was standing apart, distracted in a conversation with two men in Reach livery. It was only a minor breach of protocol, but in her poor mood, Amelia felt a sudden flash of anger at him.

For his part, Baron Tillervex showed no inconvenience, passing the prince to his other hand and offering his first to the duchess to help her down. From then on, the formal process continued as it normally would, though Prentice had still not returned from his quietly heated conversation by the time all the carriage's occupants had dismounted.

Amelia looked apologetically at the baron as the delay stretched. The baron smiled politely at his liege lady's embarrassment, and Prince Farringdon stood by passively, content under the baron's control.

"Captain Prentice," Amelia called, feeling her lips twist into a sneer and not bothering to hide the tone of annoyance in her voice. "Will your private conversation be concluded soon, or should we send to the king and tell him to wait a while longer for us?"

Prentice left the two uniformed Reachermen and walked the short distance back to Amelia. He saluted her and bowed his head.

"Please forgive me, Your Grace," he said quietly.

"Are you ready to attend to your duty now?" she demanded.

"With your favor, Your Grace, I believe I have been."

"Have you indeed?" Amelia felt her irritation rising, and while she knew little of it had to do with Prentice, it was hard for her to control. She was angry, frustrated, and resentful of the twist of fate toward which she was now marching, and Prentice was bringing it all to the surface like a minor scratch drawing unexpected blood.

"These men have requested I go with them, Your Grace," Prentice explained.

"Now?"

"Yes, Your Grace." From his expression it was clear he was asking her permission to do just that.

"Are you mad, man?" asked Baron Tillervex, inserting himself into the situation at last. "Her Grace is about to stand before the throne. What business could these men possibly have to draw you away at so vital an hour?"

"This," said Prentice, and he offered an open hand to Amelia. In the mere torchlight, it took a moment for her realize what he had on his palm. Then she saw. It was a silver rat pin. In a sudden rush, all the resentment washed out of her, and in its place, she felt a quiet shame. Of course, it would be something this significant for Prentice to make this request. Involuntarily, her eyes went to the matching earring hanging from Righteous's ear. They were just two strange little pieces of silver, but they stood for so much. Here she was, fearing what she would lose in her future, and Prentice still had an eye on the debts of honor she owed to her past. He wasn't failing her as she became a princess; he was serving the duchess she already was.

"This is the one I gave to Sacrist Fostermae and his scholar friend?" she asked him.

"Solft, Your Grace, yes. This is that one."

The one that had belonged to Sir Gant, Amelia felt he could have added, though he did not. She looked her captain in the eye, and in his serious gaze she saw reflected all the complexities of emotion she felt in herself. It helped her steel herself, and she turned to the baron and prince.

"Lord Tillervex," she said decisively, "Captain Prentice has been summoned away on a matter of honor for the Western Reach. Would you do me a further service and take up the escort of Prince Farringdon until the captain may return?"

"The honor would be mine, Your Grace," Tillervex said readily. Amelia nodded and turned back to Prentice.

"Go, Captain. Do what honor demands."

Prentice bowed.

"Should I go too, Your Grace?" asked Righteous, unexpectedly. Amelia looked to her and realized that, of course, the loyal knife fighter would want to aid in a matter of honor like this. Her husband raised his hand and shook his head though.

"No wife," he told her. "The duchess needs you here. This should only be a simple matter."

"Yes, Captain," Righteous breathed softly and then curtseyed.

This, Amelia thought. *This is what I have built, what we have built. Not a militia or a duchy, but a bond of loyalty and faithfulness. This is what nobility should be. And I swear, duchess, princess, queen, or pauper, I will never let Daven Marcus take this from me.*

The notion made her smile grimly, and she waved for her entourage to be set in order while Prentice marched off into the night with his men. No drummers led the way this time, only the royal herald.

"Of course, I'll still probably have to marry the silly brat," she muttered.

"I'm sorry, Your Grace," said Dalflitch at her shoulder. "I did not hear you."

"Never mind, My Lady. I will tell you later."

CHAPTER 52

P rentice followed the two messengers—a knight and a militiaman—into the darkness as they led the way between tents to what they said was a ruined farmhouse nearer the river. The scholar Solft had apparently been attacked in Aubrey and chased all the way back over the bridge. He'd been injured but had gotten word, as well as the rat pin, to Fostermae, who'd immediately sent these two men to fetch Prentice with word that Solft's discovery was of the utmost importance. With Sir Gant's death, the cleanup after the battle, Prince Farringdon, and the duchess's impending betrothal, Prentice realized that he'd hardly given the two clerics the least thought.

But a silver rat, especially Sir Gant's? He would honor that without hesitation.

"He made it across the bridge?" Prentice asked as they emerged from the southern fringe of the king's camp. The stars overhead were pleasant to look at. The Rampart glittered brightly, and the balmy air was sweet. It was a marvel that the creation had reasserted its glory so swiftly after the grisly events of the recent days. A part of him wanted to turn around, seek out his wife, and draw her away to go swimming with him in the wide river. They could lie out together under the stars and enjoy the world as a husband and wife should. Smiling at his simple wish, he looked down at the quilted arming doublet he was wearing at his wife's insistence. It was simple, neat, and clean, in Reach blue. Unlike his usual field armor, the only steel he was wearing tonight was his gorget of blued steel and the attached white steel pauldrons on his shoulders that identified him as Captain. He felt he needed that because the weapon he was carrying was his old sword-breaker, the edged and flanged metal bar that looked like a baton and was able to do savage damage to the blade of any sword. It was a peasant weapon, but he could not bring his partisan into the king's presence, and his captain's sword had been lost on the other side of the Murr. The sword-breaker was all he had left to suit the occasion.

"It surprises you that he made it this far?" asked the bannerman wearing the duchy's White Lion tabard over a byrnie of bright mail. Bannermen were knights who often provided their own armor, even though they wore the duchess's colors and not their own. The mail looked old-fashioned to Prentice, but he supposed it was a family heirloom or something similar. The man wore his hair like a knight, though—long and tied back simply—and he carried himself with the broad-shouldered uprightness typical to his rank.

"Not really," Prentice said, answering the knight's question. "I only wonder that there were no guards on the bridge to help him if he was pursued by Redlanders."

"By what?" asked the bannerman. "Oh, yes, the invaders. I couldn't say, Captain. I only know what I was told. Our camp is far from the bridge, as you know."

"Maybe they'd gone under the bridge to drink," offered the militiaman, a short, solid type, with dark hair that looked like it had been hacked off with a kitchen knife. "You know what lazy sods ordinary sentries are."

"Yes," the bannerman said with a laugh.

Prentice did not share their amusement, though. He had gone to great lengths to instill in all his men the importance of strict discipline among his sentries. Convicts could not be allowed to escape or shirk. He did not like the idea of men skiving off and going drinking, even as a joke. He was about to rebuke his man when he noticed something that surprised him. The common soldier was wearing the typical linen gambeson of a militiaman, and he had a sword belt around his waist, his basket-hilted sword swinging comfortably. Unusually, though, the man had a polished steel pauldron on his left shoulder, indicating that he was a corporal. At such a rank, he should have had his own brigandine, much heavier armor. Perhaps he was one of those recently promoted after the battle. Prentice was about to ask the man about it when he caught the flash of the bright shoulder armor in the moonlight and saw the embossed claw in the steel.

"How much farther is it?" he asked them.

"Not far, Captain," said the bannerman. "Just down there. You can make out the torches. We sent a small guard of men to hold the whole place until you came for the scholar. That was what the sacrist suggested we do."

"Good thinking." Fostermae probably would suggest something like that. "How many men?"

"Only a half dozen or so."

"But only two of you came to fetch me? Couldn't you loot enough uniforms for everyone?" he asked them. Prentice stopped walking and they continued a few more steps.

"I'm sorry, Captain?" asked the bannerman as he turned back. "I don't understand."

"Yes, you do."

The two men exchanged a glance, the shadowed eyes no more than dark pits in the night. Then the militiaman spun in place, drawing his sword in a smooth motion, aiming an arcing sweep straight at Prentice's throat. Prentice had already worked his sword-breaker free of its sheath however, and he intercepted the stroke with a simple check that rang in the still air like a gong being struck.

"Heretic bastard," the false militiaman cursed, pulling his sword back while his companion drew his own blade. Prentice wasn't interested in talking, and he kept his 'breaker tight on the man's sword, controlling it and then planting a savage kick into the side of the man's knee, which flexed the wrong way and then cracked sickeningly. He collapsed with an agonized cry, and Prentice leaped away. He brought his weapon back to guard and crouched low to try and keep his other enemy silhouetted against the sky. There was enough light to make out the bannerman's shape, but only just, and swordplay was a difficult enough art in full visibility.

"You should have brought a lamp," he mocked the knight as the man waved his sword in Prentice's direction. "Or did you really think you could get me all the way to your ambush without me seeing through your disguise?" In truth, they almost had, but that was a worry for a later time. He had to survive this first.

"It doesn't matter, heretic," the knight spat. "We're close enough now. They'll have heard us and will be here with enough light to take your head before you know it."

As if to support his comrade's claims, the man with the broken knee tried to roll over and get to his feet but then all but screamed with the pain of his injury banging against the ground.

"They'll hear that for sure," Prentice said and leaped back as the knight shuffled forward. He didn't see the blade but heard the sweep cut the air.

"It won't matter. By the time they arrive, you'll be dead by my hand. Then Sir Pallas will gut your fat heretic friend and Mother Church will be avenged."

Well, that tells me who they are, Prentice thought. *Church knights in league with his brother.*

From farther over the meadow, in the direction of the torches and farmhouse, there came shouts as the rest of the ambushers started to follow the sound of combat and the injured man's cries of pain.

"This is a lot of effort for one man," said Prentice, "even a heretic as famous as I. A quick shot from a hunting bow would be so much easier. Or a swift shank with a poniard from a paid-off servant."

"We are warriors of God, not assassins."

"You are liars and thieves, wearing stolen uniforms and dead men's glory!"

The knight snarled and charged, but Prentice dodged away again. He swung his sword-breaker optimistically but utterly missed in the dark.

"Whatever meagre glory we have stolen will be forgotten when we burn these petty rags," the false bannerman spat. "As will you and all your kind! We are not the only ones doing God's work tonight."

The knight lunged again as he talked, and Prentice, hoping he did not misjudge, dropped nearly flat to the ground, letting the cut pass over his head. Then he sprang up, leading with his sword-breaker. By chance rather than design, his weapon engaged the knight's and the ridges of the 'breaker caught the edge, causing the blade to twist in the man's grip. The knight tried to draw his weapon back, but the catch held it a fraction too long, and Prentice let his leap carry him past the engaged blade. He slammed bodily into the mail-clad man and drove him backward. As they fell, Prentice on top, he smashed his free fist repeatedly into his opponent's face, beating the man unconscious. Then he held himself completely still as the rest of the abortive ambush party came charging up, weapons drawn and torches held high, following the pained groans of the man with the broken knee. There were five of them, and four wore White Lions uniforms, stolen from the dead. Now that he knew to look, Prentice could see a number of tiny errors that only a true militiaman would pick, and he cursed himself for not noticing sooner. The one man who was not in stolen garb was his brother, Pallas, who wore his Church knight tabard and armor.

"Where is he?" Sir Pallas demanded of his wounded man. The fellow huffed and gasped as he tried to speak through the pain.

"Run off. Halleck went after him. I…I heard 'em talking and fighting, not far."

"Start searching! And take him alive," Pallas ordered his men. "The Inquisition allowed me the honor of his arrest to cleanse my family's stain. They will punish us all severely if we let him escape."

"Do not fear, Brother," said one of the others. "After tonight, there'll be no refuge for him to hide in."

Why? Prentice thought. Did they think the duchess wouldn't defend him? He had no doubt she would do all she could to protect him, even if that just meant sending him into exile in the Reach somewhere, hidden under a new name.

Unless.

Cursing fate that he could not save Solft and silently praying the scholar would not be murdered for his escape, Prentice slithered a short distance away and then turned and sprinted into the night. Tripping and half tumbling over the unseen ground in the dark, he pelted back toward the king's camp—back to the duchess, his friends, and his wife.

CHAPTER 53

"Well, at least it looks like a celebration," Amelia said to herself as her entourage began to fan out across the grass and crushed stone pathways, entering into the king's triumph gala. Rumors were already circulating about the sullen, richly dressed man who had ridden with the duchess in her carriage. Amelia was happy for those whispers to travel throughout the courts. She wanted every single eye fixed on her with avid curiosity when she presented Prince Farringdon to the king.

The garden was lit with lanterns, candles, and torches hanging from any available point. Flowers and ribbons were strung from the branches of every tree. Royal guards in red and gold livery lined the entire courtyard, and double sentries were posted at every entrance. King Chrostmer might resent the nobles grasping for a share of his wealth, but he had spared no expense for this victory revel.

At the side of the paved court, a firepit had been dug in the grass, and potboys, stripped to the waist and running with sweat, turned whole sides of beef, lamb, and pork on spits over the coals. The rich aromas wove through the air like another voice in the endless conversation. Despite the bitter state of Aubrey just across the river, the highborn of Denay and Rhales were determined to rejoice in the Grand Kingdom's victory.

Especially so, Amelia guessed, since they would not be footing the bill.

Projecting as great an air of dignity as she could, Amelia took her time moving into the crowd. This was not like the morning of the war council. She had no desire to make a huge impression on these folk. In truth, she would rather spurn them all as they had so often spurned her. It surprised her then when she received so many nods or smiles of acknowledgement.

"It seems you are at last accepted among equals, Your Grace," said Dalflitch, easily noticing what Amelia also had.

"They've heard the prince is commanded to seek my hand again," Amelia said, having to work to keep a polite and, she hoped, unreadable smile on her face. "Now they have to curry the favor of a future queen. Is this how you imagined it would be for you when you dreamed of Daven Marcus's hand?"

"I think I imagined myself a good deal crueler and less dignified than yourself, Your Grace," Dalflitch admitted, her sweet voice and perfect smile at odds with the regret Amelia saw in her eyes. "I had a number of petty vengeances I planned to take, I fear."

"You are no longer that venal creature, My Lady," Amelia told her.

"Loving a former convict will do that to a woman."

"Are you speaking of my man again, Lady?" asked Righteous, coming from a pace away and only catching the tail of the conversation.

"No, My Lady," Dalflitch said smoothly. "I was speaking of mine."

"Oh well, of course," said Righteous.

At that moment, Spindle came up behind Righteous and whispered in her ear. The two of them moved away a pace to speak privately. In the meantime, Amelia continued forward to the pavement and noticed Daven Marcus standing between two royal house-guards in full armor, gilded and burnished so that the gold and steel flashed in the firelight. The golden eagles on their chests seemed almost to be leaping from flames, so vibrant were they. The prince himself was dressed in doublet and hose. Sighting the Prince of Rhales, Amelia couldn't help looking back to Farringdon, standing forlornly in Baron Tillervex's grip. Like the Veckander, Daven Marcus had a miserable expression on his face and his head downcast, but the comparison of the two nearly infuriated Amelia. She felt her hands clench, and she had to force herself to relax them in case anyone should see.

Farringdon's had his life ripped from him and been tortured by deviltry, you monster, Amelia thought as she looked at Daven Marcus. *All you have to do is marry a rich widow who's still younger than you. How hard is that?*

At least the prince was wearing royal red like his guards rather than the insulting outfit he'd had made for his previous wedding plans. With quiet breaths, Amelia took control of her emotions once more. It occurred to her that Daven Marcus's mood might be a tool she could use to her advantage. If he could be provoked to insult her publicly, or better yet to completely disdain her, it might let her gather some support amongst the courts to oppose the marriage. It was a threadbare hope, but she worked her thoughts through it, nonetheless. Prentice always reminded her that she was a champion at the social combat of the nobility, but in this fight, she felt far too alone, like David against the Philistines.

Even David had five stones, she thought. *Tonight, I have only the one.* She looked again at Prince Farringdon and thought how poor a weapon he seemed to her now. Then she remembered it was not the sling stone but the heroic David's faith in God that had slain Goliath. *Very well, Lord. I will sling my stone if you will slay the giant.*

A goblet of wine was presented to her by a steward and Amelia accepted it, indicating that another should be offered to Prince Farringdon. The young man took the cup but did not drink. The courtly folk moved about in their endless, shifting politicking, and Amelia found herself feeling once again an impatience to see the battle begin.

Just sound the charge.

But the king had not yet arrived for the feast. His throne stood empty on its dais. Amelia looked about for Lord Ironworth. Even with the battle over, the king's knight marshal would still have an important role in tonight's festivities. He would know if the king were delayed or merely making his lessers wait upon his majesty. She was about to go searching when she heard Dalflitch beside her.

"Speaking of petty revenge, Your Grace."

Amelia turned to see her former handmaid, Lady Kristen, approaching, wearing a fine gown of red and black silk. She carried a golden goblet, which was mirrored in a bejeweled brooch that she wore on her breast. It was a marker of the man Kristen had married, Baron Robant. Daven Markus had awarded Robant a golden goblet as a trophy for killing one of Amelia's most loyal nobles in a duel. The man had adopted the symbol as part of his livery.

"Duchess Amelia, so good to see you," Kristen said unctuously, and Amelia felt her skin crawl. She noticed her former maid did not bother to curtsey as protocol demanded.

"Kristen, what a pretty dress," said Dalflitch, her smile equally as calculated as Kristen's. "It must be nice not to have to wear my hand-me-downs all the time anymore."

Kristen's eyes narrowed hatefully. "My husband's colors and my prince's, as is fitting. And you may call me My Lady, Dalflitch. I am a baroness, after all."

"Truly?" said Dalflitch casually. "He hasn't tired of you and cast you off yet?"

"No. Unlike you, I know how to keep a man."

"Oh, silly girl, keeping them isn't the problem. It's finding one worthy of keeping."

Kristen cocked her head to one side. "Truly? I'd heard you'd taken to warming your nights with a mongrel. A crippled one at that."

"And still a better man than your husband in every way," Dalflitch said with a smile and without losing a beat.

"You sow," Kristen spat back, all but snarling as she lost her temper.

"Oh, shut up, Kristen," Amelia commanded the young woman, and the flatness of her tone cut through all the snide contempt of the conversation. "None of us cares what you think or say. You betrayed me and the Reach, and for all of it you have your title. Beyond that you are nothing to us."

"The Reach belongs to the prince by right, you wayward slattern," Kristen said, recovering her poise but no longer bothering to veil her contempt. "After tonight we will see who has risen how far and who has risen only to fall."

Amelia shook her head with a pitying smile. She was about to speak when Viscount Gullden presented himself so suddenly that it bordered on rudeness.

"You wanted to see me, Your Grace?"

"I'm sorry, Lord Gullden?" Amelia said, blinking. Baroness Kristen scowled at being upstaged by the newly arrived viscount, but there was nothing she could do about it. Gullden outranked her. Instead, the young woman showed her displeasure by turning on her heel and withdrawing without leave. Amelia was glad to see the petty girl go but was still puzzled by the viscount's arrival.

"Lady Righteous said that you needed to speak with me, Your Grace."

"Did she, My Lord?" Amelia tried to think why Righteous would say such a thing. "I was about to look for Lord Ironworth, Viscount. Perhaps she was confused about whom I was seeking."

"Oh, well, no trouble, Your Grace," said Gullden politely. "And I can save you further trouble. Word is that Baron

Ironworth has been summoned away on some unknown business for the throne."

"Indeed? What a pity."

Amelia knew the knight marshal would do nothing to interfere with the king's plans for her marriage. His loyalty to the throne was absolute. But at least she could have counted on him to be a neutral voice if she had to try some verbal ploy against Daven Marcus when the king arrived.

There was a blast of trumpets at that moment and King Chrostmer emerged from the manor behind his throne, escorted by two of his own house-guards. He was wearing fine silk, red and gold like his son and his retainers, but visibly more ornamented with feathers made of cloth-of-gold as well. On his head he bore his crown, and he smiled as the entire assembly welcomed him with bows and curtseys. Being farther back in the crowd, Amelia risked a longer look, and it seemed to her that the sovereign's smile was forced rather than genuine. Victory revel or not, the king did not expect to enjoy his feast. He gestured to allow the gathered worthies to stand freely once more. Everyone waited on him, but after a long moment he only said, "Continue."

It seems his majesty is in no hurry to address the evening's business, Amelia thought as the conversations recommenced around her. She raised her head in the hope of catching the king's eye, but his attention was turned to a steward serving him wine. Then she heard a splashing sound next to her and she turned to see Lady Righteous standing beside Prince Farringdon, holding his arm while his drink spilled on the stones.

"The prince has had too much to drink, Your Grace," said Righteous. "I think we should take him away as soon as we can."

"My Lady, you jostled his arm yourself," Baron Tillervex protested, still holding Farringdon's other arm. He turned to Amelia. "Truly, Your Grace, he's not touched a drop."

"Forgive me, My Lord," Righteous impudently argued with a tone of perfect politeness, "you are mistaken. Her Grace must escort the prince away immediately. You and Viscount Gullden will no doubt wish to escort Her Grace and her ladies as well."

"Is this why you wanted me, Your Grace?" asked the viscount.

Amelia shook her head. What she wanted was to present Prince Farringdon to the king, get him to bend the knee, and make sure everyone knew it was she and her household that had served the Grand Kingdom so well in this historic moment. They might forget her soldiers' contributions, but they would not forget this. If she had to go into this foul marriage, she would go in as the Lioness of the Western Reach, teeth bared and roaring. But that required timing, and Righteous's odd behavior was interfering with that.

"Lady Righteous, you will be silent," she commanded quietly. "The king will call me soon."

"No, Your Grace," Righteous said flatly, and everyone around them reacted in surprise. The baron and viscount gawped in offended disbelief, and Dalflitch actually hissed, trying to warn Righteous to silence. Amelia looked about and realized that in the close crowd they were beginning to draw unwanted attention. Hadn't Righteous learned better than this? How could she be this boorish at such a vital moment?

"You forget yourself, Lady," Amelia whispered, and she was about to ask the viscount to take her away when Righteous pressed herself to stand directly in front of the duchess.

"It was Lady Spindle that noticed," she said, speaking quickly, voice rising so that Amelia became even more uncomfortable. "You know how fascinated she is with the nobles' pretty animals."

"What are you jabbering about, woman?" Baron Tillervex demanded, and Amelia lifted her hands in exasperated disbelief. She turned to speak to the viscount.

"It's the eagles, Your Grace," Righteous said, seizing Amelia's hands and leaning in earnestly. "Only the king has a crown over his." She looked about herself with slitted eyes, like a hunted animal.

"For God's sake, Righteous, I know this." Amelia tried to pull her hands away, but her lady's grip was like iron. "This is neither the time nor place for discussions of embroidery. And even if it was, what has that to do with the prince's drink?"

"No, Your Grace, you must listen to me." Righteous seemed in a near panic. "Of all the eagles at the feast, only the king's has a crown over it."

Amelia was about to order the viscount to take Righteous into custody when she was stopped by Dalflitch's quiet hand on her arm.

"Your Grace, look around," said the other lady in a near whisper. Amelia blinked. "Lady Righteous is correct. Every single eagle."

She looked about then, puzzled, but recognizing that something must be wrong for Dalflitch to side with Righteous in this breach of protocol. Her eye sought out the men in their red and gold livery, from the guards escorting Daven Marcus to the ranks standing around the garden and the double sentries at every gate.

"Oh my God," she said when she realized. "They're all the same."

Every single armed guard at the feast was wearing the livery of the Prince of Rhales.

CHAPTER 54

"The nearest gate is this way, Your Grace," said Righteous pointing to a different direction from where they entered. "Lady Spindle's gone to fetch the carriage around. We should be out quick."

"Uh...yes, good thinking." Amelia felt her mind running to catch up with events. She turned to her two noblemen, who looked even more perplexed than she felt. "Lady Righteous is correct, gentles. You must escort us and the prince back to the carriage."

"But Your Grace..." Baron Tillervex began to object.

Amelia cut him off. "You must do me this service, My Lord. I swear I will explain all when time allows."

"Daven Marcus, the Prince of Rhales," announced a herald's voice from the direction of the throne.

Every eye turned and Amelia used the distraction to begin pressing toward the escape path Righteous and Spindle had planned for them. The assembly was shifting toward the throne, seeking to hear for themselves this latest public conversation between king and prince, father and son. At a much simpler level, Amelia couldn't blame them. The last time the two men had spoken publicly had been a feast for the gossips. Who knew what would happen now? Amelia felt she could make a good guess, but she had no intention of waiting to see it.

"We should get word to the other Reachermen," she said, realizing how many of her subjects were scattered around the garden.

"Later, Your Grace," said Righteous, taking Amelia by the hand and pulling her along with undignified haste. "First, you must be seen to safety. The Veckander prince, too."

They were almost to the gate when there was a murmur through the courtiers. Amelia looked back over her shoulder to see that Daven Marcus had mounted the dais to stand in front of his father. She was forced to turn back as Righteous continued to drag her, but they were both brought to a sudden halt as a dark-haired man in royal red stepped into their path.

"You can't leave now, Duchess. You'll miss the important part."

"Baron Robant," Amelia gasped. Being Daven Marcus's attack dog, Robant's presence wearing the prince's uniform instead of his own house colors confirmed that they were caught in the midst of a dire conspiracy. "What is he planning?"

"The prince? He feels it is time for Rhales to come fully out of the shadow of Denay." He pointed back towards the throne. "Watch closely. This is the true history of the Grand Kingdom you're witnessing."

Daven Marcus embraced his father with a smile. The two men stepped apart, and the king looked over the prince's head so that while he spoke ostensibly to his son, he did it for the whole court to hear.

"Son, you have heard our advice regarding your desire to marry," Chrostmer declared.

"I have, Father," Daven Marcus bellowed back at the king only one pace from him. He was beaming with a broad smile.

"And what have you decided?"

"I have decided I will not do what you say!" the prince said, eyes widening in triumph. "I will not do what you say ever again!"

Then he stepped forward and thrust a dirk into his father's belly right up to the hilt. The king staggered back in shock, hands around the dagger's handle while his lifeblood flooded out through his fingers. Daven Marcus pushed him backward and he slumped into his throne. The prince pried his father's weakening fingers from the hilt and then tore the blade free, widening the wound. Then he took aim and thrust again, this time into King Chrostmer's eye. In near silence, the monarch died.

Pulling the blade free once more, Daven Marcus turned to the disbelieving crowd and lifted his blood-soaked hands into the air.

"The lover of heretics is dead!" he declared. "Mother Church is avenged, and the rightful man will sit the throne."

"King Daven Marcus!" The shout went up from every man dressed in the royal livery. Even Baron Robant joined in. It echoed off the walls as Daven Marcus took the crown from where it had fallen from his father's head and placed it upon his own. Then he hefted his father's body out of the bloodied seat and sat down to smile over the aghast feasters while the shouting continued.

"King Daven Marcus! King! King!"

The chant persisted for some time, but when he saw Amelia looking for a way past his interference, Robant stopped shouting and gave swift orders to the two house-guards standing with him. All three men drew their longswords.

"This is madness," Amelia protested loudly, though she could barely hear herself.

"You will come with me, Duchess," Robant told her, snatching her hand out of her lady's grip while the two other guards each grabbed at Dalflitch and Righteous. Viscount Gullden moved to intervene, hand ready to draw his dagger, but Robant held him at bay with the point of his sword.

"Do nothing foolish, My Lord Viscount," Robant warned. "Your bloodline has a habit of overreaching, to fatal consequence."

Gullden's eyes went wide, and Amelia knew that he had recognized the baron now as his brother's killer. "I'll have your head!" he declared savagely.

Baron Robant only smiled. "You can try now, if you desire, or wait until I've finished my duties to the prince. I'll gladly indulge your death-wish in either manner."

There was a moment when it seemed Lord Gullden would draw his dagger and try there and then, but it was interrupted as Righteous suddenly fell sideways, sighing loudly and collapsing against the guard who held her hand.

"What in God's name?" Robant demanded.

"Can you not see? She's fainted?" said Dalflitch.

Robant sneered at her then looked to his man, half pulled down under Righteous's weight.

"She's naught but a mutt's bitch," he said to the man. "Can you not hold her up?"

Before the knight could respond however, the shouting ceased, and everyone turned to see that it was because Daven Marcus had raised his hand for silence. A hush reigned over the yard such that Amelia could hear her own heart beating in her chest.

"So, who will be first to bow the knee to their new king?" he asked loudly, slouching, one leg crossed over the other on the throne. "I had heard there were some genuine worthies before us tonight. Surely one of you wants the honor of being first."

"That's your cue," said Robant to Amelia before turning to Baron Tillervex and nodding at the Vec prince still in his grip. "Bring him. He has an engagement with history."

Before they could be moved though, a voice from somewhere else shouted, "Murderer!"

The prince turned his eyes in that direction and pointed to the guards who had, only a moment ago, been posing as his jailers. "That one, bring him!"

The two men in full armor strode rapidly into the crowd, shoving nobles aside. They laid hold of a man Amelia didn't recognize and, ignoring the cries of a woman with him, dragged him in front of the prince on the throne.

"Did you have something you wished to say?" asked Daven Marcus, looking down on the man.

"You are a kingslayer!" the man declared, and he spat on the ground in front of him. "Hell awaits you!"

Daven Marcus shook his head sadly, as if sorry he was forced to this moment. "No, My Lord," he said. "Hell awaits you, as well as any rebel who dares to oppose God's will and his appointed high king."

With that he nodded to the guards. Although the nobleman tried to wrestle free, one man-at-arms forced him to his knees while the other took out his longsword, and with a smooth motion, cut the man's throat. It happened in mere moments, and there was audible shock at the brutality of it.

"I trust that's the only rebel in the Denay court, but let us be sure," said the prince with a cold sneer. All around the courtyard every man-at-arms in royal colors drew his sword. Clearly, this was another signal the prince had prearranged, intended to intimidate the mostly unarmed nobility into submission.

"Now to the Veckander business," Robant said quietly. "Bring him, or I'll end your precious Lioness right here." He turned to see that the man who was wrestling with Righteous was still bent over her fallen form. With his sword in one hand and Amelia in the other, he kicked at the man to get his attention. "Stop faffing about."

The kicked man-at-arms fell sideways, revealing a long cut through his surcoat at thigh level, and then Righteous erupted from the ground, leading with her favorite fighting knife. She slashed straight at the hand Robant was using to hold Amelia, and it was a credit to the baron's skill and reflexes that he managed to withdraw it before she severed it at the wrist. Nevertheless, she caught him somewhat with the edge and he recoiled, cursing as blood flowed. Righteous pushed herself between him and the duchess, one hand leading with her blade while her other ripped at her skirts, tearing them away to reveal trousers underneath.

"You bitch!" Robant spat and shoved his bleeding arm up under his other, trying to staunch the flow while keeping his sword in guard and ready to strike. The unexpected disturbance drew the prince's attention at last, but like the first drops of rain that prelude a sudden downpour, this one little fracas at the edge of the crowd disrupted the knife-edged calm. In seconds, the entire feast was in uproar. Men-at-arms laid about with swords as the crowd scattered in panic. Some screamed as they ran, while others, many of them old warriors and veterans of dozens of battles, drew their own daggers and sought to sell their blood in one last sacrifice for their slain king.

Robant thrust at Righteous, but it seemed he wasn't sure whether to aim for her or the duchess she protected, and it was not difficult for Righteous to keep herself and her liege lady safe. In the meantime, Baron Tillervex snatched up the longsword dropped by the man Righteous had killed and turned it on the man holding Dalflitch, keeping protective hold of Prince Farringdon, who flinched from the noise but still did not rouse from his fugue. The prince's man cast Dalflitch aside and actually saluted his new opponent with his longsword, as if they were meeting on a field of honor. The gesture was so incongruous that it seemed to Amelia that Tillervex almost froze. It would have been a fatal opening, but the saluting knight was suddenly blindsided as Viscount Gullden crashed into him, stabbing him in the neck and face with his dagger. The man fell, dying, and Gullden swiftly recovered his dropped sword.

Lord Robant all but screamed for more men, but the chaos was rising around them like a torrent, and Amelia found herself pressed into a tight knot with Lady Dalflitch and Prince Farringdon as Righteous, Gullden, and Tillervex formed a defense around them.

"The gate!" Righteous pointed the way. The opening was so close, but getting there through the riot of bodies would be like swimming through the rapids of a flooding river, even if there weren't royal soldiers also trying to bar the way. Amelia swallowed her terror, feeling tears rising in her eyes even as she tried to stop them. This was not a time to give way to fear, but she almost felt she could not help it. Was this what battle was? How did any man or woman survive it and not despair?

"There's too many," Lord Tillervex shouted as he slashed at a man who attacked him from the side.

"We must save the duchess," Gullden replied, and he seemed about to push the prince away. Amelia stopped him.

"No, My Lord! The prince must survive. On my honor!"

Viscount Gullden looked from his liege to Baron Tillervex and then back. "Our lives and our honor," he pledged and then turned back to the fighting around them.

"Enough of this!" Daven Marcus screamed over the melee, though no one seemed to be listening. "Kill them all! Let Denay bleed!"

Amelia could hear him but steadfastly refused to look, concentrating on staying close to her bodyguards. His voice in her ears sounded like the shrill cries of a rabid devil, a creature more suited to the night of the Red Sky. Then suddenly, it was like an eagle's cry, the mad cackling of a wretched, plague-ridden eagle. She had heard that sound once before in the midst of a vision in her own great hall in Dweltford. That time it had been the prince, and here it was again. She wondered if she was having another vision, or if the insanity around her had damaged her nerve, bringing the memory back too forcefully to resist. She pressed her hands to her ears and clamped her eyes shut, trying to keep the monstrous visions at bay. Then she heard Righteous, leaning in close to shout in her ears over the din.

"Don't give up now, Lioness. The rest of the pride's coming."

Amelia looked up to see the press of bodies pulling back from around her, and ahead, just inside the gate, were three new figures like avenging angels falling on the prince's sentries from behind and slaughtering in fury. One was Lady Spindle, long poniard in hand like her namesake. Her mask had fallen off and she snarled so wildly that men who saw her scarred visage paused in fear, which only made them easier prey. Beside her were Prentice and Turley, using their force and skill to drive a path to their liege through the chaos. Turley laid about with his hefty mace, while Prentice wielded his jagged sword-breaker in one hand and a dagger in the other.

"This way!" shouted Righteous, and the two little groups merged.

The number of defenders around her suddenly doubled, Amelia felt herself passed from one hand to another and thrust through the gateway. Then they were out past the wall.

"Stop them," Daven Marcus's cracking voice screamed. "Don't let the witch escape."

Amelia was pushed toward the carriage, and she clambered, tearing her skirts as she did, but finally made it to relative safety. Behind her, Righteous and Spindle ushered Dalflitch up as well.

"Her Grace is safe, husband!" Righteous shouted.

"Farringdon!" Amelia cried out, fearful they would drive off now without the prince.

"We have him," came Gullden's voice as he and Baron Tillervex all but carried the prince through the gateway. They were almost clear when a wild slash caught the baron's calf, causing him to fall. Viscount Gullden continued dragging his charge to the carriage, while Prentice and Turley felled the attacker with a rain of heavy blows. Then they looked to Tillervex who cursed in pain when he tried to stand, almost losing his sword in the process.

"Take the reins and be ready!" Prentice commanded his old friend. "I'll bring him."

Turley dashed to the carriage and threw his mace under the driver's board as he leaped up. Scrambling with only one good arm, he managed to find his seat and seize the reins readily. Prentice put his arm under the baron's shoulder, but before the two men could take even a single agonized step toward the carriage, Lord Robant appeared just beyond the gate, accompanied by three more house-guards.

"Save Her Grace," said Tillervex, and he pushed Prentice away. Sword in hand, he half staggered as he threw himself at the gateway with a furious battle cry. "Treacherous bastards!"

Amelia couldn't watch as Robant's men engaged the heroic nobleman, but she felt the carriage rock one last time as Prentice leaped onto the backboard.

"Go! Go!" the captain shouted.

Turley cracked the leather reins like a whip, and the carriage began to rumble into the night. Folk still about in the evening jumped aside as they hurtled through the camp, and behind them the clamor grew as the chaos of the prince's rebellion spilled out into the Grand Kingdom army. Darkness seemed to rush about on every side as they reached the edge of the encampment, and the carriage swerved suddenly. Turley did not let the horses slow even for a moment, lashing them like a wild man.

The journey in the pitch dark, with no more than the Rampart and stars to light their way, seemed momentarily as terrifying to the duchess as the fighting in the garden. Then she realized that the darkness meant they were free of the treachery and on the way back to her tower. They were safe, relatively. That let her draw a moment's breath, and no sooner did she have that respite in her emotions than her stomach heaved within her, and she leaned forward to retch upon the carriage floor.

"See to the duchess," she heard Prentice command. "She may be wounded."

Concerned hands reached for her in the dark, but Amelia waved them away as she managed to get control of her nerves, somewhat.

"I am well," she protested weakly. "I just need to recover my wits a little."

Her ladies' hands withdrew, but suddenly out of the dark came another touch, a masculine hand, and she looked by the bare light to see that Prince Farringdon had reached down and placed his palm on her shoulder. She could not make out his full features, but his voice was soft and sincere as he simply said, "Thank you."

Amelia wanted to tell him he was welcome, but her stomach rebelled again, and she bent double once more, only just managing to keep her mouth shut.

CHAPTER 55

Prentice heard Her Grace spit and groan again, trying to retch out of an empty stomach, and he thought it was probably a good sign. Having confirmed she wasn't injured, this reaction meant her mind and body were responding to the shock of the conflict, which was healthy as long as she was permitted to recover. He remembered his first time in a melee like that. He'd not been able to keep food down for the rest of the day afterward. Of course, he'd been thirteen at the time and a young man needed to toughen up. His training master had commanded him to fast with only water for the next three days as a punishment.

Prentice never vomited after a battle again.

"What of the rest of us?" he asked the shadowed company. "Does anyone else have any injuries?"

At first no one said anything. Prentice knew they were all recovering, but there was no time to sit and stare into the space between life and death. If someone was injured, they needed to be treated.

"Anyone? Lady Dalflitch?"

"I...I believe I am hale," the lady answered.

"Thank God for that," muttered Turley, and he flicked the reins again.

"Righteous? Spindle?" Prentice continued.

"I'm fine," said Righteous. "Just annoyed is all. Thought I had that Baron Robant dead to rights. Should have taken his whole hand but only laid a little nick on him."

"Next time, my love," Prentice comforted her, imagining her grim smile in the dark. "Lady Spindle?"

"I was clipped about the head, Captain," Spindle reported, mixing a lady-like tone with a combatant's assessment. "Took my mask off and cut me some as well, I think. But it's on the scarred side, so little harm done."

"Is that all of us?"

"Save myself, Captain Ash," said a male voice Prentice hadn't expected.

"Viscount Gullden?"

"Aye."

"Are you hale, My Lord?"

"Mostly, but let me just..." answered the Reach noble. After a pause, the air was punctuated by a sudden small curse. "Dammit, yes, as I feared. I've lost the top of two fingers on my left hand. Hurts like the devil."

"Do you need assistance, My Lord?"

"Thank you, no," he replied but hissed again in obvious pain. "Just need to staunch the bleeding. I'll use the end of my scarf. Damn, but it hurts. Old Sir Nickoss always said never go blade to blade without your gauntlets. Proved right again, old man."

Prentice thought he could just make out the viscount's silhouette as the man shook his head ruefully. He assumed Sir Nickoss must have been the knight the viscount had been squired to for his training.

We all carry our teacher's lessons with us, he thought. *Was there anyone in this carriage who had not suffered in their youth?*

"How about you, Turley?" he called to his old friend.

"Shamed to say not a scratch."

"Why shamed, my love?" asked Dalflitch.

"Cause he wants you to think he's a proper man," said Righteous, archly, but without callousness. "Silly twit thinks he ain't suffered enough to impress you."

"Oh, darling," said Dalflitch, and Prentice heard the lady clamber awkwardly in the carriage. Then she was speaking quietly to her betrothed in a comforting tone.

"It is by your hand we have our lives, master steward," Viscount Gullden offered generously. "You and the captain."

"Lady Spindle and Lady Righteous too, I would say," the duchess added.

"More Spindle than me, Your Grace," said Righteous. "She spotted the prince's boys and brought the carriage. I just walked you to the gate."

"There'll be thanks and glory enough to go around once we're safe," Prentice said curtly. It was a presumptuous thing to say in front of three nobles, one a foreign prince, but he was sure the duchess would not mind. Certainly, it was good to feel the pressure of the moment ease somewhat, but they were not yet safe, and complacency would kill them if they let it. "How much longer, Turley?"

"Not too long, I think," came the answer. "That big shadow on the right is a rock spur. We turn around to head straight west now. We should run across Lion sentries in a short space."

"After we do, I'll drop off and get the camp roused."

"No, Prentice," the duchess cried. "You must come to the tower; I'll need your counsel to plan what to do now."

"What you must do now, Your Grace, is pack your things and be ready to march at dawn. You must return to Dweltford immediately, or Griffith at the very least."

"You think to give your liege commands?" Viscount Gullden asked indignantly.

"I do, My Lord," Prentice told him without hesitation. "And moreover, I will give them now to you as well."

"You presume too much."

"I haven't even begun." Prentice addressed the duchess directly. "Your Grace, you need a knight captain to rally the Reach nobles who have survived this night. I urge you to appoint Viscount Gullden, and to do it right now."

"You hope to buy my favor?" Viscount Gullden was a loyal man and competent in a fight; these were characteristics Prentice needed right now. But the man was slow on the uptake.

"My Lord, you'll forgive me, but right now I do not give a tinker's cuss for your favor. The Reach has a need, and you are called. The duchess rules, but she needs soldiers to command for her. She trusts me, and I know she can trust you. Will you answer her call?"

No one spoke for a long moment.

"Is this your will, Your Grace?" Gullden asked at last.

"My Lord, since my husband died, I have been thrust time and again into moments like this. I would give you pomp and honor, award you your status with banners and trumpets and a medallion hanging from your neck, but these are the moments God gives me, and so I do with them what I can. Will you serve me and the Reach as knight captain?"

"I do not need trumpets and banners, Your Grace," the viscount responded. "I pledge you my service willingly."

"Then you must pledge to obey my captain's orders, at least for tonight. I know it is an indignity, but it is an indignity thrust upon us all."

"If you command, Your Grace," Gullden said, and his tone made it clear how uncomfortable he was.

"It is an indignity forced upon us by the prince and his crimes," Prentice added. If he had to offend a ranking noble of the Reach, he could at least remind the man why.

"You mentioned the survival of our nobles, Captain Ash. Do you think many will be slain?" the duchess asked, and Prentice was thankful she was moving the conversation from protocol to problems.

"The prince keeps more than a few grudges with the Reach, Your Grace," he told her. "I think he plans a blood bath."

"He slew the king," said Dalflitch, and it was clear that even just saying it aloud was hard for her to do. "In front of God and everyone. I thought I'd seen his worst..."

"God and everyone," the duchess repeated, and Prentice realized that she was beginning to guess the depth of the evening's conspiracy.

"He has the Church's support, Your Grace," he told them.

"Surely not," breathed Gullden.

"They've been with him since we came south, at least. And tonight, it was Church knights wearing our uniforms who lured me away."

"They didn't have the scholar?" the duchess asked.

"I think they did, Your Grace," Prentice told her, and he felt a lump of shame in his throat. The Inquisition had a man prisoner, and he'd left him there. "I never saw him, though. I sprung their ambush preemptively."

"Good that you did," she told him.

If you say so.

"But how could they permit the prince to do this?" asked Gullden.

"Because the king wouldn't take their leash," said Righteous. "He bearded them good in front of both courts when he got the marriage and heresy settled. Now they've got him back."

"But the king is the king."

Viscount Gullden was never going to come to reality easily, and Prentice did not have time to persuade the man. During his whole fevered run through the dark back to the king's camp, he had been hoping to return to the feast to stop an assassin's dagger, something small and quiet. But this was open rebellion in front of God and man. That meant all opposition would have to be crushed. There hadn't been an attempted rebellion in the Grand Kingdom since the Vec earls had declared themselves princes and broken away centuries ago. Rebellions

failed because they needed the support of the nobility. Kill the
king and the armies of a dozen great nobles would fall upon you
like the wrath of God, not to mention the forces of the Church.

Daven Marcus had the Church on his side this time, it
seemed, or at least its Inquisition. But that still meant a host
of nobles would array against him. Unless, of course, they were
already gone. He could have them all killed, but then there were
the heirs, the ones who would inherit. Even if Daven Marcus
had the whole Denay court killed...

One unpleasant thought dominated all of Prentice's fears
about this night.

"Your Grace, Viscount, ladies?" he asked them. "Do any of
you remember who was present at the feast?"

"The king, the prince, the traitorous bannermen," Gullden
rattled off.

"No, My Lord," Prentice interrupted. "Nobles. Individual
nobles."

"Some, Prentice," said the duchess. "Did you hope for
someone specific?"

"Were there any Rhales nobles there, Your Grace? Any of the
prince's courtiers?"

"Baron Robant," said Dalflitch.

"Yes, of course him, but anyone else?"

"I do not recall, Prentice," said the duchess. "Why does it
matter?"

"I think Daven Marcus plans to kill the entire Denay court,
Your Grace. To slaughter them all, or most, and replace them
with the Rhales nobles. So many of the rightful heirs are in his
court. He may have their whole loyalty in this."

CHAPTER 56

"Such a thing is monstrous even to contemplate," Viscount Gullden said.

"I fear we live in an age of monsters, My Lord," Duchess Amelia answered him.

"It would mean that the Rhales Court as a whole was willing to commit patricide. The prince is a venal coward, and now a kingslayer, but do we suppose that the entire court is the same? Would none still bear their father enough love to spare his life?"

"The prince keeps a court of sycophants and ambitious scoundrels, My Lord," Dalflitch responded. "You've met some, surely? I assure you, any folk with true honor or loving fidelity do not last long in his company. Either they remain on the outskirts of his affections, or they simply leave in disgust. I would expect that the faithful sons would rather have sat in their father's shadows in the Denay court than join the flock of vultures Daven Marcus gathers around him."

"A flock of vultures led by a leprous eagle," the duchess muttered enigmatically, and the image caught Prentice's attention. He had seen a sickly eagle before in visions and had come to think it might stand for the prince.

"You pick an apt image for him, Your Grace," he said, hoping to probe for more. "Might I ask how you come to it?"

"Just something I dreamt once," she replied.

It was all Prentice could do not to sigh in frustration. For years he had received occasional visions and dreams of beasts and angels and sometimes even the Lord himself. He had come to trust them and sometimes even wish for them, pray for them. But he had always kept them secret, fearful that folk would think him mad. Even his wife hardly knew the extent of them. Now he discovered that Her Grace might also have similar or even the same dreams. What prophecy or auguries might they have devised if they had only shared what they knew?

Of all the damnable times to discover it, he thought.

Before he could explore the notion further however, the first camp sentries challenged them out of the darkness. Turley declared the duchess's name, along with the viscount's and Prentice's. A lantern hood was pulled back with a metallic clack, and light played over the carriage. It revealed a grim-faced company, disheveled and dirty. Viscount Gullden was holding his injured hand up in the air, the severed fingers wrapped in a blood-soaked cloth.

"Sorry, Your Grace, Captain," the patrol leader apologized. "It's only orders."

"I know," said Prentice. Having his sentries apologize to ranking folk for following orders was becoming standard practice, it seemed. He jumped down from the backboard and strode up to his men, giving swift orders. "You with the lantern, escort the carriage to the duchess' tower. The rest of you will come with me." He turned to Turley. "As soon as Her Grace is in the tower, you go with Lord Gullden. It will help him to have a witness when he announces himself as the new knight captain."

"Alright," Turley said, but in the lamplight, he looked to Dalflitch sitting behind him, and Prentice knew the cause of his concern.

"Trust me," he told his old friend, then turned to the viscount. "My Lord, you must rouse the house-guard and every living Reacherman of birth still in camp. You must persuade them of the truth of what has happened this night, and they must be ready to march at dawn. Will you do this for Her Grace?"

To his credit, the viscount did not bridle at Prentice's order, but he did look to the duchess for one final confirmation before he nodded his agreement.

"And, Knight Captain," Prentice added. "I would not rush to think even a single Reacherman contemplated betraying the Lioness, but this is a night of blackest treachery. Pick the knights you trust the most and send them direct to the tower. Once the prince knows the duchess has slipped his trap, he will send men to bring her back, do not doubt."

That notion seemed to sharpen Gullden's attention, and he nodded to Prentice. "As you say, Captain."

"Thank you, My Lord. Lastly, Righteous, Spindle..."

"We know our duty," said Righteous, but Prentice shook his head.

"No. Listen, wife, I will never ask you anything more direly than this. You two stay with Her Grace and Lady Dalflitch. All four of you stay together. That goes for the Vec prince, too. No one is to be ever out of another's sight until we are marching north. Any man who seeks to separate you, no matter his birth, you separate him from his head. You hear me?"

"Yes, Captain," the two women saluted in unison, and the daggers in their hands thumped to their bodices.

"Where will *you* be, Captain?" the duchess asked him before he could turn away.

"I will be rousing your army, Your Grace," he told her. "We need to march, but we also need to be ready. If we are correct and the whole of Rhales has their hands in this conspiracy, we will likely see a company of knights sent to hound us before midnight. I want them to find the Lions ready to hunt."

"Very good, Captain. Go to."

Then the carriage was rumbling away into the darkness and Prentice broke up the patrol, sending them as runners to all the other sentries. Drummers would call them back as soon as he gave the order, but he wanted his people warned as early as possible. For all he knew, Daven Marcus was already on his horse with several hundred men-at-arms charging up behind them. He marched into the center of camp, shouting orders, sending runners to fetch corporals and drummers, and making as much commotion as he could. The sooner everyone was awake, the better.

"What's happening, Captain?" Sergeant Franken asked as he rushed up, struggling to give a proper salute while he pulled his brigandine into place, his hair a messy tangle.

"The Prince of Rhales has raised a blade against his father and killed him."

"Bollocks!" Franken swore in reflexive disbelief but saluted again, ducking his head. "Sorry, Captain. But...are you sure?"

"I've just brought the duchess back from the massacre, Sergeant. Reach and Denay nobles are being slaughtered in the king's camp right now."

"Are we going to stop them? Defend the king?"

Good man, Prentice thought. That was the kind of response he wanted from the duchess's militiamen. But he shook his head.

"The king is dead. Her Grace saw it happen. We do not know how many have pledged to the traitor prince or what forces he might command, but he has the backing of the ecclesiarchs, it seems."

"The Church?"

"Aye," Prentice confirmed. "So that will mean Church knights and the Inquisition as well. These are your orders. We are marching north at dawn. If we can be ready earlier than that, we will march earlier, but come what may, we go at dawn."

"We've never struck camp in the dead of night before," Franken said.

"Then we had better learn how."

"What about the wounded?"

Damn. Prentice had forgotten the wounded. "The ones that can walk, will walk," he decided swiftly. "Tell them to carry their weapons but to leave their kit and armor if they have to. The ones that cannot walk we will have to...uh, maybe the wagons."

"I don't think we've got 'nough wagons for all of 'em, Captain."

Prentice was sure he was right. They'd have to come up with another solution.

"Alright, I will deal with the wounded. You get the wagons loaded for the march instead—weapons, powder, the things we need to help us fight. *Then* food. If things get desperate, we can forage on the way back north, but we won't get any chances to reequip before we reach Griffith."

"You think we'll be fighting on the way back, Captain?"

"Sergeant, I think we will be fighting before midnight. I am going to put my harness on, and then I will be with the wounded. Get the camp struck and the Lions in order. The first five cohorts that you can marshal, get them down on the eastern edge of the camp. If the prince comes in force, I do not want him to get a free canter into the midst of us."

"Ain't much powder left for the Roar, Captain."

"Then we will do it hand-to-hand. This isn't the Red Sky, but do not think it is any less desperate."

With that, the two men parted to their separate duties, and by the time he reached his tent, Prentice heard the drums beating the order to strike the camp.

CHAPTER 57

With the warm, dry weather, the worst of the wounded were gathered under a simple set of tarpaulins held up by posts, like a row of tiny, rough-cut pavilions. On the ground underneath, men lay on simple bedding, mostly sleeping, though under the sound of the camp's uproar, the occasional moan or whispered prayer could be heard. Mostly it was dark under the tarps, but here and there Prentice could see some figures—men and women tending to the wounded and offering comfort where they could. Walking the length of the row, Prentice did a rough count in his mind. Franken was right, the wagons would not hold them all.

"Too many to carry away," said a voice, and Prentice turned to see Sacrist Fostermae holding a lantern nearby. "That is what you were doing, is it not, Captain? Counting how many men are here and devising whether you can take them with you when you march?" He looked around at the rushing encampment. "You mean to be gone very soon, I take it?"

Prentice's mind was a battleground of priorities. He had the duchess he must defend, the evacuation of his militia and their wounded, as well as all the strategic plans he wanted ready to defend against any assault from Rhales men-at-arms. But all of these thoughts simply stopped dead when he looked at Fostermae's dimly lit face.

"Your friend is dead," he said flatly. "Or at least soon will be. I am sorry, but the Inquisition has him."

"I guessed as much," the sacrist said quietly.

"I wanted to save him, but the duchess was in danger. I had my duty."

"Did you speak with him?"

"I never saw him," Prentice said, shaking his head.

"Then you do not know anything for sure?" Fostermae gave a gentle, compassionate smile. "Perhaps his estate is less dire than you fear. He may be well, or even yet win free somehow."

"It would take a miracle, Fostermae."

"I'm a firm believer in miracles, Captain. What kind of sacrist would I be if I were not?"

That made Prentice smile, and he hung his head a moment, feeling some of the tension leave his mind.

"Given your own experience with angels and visions, I would expect you to have more faith in them as well," Fostermae added.

"I believe in miracles, sacrist," Prentice told him. "I just do not expect them. They will come when they come." He rubbed the back of his head and suddenly wished desperately for sleep.

"You think our Lord is capricious?" Fostermae pressed. "Giving miracles on a whim?"

Prentice almost said yes and then realized that was not what he thought. He had at one time and for years as a convict, but not anymore.

"Not capricious, my friend," he said. "But He is the one who has seen the end from the beginning, so we are taught. His plans include much that I do not know, that *no one* knows. I only see what is in front of me and what the Almighty chooses to show me. My wisdom stretches no further than that. I can ask for a miracle, but I will not plan for one unless God tells me to himself. In the meantime, I have two hands, my own strength, and my own wisdom."

"I think you are wiser and stronger than you give yourself credit, Captain."

"I pray so, sacrist. I pray so."

"You lookin' for me, Captain?"

Prentice turned to see Solomon standing at perfect attention in the dark, saluting proudly. Prentice returned the salute with a smile.

"I wasn't, Solomon, but it is good to see you."

"You need a drummer? I can fetch me barrel and sticks, right quick."

Prentice shook his head. "No lad, I have heard you are doing good service to the Lions here."

"I'm just doin' runnin' and fetchin', Captain. Ain't nothin' special in that."

"You might not think so, lad, but the militia runs on service like yours. It might be only water or a bandage to you, but a man dies of thirst or bleeds away for want of them if you do not do the fetching." Solomon puffed with pride at that praise. "Now, if there is a healer in charge, or someone who arranges the care of the wounded, go fetch them."

Solomon dashed away, swinging under a guy line and between two of the tarps.

"He adores you, you know," Fostermae said while they waited for him to return.

"He has a good heart and steady courage," Prentice said, recalling Solomon's bravery in the battle. "He served well under the Red Sky."

"And you will take him with you into more battles?"

"Eventually, perhaps, but the boy has earned a few days' rest." The memory of his own childhood rose in Prentice's mind. He did not recall any of his masters feeling this affectionate or merciful. But mercy was a worthy thing, and he wanted Solomon to see some. That prompted his mind, and by the time the drummer boy returned with a bent-backed old man in a finely trimmed grey beard, Prentice knew what he had to do.

The old healer introduced himself as Malaster.

"These men cannot march, can they, Master Malaster?"

"I see your camp in uproar, Captain," the old man replied in a surprisingly strong tone for so elderly a body. "You mean to leave and right quick, but no, absolutely not. These cannot march. With the dry air, best they not be moved at all, at least not for some days. No rain or even dew, nothing to bring the rot into their wounds. They're safest where they are."

"And do you plan to tend them until they are well?"

"Some, but for most I will wait until they can walk on their own and then leave them to it. The body heals itself good enough once it reaches a certain wellness."

Prentice couldn't argue with that. "You have other healers here with you," he said. "Will they stay too?"

"A few will, I think. Others have already gone to pack their bags and march with your lot, if that's what you're worried about."

Prentice wasn't, but he did not fault Master Malaster for thinking he would. He shook his head. "What I wanted to ask of you, Master, is that you protect these men as we go."

"Protect? I'm not one of your soldiers."

"And I do not seek to treat you as such. I only ask that you do a kindly service to these injured men and look to their needs. The White Lions must march tonight. You will learn the why of it soon enough. The whole Grand Kingdom will know."

"What is to become of these then?"

"They will be given leave from their service, at least for now. I will see you are given a purse to pay for their needs and a promissory note to the duchess's seneschal for any further costs you incur."

"Some of these men are convicts," Malaster said, eyes narrowed.

"The ones who return when they are well will be restored to their pledge and can serve the rest of their time to their honorable absolution."

"And those that don't return?"

"Them I trust to God."

As he said the words, Prentice scowled. He was the Reach's jailer, the man who was entrusted with the fate of every convict, to make soldiers of them for the purging of their souls. And here he was, allowing that any convict who survived his wounds could simply walk away if they chose. It was certain that some would definitely flee. But somehow, he was sure that many would not. Any convict who completed a seven-year stint with the White Lions was entitled to freedom and a parcel of land in the Reach. The officers would muster out with silver as well. He was sure that some of these wounded would fight hard to return to that promise—the gauntlet run that ended with an honorable life.

After all, it was the path that had led Prentice off the chain, and he had made it clear to all his militiamen that if he could rise to become Captain of the White Lions, then any man could.

"Alright," said Master Malaster, rubbing his chin thoughtfully. "I'll do as you ask, at least until the end of summer. Autumn and winter see me needed amongst the lesser folk."

"Thank you, Master," Prentice said, bowing his head respectfully. "If when winter comes you find yourself in the north near Dweltford, call at the duchess's castle. I promise you will find a warm bed and hot meal there."

The healer cocked a suspicious eyebrow. "A healer goes where he will."

"Of course. We would not seek to bind you. I only pledge our thankfulness with more than words."

"That would be alright, I suppose," Master Malaster allowed, apparently mollified. "Back to my duties then. Send that purse when you're ready. I'll be here."

The healer stalked away among his sleeping charges, and Prentice turned back to Fostermae. "Will you be coming north with us, sacrist?"

"Not tonight, if you'll permit, Captain. I need to stay and pray with these men. Master Malaster and his fellows are blessed and skillful in their arts, but there are some here not long for this world nonetheless."

Prentice nodded and shook Fostermae's hand as a gesture of thanks. Hands clasped, both men shared a moment of unspoken communication. They both realized that the night was not over and each likely had their own appointments yet to keep with the angel of death.

"What about me, Captain?" Solomon asked loyally. "You want me on the march?"

"Not tonight, Solomon. Sacrist Fostermae and the healers will need a runner for a while yet. But he will bring you back north when he returns, won't you sacrist?"

"Of course," said Fostermae, and he ruffled the drummer's hair. Solomon was not consoled though.

"I want to be at your side, Captain," he said, his voice cracking with emotion. "I'm your drummer! I earned the right!"

Prentice felt his heart clench. He remembered the tears on Solomon's face the night they fought on the Redlander bridge. This boy knew firsthand what battle was. And now he wanted to march back into that terror again, all for the honor of standing beside his captain. Prentice reached into his belt and drew out the silver rat pin that had been used to lure him away just a few hours before.

"Do you know what one of these is, Solomon?" he asked, holding the simple piece of jewelery up in the lamplight.

"I do, Captain. It's a sign of special service. You have one on a chain around your neck and your wife has one, too. They say only the best of the duchess's servants ever gets one."

"That's right. This one belonged to Knight Captain Sir Gant, and he was wearing it when he died. Did you ever know a more honorable or powerful knight in all your life?"

Solomon shook his head, his eyes focused on the pin.

"And you likely never will, lad," Prentice continued. "This pin has a tale behind it more than that even. It is precious to the Western Reach. But I cannot keep it. I already have my own." He reached for the chain around his neck and pulled out his own pin, holding it up beside the other one. "So, I need someone I can trust to carry this one."

He handed Gant's pin to Solomon, and the boy held out his hand reverently, seeming almost afraid to take the simple piece of metal. Prentice put the pin into Solomon's grip and closed his fingers around it.

"You are my drummer, Solomon, and my loyal man. I entrust this to you because you have earned the right. I know you understand its importance. It is not a gift; it is a duty. When Sacrist Fostermae brings you back north, I will tell you the whole of its tale—who has held it and how it has been used. Until then, keep it safe and continue in the loyal service you have already shown."

Then Prentice stood back and saluted his young charge. Solomon returned the salute with such eagerness it was a wonder the boy didn't pound the breath out of his own chest.

CHAPTER 58

"I'm so glad you had those curtains and this wall installed, Your Grace," Dalflitch said from across the duchess's chamber. "Imagine how troublesome these few days' stay would have been without them."

"You jest, Lady Dalflitch?" Amelia asked, her brows narrowing.

Dalflitch shrugged apologetically, and Amelia realized that she would actually rather an attempt at levity than to continue in the grim atmosphere that had gripped them since the feast. No one was likely to laugh, but to relieve the tension even a little might be a worthwhile goal. And as she thought about it, it *was* a trifle ridiculous. So much effort had been made to make the chamber suitable to her rank and comfort, and she would barely have stayed in it a week. She wondered what the carpenter and his apprentice would think of that. Then she remembered the switchback path Prentice had had the militia digging out of the side of the hill beneath the tower. All for what?

Prince Farringdon sat on a chair a short distance away, facing out the tiny window. There was nothing for him to see except the dark of night, but Righteous and Spindle had placed the man there as soon as they arrived, and one or the other stood guard at his shoulder as the rest of the ladies changed their clothes. Care was taken to see that he did not look about indecorously. Any other noble might have bridled at such treatment, but the prince sat quietly through the entire procedure. Since the carriage ride in the dark and his word to Amelia, the young man seemed to be more aware of his surroundings than ever, but he was still far from fully alert.

"I trust you'll forgive me, just this once, Your Grace," Righteous said as she presented herself to Amelia. "But Lady Spindle and I mean to wear trousers today and we will not be dissuaded." Both women had kept the striped pants from under their skirts that fitted their legs in unladylike fashion. Above those, they wore arming doublets with gorgets and gauntlets, and instead of hoods or veils, they covered their heads with fitted, open-faced sallet helms. Each had a sword belt with at least two fighting daggers in sheaths, and Righteous also had a Fangs' sword that hung from her hip, seeming too heavy for the slight woman. They made a martial pair, but as she looked them over, Amelia was surprised that her first thought was that they were under-equipped. Any men-at-arms that Daven Marcus sent for her now would likely be nobles clad in the finest armor, sealed in polished plates from head to foot.

From the ground floor of the tower there came a clamor of voices, and without being bidden, Righteous and Spindle took up a place on either side of the door, daggers in hand, when someone knocked. When they were ready, they nodded, and Dalflitch opened it to find one of the stewards looking flushed and uncertain.

"Forgive me, Your Grace," he said, tugging his forelock. "Turley said I was to tell you the minute knights arrived sent by Lord Gullden. They're here to be your guards."

"Then we only await the captain's orders to join the march," Amelia said.

"If that's good, Your Grace, and you're ready, I'll have the others come and start clearing out your furniture."

"Oh, I'm ready," Amelia started to say, looking to Dalflitch. While Righteous and Spindle had dressed for a fight, she and her other lady had changed into linen dresses of thicker cloth more suited to hard travel, and both had light summer cloaks about their shoulders. Then she fully heard what her servant was saying, and her eyes went wide. "Clearing out the furniture?"

"Yes, Your Grace. Sooner we start—"

"You'll do no such bloody thing, man! See to your people. Every bit of food you can carry, nothing else. Then get yourselves direct to the camp to join the march. If I see a steward weighed down with so much as a chamber pot, I'll order the man beaten, do you hear me!"

"Yes, Your Grace," the shocked steward stammered, recoiling from his mistress's unexpected anger.

"We are in a flight for our lives, man. Furnishings be damned!"

The man backed out, tugging his forelock repeatedly as he went.

"That caught him by surprise, Your Grace," said Dalflitch.

Amelia smiled.

"Two of my father's oldest stewards went back for mother's portrait when the Blood Sect forces breached the castle," Prince Farringdon said quietly but clearly, and all the women turned to look at him in shock. "Father called after them, but they didn't hear him. I promised I'd get them to safety, but by the time I found them it was too late. We tried to fight our way free, but there were too many."

"Were they killed?" Amelia asked as she approached his chair and stood beside him.

"I don't know." The prince blinked and then turned to look at her directly. "The invaders beat me senseless. When I awoke, I was in prison and they were gone."

He stopped speaking, and Amelia and her ladies waited quietly to see if he would say more.

"What a pleasant tale," Dalflitch said when it became clear he would not.

"Your jests need some work, My Lady," Amelia quipped.

"I will do what I can, Your Grace."

For the next hour or so, by Amelia's reckoning, they waited in their chamber, speaking little and listening tautly to every sound that came from below. Despite her commitment to try harder, Dalflitch did not make any more attempts at levity. There was a long silence so deep that Amelia could hear her breathing, which was finally broken by the return of the steward.

"Beggin' your pardon, Your Grace," he said as he entered. "Only, it's just the number of knights waiting down below is growing, and while they're all your men, they're awful antsy, if you'll forgive me saying so."

"Is there trouble?" Dalflitch asked.

"Not so much, but more than one has made a polite request to come up to speak with you direct. And some of them is getting' less polite about it."

"Tell them to curb their impertinence," Dalflitch told him, and the servant blanched. "They are sworn to the duchess's service, and they'll have to summon the patience expected of them in this difficult hour."

"I...um, that is..."

"Tell them as soon as word has come from the captain and knight captain, we will be with them."

"I tried to say that Your Grace, but..."

"But?"

"Well, I'm just a steward, and Master Turley, well he normally spoke with the house-guards, and knights, and what all."

"He set you to watch the household in his place," Dalflitch said, advancing on the man imperiously and showing her impatience. "You do as he would do."

"I would, but, well Turley, he's...he's got a way. He knows how to speak, you know, Your Grace." The servant tried to look around Dalflitch to speak to his liege lady directly. Apparently, he felt he'd get a more sympathetic response from her. "I just ain't got his way with the words, is all. I don't know how to tell 'em off polite like. They'll not take it kind from me."

"It is true that my chief steward has something of a silver tongue," Amelia admitted. "I'm sure you'd agree, My Lady."

"If you say so, Your Grace."

Amelia watched the earnest servant wringing his hands. The more she thought about it, the more she realized how wrong it was to expect the poor man to hold demanding nobles at bay on a night like this, with tensions running high and rumors doubtless abounding.

"Perhaps we should make an appearance," she said. She saw Righteous and Spindle flick her uncertain glances. Their task was so much easier up here than amongst a crowd of men-at-arms, but Amelia felt a growing confidence. If there were men down there who meant her ill, they would not have waited patiently all this time. They would have rushed the stairs and tried to take the chamber; she was sure of it. And even if there were patient assassins waiting in the company below, there were almost certainly loyal men and true there as well. Any attempt at rebellion would find them taken down swiftly.

"Go and tell them we are coming," she told the steward. "We are ready to travel and will await word from the captains with my sworn men."

The steward left and the duchess's little clutch of household worthies readied themselves. Lady Dalflitch took the prince's arm to guide him, and in what was becoming an ever more standard violation of protocol, Righteous went ahead like a herald, hand on her sword hilt. The entourage went down the steps slowly, as if expecting attack. As soon as she could see the floor below, Amelia began scanning the upraised faces of knights in armor. Most had their helmets under their arms, and those that did not removed them upon sighting her. Amelia looked from man to man. She saw uncertainty in their expressions, anger, and perhaps a little fear. But what she did not see was hatred. As near as she could tell, she was safe in this room.

"Gentlemen, sirs, My Lords," she greeted them as she reached the dais in front of her chair. Steel clashed as every man-at-arms went readily to one knee. "It is good to see loyal men and true on a dire night like this."

At her signal, they retook their feet. Amelia looked at the chair behind her, but before she could sit down, one of the knights spoke up.

"Your Grace, can you tell us, is it true? Is King Chrostmer truly dead?"

"Sadly, sir, he is indeed."

There were troubled murmurs before another called out the next question. "And slain by the Prince of Rhales? That is what we have been told, but surely that cannot be?"

"I saw it happen, sir," Amelia said, nodding sadly.

"But..." the man began to protest.

Righteous cut him off. "He buried his poniard in the sovereign's eye," she said flatly. "Right to the hilt."

There were grief-filled groans at that news. Such treachery in the royal family was unspeakable. Men looked aghast at each other. They were bereft, and their duchess could not blame them. The foundational truths of their society, their nation, and their own individual duty had all been attacked this night, and she could not fault them for not knowing how to respond.

She barely knew herself.

At that moment the tower door boomed open, and every eye turned to see Turley, Prentice Ash, and Viscount Gullden enter. The chief steward and two captains took the room in at a glance, and then, sighting her on the dais, Prentice began to lead the trio directly to Amelia. As the armored crowd parted for the three men, their duchess realized that though she lacked a plan for a night like this, there was still something she could do. She could trust the men and women God had sent to defend her so many times in the past.

It had always been enough up 'til now. Lord willing, it would be enough for this monstrous night as well.

CHAPTER 59

"Captain Prentice, Knight Captain Gullden," Amelia greeted the two men as they knelt before her. "What word do you bring?"

The two men looked at each other, and Prentice nodded his head to his noble counterpart, giving the man place to speak first. Amelia marveled at his thoughtfulness. Sir Gant would have deferred to Prentice without hesitation, such was the respect and affection between the two men, despite their differences in rank. But the viscount was new to his role and needed to earn the respect of these other gathered nobles. It would not do for them to see him take second place to a man of no birth, even one as respected in the Reach as Prentice Ash.

"Your Grace, every noble of the Reach is mounted or has his horse in the care of his squire. We will ride at your command." Obviously, the other knights and nobles in the room with them were the ones Gullden was referring to when he mentioned squires. Was he reassuring his peers that there was no plan to leave them behind? Amelia wondered. "Tents are being struck and luggage packed, but whatever is not ready when you give the order will be left behind. Everyone understands that."

The armored men in the room beat their gauntlets on the hilts of their swords as gesture to show they agreed.

"Are all aware as to why we must leave?" she asked. Viscount Gullden nodded solemnly.

"They have been informed, Your Grace, though many struggle to accept it." The nobleman nodded in Turley's direction. "Your chief steward did me good service in lending his testimony to my own, but nonetheless, there were five or six who insisted on seeing for themselves. They rode to the king's camp."

From his expression, it seemed to Amelia that the viscount was leading to something dire, so she nodded for him to continue.

"A squire that rode with them returned not a quarter of an hour ago with a hateful tale, Your Grace. The knights were told that it was you who slew the king."

"What?!" It was so preposterous that Amelia nearly laughed before she realized that Viscount Gullden was in deadly earnest. She swallowed at that. "A hundred pairs of eyes saw the prince plunge the dagger," she declared, protesting.

"I was there, Your Grace, and will swear to it until my dying day. But already there is war in the Grand Kingdom camp. The squire says his master met with royal men-at-arms and was persuaded. Others were doubtful but were willing to hear the prince tell his side."

Amelia looked from Gullden to Prentice to Turley. Each man in turn met her eyes with a grim expression. "How can he do this? Prentice, do you understand it?"

"From what the squire tells, Your Grace, the prince has been sitting judge in a court of lies since the moment you escaped," Prentice explained. "He has taken the Denay court captive and is forcing them at sword point to put their names to a testimony against you. Accusations of murder, treason, and witchcraft are being heaped one upon another. Men perjure themselves or their wives and heirs are dragged before the prince and put to the sword."

A renewed wave of muttering, more angry than confused, swept the room. If it was true, this was unforgiveable news.

"In the meantime, the Rhales court and their men-at-arms sweep the Kingdom camp, seeking dissenters. Any attempting to escape are being hunted, and the prince has extra help."

"Extra help?" Amelia asked, but Prentice only gave her a raised eyebrow. It puzzled her for a moment and then she realized. Church knights were assisting the prince. It was obvious once she thought about it, and she was thankful for Prentice's reticence. News that Mother Church had sided with the usurping prince might have been a truth too far for many faithful men present.

"Thank you for your service and this news, dreadful though it is, Captain, Knight Captain," she said loudly. "As to the men who have gone to the prince in all this uncertainty, they are not to be faulted for their doubts." Amelia could see the surprise on many nobles' faces, but she felt she had to say it. It would be unjust to judge a man forced to choose between his liege and his liege's liege in a chaotic state of affairs like this. "This is a night unlike any we have ever thought to face, and we have all seen the blood-red sky. If any other man is uncertain, if any finds himself unsure and fearful that perhaps I have the wrong of the story, or if you fear that the rebellion is mine and not Prince Daven Marcus', then I release you to take your leave without rancor. God will judge between the prince and me. You must all look to the wisdom he gives you until the light of righteousness divides truth from lies."

She looked them over, but not a single man moved to leave. She took that as a good sign.

"Well then, Captain Ash, how go the plans for our march?"

"The militia will soon be ready, Your Grace. If it would please you to accompany us now, we will escort you to the camp and march from there."

"Not by my carriage?"

"I would prefer you rode, Your Grace. Your horse is saddled and awaits you. She is a better seat for a journey in haste."

"And what of my ladies who have no horses to ride?"

"Our wagons are uncomfortable but safe, Your Grace."

None of Amelia's ladies-in-waiting offered so much as a frown at the news.

"Then we should go, now."

"As you command, Your Grace," said Gullden and the new knight captain turned to give orders to the gathered knights and nobles. Not one raised any objection, and the heavily armed escort was assembled in moments.

"That was well spoken, Your Grace," Prentice whispered to her as he held out his hand to help her down from the dais. "A leader with truth on their side does not fear the judgement or the momentary doubts of their subordinates."

"It is also pleasing to confirm that none here doubt me," Amelia said quietly in return.

"I suspect they would not have taken that moment to leave even if they did, Your Grace."

"But I gave them leave. I meant what I said."

"I am certain that you did," Prentice said with his characteristic wry smile, though his eyes were cold. "Even so, I doubt any man here would risk his fellows' disdain by turning his back on you publicly. Loyalty and honor are often competitors for a nobleman's affections. More likely, if they have doubts that are too great for their consciences, they will quietly fade into the dark as we head into camp or else drop back unobtrusively once the march is underway. Easier that than publicly splitting from one's liege in the midst of a crisis."

Prentice's words made sense, but that did not mean Amelia liked hearing them.

"Will many be like that, do you think?" she asked, fearful now that some of the men-at-arms nearby might be able to hear them.

"I would not think so, Your Grace," he said and smiled again. "But on this night, who could say for sure?"

CHAPTER 60

"We will go down the switchback path," Prentice told them as they left the tower. "It will be difficult in the dark. Take care where you step."

Amelia and her closest entourage were only just out of the door when the sound of a horse's whinny echoed in the darkness and she looked north to see men on mounts carrying torches. The flames of their lights glinted on the steel they were wearing, and as she watched, it seemed more joined them from behind so that there must be at least a dozen knights waiting on the old road to the tower.

"Friends, Knight Captain?" Prentice asked Viscount Gullden.

"I do not think so, Captain Ash," Gullden answered.

"Good thing we have this other path then, Captain," Amelia said. "Compliments to your foresight."

"The compliment belongs to Felix," Prentice answered gruffly and then paused and turned back to Amelia. "Forgive me, Your Grace. And thank you for your compliment."

Looking to the foe waiting in the distance, Gullden slapped Turley on the shoulder. "Looks as if we'll need that plan steward," he said.

"Quite so, m'lord," Turley replied. "I'll get to it."

"Good man. We'll go hold them while you do."

"Plan, Prentice?" Amelia asked, wondering what they were talking about.

"To cover our retreat, Your Grace," Prentice said. "We are going to fire the tower and your carriage in front of it. Their horses will not want to ride close once it is burning hot, and the ridge here is too narrow to ride around in the dark."

"Burn my tower?" The idea seemed so extreme, destroying an edifice that had stood for centuries to slow the pursuit of a dozen men.

"It can be rebuilt, Your Grace," Prentice reassured her. "We have set lamp oil and plenty of fuel inside. It will go swiftly." He turned to the viscount as the knight captain gathered a company of knights to distract the men on the path. "Do not go too far toward them, My Lord, and be ready. When you sight the flames, you will not have much time before it will be too hot to get past."

"Fear not, Captain," Gullden replied with a smile. "When we come back, we will be running like broken rogues." Then his face fell, and Amelia knew he realized he had just insulted Prentice. He corrected himself. "We'll hold them off like Reach Lions until the flames take, then we'll run like broken *Kingdom* rogues."

"I know you will, My Lord," said Prentice, smiling without offence.

Viscount Gullden strode into the dark, accompanied by a dozen men-at-arms, weapons drawn. "Ho there, you on the horses," he bellowed. "Stand and be recognized."

"Prince's men," came the return call. "Come to arrest the witch from the west and fell any man as stands between us and her."

"Fell? What are we, sir? Trees?"

Amelia wanted to hear more, but already she felt herself being forcefully ushered along the narrow side of the tower toward the freshly hewn, switchback path down the bank of the ridge. The path was more rock than earth, and with the darkness and hurrying, she slipped with almost every step. Nevertheless, strong hands guided her, and she was passed from escort to escort. Behind her there were shouts and the clash of steel, and she knew Viscount Gullden was now fighting for his life. She was about to make the second of three turns when she heard Turley shout from above her.

"Now's the time! Go, like the clappers!"

Amelia looked up and saw light licking at the edge of the path. Then there came a sound of rushing armored feet, steel boots clashing on stones. A handful more steps and she realized that there was more light in the night. Another few paces and she had reached the last switchback of the short path. Then there was a thump and the ground beneath her shook. A bright gout of flame burst over her head, and dust and splinters fell from above them.

"That's the powder and oil going up," Prentice said matter-of-factly. "We won't be fighting at our rear guard now."

"I thought you said we had no powder to waste," Amelia said breathlessly as they rushed down the last cut slope to the grass at the ridge's foot.

"It was not wasted, Your Grace."

The crowded company of armed men began to disperse somewhat around them, and as uncomfortable as the press had been, a sudden rush of irrational fear jumped in Amelia's heart. Then her ladies were beside her again, Prince Farringdon as well, and she was able to force the emotions back down within her. As they marched and stumbled into the camp proper, she looked over her shoulder to see the tower burning above, the flames already leaping through the roof, like a chimney with a roaring fire beneath it.

"What now, Captain?" she heard herself ask. She felt like a twig fallen into a river, bouncing along wherever the water took her. At least for now, she surrendered herself to fate and the plans of others. All the maneuvers and stratagems she had prepared for Daven Marcus and his allies, every defense against their ambitions and deceits, this night made them all irrelevant. And at every turn, it only got worse.

"Now, Your Grace, we get you safely back north," Prentice told her as Turley and Viscount Gullden returned.

"Worked a charm there, steward," the knight captain congratulated Turley who returned the thanks with a tug of his forelock. "They thought they were going to ride right into the tower, I think. Their horses surely were having none of that once they saw the flames."

Lady Dalflitch grabbed her betrothed around the neck and placed a kiss on his sooty cheek. He hugged her a moment, and it cheered Amelia to see something good in this fell experience. Then he tried to detach himself.

"I got other duties tonight, my love," he said.

Dalflitch wanted none of it. "No," she cried. She turned to Amelia. "No, Your Grace, please. I cannot let him go again like this. Please, not tonight."

Amelia understood her lady's desire. "Prentice..." she began to command, but he interrupted her.

"He has duties to Your Grace," he said sternly, and for a moment, Amelia remembered how he had sometimes been when they first met, like a demanding tutor who had helped her order her thoughts and build her abilities as duchess and a ruler. But she was no longer that learner. She was duchess in her own right, and she was tired of the hours of waiting while others took all the decisions. Perhaps it was not the wisest moment to intervene, not the most useful decision to take, but she felt that she had to do something, and she chose this.

"Master Turley will stay with us, Captain," she ordered. "His primary duty is to my household and staff, and he can fulfil that duty here." For a moment she thought he might argue with her, but Prentice only bowed.

"I can swap," said Righteous suddenly.

"No, you can't," Prentice told his wife, but Righteous ignored him and looked to the duchess for approval.

Amelia blinked. She was happy with Prentice's command. She wanted to gather every member of her household as close as she could, to somehow have them in sight and keep them safe. But even as she thought it, she realized that was exactly what everyone around her was seeking on her behalf. Moreover, she knew they could not do it while keeping everyone under her wing. Safety—their safety and hers—required people to go and do what was needed. As duchess, she had to release them to their duties.

"You could use another corporal, couldn't you Captain?" she said. "A ferocious blade and competent; you've said so yourself."

"Her duty is your safety, Your Grace."

"And my safety is well seen to. Look about, Captain. I stand in the midst of the army you built me. Until we reach Dweltford Castle, I am as safe now as I can be." Amelia directed her words at Prentice, but she knew that, in fact, she was equally counseling herself.

"As you command, Your Grace," Prentice relented with a bow.

"We all know our duty," Turley told him, putting his hand on the captain's armored shoulder.

A moment later and a steward presented Amelia with Silvermane. She took the bridle and stroked her mount's neck, speaking soothing words. The poor thing was skittish enough at the best of times. This night, with all the torchlight and shouting, the mare was almost unruly. Once she was certain her mount was reassured, Amelia was helped into the saddle. A short distance off, another mount was brought for Prince Farringdon. He allowed himself to be led to the saddle and placed his hands on the leather, then paused as if perplexed.

"This is not my saddle," he said to no one in particular. "This is not my horse."

"Forgive me, Highness, it is the only horse we have to offer you," Amelia said politely, as if inviting him to a pleasant afternoon's ride in open country. "Perhaps later we can find you your own mount, but I would be flattered if you would take this one in the meantime."

"You are too kind, My Lady," said Farringdon, and he put his foot into the stirrup.

"Her Grace," Spindle said reflexively from the ground behind the prince. Amelia wanted to rebuke the woman; this was not the time, not with the fragile prince, but Farringdon accepted the words with complete aplomb.

"Of course, Your Grace," he said and bowed as he settled himself into the saddle. "We have so few duchesses in the Vec. I forget."

Amelia felt a crazed laugh try to bubble out of her chest and she squashed it down. Perhaps it made sense that the calmest man on this mad night should be the man who was already closest to madness. She watched as Turley escorted Spindle and Dalflitch to a wagon that was waiting some distance off and then looked to her two captains.

"At your command, gentles," she told them. They both bowed and went to the business of the march. Viscount Gullden mounted up himself and drew up a close escort of thirty knights on horse in full panoply, with lances and shields. They arrayed like a tourney-day parade, and it might have seemed a bright and cheering sight at another time.

Prentice marched away with his wife to give the final orders for the march, and the drummers beat again. Silvermane shied, and Amelia leaned forward to calm her once more.

Then the cry went up along the line: "Camp is broken. The march commences. North to Griffith."

Amelia looked up and thought perhaps the sky was lightening. "Come, dawn," she whispered. "End this unholy night."

CHAPTER 61

"Two columns, side by side, forty-pace gap. See that every corporal keeps his cohort in discipline."

Even as he gave the order, Prentice knew it was unnecessary. It was the same order he'd given an hour ago and the hour before that. It was the tension that made him repeat himself. And now that the sun was risen and the torches and lamps had all been doused, it was so much easier for the entire company to keep formation. On the open ground, they marched in two long columns with the wagons down the middle. Knights rode on the outer sides in skirmish companies to prevent sudden flanking attacks or ambushes. These meadows were the best terrain to march in such a defensive formation, and that was one advantage they enjoyed.

Not that it relieved Prentice's tension much. Now that the sun was up, he kept an eye on the foothills of the Azure range only a few leagues to his right. The mountain range was still little more than a long escarpment this far south, and he knew it was riddled through with gullies and gorges that would allow horses and men-at-arms through from the east. A day and a half's march north and the mountains would be an impassable wall that would shield the Reach forces from the Grand Kingdom proper. Until then, these lesser hills were just a curtain behind which whole armies might hide.

A league away to the west, the Dwelt flowed, and Prentice wondered if there were any Redlander boats to be found there, hiding. He gave word to Viscount Gullden to send men to flush the riverbanks, just in case. He doubted they could be there in strength enough to threaten the White Lions, but Prentice was taking no chances.

By mid-morning the air was heating up and the flies hounded the march like a cloud of pestilence. Prentice sent a runner from his position near the head of the march to check on the duchess in the middle of the formation and received word that she was well. He made sure she was aware that he intended to keep the march going until evening. The farther north they were before they stopped to rest, the safer they would be.

"We'll start getting waterskins passed down the march," he told Sergeant Franken. "And make sure everyone knows there'll be nothing to eat until evening."

The sergeant saluted, and his grim expression told Prentice everything he needed to know. All around him, the bright and glorious army he had marched south was dirtied and shabby, but though the gloss was off them, they were resolute, and he knew these were the victors. They had stood against the Redlander bridge under the blood-red sky. They had thrown back the wave, and though they were less than four thousand now, that was enough.

"Dust cloud," Righteous said next to him, and he looked to see her scanning the sky to the south. Their own march was stirring a mass of dirt into the air, but that settled behind them slowly as they passed. Prentice moved out of the line of the march several dozen paces to be sure. It looked like she was right. Leagues behind them, there was fresh dust rising.

A squire on horseback, wearing a gambeson with the collar unlaced over his bare chest in the heat, rode up at that point and saluted without dismounting.

"Word from the knight captain," he said. "Enemies sighted on horses."

"We've seen them," Prentice confirmed and started doing calculations in his head. If they were mounted men, they would overrun his own force quickly. How much time would he have to prepare or find better ground to defend?

"Not that way, Captain," the squire corrected him and pointed to the hills to the east and slightly north. "In the hills up there."

"That is ahead of us," Prentice muttered. That changed everything. "How many?"

"Many. Not quite half our company, but maybe."

More than a thousand men on horses? How had the prince sent so many so far north so quickly? "What's ahead of us?" he asked the squire. "The next league or two north?"

"Just meadows, rolling slopes and some rivulets. Nothing you could call a hill or a stream. Nothing to defend, Captain."

Prentice wasn't too worried about that. He'd make a defense out of the wagons.

"Go straight now to the knight captain," he ordered the squire. "Tell him that if it pleases, I think he should begin to pull all the riders into a coherent force and, with my compliments, inform him that we will be double marching hard north for the next half hour."

"Double marching, Captain?"

"They will want to attack us from the front and the rear, pincered. I mean to try and get them all south of us before we form up."

"I will inform the viscount," said the rider, and he spurred his horse away.

"Double march?" Righteous asked Prentice.

"Give the order," he told her, and she went to pass the word to the nearest drummers. The command was just beating out when Markas came up, the company colors furled about their standard pole.

"We forming up soon, Captain?" he asked.

"Not just yet, Markas," Prentice told him. "We have a hard march first. But stay close."

The rhythm of tramping feet increased around them as weary but resolute militiamen lifted themselves to the new pace. Soon, this was accompanied by the bellowing of complaining bullocks as the wagon drivers whipped the animals up as well. Sweat dripped down Prentice's back under his armor as he kept up with his soldiers. Every dozen paces he looked back over his shoulder and the rest of the time he had an eye on those hills where a thousand riders lurked. Then he spotted a glint on one of the hilltops, a flash of metal in the late morning sun. It was not even a half a league away and still slightly north of them. With every step, Prentice scrutinized that glint, dreading a horde of knights riding over the crest and sweeping down on them, cutting them off. Soon he found himself almost willing them to come, but the glint remained unmoving. Whatever was there, it was not riding out to intercept them. The vanguard drew even with that hill, straight west of it, and still nothing happened. Prentice stopped to watch that point, and soon the wagons were passing behind him. The militia was almost halfway past.

"Is all well, Captain Prentice?" the duchess called as she rode by in the midst of her escort.

"I could not say yet, Your Grace," he called back. "I will see you informed when I know anything with certainty."

"Very good."

Then the duchess and her escort were north of him.

"Riders," came a call behind him. "There!"

Prentice looked to the south. Not more than a league away, a column of mounted men-at-arms emerged from behind a slope just south of the hilltop he'd been watching, banners flying as they trotted westward. There were easily a thousand, and Prentice was pleased to see them behind him at last. Whatever was on that dreaded hill, all the Grand Kingdom knights he knew of were now on one side of his forces. His pleasure was short lived, however, because now they would have to give battle.

"Drummers," he shouted, and in an instant two lads were next to him. He gave them orders, and complex patterns began to rattle out, picked up and echoing over the spring-green meadows. The vanguard cohorts stopped marching and dispersed to assist in redeploying the wagons. The north-south line of vehicles was turned and rapidly maneuvered into an east-west line across their path, with the ends curved northward, so that the line was like a broad, flat horseshoe. The trailing third of the column marched around the rapidly forming defense so that by the time the Grand Kingdom knights had formed themselves up in a three-row formation for a charge, the entire White Lions company had marched north and was now concealed behind the wagon fortification, which was rapidly pressing together to close its gaps.

"It was not even a month ago that no one had ever seen one of these wagons," Prentice said to himself, proud of the White Lions rapidly incorporating the vehicles into their tactics. He clambered up the middle wagon as all along the line the reinforced sides were dropped into place and the wooden wall hardened against assault. Looking south, he watched the knights and realized how the prince had sent such a large force so far north so swiftly. Many of the banners and pennants showed the black and gold double-overlapping crosses of knights of the Church. These were the forces that had sat out the Battle of Red Sky with the prince, never coming as far south as the Murr River. That was why they could be this far north so quickly.

"Are they just going to stand there or are they going to throw down?" asked Righteous as she sprang up next to her husband. She was fitting a buckler shield to her off hand.

"I do not know," Prentice answered, trying to puzzle out the knights' plan. Why come out now? A pair of Roar gunners took firing positions on his wagon, one of them a corporal, and behind them pike men hefted their weapons, points ready to strike down over the top. A corporal of the Roar ran up from along the back of the wagon line.

"Oy, Captain," the man called rudely, though he saluted perfectly. "Sergeant Franken says to remind you that the Roars's only got about one shot each. We can't do like we did at the river."

"Tell Franken thank you and pass the word to hold that one shot. Every gunner fires on my command only. You pass the word as you run back. On my command."

The man saluted and ran off.

"Us Roar're just going to be meat in the middle after that one shot, Captain," said one of gunners beside Prentice.

"You take one knight each with that shot and none of the rest of us will have anything to do," he threw back at the man. "Make your shot count, and we will do the rest."

"Right you are, Captain."

The men around him smiled, steeled by their commander's confidence, at least for a moment. Yet the knights remained like statues, completely still in their ranks. Prentice took a glance over behind himself and saw that the duchess, the wagoneers, and other non-combatants were now gathered in the safety of the horseshoe formation, with cohorts of Fangs and Claws guarding the open end of the shoe. Beyond that, Knight Captain Gullden had formed up the knights of the Reach, about two hundred in all, on one side. It was a strong company of heavy horse, but their mounts had already been riding all morning without changeovers. Their horses would have the strength for maybe one full charge. They would be best held as a reserve.

"Here they come," muttered Righteous, and Prentice looked back south as trumpets sounded and the Kingdom force spurred itself to the charge. A wall of steel and brute strength flowed toward the wagons, the pig-headed majesty of the Grand Kingdom's traditional battle formation. Prentice shook his head. What were they going to do, try to ride over the wagons?

They might as well charge at a solid wall. He did not give the order to fire; there was no point, not until they were as close as they could get. With only one volley to shoot, best to leave it to the last possible moment.

The charge was just beginning to shake the ground as it drew near when the knights did something completely unexpected. They reined in.

"Do they normally do that?" asked Righteous.

"No, they do not," said Prentice. His eyes narrowed and he stared at the Kingdom line as it came to a halt no more than thirty paces away. He could see individual faces amongst the armored figures, with many visors up, and in the middle of the line was the king's knight marshal, Lord Ironworth. Prentice could scarcely credit it.

Why was he with these Church knights?

"Do we fire, Captain?" asked one of the gunners. A curlicue of smoke rose from the man's burning long-match. The smell of it, and hundreds of its fellows, wafted around in the fresh morning air.

"No one fires until the signal."

A shout went up from the Kingdom forces, and with expert precision, the entire company turned to its right and started to trot around the wagon line.

"What is it? A parade?" asked Righteous.

No, not a parade, Prentice thought. But what was it? Perhaps Ironworth wanted to draw out their knights first, knowing they were a smaller force. If he could detach them and break them before he faced the militia proper, that would be to his advantage. In short order, the enemy knights were at the flank, showing no sign of attacking but continuing northward, as if the fortified wagons were a feature of the terrain, rather than an enemy to defeat.

Prentice jumped down and rushed through the inner part of the portable fortification to the Reach knights. Viscount

Gullden was already watching for some kind of signal and rode toward Prentice as soon as he caught sight of him.

"There are at least a thousand, My Lord," Prentice called to him as they approached. "Knights in full steel ahorse."

"What do you think best, Captain?" asked Gullden as he reined in. He winced with pain and flexed the fingers of his left hand. He had a gauntlet in place, but under that, the freshly injured digits must have been giving him no small discomfort. Prentice was impressed with the man's resolve to fight and surprised he was so willing to take advice.

"Wait until we see their array, My Lord. Once they pick their order, ride to the river. Either they will be forced to split their force to pursue you, or else they will ignore you to engage us. If they do that, then you may turn and bite their flanks at your leisure."

"What if they pursue us in force? They are five times our number of horse."

"If they do that, My Lord," Prentice told him, "you will hear the drums beat the double march again and we will be running to support you. With God's blessing, we will catch them between us, hammer and anvil."

"Do not tarry, if that happens, Captain. We are brave Reachermen, but we will not hold long against those odds."

"We will be coming as fast as our legs can carry us, Knight Captain."

The two men saluted and parted to their respective commands. Prentice stood in amongst the pike and halberd cohorts of the Claw infantry, facing north as the enemy knights formed up into a single company. In amongst the Claws were the Fangs, their swords ready for the close-in fighting. Prentice wished he could bring some Roars to support his flanks, but he left them on the wagon wall to watch and oppose the other force still kicking up dust from the south.

A half dozen knights detached themselves from the Grand Kingdom's ranks, two bearing long pennants, one royal red, and the other green with black and gold—the throne and the Church. They walked their horses into the space between Kingdom knights and Reach militia, planting their pennants in the ground. Then a trumpeter blasted a long, complex flourish. One of the knights removed his helmet to clearly show Lord Ironworth's grim countenance.

"What's that about?" asked Righteous.

"Parley," Prentice told her, looking at the knight marshal. "They're inviting our commanders out to talk with them before we get down to the fighting."

"Oh, I get that. Got to show your brass before the barney."

Prentice smiled at her street fighter's understanding of nobles in battle. "Go tell Her Grace they've called for parley and see if she wishes me to go with her or in her stead."

"She won't be daft enough to go out there herself, will she?"

"I hope not, but it is her right; she is the Lioness."

Prentice watched the knight envoys waiting patiently for a reply to their trumpet. If he forced them to wait long enough, they would likely just turn around and the battle could commence. That was his preference. There was nothing that needed to be said here. Behind him, he heard men shuffling and making way, and then Duchess Amelia's horse appeared beside him in the ranks.

"Come, Captain Prentice," she said. "Let us see what these men who have invaded my lands have to say."

CHAPTER 62

A melia knew it was not strictly correct to name Grand Kingdom knights as invaders, even in the Western Reach, but these were her lands, and these men-at-arms were arrayed against her and her forces. They were making themselves enemies. She geed Silvermane forward and Prentice marched at her horse's shoulder, his long spear in hand. Behind them came the White Lions' standard-bearer, his blue and cream banner flapping against its pole. The ranks parted for them, and they emerged onto the open ground. From her left, Viscount Gullden and another Reach knight she did not know rode up to take a place beside her. She welcomed them with a nod.

"Dignity, Your Grace," she whispered to herself and straightened her shoulders reflexively. She felt her fingers beginning to tremble on the reins, and with every step her horse took she felt more and more adrift, like a swimmer in a storm. She had stood on battlefields before but never in the midst of two armies like this. It felt frightening enough to be surrounded by grim-faced militiamen setting themselves to fight. But to emerge from their protection to meet with enemies far ahead of their lines? It threatened to overwhelm her. Amelia knew that these men were offering parole and would be honor-bound to never attack under this truce, but only a day ago she had also known that no prince of the realm would ever slay his father in front of hundreds of witnesses. She was much less comforted today by what she "knew."

Amelia reined in Silvermane only a handful of paces from the enemy representatives. Beside her, Viscount Gullden and his man did the same. Lord Ironworth sat in the middle of his little group, but the other knights still had their helmets in place, though some opened their visors at her approach. Amelia recognized Prentice's brother Pallas as one of them, wisps of the man's fair hair emerging around the helmet's edges. Every man's armor was polished to near whiteness, and they flashed in the high sun so brightly it made her blink.

"Lord Ironworth," she acknowledged the knight marshal.

"Duchess Amelia," he responded. "You know why we have come?"

"In truth I do not, My Lord, though I could hazard a guess. Perhaps better if you tell me yourself."

Ironworth nodded. "I have a warrant for your arrest from the hand of King-elect Daven Marcus."

"You are mistaken, My Lord," Amelia said through gritted teeth. "Daven Marcus is a kingslayer and cannot ever be king."

"Stop your lying mouth, witch!" Sir Pallas spat venomously.

"Curb your own tongue, sir, or answer with steel!" Viscount Gullden intervened with equal fury. "You insult the Duchess of the Western Reach in her own lands."

"She is..." Pallas made to respond, but Lord Ironworth held up his hand to stop a further intemperate outburst.

"We have heard that you claim it is the Prince of Rhales who slew King Chrostmer," he said calmly. "Yet his highness has the testimony of dozens of witnesses signed and sworn before ranking ecclesiarchs that it was you."

"It was Daven Marcus. I saw it with my own eyes," Gullden insisted, and Amelia could hear the tension in his voice. She wondered if he was having as much difficulty controlling his passions as Sir Pallas clearly was. She turned to him.

"My Lord, if you please?"

Gullden bowed, and Amelia heard one of the other Church knights scoff. "See the power she wields over them. They are all ensorcelled."

It took all of Amelia's self-control not to laugh at that preposterous claim. The nervous impulse rose in her chest, prompted by her fear as much as the ridiculousness of the words, but if they wanted to accuse her of witchcraft, then cackling openly was not the way to dissuade them. She forced herself to swallow and set her mouth in a firm line, expressing no emotion.

"I am no witch."

"Nonetheless, Your Grace," Ironworth said, his expression making it seem that he was uncomfortable with claims of witchcraft, along with everything else about this moment. "I am commanded and cannot shirk my duty. The King-elect has made his will plain. You must accept my authority and submit to trial. It is the only way."

"I have already suffered once under Daven Marcus' idea of a trial," Amelia told him flatly. "I will not ever do it again."

"Think of your men, Your Grace," Lord Ironworth asked earnestly. "Will you make them suffer and die for your rebellion?"

Amelia could not think what to say in response to that. She hated the idea, but as she searched for a way to express her regret at being forced to this point, she heard Prentice whisper beside her.

"Go back, Your Grace. Go now."

"What?"

"Now, Your Grace. Please trust me!"

She looked down at him and realized that he was staring at his brother. Her mind wanted to understand, to see what her captain was seeing, but she knew better.

"This cannot be resolved with words and trials, Lord Ironworth," she said, and she wheeled about quickly to head back to her lines.

"No! Stop her! Don't let her escape," she heard someone shout. Then there was a slap against Silvermane's haunch, causing her spirited mount to surge, and she failed to hold the mare to even a canter.

"Go, Your Grace!" Prentice shouted, and she was sure it was he who had slapped her horse. Then she heard Lord Ironworth's powerful battlefield voice.

"Cease this. We are under truce."

"To hell with truce," called Sir Pallas. "No word of honor binds to a witch or a heretic. Ride them down."

"This is a disgrace!" bellowed Ironworth, but it was swamped by the sound of steel crashing and scraping. They had come to blows.

Her men-at-arms were fighting behind her, but Amelia could not spare even a glance over her shoulder. It was such a short distance back to the White Lions' line at a gallop, yet Amelia wondered if any journey in all her life had seemed to take so long. Unbidden memories of her flight across the western grasslands fleeing the prince's hunters rose in her mind, threatening to overwhelm her. Then the ranks were opening to admit her and pikes set to defend her. She looked over her shoulder then to see one Church knight who had cleared the conference come hammering up, sword drawn, only to rein in at the hedge of steel points. He turned his mount back and forth, as if seeking a way through, then wheeled about to return to his own side. He was completely unready for Prentice and his standard-bearer who were themselves retreating at full pelt. The White Lions' banner struck the mounted churchman in the face, doing no damage but momentarily confusing him while Prentice rammed his spear upward at the man's chest. The steel point scraped up the armored breastplate with a sharp squeal. Then its pointed wing caught under the man's armpit, and he cried out in pain as he was nearly thrown from his horse. The trained war mount reared to protect its rider, and Prentice and his man were forced to dodge free of its steel-shod hooves. Then they were safe under the pikes, and horse and rider retreated across the field.

Looking back to the broken parley, Amelia saw Viscount Gullden spur free of the chaotic melee but realized that his companion had not been so fortunate. Another man had been killed protecting her life.

"What happens now, Captain?" she asked as Prentice returned to the ranks.

"Now, Your Grace?" he answered. "Now you return to the safety of your escort and we make those bastards pay for their treachery." Around her Amelia heard the militiamen growl like furious animals. It was so visceral and full of rage that she had to remind herself they were on her side.

"One of those bastards is your brother," she said to Prentice quietly. He did not spare her a glance.

"Not anymore, Your Grace."

CHAPTER 63

"We're in it now, husband," said Righteous, holding out something in her hand.

"What's this?" he asked, taking it from her. It was a folded piece of blue cloth. Opening it, he saw it was embroidered, but he couldn't make out the pattern.

"It's a lion," she told him. "I was making it as a lady's favor, you know, so you could carry it into battle like them proper knights. I used it to wash your face the morning after."

"Oh," he said, not really paying much attention.

"It's not finished," she snapped as her eyes narrowed. "It's supposed to be all rearing up like a proper Reach lion." Prentice tried to spare her a smile, but he was distracted watching the enemy knights forming up. They would charge soon, he was sure. He passed the cloth back to Righteous.

"Perhaps you should keep it then, until it is done."

"Nah, I ain't like to finish it now. 'Sides, I figure you don't need a little snot cloth. You want your wife to look after your proper needs."

Still not paying her his full attention, he was surprised as she suddenly hefted a weapon belt around his armored waist and buckled it in place. Blinking, he looked down as she fitted the belt to hang correctly. There was a sheathed fighting dagger on it with a broad cross hilt.

"You love them big polearms like your partisan," she told him. "And you keep losing swords. But you need something for close work. It's not my favorite, mind; I'm keeping that for me. But it's a good one, and I made sure it was sharp for you."

"It is a favor I shall treasure," he told her, affecting his most high court accent. "I shall wear it near my heart, Lady, to remind me of your kindness." He leaned in to kiss her.

"Shut up, you daft bastard," she said as she blushed, but she accepted the kiss. Then the sound of the trumpet echoed over the field, and Prentice returned his full attention to the battle.

"The charge is coming," he said, but as he watched, he realized that instead of the typical knights' charge, Lord Ironworth was instructing his men-at-arms to dismount. In short order, at least four out of each five knights climbed out of the saddle to fight on foot, their warhorses led away to be cared for by squires and pages. The remaining mounted men withdrew a short distance, reforming into a smaller horse company about the same size and strength as the duchess's Reach knights.

"That's not usual, is it?" asked Markas, leaning on his standard pole and still recovering his breath from carrying the heavy banner back on the retreat.

"No, it is not," said Prentice. He stared as he watched. At every turn, Lord Ironworth surprised him. What were they doing? The knights on foot reformed themselves into a single cohort about the same frontage as the White Lions, but in narrow columns, as if they were deliberately lining up like arrows to be fired into the Reach militiamen. Then Prentice noticed that the two or three warriors at the head of each column was carrying a heavy sword, longer than a longsword by half again at least. The blades were almost as long as their wielders were tall. The massive things were surely heavy, but the men carrying them hefted them powerfully enough. Prentice was reminded of the heavy blade Lord Ironworth had boasted of at the king's war council, and then he remembered the charge at the wagons that had stopped close but never attacked. He whistled in appreciation.

"Damn me, but that man knows his business."

"What? What's going on?"

"The duchess told Ironworth we have no powder for our guns," he told Righteous and Markas. "That was what his false charge was for. He wanted to confirm we couldn't fire the Roar at him. Now that he knows he doesn't have to fear our fire, he is going to take away the Claws' advantages as well."

"How?"

"Those heavy greatswords his line leaders are carrying. He will have told those men to aim for our pikes, knock them aside, perhaps even break them outright. Those knights will advance slowly, clearing our pike hedge for the men coming in the columns behind."

Prentice shook his head in grim appreciation of the knight marshal's strategy. At the Battle of the Brook, he and Lord Ironworth had stood together against massed ranks of Redlander spearmen and had learned an appreciation for the tactic. Prentice had adopted and improved upon it to build the Reach's White Lions. Lord Ironworth had studied its challenges and developed his own response, it seemed. As Prentice watched knights who normally would be rash for personal glory advance in tight formation, he knew they were about to see who had the better strategy.

"We're in for a hell of a day, lads," he shouted, and no sooner were the words said when another trumpet blast sounded. The enemy knights continued their patient advance and nothing else seemed to happen for a moment. A dull whoop sounded far off, almost too low to hear over the creak of leather harness and the ring and jingle of armor all around them. Prentice's mind barely registered the sound. He was concentrating on watching the initial clash between his pike and Lord Ironworth's pike-fighting strategy. Then there was an explosion of wood shattering, men and animals screaming in agony, and the ground trembled.

"What the hell?" Prentice looked about, wondering if the southern pursuers had reached them so soon when he saw a gout of fire from the hill where he had observed the metallic glint earlier. A second stone cannonball slammed into the ground to their east and sent a spray of earth on the wagons as it bounced over the eastern end of the fortifications and then into the space where the bullocks were corralled. Four of the beasts died in the impact and blood and bodies were scattered westward.

"The Bronze Dragons," Prentice cursed. How had Ironworth managed to get the king's cannons so far north so quickly?

The knights finally reached the hedge of pike points, and the clashes began as their greatswords hacked at the shafts. There was another thump and another cannon shot sailed toward them.

The battle had begun in earnest.

CHAPTER 64

Prentice grabbed a drummer and pulled the boy's instrument from over his shoulder. "Go now, straight to Sergeant Franken. Tell him to take two cohorts from the wagons and clear those cannons off the hill! You understand?"

The boy nodded, but Prentice made him repeat the message back to be sure before he sent the lad off. Then he turned to Markas and Righteous, handing his partisan to his wife. "Hold this here. I'll be back in a moment."

"Where are you going?"

"To try and pry open the jaws of this damned bear trap before we lose our leg!" he shouted and didn't wait to see if they understood his meaning. Rushing behind the ranks of his troops, Prentice crashed at his best pace in his heavy armor to the flank where Viscount Gullden was holding the Reach knights in reserve. He had to get to him before the knight captain followed their earlier plan.

"My Lord! My Lord!" he screamed, desperate to be heard over the din of battle. It looked like he might be too late as he reached the flank and saw the Reach knights turning their horses about. The gap between them was only twenty or thirty paces, but it was open ground. Ignoring the sudden memory of running to protect the duchess over open ground not a quarter of an hour before, Prentice burst into the space and rushed, hands waving and voice cracking, toward the Reach knights.

Gullden was already looking away, but some other men-at-arms saw Prentice running and they spurred their own mounts to catch up with their leader. The viscount reined in his force and trotted to Prentice. As the two met, there was another whoop and more crashing of shattered wood.

How much longer would the wagons last under this kind of assault?

"Those cannons," Prentice pointed to the hill and the column of smoke rising from the firing. "They have our range. We will be smashed to firewood and bloody rags in short order. I have sent men to stop them, but I swear to you Lord Ironworth has already thought of that. His reserves on horseback will be watching and will ride them down."

"Your Lions are trained to fight against the mounted man," said the knight captain.

Prentice wanted to curse the loyal but slow-witted nobleman. "Yes, My Lord, but not mounted men and cannons at once. They must either rush to the cannons out of formation and vulnerable to the Kingdom knights or else hold formation and make ideal targets for the dragons."

"You wish us to ride to the Bronze Dragons?"

That would have been ideal, but Gullden's already curled lip at the prospect told Prentice he'd been right to send his infantry first. Riding down cannoneers was not the Reach knights' idea of glory in battle.

"My Lord, if you would be the finest of hunting hounds and make the Kingdom knights still ahorse your prey, I believe you would do the duchess your best service."

The viscount smiled at that and waved chivalrously at Prentice. "That we can do, Captain."

Turning to look, they could see the Kingdom's mounted reserves were already headed east behind the line of battle. They must have seen Franken's detachment making for the cannons on the hill. Viscount Gullden waved his men around and headed south to circle in front of the wagon line and then intercept the enemy horsemen. Prentice did not wait to watch them go. Another cannon ball sailed wide over the battlefield, and he wondered if the Bronze Dragons had sighted his men coming and tried to aim for them. Whatever was happening, he'd set every soldier to their task and had nothing left but to return to his own post.

Righteous handed him back his partisan when he arrived through the ranks. "What's the word?" she asked.

"We win this, or we die here."

"Fangs out!" a corporal somewhere on Prentice's right shouted.

"Damn, that's too soon," was all he could think to say. The Fangs were not supposed to engage the enemy until they were well inside the range of the pike and were hard pressing the halberds. If a corporal was putting the swords into the fray, he'd either lost his nerve and ordered them early, or the enemy had pressed deep too quickly on that part of the line. Neither prospect was desirable.

"You didn't think to put your helmet on at some point, husband?" asked Righteous beside him. He rubbed his gauntleted hand over his scalp and smiled to himself ruefully. In fact, he had not.

"It's back in the luggage, I think," he told her.

"I'd offer you mine," she sniped, "but I don't think it would fit over your fat head."

There was a sudden shift around them as men closed ranks and pikemen farther back in the company lowered their weapons to fight over the shoulders of their comrades in front. Another cannonball struck behind them, and a high-pitched scream made Prentice afraid that it might be a woman injured because that could be Her Grace. If the duchess died, the whole battle would be for nothing.

"Their armor's too strong!" someone on his left shouted, and the press of men shifted again.

"The hell with that!" he shouted back. "Second rank cohort there, up in support."

Men shuffled forward on the left to support the hard-pressed front. Prentice couldn't see over the shoulders of those militia, but he could sense the desperation on that side of the battle. Without thinking, he found himself moving in that direction and then felt his wife step in his way.

"Captains command," she shouted at him through the noise and chaos. "Corporals and sergeants rally lines."

He wanted to tell her he loved her. Tell her she was his wild bramble rose and no woman would ever be as beautiful and precious to him as she was.

There was no time.

"Go," he commanded, and Righteous was away to rally the left flank.

There was a cheer in front of him and Prentice guessed that one or more of the penetrating greatsword wielders had finally been felled in that part of the battlefront. Then a wild cacophony of steel told him that the joyful moment had been short lived. He could hardly see amidst the sweat and press of bodies, and the dust that the battle kicked up was starting to choke the air so that even breathing was difficult.

"I need to learn to bloody ride," he swore to himself. From horseback he would have a better view of the field. In smaller battles, or with the wagons to climb upon for a better view, it had never mattered before. Now he was being forced to guess. In front of him the metallic rage rose and fell, and he felt as much as saw that cohort thinning as men were being injured. A Fang staggered back between the lines, blood spilling down his gambeson from a slash that opened his cheek from eye socket to jaw. The man almost collapsed as he lurched past, and the gap in the company out of which he stepped seemed to go almost all the way to the front. Prentice could see Grand Kingdom knights hard pressed on every side, laying about like men clearing wild thorn bushes but managing to stay upright and in the fight because of their heavy armor.

"Stay here," he ordered Markas and his drummers. "I need a better look."

He pressed into the gap, his long partisan held high and forward, to join the fight. Through the ranks he moved, slowly, waiting for shifts in the flow of battle to find spaces ahead. Corporals and line-firsts shouted at men to close the gaps, but Prentice watched for his moments and soon found himself only two ranks back from the front. He stood beside a line-first Claw with a halberd. The man drew his weapon back for a moment and grounded it, then paused to pull his left gauntlet back into place. Prentice thrust his partisan into the gap the man's weapon had left.

"Captain," the militiaman exclaimed, surprised to see his commander. He moved to salute reflexively and nearly lost control of his halberd.

"See to your gauntlet, man," Prentice shouted at him. "I have you covered."

The line-first pulled his armored glove back into place and took up his weapon again, hefting it over those in front to fall on the enemy.

"It's getting a might hairy here, Captain," the man shouted, and Prentice could hear the uncertainty in his voice.

"They want our colors," Prentice shouted back, looking at the White Lion banner flying from its pole. "We need to push them back."

"Be nice if we can do it," said the man and recoiled as a broken piece of a blade flew through the air and bounced off his helmet's cheek plate, narrowly missing his eye. Prentice could see the front now and it took him a short moment to assess the situation. As he feared, the lead knights had hacked paths through the pike hedge, and the ones following had started to fan out closer to the front, using longswords and pole axes to hammer at his militia directly. The one thing that was slowing them was their insistence on using weapons better suited to open combat. The Grand Kingdom knights all wanted space to swing their blades. Prentice's force was more comfortable in the tight press, with long pole weapons closing off side movement. Nevertheless, the knights were making progress. Man for man, a knight was a more well-trained warrior, and there was no doubt Carron Ironworth would have told them what to expect.

Prentice was about to return to his command position by the standard when the man in the line in front of him fell with a loud groan, and a knight in fluted steel swung his greatsword in the sudden gap, causing men on either side to shy. The gap widened, and without thinking, Prentice stepped forward, standing almost directly on the felled militiaman and thrusting with his partisan. The knight did not see the attack coming, but Prentice's weapon was out of position, and all he managed to do was bang the haft on the man's helmet. The knight swept the polearm aside with his sword and made to swing it back to hack Prentice down on the return stroke, but Prentice released one hand and thrust his weapon further forward. He closed the distance between them for better leverage, even though it meant standing on the fallen man beneath him. That unexpected motion allowed him to catch the enemy's sword by its crossguard, and for a moment the knight's hands and arms were twisted around his body. He wrenched at his blade hilt to try and disentangle the weapon, but in that space, Prentice snatched his wife's dagger from his belt and hacked, reverse-grip, up under the man's upraised arm where the armor was only thinner mail. True to her promise of sharpness, Righteous's blade cut cleanly through and into flesh. The knight screamed at the sudden agony and his arm fell limp almost instantly; the blade had cut to the man's tendons. The greatsword fell from the wilting grip, and the armored man staggered back. Prentice planted a kick on him and sent him over on his back, entangling his fellows behind him.

"Close ranks and push," Prentice shouted at the men next to him and then over his shoulder as he watched knights trying to rescue their fallen comrade while halberds fell on them. "Pass the word. Close on me and push!"

Men followed his orders, and he felt the gap around him diminish. There was a reassurance in the closeness of the ranks, even though it meant there was no longer space for him to withdraw to the standard. He had no choice now but to command from the front. He was pleased when he heard the drumbeat behind him pass the order for all the ranks to pull together. Then came the sound of the slow advance. It was a familiar beat; every White Lion would know it. It was a rattle and a heavy stroke. Then another rattle and another single, heavy stroke. On every singular beat, the entire company took one step forward—militiamen moving in unison as one mass.

Pushed up against the enemy so close that they were like two walls of steel and flesh pressing on one another, Prentice found himself on the front line of a test of strength. He tucked his partisan awkwardly under his arm and let the ranks behind him shove him like a part of a battering ram. The knights arranged themselves to push back, but holding the line meant giving up the usefulness of their weapons, just as Prentice had his, and that gave the Reach militia the advantage once more. The Grand Kingdom knights had not come with weapons that their back ranks could use. Prentice's soldiers had, and even as they pushed forward like a team playing a ball game on a village green, the men behind them could still bring their pikes to bear. And more than one had his own dagger as well, like Prentice, who shoved his point into any gap that let his arm move even a fraction. He never caused another wound like the one that had stopped the greatswordsman, but he still caught several enemies off guard with the bite of short steel.

Prentice had no idea how long the press went on. At some point, his grip on his polearm failed, but the weapon stayed tucked where it was, so tight was the crush. There were moments he was so close to the enemy that he could hear their whispered prayers for safety or strength, and some spat through their steel visors at him, cursing and swearing. More than once, it was almost too close to breathe, the pressure keeping the air from his lungs. Then the weight would shift a fraction and he clutched at a moment's gasping breath. And still the drums went on. Sometimes they would try to step with the single beat and find no purchase, the lines unmoving. There was grunting and groaning, screaming and crying, and over it all echoed the whoop and crash of the cannon fire. But all of that faded, and soon in Prentice's mind there was no space for other sounds, no other thoughts but the drums, beating the gradual advance one step at a time.

On it went, a crushing, exhausting, shoving match.

Then from his right, Prentice felt a sense of relief for a moment, and the Grand Kingdom broke, the knights scrambling back as the weight they were pushing against overwhelmed them. Prentice wanted to order a charge, to see the enemy driven off, but he scarcely had the breath. His mouth was dry from dust, and he had a thick lip from a hit he couldn't remember receiving. He watched the knights falling back and heard their trumpets sound, rallying them. They slowed and began to reform their lines even as the Reach militia continued to close up their ranks. Prentice knew this moment all too well. The Battle of the Brook had had a moment like this when both armies paused from grinding each other down and took a moment to draw breath, to see if their enemy still had the will to fight.

They watched each other over a distance of no more than thirty paces, the wretched ground between them churned to mud and strewn with the dead and wounded of both sides. Moans of pain filled the air and men heaved breath into their weary lungs, but the space otherwise seemed so strangely quiet. This was the moment the battle would be won and lost, and both sides stared at each other, unable to tell yet which side would be victor and which had suffered in vain.

CHAPTER 65

The second cannonball caused Silvermane to rear in terror as it smashed apart the poor bullocks, and Amelia felt herself nearly thrown from her panicky mount. One of her escorting knights seized her reins and held the mare tight. Amelia wanted to calm the poor creature, but it shifted so under her that it was difficult to hold on. After a moment's thought, she dismounted and pushed herself clear.

"Your Grace, you must remount," another escort tried to insist. "If we are forced to flee, you must be ready."

"If we are forced to flee, good sir, then she will be more threat to me than the stones that are falling about us."

A wagon on the line suddenly burst apart like a rotten barrel dropped from a tower, and the knight gave Amelia a disapproving look, but she would not be dissuaded.

"This is a moment for nerve," she said. "My dear mare is not suited to it at all. Keep her safe if you can, but she is no help to me now. I do not expect miracles."

Many of the knights watched her suspiciously as she strode away from the mounted company. She was sure that several of them would like to go with her and remain a close escort, but they had enough problems keeping their own mounts calm. Amelia felt for them, but their fears for her safety were a little pointless now. Anywhere they were in this wooden fortification could be smashed by a giant's hammer from the hilltop at any moment. There was no safety for her to go to.

Another ball bounced off the ground and skipped almost over the entire wagon line before clipping the top of one on the western side and knocking men apart like skittles. Amelia shrank from the violence of it, then forced herself to stand upright once more. If she had to be in danger, she would face it with at least as much dignity and discipline as the men just a stone's throw away who were dying to keep her alive.

"A stone's throw?" she scoffed at herself bitterly. *If only I could throw a stone like those damned Bronze Dragons.*

"Your Grace?" called a voice, and she saw Lady Dalflitch approaching, accompanied by Turley and Spindle. "You're still safe?"

"So far, m'lady," Amelia said. "You too, I see."

"I set all your house servants to act as runners for the Lions," Turley said, tugging his forelock. Dalflitch and Spindle curtseyed, and Amelia finally did laugh, allowing the insanity of her circumstance to have free rein for just a moment. These were her closest servants and friends, or most of them. She longed for nothing so much as to keep them safe. But where was safe? Where could be safe, when the rulers of faith and monarchy had relinquished their duty to pursue lies and murderous ambition?

"What should we do, Your Grace?" Dalflitch asked. "What should we do?"

Amelia looked about and saw wounded men being dragged by comrades away from the damaged wagons.

"We do what is right, regardless of life or death," she said.

They looked around with her, following her gaze, but clearly did not understand her meaning. Amelia let the mad laughter die out of her and she felt her face set into a serious frown.

"We find water and whatever cloth we may for bandages," she commanded, "and we begin to see to the wounded."

"Even you, Your Grace?" Spindle asked, seemingly aghast at the notion.

"Especially me."

Amelia led them to the first clutch of wounded they could find, and they began to care for them as best they could, cleaning and binding their wounds. At first, militiamen responded with shock, and between the crash of the cannon fire, she was forced to reassure every one of her soldiers that it was alright for her to humble herself to their care. Even the wounded tried to fend her away, as if her embarrassment were somehow worse for them to bear than their own wounds.

And still the cannonballs fell.

By the time Amelia pulled her own hood and veil from her head and handed it to Spindle, her maid was past her misgivings about status. The lady took the finely embroidered cloth and used her knife to cut it into strips for bandages. Around them the number of wounded grew as men were being dragged from the meatgrinder to the north where the two infantry forces were in a knock-down, drag-out brawl to the last. Hundreds of men lay about, wounded, moaning, crying, and praying as the warm sun moved westward toward mid-afternoon.

Then a corporal ran up to Amelia as she knelt to help a man missing his hand sip water from a wooden cup. The junior officer went straight past her at first, then turned about and looking at her, his eyes went wide in shock. As she wiped the sweat from her face and noticed the blood and filth on her hands and dress, she could not blame him for his disbelief.

"Your Grace," he said as he stood before her and tugged his forelock, following that up with a salute. "I...uhm...you need to know. That is...if you could help..."

"Speak you plain, Corporal," Amelia told him.

"Sergeant Franken's gone to the cannons on the hill," the man explained. "He told me to hold men on the wagons 'cause of the other army coming up from the south behind us. 'Cept he didn't say what to do when that army got here."

"So?"

"So, they's here, Your Grace. Leastwise they soon will be."

"You should take this news to Captain Prentice," Amelia told him.

"I sent a runner already. He come back saying no one near the banner's seen the captain since around midday." The man looked up at the sun, and Amelia followed his eyes. By her reckoning, midday had been at least an hour ago. If no one had seen Prentice in that long, it was likely he was lost. He could well be one of the dying around her if his wounds were so grave as to ruin his face, though she was fairly certain his armor would identify him well enough.

"How far is this army?" she asked.

"'bout a league, Your Grace."

"Then I'd best see them."

She stood, finally, and brushed her hands on her wretched skirts before waving the corporal to lead the way. No sooner had she taken the first steps than she realized Prince Farringdon was beside her. He seemed as filthy as she, and his bright green surcoat was hacked all along its bottom edge where strips had been cut away for bandages.

"Your Highness," she said with a reflexive nod.

"Your Grace," he replied, nodding in return. "If I might accompany you."

"It seems you already have been, Highness. Your aid is most welcome."

"Too kind, Duchess."

"I am summoned to the battlement, Highness," she told him, pointing to the wagons. "It could be dangerous."

"It all seems most dangerous already," he replied, and Amelia was amazed. The man had been tortured until his mind seemed broken. Now, a day of growing insanity seemed to be healing his thoughts like a balm. "Moreover, my father spoke more than once of the stories of your new hand-gunners, Your Grace. I would value a chance to see them at work. The Lioness' Roar you call them, do you not?"

My roar? she thought. *Perhaps, but not mine alone. For if they are mine alone, then they have died only for me. Let it not be so.*

She forced herself to smile at the prince, and the obligatory courtesy almost made her cry. "My gunners have enough powder for but one shot, Highness."

"Well then, I certainly must not miss it."

Amelia shook her head and took an offered hand to clamber up on one of the undamaged wagons. The line of the wooden battlement was broken in at least three places, men clearing wreckage and setting themselves up in formation in the gaps. She stood on the platform as she had seen her officers do, as Prentice did, and looked south. There, now only two hundred paces away, was a force of knights easily the equal in size of the one commanded by Lord Ironworth. They were arraying in a battle line, with numerous pennants along its length. Amelia quickly recognized most of them as those that had hung in King Chrostmer's audience hall, but she was sure a few were not present.

Had those nobles escaped Daven Marcus's purge, or were they already slain at his command?

Out in front of the formation, a group of the finest-equipped knights were all consulting with one another, and Amelia thought she saw Baron Robant's dark-haired head amongst them. One of them pointed to the east, and she looked to see that Viscount Gullden's company of Reach knights was engaged in a wretched melee with Lord Ironworth's mounted reserves. A trail of dead men and horses traced the path of the desperate fight over the eastern half of the field, and still the combat continued. Were even a quarter of either sides' men-at-arms still alive? It was impossible to tell in the dust and confusion.

"Oh, that's a good sign," said Prince Farringdon, climbing up next to her on the wagon. Amelia whirled on him, shaking.

"Are you truly mad?" she demanded. She could feel her breath heaving in her breast. She was so enraged.

"I only meant your men on the hill, Your Grace," the prince said politely and pointed over her head. She looked up to see a cohort of White Lions marching down slope in formation, carrying what looked like a banner on a pole. It was royal red, but the animal on it was not the golden eagle of the king or prince. It was a darker metal beast—a bronze dragon.

The cannons had stopped firing.

CHAPTER 66

"We've been here before, My Lord," Prentice shouted as he saw Lord Ironworth take up a position in the center of the enemy line, almost directly across from himself. "Of course, we were on the same side then and there was a brook between the lines."

This was exactly the kind of moment that had inspired Prentice to put his Roar gunners in amongst his other soldiers. Even a single volley, fired at the tired enemy now, would decide the battle. But he had no gunners, no powder for the Roar. Lord Ironworth removed his helmet and shook his sweat-soaked hair.

"It should not have come to this Prentice Ash," he called back.

"I have no control over the actions of liars and kingslayers, Lord Ironworth. We were not the ones who broke the parley truce," Prentice answered him. "I am sorry duty binds you to such men. Your honor deserves better."

Knights in the enemy lines scowled and spat, and the whole company grumbled at the insult, but Prentice only scoffed at their displeasure. If they did not want to be insulted, they should have acted more honorably. Lord Ironworth looked at the men beside him and then back to Prentice.

"If you yet respect my honor, Captain, then let us finish this as men of honor."

Prentice blinked, astonished. He shook his head. The enemy had just tried to assassinate his duchess.

"I am a man of no birth, My Lord. I have no honor to bind to your word. How can you trust me?" *And how can I trust you?* he thought as well, though he did not insult Lord Ironworth by saying it.

"We have the honor of a victory between us," the knight marshal called. "We stood together at the Brook, and we have blooded each other well and truly this day. I acknowledge your mettle and your skill, Captain. It is only rank of birth that separates us."

"That and a space of twenty-five paces full of blood and death," Prentice muttered. He looked at his men. They were tired and frightened, but he could see their resolve. If he ordered them to, they would charge to the attack once more and the grinder would begin again. That was the sensible thing to do. He had the numbers still. It would not be easy, but they could win eventually, he was sure. And honor duels were the stuff of nobles' dreams. He'd hated the foolishness of them ever since the duel he'd fought that condemned him to be found a heretic. But if he could defeat Lord Ironworth, then no more of his men would have to die.

"Alright, My Lord," he shouted, and the men around him cheered. He handed off his partisan, sheathed his dagger, and turned to a Fang standing nearby. "Give me your sword and buckler," he commanded.

The man handed them over readily.

Prentice stepped out of the line, and he watched Ironworth do the same. The knight marshal made to put his helmet back on his head, but seeing that Prentice was bareheaded, the noble removed the protection and handed it to one of the knights in the line behind him. As his eyes scanned the enemies watching him walk forth, Prentice realized he could see his brother amongst them. Pallas's armor was sprayed with blood, and he hefted his longsword like a man eager to return to the fight.

"Lord Ironworth is a righteous man," Prentice told his men, turning to face them as he fitted the small shield onto his hand.

"Trust to his word if I fall. He will accept your surrender." He looked up and down the line, hoping to see his wife, but he could not find her.

Pity.

As he stepped out farther from his line, a word of the scripture sounded suddenly in his mind: *Unto God belong escapes from death.* He looked around to see if the sudden thought was a precursor to one of his religious visions, but there were no divine lions to be seen, no angels or sons of God, just the warm afternoon sunshine and the attentive eyes of two armies.

"Well, Lord God," he whispered, "I have escaped death too many times to doubt you now. But if you have only one more of those left in your plan, then please give it to my wife. She should not have to die on this field just because she married a wild bastard like me. Oh, and give her a baby, if that suits you. I think she would really dote on a babe if she got the chance. Of course, if you can give me victory, that would be quite sweet."

Victory? Against the Grand Kingdom's greatest living hero? It was all Prentice could do not to sneer at the thought. But he would not approach this opponent with anything but respect. How could he?

The two men drew to almost within combat range.

"We will give quarter, if it is asked?" Ironworth said.

"We will," Prentice replied. He knew the knight marshal was only being polite.

"Do you require any other terms?"

"Only that my men receive mercy if I lose," Prentice said. *If? Ha!* "No slaughter. They have no ransoms to buy any parole."

"If they will surrender their arms and armor, I swear they will come to no harm."

"You will rein in the dishonorable ones? The men who break parleys?"

Ironworth scowled and looked ashamed. "I swear it. I will not allow a humiliation like that under my command again."

"Thank you, My Lord."

The two men watched each other for a long moment. A quiet breeze blew the stench of death over the field. Neither man wanted this, but neither would shirk his duty.

"The hour grows late," Ironworth said at last, and he raised his heavy, single-edged blade in salute as though it was a longsword.

Prentice saluted him in return, White Lions' fashion. It was more respect than any noble had likely shown a low-born man on a Grand Kingdom battlefield in more than a hundred years. Prentice set himself, shield leading, but even as he did so, Ironworth was charging, blade in a low guard but flicking upward as soon as he was in range. With a desperate deflection, Prentice used his shield to put the edge away safely, but even before he could think to respond with his own sword, Ironworth was slashing with a backstroke that rose up before turning again, this time thrusting with the point. Prentice had the measure of the attacks, but only barely, and in this first pass, he had no hope of returning the assault. He broke away a moment to reset his guard and marveled at Ironworth's opening gambit. The man was over fifty.

What must he have been like in his prime?

The knight marshal came on again, and the knights on his side of the field began to shout encouragement to their leader. The Lions started to cheer for Prentice in response. Some were banging on their shields, and amidst the noise there was something else, like the crackling of a campfire, but Prentice hardly noticed. He parried hard against the second pass, slashing only once and reaching nowhere near the knight marshal. The third exchange was equally one-sided, and though Ironworth led with a low guard again, as he had on the first, his combination of strikes was completely different. The man was a master, and his technique showed it.

My wife shouldn't have to see me die like this, Prentice thought, and for some reason, he was sure she was watching. It must be killing her to not charge out like a wildcat, dagger

in hand, slashing at his opponent like a storm. The idea made
Prentice smile, in spite of himself, and he realized that Lord
Ironworth could see it. His eyes met the knight marshal's,
and the nobleman sneered angrily. He thought Prentice was
mocking him. Prentice wanted to apologize, to explain his
actual thoughts, but the ridiculousness of that feeling only
made him smile more broadly, and that amusement triggered
the icy cold he often felt in life-and-death situations. Up until
now, the duties of the captaincy, the fear for his men and
his wife, had choked off his calm, kept him on edge through
the whole battle. This one sudden moment of grim humor
disrupted all that, and immediately he was just one man facing
another. It was dire still, no less desperate, but he was no longer
afraid. In truth, he more feared the earbashing he would get
from Righteous if he survived the duel. That made him want
to laugh once more, and he felt better than he had for hours as
Lord Ironworth attacked again.

"You do not have my measure yet, Captain Ash," the
nobleman declared, and Prentice knew he was right, but he no
longer cared.

An idea occurred to him, and he backed away, using his
sword to defend while he dropped his buckler hand to his
belt and drew his dagger out again. It took him a moment
to settle it into his grip, with the shield grip also across the
same palm, and the distraction left him open. Ironworth's
heavy blade slipped through his guard and clouted his side
before jumping up, aiming for his inner elbow—a less armored
target like an armpit or the back of a knee. The heavy blade
cut the leather of Prentice's brigandine on the side, though
it deflected off the steel scales underneath. It was sheer good
fortune that the cut to his elbow did not sever his arm, the
edge of the blade catching on the steel cuff of his gauntlet. The
two strikes opened Prentice's arms wide however, completely
out of position, and he pinwheeled as Lord Ironworth stepped
in and shoulder-barged him off-balance. With no possibility

of recovering his form before the next slash, Prentice sprang backwards and tumbled over the ground just outside the reach of the follow-up strikes. He rolled up onto one knee and grimaced at a sharp twinge in his left shoulder. He had not fallen well.

Prentice could tell from the man's expression of professional scrutiny that Lord Ironworth had seen the pain in his face. Experimentally, he rolled his injured shoulder and saw the recognition in his opponent's eyes. Ironworth knew his weakness now.

Time to make it my strength.

Prentice took his time regaining his feet, letting his fatigue show. He did not have to act tired; he was already exhausted. He put his sword lead out while holding his shield hand back, as if he didn't trust its strength. He drew in a heavy breath and let his arms sag a little.

Lord Ironworth stepped sideways as he approached, and Prentice could see he was wary. He was too old and too wise to be easily fooled. His heavy blade shifted from a low guard to high, and Prentice felt himself being scrutinized further. The older master would not rush to the final pass. He would wait and make the right strike.

I'll have to bait the trap then, Prentice thought.

With a wild lunge, he made a thrust for his opponent's legs. Ironworth stepped back out of the way, keeping his blade in its high guard. Prentice regained his stance and watched. Like a stalking predator, the knight marshal kept circling. Prentice thrust again as wildly as before, putting himself so out of position that he had to scramble to keep from falling over. Nonetheless, his blade managed to scrape the steel on Lord Ironworth's thigh, and the nobleman was forced to flick his blade away with a dropping parry. And still the hunter circled.

Prentice felt cold resolution in his mind. The moment had come.

He thrust a third time, so wildly that he ended up on one knee. Lord Ironworth stepped inside the thrust, and his heavy blade descended in a diagonal strike that would sever Prentice's neck, perhaps not beheading him but certainly killing him. Even if he tried to pull back, as he had before, the blade would follow faster than he could withdraw. But Prentice had no intention of withdrawing. As the heavy sword slashed downward, he raised his shield and dagger in a twisting block. Not as weak as he had made it appear, Prentice's buckler caught the falling blow, and the short blade pinned Ironworth's own against the shield's edge. Now, instead of pulling back, Prentice surged upward. The pinned weapon was pushed aside, and since rising brought him in too close to swing his sword properly, he punched Ironworth in the face with the weapon's basket hilt. The pommel scraped across the nobleman's brow, and he staggered backward with a curse. To his credit, he reflexively twisted and freed his sword as he withdrew. Even as he reset his guard, however, the injury to his brow began to bleed profusely, running down into his eyes. He tried to wipe it away, but still it flowed, blinding him.

Prentice edged closer slowly, wary that even in this state, Lord Ironworth was a deadly opponent, and his shield arm ached brutally. Catching the killing blow had sent the full force through his shoulder, making the injury worse. Ironworth sensed him approaching and slashed a complex combination of strikes, but unable to see, it was a desperate maneuver. Prentice was able to parry more easily and step clear. His riposte struck cleanly on the breastplate, scraping and pushing the knight marshal back but catching on the fluting of the steel before it could drive up towards the vulnerable throat and face. Lord Ironworth withdrew again.

Now Prentice led the attack for the first time, and he pressed until he had the armored man out of position and was able to plant a trip behind his leg. Ironworth went down on one knee and Prentice was able to follow up with a punch of his buckler.

The shield's edge broke the knight marshal's nose and made the bleeding from his forehead worse. Then Prentice dropped his hand so that the dagger's edge laid against Lord Ironworth's throat.

"Yield, My Lord," he commanded. "You cannot continue the fight in this condition, not from here."

Prentice swallowed and inwardly he prayed that this singular champion would accept defeat in this moment. A proud man might refuse to surrender, bound by honor to fight to the death. And the great Ironworth, in his prime, might even have been able to come back from this degree of disadvantage. But Prentice knew he had the older man, and he hated the thought that he would have to end Lord Ironworth's legend like this. With a heavy sigh, Ironworth bowed his head and turned his weapon point down.

"Captain Ash, I yield," he said. "I offer you my sword and concede your victory."

Prentice felt his chest convulse in such a savage sigh of relief that he thought he might start to weep. He thrust his own sword, point down, into the churned ground and symbolically put his hand on Lord Ironworth's hilt.

"I accept your parole, My Lord," he said formally. "Let there be honorable peace between us and our forces."

"Haven't had to yield since I was twenty," Ironworth said with a rueful smile and released his sword, pressing the leather palm of his gauntlet against his forehead to staunch the bleeding.

"No! Never!"

CHAPTER 67

As Amelia watched, Sergeant Franken's small unit marched toward the fighting knights, shouting orders and pointing their pikes at the men ahorse. She was sure it must be a tense and confused experience. How could the militiamen tell the Reach knights from the enemy? All were so filthy with dust and blood. The Reachermen were too canny for that problem, however, and any man who did not yield to them they unhorsed and subdued. In the end, only three or four men galloped free while the remaining mounted Reach nobles took custody of every man who yielded.

The fleeing knights wheeled about a short distance from the ended melee and, realizing that the second army had arrived from the south, rode to the newly arrayed Grand Kingdom contingent. As the duchess watched, they consulted with the commanders of the second force, and then a new company of knights was detached to harass Sergeant Franken's militiamen. The Lions formed up as usual to receive an enemy charge, and as the knights rode at them, their Roar fired its serpentines. The sound of iron shot punching through armor could be heard even over the hammering of the horses' hoofs.

"There is your one shot, Highness," Amelia said without turning to the prince. A number of the knights fell, but too few to her eyes. The gunners withdrew into the body of the pike and halberd men and the knight charge balked as the majority of the horses simply refused to force themselves onto the sharp steel points. The few men-at-arms that did press in were outmatched by the number of weapons they faced and were either driven out or fell before they reached the infantry men. Most of the knights withdrew from the initial clash to reform the charge again. As they did, the Roars burst out and fired another volley upon them, which harassed them and made it harder to reform their line. More fell, and horses with them.

"A second shot, Your Grace?" asked Prince Farringdon. "Is that not unexpected?"

It was. Amelia looked at them and then at the men around her. She remembered hearing Prentice say so many hours ago that he might concentrate all the remaining ammunition in the hands of a few Roars so that some would be able to fire as they were supposed to, but most would be left completely without the power to fight. Had he done that? And had Sergeant Franken taken those men with him to attack the cannons on the hill? If that was the case, then the gunners crouched around her were effectively unarmed. She suddenly felt so much more exposed standing on the wooden battlement, and half the men around her could not even fight.

"Do you even have shot?" she asked the nearest gunner. The man saluted as if she were any other officer.

"We got our one shot of powder each, every man here."

"Then how do they keep firing?" she demanded as a third and fourth volley ripped into the Grand Kingdom detachment and the entire smaller force began to break apart, trying to reach a point out of the gunners' range.

"We all got plenty o' shot, your ladyship. It's only the powder we wanted for."

Amelia was about to ask what the difference was when she realized the man's point. Franken and his men had replenished their powder from the Bronze Dragons' stores. Studying the little force in the distance, she noticed a handful of men in the middle of them, clutched around the stolen banner and carrying heavy burdens. She guessed they were sacks or barrels of black powder, and her heart leapt. Franken and his men were returning with hope for her entire army. As she watched, she realized that in between the moments of firing and receiving the charge, the militia were moving in slow increments back to their wagon palisade. They would be here soon.

It seemed the Grand Kingdom army from the south had seen their movement as well, and after the smaller contingent had withdrawn almost to their original line, a trumpet was sounded. Nearly half the entire army turned and began to array for a charge. Amelia's heart was suddenly in her throat. Pike and shot were an effective tactic, but Franken's force was too small to repel what must surely be at least a thousand mounted men-at-arms. The Reach knights whom Franken had rescued would be small help, as they were concerned with prisoners and their own wounded. Besides, there were fewer than fifty of them still mounted. The massive enemy force formed up, and at their head she saw Baron Robant, riding with a pair of trailing royal red banners—the eagles of Rhales and Denay.

Amelia clambered up onto the front of her wagon and leaned out so far that she almost fell.

"Lions of the Reach!" she cried, the fury and passion in her voice making it sound shrill in her own ears. "Eagles hunt the pride to the east. Bring the birds down! One shot is still one shot with which to hunt!"

All along the wagon palisade, militia turned to look at her as she screamed her command again and again. She knew she must look like a harridan, like the witch Daven Marcus and the Church accused her of being. The Grand Kingdom knights must have thought her mad. She did not care. The force was gathering itself. Then a clutch of ten Roars, led by a corporal in a nearly pristine gambeson, rushed out into the open a short distance and lined to fire. Their long-matches trailed thin smoke behind them, as if the men had all shared a pipe of tobacco together. They aimed for what seemed like an eternity, and then they fired as one. It was at an oblique angle across the front of the enemy company that was already starting to walk their mounts toward Franken's men. The shots were lost in the mass, but at least one man in the front rank fell. It was not enough. The gunners rushed back into safety, their one shot expended.

Two other groups stood out, and they too aimed at the eagles. The next volley seemed as useless as the first, but the third hammered one of the standard-bearers riding behind Robant, and his horse. Man and mount staggered and fell, and the long banner on its standard pole fell across the baron, tangling around him. He signaled his trumpeter to order a halt while he disentangled himself, and as he did so, an unseen pair of gunners still concealed in a wagon at the corner of the fortifications fired at him. Amelia neither saw nor heard the hit, but she guessed that it must have struck him on the shoulder because he lurched that direction and nearly fell from the saddle. At the long distance, it was likely the iron shot only bounced off his steel, but she hoped it had hurt him. Behind her she heard more serpentines fire, and she looked to see that some other knights had drawn close, perhaps hoping to exploit the distraction of events on the opposite flank. The ringing of shot on armor seemed enough to dissuade them, and they pulled back a moment.

Then there came a cheering, and Amelia realized Franken's militiamen had reached the wagons and were being dragged inward, safe from a knight's charge at last.

"Help me down, Highness," she ordered more than asked, holding her hand out. Prince Farringdon assisted her dismount from the wagon to the ground, and she did not pause to thank him. Hiking her skirts, she ran to where Franken was ordering his newly returned men and found him taking a deep drink from a water skin. He was black with soot stains and had a serpentine leaning, butt down, against his leg. When he saw his liege lady approach with indecorous haste, his eyes widened in his filthy face, and he threw away the skin to give a salute.

"Your Grace?" he almost stammered.

"You bring powder, Sergeant?" she asked, all manners and presentation forgotten in her eager hope. She looked past him to see men already sharing powder from several barrels and Roar gunners rushing to refill their horns.

"Just handing it out, Your Grace," Franken reported.

"See that it's distributed along the line evenly," she commanded, pointing behind her. "Many spent their one shot to save you."

"Was that you we heard ordering the shooting, Your Grace?"

"It was, Sergeant. And now I'll give you more orders. When you have fifty men rearmed, send them north to support Captain Ash! His men have gone too long without the help of the Roar."

If he even still lives, she thought. She looked north and realized the sounds of fighting had faded away. Did that mean it was over? There were some shouts, she thought, but not the clashing cacophony of wild battle. Was it too late?

"With haste, Sergeant," she commanded. "With haste."

CHAPTER 68

P rentice hardly had to look to know that it was his brother screaming in indignant rage. Longsword raised, Sir Pallas pulled down his visor and rushed out of the Grand Kingdom ranks toward the two duelists alone on the battleground. Lord Ironworth rose to his feet in indignation and turned to face the charging Church knight. One hand remained on his head, but he held his other out to halt the man's rush.

"Quarter was asked and given honorably, sir," Ironworth bellowed, obviously appalled at yet another breach of battlefield etiquette. He stepped into Sir Pallas's path to prevent him attacking his older brother. "This is shamef..."

Prentice was never Pallas's first target. The young Church knight swung his sword in a furious arc and hacked Lord Ironworth's neck at the shoulder, even as the knight marshal was trying to order him to stand down. The knight marshal's head was almost completely severed. From the Grand Kingdom side there came a groan, as if the entire army suffered a moment's anguish together.

There was a gout of blood, and Prentice leaped back, his hand reflexively seizing Ironworth's surrendered heavy blade and bringing it into guard. Pallas launched himself over Ironworth's falling body and scythed at Prentice. The younger brother was well trained, and Prentice had no doubt he had probably dreamed of this moment since his first days at Ashfield

Academy—the moment when he avenged his family's dishonor. He'd probably trained harder than any other student there.

But Prentice had been fighting just to survive for over a decade. He had seen the limit of honor and the desperation of men facing monsters and sorcery. He'd heard the screams of the dying and lived in terror of the bite of steel for almost as long as Pallas had been alive. And before he was hard forged in that fire, he had also trained harder than any other student at Ashfield.

He deflected his brother's first attack and then caught and checked the next one. Before Pallas could retract his longsword, Prentice used Ironworth's heavier blade to sweep it out of the way and followed up with a kick that almost spun Pallas completely about. The younger man had no chance to recover as Prentice slammed the pommel of the heavy sword down to hammer on the back of his helmet, and Pallas went sprawling on the earth. He tried to scramble off, but Prentice overran him easily, and stomping down on his brother's hand, forced the sword from his grasp.

Prentice kicked it away.

"You just killed the Grand Kingdom's greatest hero, you fool," Prentice said, allowing his brother to roll over but keeping his newly acquired sword pointed straight at him. "In a moment of honor." He looked up at the enemy line, their faces twisted in despair. "Is this the glory of Daven Marcus? Is this the victory your men of God promised you?"

There was a noise behind him and suddenly at least fifty Roars rushed around the right flank of the White Lions. He looked and saw them form up, serpentines at the ready.

"We found some more powder, Captain," a soot-faced Sergeant Franken shouted from the center of their line. "The Bronze Dragons had it. They didn't want to share, but we swayed them."

Prentice wanted to cry with relief. He looked at the enemy, and he could see their consternation. Lord Ironworth would have explained the effectiveness of massed gunner fire when he made them test whether the Lions still had powder.

"This battle is over," he shouted at them, his voice cracking, and he was forced to spit blood and dirt from his mouth to be clearly heard. When had he bitten his tongue? "Any man who surrenders his arms and armor will be given parole. Your horses are forfeit. If you cannot surrender..." he looked down at his brother, cringing on the ground, "then run and do not stop until you have the Azure Mountains between you and the Reach. When the sun sets tonight, the Lioness puts a bounty upon your heads. Any man who brings her the head of a knight from the east will receive the head's weight in silver."

It was a grotesque threat, and Prentice was almost certain Duchess Amelia would never consent to such a thing, but he wanted any man too proud to surrender to flee and not look back.

"Now!" he bellowed, pointing with the sword in his hand, and with a sudden cheer, his men surged forward. The broken knight force flinched as one. Then some went straight to their knees, weapons point down as Ironworth had. A few others turned to run, and they had to fight past their allies to get away. As the rush of his forces flowed around him, Prentice lowered his sword arm and let his shoulders slump. It was like standing in the midst of a raging flood as victory washed the enemy away, but not one of his men came near him. They all gave him respectful space until one woman charged out of the crowd and rushed around in front of him. Righteous grabbed him by both shoulders and leaped into his arms, wrapping her legs around his waist.

"That's my man," she declared loudly as she laid stinging kisses on his bruised face and lips. "My husband. He fights champions and faces down armies of brassy bastards and he ain't afraid o' nothing! He loves me. He loves me and...God, I love him."

Prentice groaned as the weight of her hanging on him hurt his shoulder. She stopped kissing him, and he realized she had a long cut down her cheek. It was not deep, but he was sure it would leave a mark alongside her brawler's brand.

"Your record," he said to her. She wiped at the injury.

"What, this?" she said. "Don't worry none about it. If anyone even speaks of it, I'll tell 'em how I got it the day my husband proved he was the greatest fighter the world has ever seen. Unless..." she paused and gave him a narrow-eyed look. "You won't hate me, now that I'm not pretty anymore?"

"I will write poems about your beauty, wife," he said playfully. "I'll swoon at the sight of your fine visage forever, sighing as a lovesick pup."

"Eww, don't you bloody dare." Righteous hopped down and Prentice groaned again in pain.

"I prayed for you," he said. "That you would survive the day."

"I prayed for you, too," she told him shyly, as if the admission embarrassed her. "I think we might need to start taking ourselves to church again once we get back to Dweltford."

"I am sure Fostermae would be glad to welcome us into his congregation."

"He'll be the first sacrist that ever was pleased to see me in a church."

Prentice cocked his head in amusement. Suddenly Sergeant Franken was standing next to him, and Markas as well, saluting with a loudly thumped fist on his chest.

"Captain, good to see you still breathing, if I can say. The duchess, she was fearin' you might not have made it this far."

"I will go to her. I need to report this victory."

"She'll want some of these men to rally to the wagons too, Captain."

"How's that?" Prentice asked.

"That other army," Franken explained, "the one coming from the south? It's down there, and we're not sure what to do about it. They're making little attacks, but so far, I think the Roar's got 'em scared. Can't say for how long though."

Prentice sighed and hung his head for a moment. He was exhausted. His body ached. He'd forgotten about the second force and had no will to fight another battle the same size as the one he'd just won. Looking down, he realized his brother was no longer on the ground in front of him. He had no idea whether he had surrendered or fled. His mind was still recovering from the battle and the duel, it seemed.

I'll have to find out later, he thought.

Still on the ground before him, though, was Lord Carron Ironworth's body and his nearly decapitated head. Regarding the fallen hero, slain by his own man-at-arms, Prentice knew what had to be done.

"Help me find Lord Ironworth's horse," he told Franken and Righteous. "It is time to end this."

CHAPTER 69

A melia watched as another sortie of knights rode past the wagons, pennants streaming behind them. It seemed they were testing the range of her militia's guns and their willingness to use them. It had been like this for a while. Twice they had charged en masse, but the Roar firing repeatedly from the wagons and the pikes over the top meant that it was almost impossible for the heavy horsemen to do much damage before they were forced to withdraw. Once, they had made an effort to aim for the gaps in the line where damaged or shattered wagons seemed to offer the possibility of breaking through, but the pike and halberd of the Claws made that charge just as fruitless as the others. The duchess had heard the tales of the Lions' first ever battle against knights commanded by her rebellious bondsman, Baron Liam, and how that had been a slaughter. These nobles were not as reckless as Liam's had been, but they were no more successful for all their caution.

"They seem persistent," Prince Farringdon mused aloud, and Amelia couldn't tell if he meant it as a criticism or a compliment.

"Any more word from Captain Ash?" she asked of a filthy youth who had arrived a short while before with the news that Prentice was alive and would attend her presently.

"Nuffin', yer Grace," the boy told her. "I can go ask again."

Amelia nodded.

"The forelock, lad," the prince called after him as he turned to go. "Never forget your manners."

The boy turned on his heel, tugged his forelock and then sprinted away.

"Thank you, Highness," Amelia said.

"The spiritedness of youth," Prince Farringdon replied, as if speaking of a boisterous squire on a feast day. "He's likely just over excited to be waiting on his liege lady. He'll drink free on the tale for years yet, I'd bet."

"Prince Farringdon, your calm has been of great assistance to me this day," Amelia said with feeling. She meant it.

"Your appreciation touches me, Your Grace. As a sojourner in your land, I am pleased that I might offer any blessing to you that I can." He paused and a sudden deep expression of realization seemed to dawn in his eyes. "A sojourner, an exile, and a vagrant without home, throne, or family." A single heavy tear traced a path through the dirt on his cheek, and he brushed it away. "I will be quiet some while now, I think, Your Grace. With your permission?"

Amelia nodded. What else could she do? On this wretched day, Prince Farringdon was still the most abused of them all. If silence let him keep his dignity, then so be it.

"Your Grace?" Amelia heard a feminine voice call, and she looked down to see Spindle approaching, barely recognizable save for the polished salet she still wore on her head. She was pointing behind her, and Amelia looked to see a small company of her militiamen leading a man on a horse. As she tried to identify the rider, she realized that the knight in armor had no head. The body was tied upright into the saddle by leather belts. Blood smears ran down the breastplate, as if a gruesome jug of gore had been poured over it. Studying the horrific figure, Amelia realized that the man's head was tied to the saddle by its hair. From a distance she could not make out the face, so distorted was it in death. As the strange cortege approached, she saw that it was Prentice who led the horse by the bridle.

"What is this, Captain Ash?" she asked, looking down as he stopped behind her wagon.

Prentice's expression was cold and grim. "This is Carron Ironworth, Your Grace."

Amelia's hand went to her mouth.

"You cannot do this, Captain," she said, horrified. "Lord Ironworth was an honorable man. We cannot defile him in death in this manner."

"It is not we who defile him, Your Grace," Prentice answered her enigmatically. "Do you trust me?"

She wanted to ask him why? To demand an explanation. To order the knight marshal's body taken down and prepared to lie in state, as a hero of his status deserved.

"I do trust you," she said instead. "But tell me what you propose."

"I propose returning the baron's body to the folk who should have shown him better honor. They owe him more than we do."

"You do not think this will provoke them?"

"It might, Your Grace," he conceded. "But I intend it to rebuke them. Not every man out there is without honor, Your Grace. They have been knitted to the Prince of Rhales's treachery by it. We will be best served to give them the chance to cut the tie by themselves, or else we risk forever being heretics in their eyes. Heretics and witches."

Amelia wondered what he planned, exactly. How could those knights out there not be infuriated by this treatment of the king's greatest champion? But then how was this worse than the treatment the king himself had received? And what would they do if it did infuriate them? How would that be any different to what they already faced?

As she thought about it, Amelia realized that there was also an issue of morale to consider in this savage act. How would knights of the Grand Kingdom feel if this is the fate of their greatest when they faced the Lions of the Reach?

"Do what you think is right, Prentice," she told him, and he bowed.

Looking behind him, he took a long strip of white cloth from Righteous, who was waiting with it there. It looked like it had been cut from the tabard of a Church knight. Prentice arranged it to hang around the body, and as he did, Amelia saw that there was writing on it, possibly scribed there in the corpse's own blood. It read, "Baron Carron Ironworth, Knight Marshal of Denay and the Grand Kingdom, dishonorably murdered under flag of truce by Sir Pallas, knight of the Church, of the Order of the Black and Gold Crosses."

Amelia gasped as she read it. Prentice's own brother had killed the king's champion? No, *murdered* him? That was no small accusation. If Prentice's conviction for heresy had shamed his family, Pallas's actions had doomed them all. They would be driven from godly society, and that only if they were not avenged upon directly. She watched as Prentice retook the horse's bridle and led it toward one of the gaps in the wagons. It required a moment to lead the poor creature over and around the wreckage, but soon he was past the wall and out into the space between the two forces. It was nearly late afternoon, but the summer sun was still bright. Everyone near the wagons leaped up or pressed into a gap to watch as Prentice walked the horse and its dead rider out several paces and stopped.

The Grand Kingdom army was still, its leaders watching intently. No one moved. Prentice pulled Lord Ironworth's sword from its sheath on his saddle and thrust it point first into the ground. Then he slapped the horse on its haunches, and the disciplined steed whinnied once before it began to walk forward. Prentice lifted a leather speaking trumpet to his lips and addressed their enemies.

"Knight Marshal Baron Carron Ironworth is dead," he shouted, and an audible sigh of grief heaved up from the knights gathered. "He was defeated in honorable combat by me and had received quarter with grace. Then he was murdered by Sir Pallas, a man of his own command, a knight of the Church. Lord Ironworth's blade was in my hand when Sir Pallas took his head. The knight marshal's army is broken, and their remnants are either fled or have offered their parole. I return Lord Ironworth, his armor and his horse, to you for righteous burial. I will keep his sword, as it was already surrendered to me. I will bear it in his honor and use it to avenge him and my duchess against any who serve the kingslayer usurper and the lying clergy who turn their backs on God to protect him. The pride of the Lioness offers you the chance to contemplate the implications of your duty. Leave in peace if you wish." Prentice paused a moment to allow them to consider his words. "Or, if you prefer, stand and face the White Lions and the man who defeated Carron Ironworth."

He seized up the sword and raised it over his head.

Almost without thinking, Amelia shouted a command across the palisade. "Lions, roar!"

Not quite as one, but very nearly, every gunner fired a volley into the air. It hadn't been planned, and so it was not so well orchestrated, but it was a clear salute to a fallen noble hero and the man who had defeated him.

CHAPTER 70

The White Lions watched the second Grand Kingdom army across the palisade as the afternoon wore on. A handful of those who had fled the first force's defeat were seen to skulk in a wide arc around the battlefield and join the southern force, but whatever tales they told must have only served to reinforce the second force's uncertainties. Sundown came and, with it, no assault. Soon after it became fully dark, there was a sound of movement out in the field, and men on the wagons lifted torches, fearful of a raid, but there was none. Sentries were posted and men had rotated through the night so that as many as possible gained some rest. Dawn would reveal that the entire enemy army had withdrawn, and riders from the Reach would track them half a day southward, finding nothing. Daven Marcus's invasion of the Western Reach was broken, and as they had two years earlier, his forces withdrew from the west in ignominy.

"The withdrawal is good news," the duchess said, looking over her entourage. In the two days since that dawn, Prentice had sent men to fetch water from the river, and now Duchess Amelia resembled her noble self.

"It will take time for another army to be raised, if that is Daven Marcus's intent, Your Grace," Prentice added, his voice somewhat thick and slurred due to the injuries to his mouth and tongue.

He'd had chances to wash his face and hands, but the rest of him was covered in filth, and he knew he stank. He was glad they had no tents in which to meet. He could not imagine how unpleasant it would be to stand in a closed space with him right now.

Like a convict again, he thought.

"Let him take all the time he wishes," said Lady Dalflitch. "Another twenty or thirty years will suit perfectly."

"Indeed, My Lady," the duchess agreed. She turned to Prentice. "How long until we march again?"

"I encourage you not to rush us, Your Grace," said Prentice. "Things are not terrible here."

"Are they not?" she demanded. "Are we not spending the nights under the stars? Is food not limited? Am I not surrounded with the remnants of an army that desperately needs rest and healing and safety?"

"Safety we have, Your Grace, at least as much as we need. The kingslayer's arrogance has been rebuked and his forces are broken." Prentice refused to name Daven Marcus by any title except kingslayer. His patricide had disqualified the vile man from any term of respect, as far as Prentice was concerned. "From speaking with the prisoners, smashing the Lions and capturing your person was supposed to be the task of the second force alone. We were not expected to ever encounter Lord Ironworth's company, let alone break them. The Bronze Dragons were being sent to Griffith."

"How can that be?" asked Viscount Gullden. He had survived the savage fight between the two mounted forces, but one of his legs was so badly wounded that it had nearly needed amputation. The limb was thickly bound and splinted, and he used a piece of a broken lance to get around, having to hold it in his injured hand. His pain was so great, even with white laud, that he begged leave to sit in his lady's presence. The man had to be in agony, but he steadfastly insisted on attending his liege and serving as he was called.

"You mean to ask how they came north so quickly?" Prentice said.

"Yes. We rushed to our march. We have no tents and few supplies because of our haste. Yet Ironworth had those brute engines up north and across the Azures ridge in the same time. It beggars belief."

"He was sent ahead of us, My Lord," Prentice explained. Viscount Gullden's question was a sensible one and had been amongst the first Prentice sought answers for, once it was clear that the battle was truly over. "With help from some inside the Inquisition and the ecclesiarchy, Daven Marcus had been plotting his rebellion for some time. When the king imprisoned him in the days before the feast, he set about gathering his forces almost immediately. He falsified the king's name on orders, and since so few knew the extent of the rift between Chrostmer and his son, no one questioned it."

"How could so few have known?" the duchess demanded.

"The king worked to keep it quiet and put it about that they were reconciled. The feast was to be an announcement of their reconciliation in victory."

"That was what I was expecting. I walked into that night trying to find a way to slip out of a betrothal."

"Well, the traitor granted you that at least, Your Grace," said Dalflitch, and many smiled in amusement.

"Lord Ironworth was already marching the cannons north when the feast began, Your Grace," Prentice explained. "He thought he was marching on the king's order. After Daven Marcus sank the dagger, perhaps even before he began his show trials, he sent a messenger directly to Lord Ironworth ordering him to join up with a force of the Church and to march onward to Griffith to demand their surrender or put down their rebellion."

"What rebellion?" demanded Gullden.

"I think the Prince of Rhales expected my lands to rise against him once they learned he'd had me executed," the duchess explained.

"Bastard!" the viscount spat at the fire they were standing around, then bowed his head in apology. "Forgive me, Your Grace." The movement caused him to wince in pain, his eyes screwed tight.

"None needed, My Lord," his liege replied. "Soon enough, I believe Daven Marcus would wish for so honorable a title as mere bastard, though I suppose we should not defame his mother or father so." She turned to Prentice. "What else have you learned, Captain?"

"That there are tales that many nobles have escaped the night of treachery and returned with their forces to their own lands, including Count Lark-Stross and Earl Lastermune. They will carry their version of the night into the Grand Kingdom and Daven Marcus's liar's fable will not be allowed to stand. There are already expectations of rebellion if he tries to hold the throne. Such men might make good allies if the kingslayer continues to harass your lands."

"Worth considering," said the duchess with a nod. "Though neither noble has much cause to make any pact with me."

"I think we will find that many old friends are now enemies, Your Grace."

"But are any enemies become friends?" asked Dalflitch.

That was the question. Prentice shook his head and shrugged, which made his shoulder twinge painfully. "We won't know for some time, I would expect, My Lady."

"And you think it safe for me to remain here, Captain?" asked the duchess.

"Not you, Your Grace. With your permission, I think we should have you and your ladies, as well as Prince Farringdon, mounted and heading north as soon as possible. We have a mountain of prisoners at this point, and while they have all given their parole, I think we can agree honor has been in short supply among Kingdom nobles of late. I would not be surprised if some conspired to slip their guards and do you harm."

"So instead, you want to send us ahead alone?"

"Not alone, Your Grace," said Prentice, "but with every remaining Reach knight and five hundred Lions, with all the powder. There are riverfolk villages at a number of stops between here and Griffith, and I've already sent riders to the town to have supplies fetched. We need you safe inside the walls there at the very least. The rest of this force can afford to move more slowly."

In fact, it would be better for their wounded if they did. Everyone present understood that, and Prentice knew he did not need to say it. He waited while the duchess looked to each of her other advisors. He was confident they would agree with his plan.

"Tell me, Captain, for you have more experience than I," the duchess said after a long period of silence. "Do victories often leave the victor running for safety like a whipped hound?"

"More often than sagas and histories like to admit, Your Grace."

She hung her head and sighed. "Well, at least I am now the proud possessor of hundreds of warhorses."

"Not to mention suits of armor and weapons," Dalflitch added. "You could raise a new cadre of knights tomorrow, should you desire."

"Armor is not like a dress," the viscount observed sourly. "It must be fitted. Adjustments must be made. It cannot simply be handed from one man to the next."

"Neither can a dress," the lady responded, equally harshly.

"Do you compare the difficulties of a maid's clothing with the burdens of a man-at-arms, Lady Dalflitch?" Gullden demanded, his voice rising and becoming shrill with his pain. "In this company? You have your life by the bloodshed and pain suffered by so many men, and you want to complain?"

"I make no complaint..."

"Peace Lady, My Lord," the duchess intervened. "We have fought a war, and all suffered for this weary victory. Let us not turn our sufferings upon one another."

Dalflitch curtseyed and Gullden apologized.

A squad of Claws marched past, their boots tromping. Every man saluted Prentice as they saw him, and he returned it.

"And no matter how much armor or how many horses I have, only a prince or a king can knight a man. Whoever we have lost, we will have only squires to replace them for some time, I suspect."

That could cause problems, Prentice thought. Knights were the only source of cavalry the Reach had. His White Lions had soundly knocked them off their historic pedestal, but they were still useful, even necessary. The melee between the two reserves had proven that.

"Very well, Captain, we will follow your plan," Duchess Amelia said at last. "Everyone go to your duties and be ready to leave when Captain Ash gives word."

They all bowed and left, Viscount Gullden struggling so to keep up with his splinted leg that a squire was called for him to lean upon. He departed, hissing with discomfort at every step. When he was gone, Prentice made to leave as well, but the duchess called him to remain a moment.

CHAPTER 71

"You plan to send Righteous with me, I take it?" Amelia asked.

"I do, Your Grace."

"She will object."

"I will persuade her, Your Grace," Prentice assured her, and Amelia believed him. They both knew his wife. She was unruly by nature, but it was clear that she adored her husband. It reminded Amelia of her own love for her dead husband. And Righteous understood the importance of doing her duty. Amelia smiled, glad both husband and wife had survived the past dreadful days.

Prentice was waiting on her to see if she would say anything more, but memories flooded her mind for a moment.

"I was terrified, Prentice," she said quietly, staring into the fire. "I remember fleeing from the Redlanders that first day when they ambushed my barge. I thought I knew what fear was like, what it meant to be scared. But to have to stay in place when at any moment a cannonball could have ripped me apart like a doll in a dog's mouth—I never imagined there could be such horror."

"There are tales being spoken of your courage, Your Grace," he told her. She snorted derisively, but Prentice persisted. "You are their liege now more than ever. Your hands had the blood of the fallen on them. There are men boasting that their wounds

536 EAGLES OF THE GRAND KINGDOM

are bandaged with strips from the Lioness' own dress. And when your officers were all at other tasks, your orders stopped a charge. Die today and the Reach will have you sainted within the year."

"I'd rather live another year and not get the halo."

Prentice laughed. At least they still shared a sense of humor.

"Do we have much chance of that, do you think?" she asked. "Of living another year?"

Prentice shook his head. She wanted him to reassure her, but she knew that no one alive, not in the Grand Kingdom or the Western Reach, not in the Vec or far Masnia and Aucks, knew the answer to that question.

"Daven Marcus has set fire to the Grand Kingdom, Your Grace," he said. "All just to bring it under his heel. I do not know if we can put out the fire, but as long as he lives, I believe he will keep throwing more fuel on the blaze."

"Can I keep him from burning my house along with his own, though?"

"You have done so up until now, Your Grace."

"Only by the grace of God," she declared without thinking.

She thought that would be the end of their conversation and she waved him away. He accepted the dismissal with a bow, and then, just before he turned, he asked one last question.

"You mention God, Your Grace. Do you believe he speaks to those he grants his grace sometimes?"

"Do you mean prophecy, Prentice?" she asked him. They spoke so often of so many notions, but theology was not normally among them. She felt her eyes narrow as a feeling of shrewd caution overtook her. The widow in the wood had given her a prophecy during Daven Marcus's previous campaign, and though she remembered it word for word, she shared it with no one.

"Prophecy, yes, but also visions and dreams," Prentice explained.

"Visions?"

"You know that I have had visions and dreams, Your Grace. Troubling ones and guiding ones," he said cautiously.

"You have mentioned it to me," Amelia agreed, remembering something of the sort. There had been all manner of strange religious rumors circulating since the Redlanders had come from the west. "You are one of those who saw the angel at the Battle of the Brook, aren't you?"

"I am, but there have been other visions as well. I especially have seen animals, Your Grace. Animals that stand for other things in our world. Animals like the ones you have seen in your visions."

Amelia sucked in a gasp, and she felt her limbs beginning to shake. "How did you know?" she asked softly.

"I guessed, Your Grace," he admitted. She waited for him to say more, but he was quiet, meeting her eyes. It was a strange moment of fellowship between them as each silently realized that they shared something of which they had never spoken, something significant and deeply troubling.

"What do they mean, do you think?" she asked.

"I understand some," he told her. "And that scholar Solft, whom the Inquisition slew, he seemed to have some other notions that I think are reflected in some of my visions."

"Is that why they killed him?"

Prentice blinked. "I had not thought of that, Your Grace." He looked away a moment and stroked his scruffy chin thoughtfully. Then he looked straight at her again. "I could not say, Your Grace," he told her. "The few things that Solft shared with me are at odds with the teachings of the Mother Church but hardly worth killing the man over. Unless...unless there was more."

"What more?"

Prentice shrugged. Amelia sensed they were both on the verge of some important understanding, some revelation of deep significance, but she had no idea exactly what it might be.

"These visions and dreams, Prentice," she said. "Do you think they are from God? Could the devil have a hand in all this?"

"If the devil did, Your Grace, I do not think he would send visions to help us fight sorcerous beast armies and usurpers. A house divided against itself cannot stand."

As soon as he said this, he blinked like a man awakening from sleep.

"You've thought of something?" she asked him.

"Perhaps, Your Grace, but...as it began, so will it end."

"What was that Prentice?" It sounded to Amelia as if he was quoting something, but she did not recognize the reference.

"A thought, Your Grace, or a word of wisdom. I am not sure."

Whatever it was, it seemed alive in his mind. She watched his expression as his brow furrowed and his eyes searched empty space, as if reading a book that was not there.

"Tell me, Your Grace, have you seen the Redlander serpent?"

Amelia nodded hesitantly and swallowed, remembering the terror of the vision. Even having just suffered two horrific battles in so few days and all the fear that came with them, still the vision of the serpent made her mouth dry as she recalled it.

"You have seen it, haven't you?" Prentice pushed, obviously reading her expression as well as she did his.

"A gigantic snake with many heads, all of different beasts." In her mind she could see it rearing over her again in the midst of her feasting hall, threatening to crush her and all her people in its coils.

"Five heads, Your Grace, the animals of the Redlander magic—serpent and insect, bull, stag, and wolf. But with a severed head as well, a stump cut off. A missing sixth head."

Amelia shrugged. She did not remember a severed stump among the beast's many necks, but something about Prentice's manner, the way he looked at her, confirmed that he had seen the same serpent as she.

"I am certain the creature is the Redlanders, Your Grace," he went on, "or stands for them. I saw it first when they invaded, when we marched with Prince Mercad. And I've seen the angel of the Lord, fighting with the beast—many times in the form of a lion."

"When I saw it, lions came to my rescue—a mighty one the size of a pony and a smaller pride with it."

"White lions?"

"Yes, Prentice. The smaller ones were ordinary white, as any animal might be. But the large one...?"

"Had a mane that looked like it was made of moonlight?" he finished for her. She nodded and felt a taut eagerness growing in her that seemed reflected in Prentice's own manner, as if now that they had cracked the dam and started to reveal their secrets, they had to force the whole flood out in one go.

"What does it all mean?" she asked him again.

"I think Master Solft had a sense of it, Your Grace and now I doubly regret his death. When we first met, he shared something with me, evidence of a secret history of the Grand Kingdom, something over a thousand years old."

Amelia listened avidly as Prentice outlined the three heraldic animal illuminations the scholar had shown him and their implicit tale of a kingly lion hunted to its death by six usurper kings.

"Is this why you think the end is as the beginning, Prentice?" she asked him, putting pieces together in her mind. "The Grand Kingdom began with a usurpation and so is cursed to end the same?"

"I think it might be more than that," he said. "I have a notion that I have kept at bay in my thoughts, Your Grace, because if it is true, then the whole history we know of the founding of our land is false."

"What?"

"A serpent with six necks but only five heads, all of them beasts. And now an illumination that tells of six kings overthrowing a seventh. Six heraldic beasts that crown an eagle king, the only beast the Redlanders do not have amongst their fell numbers. Somehow, they are connected, I am certain."

"You think the Redlanders are in league with Daven Marcus?" It was the first thought that came to Amelia, but as soon as she said it, she knew it was wrong. In saying it, though, her mind began to make connections as Prentice's had done. "She said she had seen them when they came from the east, when the wood was a vast forest."

"'She,' Your Grace?"

"The widow in the wood," Amelia told him. "An ancient prophetess who lived out on the shore of the salt sea. I met her before. She prophesied over my life. It was she who told me the Redlanders' name and the story of their beginnings. She said they had been allied with ancient fey and had come from the Grand Kingdom originally. They had been driven out, she said."

The two of them stood for a moment, pondering everything they had shared. It was still only afternoon, but to Amelia it felt as if the sky had darkened, even though it was clear and blue. It was as if the air around them was heavier somehow, and all the sounds of the camp were dimmed.

"The Redlanders were the houses of ancient nobles," she said, as the picture in her mind began to resolve.

"Ancient kings," Prentice corrected, "who unified first under a lion and then helped an eagle to usurp him."

"The eagle of Denay." As soon as the words were spoken, Amelia was certain it was true, like the prophecy the widow had told her. Whatever her doubt about the words' meaning, she felt none about their truth.

"And you say the other houses were driven west?" Prentice continued. "Later. How much later, I wonder?"

That, Amelia could not say. "But they were allied with the fey, so that must have been during the crusade that purged the inner kingdom."

"So, at least a millennia ago," he mused.

One objection leaped solidly into Amelia's mind. "But the lion king, it cannot be the Reach lion," she said, remembering the details of her dead husband's heritage. "Duke Marne's family received the white lion only three hundred years ago. Well, three hundred and twenty-six." Amelia had diligently studied her husband's family history as she prepared to wed. She had hoped to show respect for him by it.

"But from where did his family acquire the livery?" asked Prentice.

"It was won by an ancestor in battle, a sworn man of a Baron named Hectamiln. He received a parcel of land with a mill and their slow climb began. Marne's second cousin still owns the mill."

"Forgive me, Your Grace, that is not what I meant. But as I think, a white lion need not be too rare a symbol for a noble house. It is possible that the king who carried it was overthrown, his heraldry purged from every codex and record, and then, over time, forgotten completely. Many ages later, a new knight comes along and is awarded his own heraldry. Unknowingly he is bestowed a white lion and the symbol is restored, even if the kingly house is not."

That certainly made sense to Amelia. Nonetheless, it seemed like they were only understanding a fraction of the whole, like the evidence of Master Solft's little pictures. Even with all the visions put together, all their revelations shared, they still only had images from the edge of the page, mere illuminations of a document that was dense with facts and truths.

"Beggin' your pard'n, Your Grace, Captain?" asked a voice, and the heaviness lifted away like a cloth flying in a breeze. Amelia turned to see a militiaman standing by. He tugged his forelock to her and saluted Prentice.

"What is it?" she asked.

"There's some folk come up from the south looking to speak with the captain."

"They should speak to me," Amelia said coldly. Her first thought was that any person from the south would be sent from Daven Marcus's rebel army so she should be the one to receive them.

"Are they nobles?" Prentice asked his man. The soldier shook his head.

"I don't really figure. At least two is sacrists, and one's a boy, so he is."

"With your permission, Your Grace," Prentice said, bowing politely. "I can speak with them and will bring them to you, if need be."

"Alright, Captain," she allowed with a nod. In her heart, Amelia wanted to continue discussing this mystery. Now that she knew she was not alone in having the same visions and revelations, she wanted to keep deliberating over them until every detail had been uncovered. But the needs of her army and her lands must come first.

Prentice bowed again and left with the militiaman.

Amelia looked down at the fire beside her for a moment. She knew better than to seek divination in the flames, as some said witches did, but she found it soothing to stare at the dancing light and heat. Ending as it had begun, that was what Prentice had said, but what was ending? The throne in Denay? The invasion of the Redlanders? Or the Grand Kingdom entirely? And in the midst of this, what of Mother Church, which seemed bent upon holding up the usurper Daven Marcus and, if all this was true, had been suppressing the secret of their history, potentially for thousands of years?

No, whatever this was, to Amelia it felt nothing like an ending. It seemed it could only be a beginning.

CHAPTER 72

"They rode in just a short while ago, but some of 'em being wounded, we looked after 'em first 'fore I come to fetch you," the militiaman explained as he led Prentice across the camp.

"Very good," was all Prentice could think to say.

All around them the duchess's militia licked their wounds, and those men who were hale moved about, tending to the injured. Foraging parties were already coming back with some food, especially wild greens and grains, and animals killed or injured in the battle were butchered for meat. In the short term, the force would not go hungry, and one or two more injured to care for would make little difference

At last, they reached a small group of weary-looking clerics seated upon the ground. When the travelers saw Prentice approaching, they all stood up slowly. He quickly recognized Fostermae amongst them, and young Solomon, though both were filthy and their clothes torn in many places. The drummer boy saluted him, or tried to, but tears streamed onto his face, and Prentice grunted as Solomon suddenly threw himself on his captain. The boy hugged him and cried.

For a long moment Prentice stiffly allowed himself to be held by the weeping child, then he put a hand on his shoulder and patted the lad affectionately. Solomon was no milksop, no spoilt brat afraid to leave his mother's apron strings. If he was in tears, he had cause. Prentice looked over the lad's head to Fostermae and the other men with him, all but one of whom were now standing.

"What has happened, sacrist?"

"They killed them, Captain," Solomon gasped out between sobs. "All of them, and there weren't nothing we could do. I'm so sorry."

"The wounded?" Prentice asked.

Fostermae nodded sadly. "The army you defeated," he said. "They passed us in pursuit of you and all but ignored us, once a handful had made sure we were not armed. But when they returned in the night, they were of a different mind."

Prentice felt his jaw clench at the news. As a matter of course, he had ordered all the militia weapons collected from the invalided. It was a sign they were no longer combatants and, at least when they were flush with the prospect of victory, Daven Marcus's force had been happy to honor that. In all the time since he had seen Lord Ironworth's force ride out of the hills, Prentice had not thought to worry about the fate of the wounded he'd left behind. He regretted that now.

"Did any survive?" he asked.

Fostermae shook his head. "I do not know, but I doubt it. They were men in the grip of bloodlust. I saw even a healer cut down without mercy. They emerged from the night and slaughtered whatever they found alive."

"How did you survive?"

"By the aid of these two men and others who have had to go another way." Fostermae pointed to the other two men who had been standing patiently by.

"And who are they?"

Looking them over, Prentice saw that one was a sacrist, like Fostermae, with a shaved tonsure surrounded by fair hair and a simple robe, as filthy and torn as the other clergyman's. The other man was clearly a man-at-arms, heavily built and wearing a coat of mail that hung to his knees.

"We are servants of the Inquisition, My Lord," said the armored man, and Prentice pushed away from Solomon reflexively, hand ready to draw his newly acquired heavy sword. An Inquisition man-at-arms? That meant he was a Church knight. How could the sacrist have brought the man here? Was this treachery?

Fostermae moved to intervene.

"No, Captain," he said quickly. "It is not what you fear, I promise you."

"Then what?" Prentice demanded, keeping his hand on his hilt.

"They rescued my friend for me," Fostermae explained, and he stepped aside to show that the man on the ground was the scholar, Solft. His rich clothing was torn and filthy with blood and dirt, and his face was swollen and purple with bruises.

"He lives?" Prentice asked and felt a tension he hardly knew was there release inside himself. A part of him felt guilty knowing he had abandoned the scholar to his brother and the merciless Inquisition. He was thankful to discover the man had survived and angry to see what he had endured in doing so.

"I owe you thanks, then," he told the two strangers. "But if you are of the Inquisition, why deliver a suspected heretic into the care of another?"

The two men looked at each other and shared a shamed expression. The fair-haired clergyman seemed familiar to Prentice, but he couldn't think why.

He began to explain. "We are of a small clutch of troubled men," he began and even his voice seemed familiar to Prentice. Who was he? "Men whose consciences have been long pricked, but who have taken too long to act, I fear. We have watched as so many of the Church compromised themselves and their faith with the secular powers of the world. We see ecclesiarchs sell the Lord's word and barter salvation like the greediest merchants. The prince's conspiracy against the king came to our ears, and we could no longer only watch and pray. I'm sure you know it is never easy to betray oaths long held."

"Well, you have left your run too late, gentles," Prentice said bitterly. "King Chrostmer and far too many good men and women are dead for your inaction."

"Be not too unkind, Prentice," Fostermae said gently. "These men have sacrificed much to save us."

"Everyone has sacrificed to save us from the usurper's evil, sacrist. What worth the Inquisition if it waits until it is too late to act? How great are your sacrifices that I must respect them?" he demanded of the two men.

"I burned my tabard," said the armored man without emotion.

"I saw him do it," Fostermae added.

"Burned your...you're a Church knight?" Wariness began to boil over in Prentice's chest, and even though the calm inner part of his thoughts recognized what a gesture burning a tabard would be, his surface mind would not accept it. No sworn brother of the Church martial would burn his armor's over-robe. The garment was almost sacred. He wrenched his weapon free.

"They have come to aid the Reach," Fostermae insisted in a rush. "Please do not be foolish."

"Foolish?" Prentice whirled on his old friend, and the fury within him was so strong that it took all his will not to raise his sword.

"You cannot blame the captain," said the fair-headed clergyman. "He has more cause than any other I know to mistrust the sons of Mother Church." The man limped forward awkwardly and Prentice saw that under his robe, he had a wooden leg. He stumped up until he was only a pace from Prentice. "I have rehearsed this moment many times, and I never imagined it would be like this. Do you not know me, Captain Ash?"

Prentice stared at the man's face, trying to recognize him. He searched the strangely familiar features over and again but could not make them form an identity.

"Would it help if I told you I no longer hold my brother's blood against you?" the man asked, and Prentice nearly staggered in shock.

"Whilte?" he gasped.

Brother Whilte was another Church knight, one whom Prentice had known as a student at Ashfield. Prentice had fought a duel with Whilte's older brother, and when he lost, that brother had killed himself rather than face the humiliation. In revenge, Whilte had provided false testimony to the Inquisition that had helped to convict Prentice of heresy. Prentice had long thought Whilte killed at the Battle of the Brook, yet here he was, dirtier, hobbled, and humbled, but still alive. Almost involuntarily, Prentice felt himself raising his blade to strike this accursed enemy to the ground. He felt his self-control cracking and his weapon shook in his hand.

"Captain, please don't," Fostermae pleaded, but Prentice hardly heard him. He did hear Whilte's next words though.

"If you strike me, Prentice, I swear I will not resist you," the ecclesiastic said. "But I beg you please, give me first a moment to confess and repent."

"Repent?" Prentice repeated, as if it were a word in a foreign language.

"I have wronged you, Captain Prentice Ash, perhaps as much as any living man could be wronged. I lied under oath to see you convicted. I perjured my soul and swore you into suffering you did not deserve. I conspired to make that suffering as bitter and prolonged as I could imagine. I make no excuse, and though I do not expect it, I ask you to forgive me, not for the sake of *my* soul but for your own."

Brother Whilte lowered his head and held both hands out to the side, unable to protect himself if Prentice chose to bring his weapon down. One strike of the heavy edge to the man's head and his skull would split. Prentice stared at the bowed crown, shaven in the middle, and felt his teeth grind while his chest clenched with rage. In all his life he had never hated a man as he hated Whilte. He turned his head away, as if even looking at the man was overpowering his self-control, and as he did so, his eyes fell upon Solomon, who was watching earnestly, hands clasped in front of himself.

"He saved my life, Captain," the lad said, his tone pleading.

CHAPTER 73

Prentice looked from Solomon to Whilte and back again. His hand twisted, white-knuckled on his sword's hilt, and the tension in his limbs made the point of the blade shake. Suddenly, it felt too heavy in his grip, and he lowered it. He was too tired to wield it now. He could not cut this man down, no matter the hate within himself. And he did still hate him; Prentice could feel it roiling in him like a storm-tossed sea. But there had been enough blood, at least for now.

"I...I am not adept at this, Brother," he said to Whilte, who remained bowed. "But I accept your repentance and give my forgiveness, such as it is. Do not think to presume upon it though, sir. It feels like a very fragile thing inside me."

Whilte looked up with a humble, relieved smile. "I try to presume very little these days, Captain. This thorn in my flesh reminds me to seek humility." He bent down and slapped at his wooden leg.

"How did you lose it?" Prentice asked without thinking.

"When a man's pride is very strong, then the Lord needs to be more forceful to teach him the folly of it," Whilte answered and shared a glance with Fostermae, who nodded encouragement. Then he turned back to Prentice. "I lost my foot at the Brook, Captain. It was injured, and then when I fell from my horse, it became caught in the stirrup. The poor nag dragged me for leagues and knocked me senseless. By the time I was found and received a healer's attention, the rot had set in and there was nothing left but to cut the thing away. I outlived the fever and returned to the Church to serve but could no longer be a knight. So, it's a sacrist I am now."

Prentice easily imagined the brutal experience such a simple story conveyed, but he could not bring himself to feel much sympathy for the man. Suddenly within himself, though, he felt a strange obligation, as if Whilte's confession prompted one of his own.

"You lied to see me convicted, sir," he said. "But you were not wrong. I was a heretic."

Whilte nodded as if the information was not a surprise. Prentice wondered if the man understood the implication.

"I have the previous king's pardon, but Mother Church likely still counts me an enemy. You understand this?"

"Mother Church has made too many enemies of late," Whilte answered the question, shaking his head. "Some within and some without. And too many of them sit enthroned in power that no man should have over the souls of other men."

He and the other former Church knight shared a meaningful look and then nodded together in some unspoken agreement.

"The Church is on the verge of shattering, Captain," said the knight. "We know that at least two factions war with each other to control its wealth and power. It is one of those two that backs Daven Marcus and the murder of his father. In the meantime, others of us want only to serve our Lord as best we know how, men such as myself and Sacrist Whilte here. We have watched in disgust as these warring factions have so misused the things of God.

"In spite of their rebellion, there are yet men of faith in the Vec, as well as missionaries to farther lands. You have heard this, Captain, I am sure. Many have preached a faith without the ecclesiarchy, and I know you know this. We have read what they write, many of us in secret. Some words can only be heresy, no matter the sins of the Church. But others are the writings of earnest men, and sometimes even women, of true faith. There are truths being learned in secret that we believe God Almighty will see hatch forth. Something new is groaning to be born."

"There is nothing new under the sun," Prentice quoted scripture, more from reflex than any true objection to the knight's words.

"But something that is very old might seem new to men who have only lived a short time on the earth and never heard it before," Whilte countered. "True faith and honor would seem strangely fresh to a man who has only ever known the petty counterfeit that has been allowed to stand in its place."

Prentice shook his head. He and the duchess had just been trying to puzzle out the meaning of their religious experiences and here before him were men of learning, even the scholar Solft he'd been sure was lost who could help them to do just that. Amongst the brutality, blood, and vile ambition, it seemed God had planted seeds of truth to sprout at precisely the right time of the season.

"What happened to the mongrel who would lie to God to avenge his brother's death?" he asked Whilte provocatively, not quite able to put down his hatred in spite of the confessions they had shared.

Whilte did not take offense. "He was rebuked by God and lost his leg to regain his soul, Captain Prentice Ash. It was a fair bargain. More than fair, in fact."

Prentice drew in a deep breath and returned his sword to its sheath, flexing his fingers to relieve the tension there.

"You have the freedom of this camp, such as it is gentlemen," he said. "We will be here some days before we march, though Her Grace, Duchess Amelia, will be gone sooner than that. While you are here, enjoy her hospitality and seek care for the wounded Master Solft. If you are willing to accompany us north, then I believe the duchess will wish to speak with you. She...and I have some...matters of divinity that we need to discuss with theologically educated men and women."

"We will be glad of that hospitality, Captain," said Fostermae, and he and Whilte both tugged their forelocks, even though Prentice was not the right social rank for the gesture. The captain then turned to Solomon.

"As for you, young lad, do you still have that pin?"

The boy nodded eagerly as he reached into his belt pouch and held it out.

"Good man," Prentice told him. "Now let's you and I see if we can find some small beer or some other drink and share a stoup, as soldiers do after a battle. I will tell you the rest of that rat's tale and you can add the story of your escape with the sacrists to it."

Solomon rubbed his nose on his sleeve. "I'd like that, Captain."

Prentice put his arm around Solomon's shoulder.

"You've earned it, lad. You have earned it."

EPILOGUE

"He said what?" King-elect Daven Marcus demanded.

The herald bowed his head and tried to control the shaking in his limbs. Since he had first received his commission as bonded man of the royal household, he had never shirked his obligations to throne and crown. To report precisely what was said when carrying messages was his sworn duty. For the first time ever, he seriously considered changing a message that had been entrusted to him. After all, in this confused age, with so many points of honor and righteousness being overlooked, what would one more be?

But he had chosen to be truthful as he'd sworn to be, and so he was obliged to repeat himself to the king-elect.

"Earl Lastermune refuses to attend your summons, Your Majesty," he said, and he could hear his voice tremble. "He says that he will not return to either Rhales or Denay, except to attend a congress of the high noble houses to choose a true royal heir, and that he will only enter whichever city it is through a gate with your head hanging from its lintel."

"Parchment-skinned old bastard!" Daven Marcus swore, and he threw his goblet so that it sprayed the herald with wine, though the cup itself bounced off the stones at the man's feet and clattered away. Cringing, the herald did not dare move to wipe away the droplets that ran down his face. There was a long moment of silence as he awaited whatever petulant judgement would fall from the new young king.

"Oh, for God's sake, get out of our sight!" the king-elect said, dismissing him, and the herald turned and almost ran from the room. Behind him, he heard the new monarch consult with his closest man, a dark-haired former baron, now raised to duke. "How many does that make now?"

"At least half."

"We should merge the two courts outright. It's been done before."

"Not for centuries, Majesty," said the duke. "And even if you do, you'll still have to bring them to heel on the field. Or with sieges."

"At least that'll be the fun part," said Daven Marcus. "If only that waste of flesh Ironworth hadn't lost so many of the dragons. Ironworth? Turd'sworth more like."

The duke laughed, and that was the last thing the herald heard as he left the feasting hall King-elect Daven Marcus was using as his throne room. They were in the castle of an earl named Gawestead, one of the few Denay courtiers who were enthusiastic in their support for the new monarch, and still many days' travel from Denay itself. The former crown prince had been eager to return to the capital for a formal coronation, but the city fathers had closed the gates to him and his court and claimed to be ready to resist him by force. The new monarch now had no choice but to wait and gather a new army to retake his throne and capital. Word among the royal heralds was that Denay was not the only castle or city that had closed their doors to Daven Marcus.

The herald had little idea what it all would mean for the future, but he had no illusions that his once respected role in society was now one of the most dangerous professions in the Grand Kingdom. He rushed away toward the castle kitchens. He needed a stiff drink.

GLOSSARY

The Grand Kingdom's social structure is broken into three basic levels which are then subdivided into separate ranks: the nobility, the free folk, and the low born.

The Nobility

King/Queen – There is one King, and one Queen, his wife. The king is always the head of the royal family and rules from the Denay Court, in the capital city of Denay.

Prince/Princess – Any direct children of the king and queen.

Prince of Rhales – This title signifies the prince who is next in line of succession. This prince maintains a separate, secondary court of lesser nobles in the western capital or Rhales.

Duke/Duchess – Hereditary nobles with close ties by blood or marriage to the royal family, either Denay or Rhales.

Earl; Count/Countess; Viscount; Baron/Baroness – These are the other hereditary ranks of the two courts, in order of rank. One is born into this rank, as son or daughter of an existing noble of the same rank, or else created a noble by the king.

Baronet – This is the lowest of the hereditary ranks and does not require a landed domain to be attached.

Knight/Lady – The lowest rank of the nobility and almost always attached to military service to the Grand Kingdom as a man-at-arms. Ladies obtain their title through marriage.

Knights are signified by their right to carry the longsword, as a signature weapon.

Squire – This is, for all intents and purposes, an apprentice knight. He must be the son of another knight (or higher noble) who is currently training, or a student of the academy.

The Free Folk

Patrician – A man or woman who has a family name and owns property inside a major town or city. Patricians always fill the ranks of any administration of the town in which they live, such as aldermen, guild conclave members, militia captains etc.

Guildsmen/townsfolk – Those who dwell in large towns as free craftsmen and women tend to be members of guilds who act to protect their members' livelihoods and also to run much of the city, day to day.

Yeoman – The yeomanry are free farmers that possess their own farms.

The Low Born

Peasants – These are serfs who owe feudal duty to their liege lord. They do not own the land they farm and must obtain permission to move home or leave their land.

Convicts – Criminals who are found guilty of crimes not deserving of the death penalty.

Military Order

Knight Captain, Knight Commander & Knight Marshall – Every peer (King, Prince or Duke) has a right to raise an army and command his lesser nobles to provide men-at-arms. They then appoint a second-in-command, often the most experienced or skilled soldier under them. A duke his Knight Captain; a prince his Knight Commander; and the King his Knight Marshal.

Knights – These are the professional soldiers of the Grand Kingdom. All nobles are expected to join these ranks when their lands are at war, and they universally fight from horseback.

Men-at-Arms –A catch all term for any man with professional training who has some right or reason to be in this group, including squires and second and third sons of nobles.

Bannermen – This is a special form of man-at-arms. These are soldiers who are sworn directly to a ranking noble.

Free Militia – The free towns of the Grand Kingdom have an obligation to raise free militias in defence of the realm.

Rogues Foot – A rogue is a low born or criminal man and so when convicts are pressed into military service, they are the rogues afoot (or "on foot") which is shortened to rogues foot.

Other Titles and Terms

Apothecary – A trader and manufacturer of herbs, medical treatments and potions of various sorts.

Chirurgeon – A medical practitioner, akin to a doctor or surgeon, especially related to injuries (as opposed to sickness, which is handled by an apothecary).

Ecclesiarchs – ruling members of the Church. Their ranks correspond (very roughly) to noble ranks. The ecclesiarchy refers to the power of the Church where it rules with its own power, like a nation within the nation. Monasteries, churches, cathedrals and the Academy in Ashfield are all part of the Church lands, where religious law overrides King's Law.

Estate – A person's estate can be their actual lands, but can also include their social position, their current condition (physical, social or financial), or any combination of these things.

Fiefed – A noble who is fiefed possesses a parcel of land over which they have total legal authority, the right to levy taxes and draft rogues or militia.

Frater – brother (from the Latin word)

Hoi Polio – the common folk

King's Law – This is the overarching, national law, set for the Grand Kingdom by the king, but does not always apply in the Western Reach.

Magistrate – Civil legal matters of the Free Folk and Peasantry are typically handled by magistrates, who render judgements according to the local laws.

Marshals/Wardens – Appointed men who manage the movement of large groups, especially of nobles and noble courts when in motion. They appoint the order of the march and resolve disputes.

Physick – A term for a person trained in the treatment of medical conditions, but without strict definition.

Proselytize – Attempt to convert someone from one religion, belief, or opinion to another.

Pugilist - A professional boxer.

Provost – (short for provost marshal) junior officers assigned to sentries or patrol for the purpose of military discipline. In the case of the White Lions militia, the typical rank of a provost is a Line First. Roughly equivalent to military police duty.

Republicanists – Rare political radicals, outlawed in the Grand Kingdom and the Vec who seek to create elected forms of government, curtailing or overturning monarchical rule.

Seneschal – The administrative head of any large household or organisation, especially a noble house of a baron or higher.

Surcoat – The outer garment worn by a man-at-arms over their armor. Typically dyed in the knight's colours (or their liege lord's colours in the case of a bannerman) and embroidered with their heraldry.

Te tree – A tree, known for its medicinal properties.

The Rampart – A celestial phenomenon that glows in the night across the sky from east to west in the northern half of the sky.

ABOUT MATT

Matt Barron grew up loving to read and to watch movies. He always knew he enjoyed science fiction and fantasy, but in 1979 his uncle took him to see a new movie called *Star Wars* and he was hooked for life. Then *Dungeons and Dragons* came along and there was no looking back. He went to university hoping to find a girlfriend. Instead, the Lord found him, and he spent most of his time from then on in the coffee shop, witnessing and serving his God. Along the way, he managed to acquire a Doctorate in History and met the love of his life, Rachel. Now married to Rachel for more than twenty years, Matt has two adult children and a burning desire to combine the genre he loves with the faith that saved him.

Learn more at:

mattbarronauthor.com

Also By Matt Barron

Rage of Lions

Prentice Ash

Rats of Dweltford

Lions of the Reach

Eagles of the Grand Kingdom

Book 5 Coming Soon

MORE FROM THE PUBLISHER

Be sure to check out our other great science fiction and fantasy stories at:

bladeoftruthpublishing.com/books

Made in the USA
Monee, IL
30 October 2024

69025547R00329